"My daughter said you wanted to speak to me, Sergeant," Watly said placidly.

"And a delightful child she is, too," Ogiv said. He grinned boyishly. "But it's 'Chief' now, if you don't mind."

"Congratulations. Now running things, are you?"

"I have that old case to thank for it, in a way. That old case you were wrapped up in, Sen-tiva. Catching and killing that notorious murderer, Watly Caiper, did wonders for my reputation and my career. Forgive me for saying it, but Watly killing your famous poovus, and then me killing him, was the best thing that ever happened to me."

"To what," she said as if impatient, "do I owe the honor of this reunion?"

"Well, the funny thing is, it happens to be related to that Watly Caiper mess. If you remember, I got out of your hair pretty quickly after all that trouble back then. I didn't hound you, I didn't harass you, and I didn't poke too deeply. I closed the book on that Caiper incident quickly, in spite of all the loose ends and unanswered questions. Did you ever wonder why?"

Also by Peter R. Emshwiller

THE HOST

SHORT BLADE

PETER R. EMSHWILLER

BANTAM BOOKS

New York • Toronto • London • Sydney • Auckland

SHORT BLADE

A Bantam Spectra Book / May 1992

*SPECTRA and the portrayal of a boxed "s"
are trademarks of Bantam Books, a division of
Bantam Doubleday Dell Publishing Group, Inc.*

ISBN 0-553-29417-2

Published simultaneously in the United States and Canada

*Bantam Books are published by Bantam Books, a division of Bantam
Doubleday Dell Publishing Group, Inc. Its trademark, consisting of the
words "Bantam Books" and the portrayal of a rooster, is Registered in U.S.
Patent and Trademark Office and in other countries. Marca Registrada.
Bantam Books, 666 Fifth Avenue, New York, New York 10103.*

PRINTED IN THE UNITED STATES OF AMERICA

RAD   0 9 8 7 6 5 4 3 2 1

To my shrink, Pamela, a patient safari guide through the deepest, darkest jungle
    and
to my wife, Margaret, a fellow explorer in the thick underbrush of the mind.

SHORT BLADE

PROLOGUE

"There is nothing wrong with my daughter," Watly Caiper said, pulling long strands of her dark hair through the middle two fingers of her right hand.

Dr. Alysess Tollnismer kissed Watly softly on the cheek and then shook her head. She appeared to be unsuccessfully trying to form some kind of reassuring smile with the corners of her mouth. "I'm not saying there is," Alysess said quietly. "I'm just saying that little Noonie needs some help. We can't ignore what she did today. Normal seven-year-olds don't *do* that. She has a problem."

Watly rolled off the far side of the bed and wrapped her robe around herself angrily. The room still smelled of fresh sex, and Dr. Tollnismer was still naked, but Watly suddenly felt no great love for Alysess. They had made love moments earlier—a desperate, strangely passionate coupling to help forget the horror that had happened earlier that day. It hadn't worked. "Keep it down," Watly hissed. "She'll hear you."

"She can't hear, Watly," Alysess said calmly, pulling the covers up over her naked body. "Noonie's sound asleep by now. I gave her a sedative along with all the painkillers. I figured she could use one. Maybe we all could, Watly."

"What do you want me to do?" Watly asked her lover.

"I think we should try to get the child help."

"We can't risk that." Watly sat back down on the corner of the white bedspread and exhaled very slowly. "She'll be okay, Alysess."

"I know she will. She's a good kid. She's a great kid. But she needs help." Alysess reached over and touched Watly's arm gently.

"*We'll* help her, Aly," Watly said. Her voice was suddenly full of corptalk authority. "We can't risk outside help. You want psychomedics in here? Poking? Prodding?"

"So what are we going to do, Watly? Cover for her? Pretend nothing happened?"

"Nobody knows what happened except us, Alysess. Nobody ever has to. If anybody found out . . . everything would fall apart. There'd be an investigation. Public scrutiny. We can't risk that kind of exposure."

Alysess squeezed Watly's pale upper arm with her own dark brown hand. "So we cover for her, call it an accident, and do nothing?" she asked.

"Her body will heal. And her mind," Watly said determinedly. "*We* help her. *We* can help her."

"How?"

"More love. More attention."

"Love doesn't solve everything, Watly. It doesn't."

"Yes, it does, Aly. Yes, it does."

And the subject didn't come up again. Not for another two years.

PART ONE

LIT FUSES AND FOREPLAY

Things are a little out of hand here,
situation-wise.

ROULLIC NEETS

CHAPTER 1

It was dark, but was no longer stormy.

At 2:15 A.M. the rains had stopped. The rains hadn't cooled things down any like they're always supposed to. The raindrops themselves had come down warm. Hard and warm, like some defective boiler room in the sky had exploded. But the downpour was over.

Now the summer night was hot and plenty breezy. The streets of Manhattan's Second Level were slick and puddly from the recent showers, and the warm winds carried that moisture about, slamming wetness ineffectually against all the ostentatious homes and expensive office buildings. Humid air rose from the perfect whitetop on the desolate avenues, passing up beyond the golden street lamps into the dense clouds above.

The twin spires of the two Empire State Buildings vanished in the mist. In fact, only the lower of the buildings' two gleaming connecting bridges was clearly visible, lit from within. All the mismatched, immaculate skyscrapers seemed to fade into hazy oblivion as they stretched upward. The Gavy Tower, the Alvedine Hosting Building, the Trade Centers, the Chrysler Building, the

Man-With-Hat-On—all disappeared into the heavens. The torso
and legs were all that remained of the Man-With-Hat-On. His
shoulders, enormous outstretched arms, and fifteen-story head
were totally hidden in the thick clouds.

The spires, brightly painted parapets, asymmetrical towers,
blunt-tipped steeples, purple cupolas, and golden roofs of the
shorter buildings were still uncovered by the low cloud ceiling.
They glimmered from every direction, reflecting their perfectly
positioned pinspots as if waxed and buffed from the rain. Heavy
mist in the air made each lit-up building seem soft and fuzzy.
Every light, every moist reflection, every golden decoration was
haloed with a diffused glow. The line between the edge of each
structure and its blurry yellow aura was unclear, as if the buildings
themselves were soft and pliable, made of feathery blond hair. No
one walked the streets to see this. No one strolled leisurely in the
humid air, gazing at the wonder that was the Second Level of the
country of Manhattan.

An unmanned copper floated by silently, water beading up on
its polished surface as it patrolled the empty streets. Its lenses and
sensors looked and listened for trouble.

Trouble wasn't happening. Trouble never happened up here on
Second Level. There were no gates on the Fifth Avenue stores.
The jewelry shops, neo-plant and flower stores, autorestaurants,
Daviti game parlors, electronics stores, cosmetronic shops, visage-
reconstruction cafés, and clothing boutiques all had simple codelocks
on the doors—no bars, no anxiety fields, no alarm systems.

Another gleaming copper zipped quickly by, blazing cylinders
reflecting bright orange and blue in the pristine road's dampness.
This copper made a slight buzzing noise as it accelerated. It was
a soothing, pleasant sound that echoed quietly against all the
surrounding deserted opulence. It was a sound no one heard. The
Second Level slept peacefully, that one tiny buzz of security
disturbing no one.

On East Seventy-second, all the buildings were dark and quiet.
The tall trees and ornate flying buttresses stood like staunch
sentries guarding every home on the block between Madison and
Park avenues. Front steps and dark-wood entryways were lit with
warm, inviting spotlights that shimmered in the heat and mist. The
concentrated light did not travel up the buildings themselves,
which loomed in darkness, a darkness broken only by the
occasional shine of some lustrous metal gargoyle or strip of
decorative gold.

All the windows on that street were closed, except one. All the rooms on that street were carefully regulated by precisely tuned air stablers—cool and crisp and dry—except one. Just one. In that one single window, white lacy drapes billowed inward with each northerly humid gust, and then those same drapes reached out under the pane and into the dark but not stormy night with the suction of every southerly backwash breeze. It was as if that single room, two stories above the Second Level street, was breathing. Was alive. It was as if the Second Level was dead save one small inhaling and exhaling window.

Within that room was the stuff of childhood. Toys and games strewn about, homework monitors leaning into a half-sized chair and desk, dark clothes lying in little piles here and there. The walls were covered with strange, shadowy drawings, and a tiny night-light in the shape of a smiling, large-nosed face dimly illuminated one corner, which contained a hand-painted wooden rocking horse. Fuzzy replicas of extinct animals—large-eyed lions, cuddly rhinos and elephants, soft alligators, huggable bears—were piled high on one side of the large canopied bed. On the other side of the bed was a sleeping child, curled up in a fetal position—drooling a little on her pillowcase as she breathed through her mouth. One damp pale sheet was tangled in her legs. The savage-looking white scar that trailed on a sharp angle across the back of her right shoulder and partway down her arm was exposed to the thick, wet air. The scar was old—two long years old—but it still looked raw and recent. It might always look raw and recent. The girl grunted slightly, gnawing gently for a second on her lower lip.

The child's secret special name was Noonie Caiper, but everyone—except her mother and her mother's lover, Dr. Tollnismer—knew her as Noonie Alvedine. Noonie didn't like air-conditioning; it made her nose ache by morning. She liked sleeping in the heat. Noonie was nine years old, had light brown hair, and was a little short for her age. Right now she was sweating a good deal around the neck and dreaming peacefully that she was famous. A famous Second Level artist. It was a good dream. A favorite dream. A dream she'd had many times before.

In the dream, Noonie had friends. Real friends. Not just kids to play with occasionally; not just interactive-school classmates. But friends. Friends her *own* age. Not like her mother's lover,

Alysess Tollnismer, who was all grown up. Sure Alysess was a friend—a good friend, an *only* friend, a whisperer and playmate. But she was also an adult. Adults were not the same thing at all. In the *dream* all the people in the world were nine, just like her. Every one of them. And these people, young people, were people to confide in. People who knew all of Noonie's secrets. And it was okay that they knew her secrets. In the dream she was still Noonie, yes, and still nine, yes—but she could be Noonie *Caiper*, not Noonie Alvedine. The secret name was not a secret anymore. And it didn't matter. They all still loved her. And she was famous among them. Country-renowned. Admired and respected. It was spaf. Peaky prone. All of the country of Manhattan knew her. Even those below—those she'd heard countless stories of; those who lived down on the First Level—even *those* knew her and loved her. Worshiped her. Worshiped her talent. Worshiped her just for being Noonie Caiper. For being exactly herself, openly and honestly, overbite and all. Family secrets and all. Scar on her shoulder and arm, and all. There was no need for secrets anymore. The hiding was over. In the dream, the hiding was a thing of the past. But only in the dream.

Noonie's bedroom door opened slowly. There was no sound to speak of, but there was suddenly a blast of cool, regulated air and a strong shaft of light that cut into the room's darkness: light from the hallway pinlights. Now all the gray animal shapes and dark clothing lumps revealed their bright colors in the white beam of light: oranges, magentas, pinks, pale peaches, lavenders, and a lot of pastel blues. The childlike drawings taped to the walls, however, still appeared strange and shadowy. Because they *were* strange and shadowy. They rustled faintly in the new, cool breeze.

Noonie stirred, moaned a tad, and lifted her head up. She felt the cold dry air on her face and turned toward it. The shadow of a woman stood in her doorway. Tall, slender, and beautiful; wearing a diaphanous nightgown that was almost transparent in silhouette. A well-toned, womanly body was clearly visible beneath the sheer gown. It was the comfortable, familiar form of Noonie's mother, Watly Caiper, known to the world as Sentiva Alvedine.

"Mommy?" Noonie said, her voice hoarse with sleepiness.

The woman in the doorway did not answer. She stood and stared into the room blankly. Her emerald eyes were unseeing, drugged-looking. Her mouth—Mommy's mouth—opened as if trying to form words. Words that didn't exist. Words that hadn't been invented yet. She tilted her head—Mommy's head—from side to side, like an animal might if it sniffed something funny in the air. Then she raised her hands, hands Noonie had felt holding her gently all her life, and she began to scratch clumsily into her own head with her shortly clipped fingernails. The silhouetted figure scratched just behind her ears—yes, Mommy's ears—and Noonie wondered if those nails were drawing blood.

The little girl sat up in bed. She pulled her knees in close to her chest and hugged them. Even in the damp, hot breeze from the window, her body shivered. Noonie looked at the beautiful woman standing in her doorway. The beautiful woman who seemed to be dreamwalking, scraping at herself in her sleep.

"Mommy?" Noonie asked again. It wasn't Mommy. Noonie knew it was the Night Lady again. The Night Lady was back in Mommy's body. It had happened before, but never for this long. It was happening more and more frequently lately. This was bad.

"Mommy, please."

The woman took a short step into the room, her head still tilting from side to side, her hands still up and clawing behind the ears. Her eyes were not focused, but they were looking blankly in Noonie's general direction. Again her mouth opened, trying to find words, trying to find a language. It was almost as though she were searching for the part of the brain that had to do with speech but couldn't find it.

"Child . . ." the Night Lady whispered finally. And then nothing.

Noonie scrambled to the far side of the bed where the stuffed animals were. "Please come back, Mommy!" she said softly. This was just too weird. This whole Night Lady business was getting way too weird. And the Night Lady had never actually spoken before. This was a first. The Night Lady had never found words until tonight. And all the times before, the Night Lady's appearance had only lasted for a few seconds. Noonie felt really hinky about that change in particular. *Really* hinky. Why wasn't the Night Lady gone by now? How could this one visit be lasting for so long?

For a while the Night Lady continued to move her lips silently. Her mouth formed the letter *o* over and over, and her hands dug hard into her own head. Then the hands fell limply at her sides and she stepped in closer. Now words came out again. "Child . . . I . . . Short blade."

The voice was not like Mommy's voice. It came from the same body, through the same vocal cords, out the same mouth, but it was not the same. This voice was cool, like the air that had preceded her into the room. This voice was oily hard. Wintry. Unfeeling.

"*Mommy*. I don't like this!"

The woman stepped to the foot of the bed. Those blank eyes were suddenly alive, aware. They were seeing Noonie for the first time. Pleading. "I . . . I . . . Short blade. Get short blade."

Noonie shrank back farther toward the wall, trying to bury herself in the stuffed animals. She let her fuzzy elephant's trunk drape itself across her shoulder. "Please go away," she said, her voice high and scared.

The Night Lady leaned closer, putting a knee up on the corner of the bed. "Shh-short. Shhhhort blade."

"Go away!" Noonie yelled, throwing her stuffed giraffe—Mr. Necky—at her mother's face. She could see some spots of blood on the woman's fingers, blood from her mommy's head. Blood from behind the ears.

The glow of the smiling big-nosed night-light reflected brightly in the corners of the Night Lady's newly awakened eyes. She looked angry now. Dangerous and insane. "Shhhort blade!" she said as she climbed up on the bed and crawled awkwardly toward the cowering girl.

"*Please!*" Noonie cried out. But now the woman was over her, leaning in, her head still shifting back and forth like some sniffing cat.

The Night Lady reached down with the bloody fingers and clumsily stroked Noonie's hair with a faltering left hand. "Child. Chhhhild . . ."

"Where's my mommy?" Noonie asked softly, holding tightly to the elephant's trunk. She felt the Night Lady's hands—both of them now—stroking the matted, sweaty hair that fell down around her neck. "I want my mommy back."

The Night Lady's fingers stiffened and clenched up around Noonie Caiper's thin neck. "Short blade, child. Shhhort blade!"

Noonie felt her mother's hands tightening around her throat. "Please!" the girl gasped. But the long fingers gripped firmly and began to squeeze inward. Noonie felt the air being cut off. She tried to remember all the self-defense lessons, all the careful training sessions her mother had given her. It all seemed useless now. Useless against the very body that had taught her how to protect herself.

Noonie grabbed the hands that choked her and tried to pull them away. She tried to twist her body and pull out of the hold. Nothing worked.

"Shhhhhhort blade! Need . . . shhhort blade!" the woman said as she leaned over and tried to strangle the nine-year-old—the nine-year-old her own body had given birth to.

Noonie struggled still, trying to break the firm grip of her mother's hands. She yanked hard at the arms, but they were too strong and determined. She kicked outward with her legs, but the Night Lady ignored them as they slammed impotently against her thigh and hip.

"Mommy, don't kill me!" Noonie managed to squawk through the choking fingers. The child felt the room growing smaller and beginning to spin, the light from the hall dimming and turning red. That redness spread across the floor toward her. The world was fading. Noonie was getting no air at all now. Not the warm air from the window, not the cold air from the hall.

The Night Lady pressed down even harder for a moment, and then her eyes seemed to cloud over. She looked bewildered again, disoriented and confused. The squeezing fingers went slack. The head stopped tilting from side to side. The woman's hands went up to her own face, as if trying to feel for something, trying to find something. Trying to find her own face.

Noonie pulled quickly away as soon as the choking stopped. She scrambled off the bed and stared at her mother, gasping for air, coughing, and rubbing her throat.

"Noonie?" the dazed woman on the bed said.

Noonie felt her nose get hot and tingly as tears started to stream down her cheeks. She didn't want to cry. She didn't want to cry in front of the Night Lady. "Mommy?" she asked tentatively

"Oh, Noonie, baby, I'm so sorry!" Watly Caiper said, reaching for her daughter.

Noonie stayed where she was for a moment, her shoulders beginning to shake from the inevitable onslaught of sobbing. She stared into her mother's frightened eyes, unsure at first whether to trust them. *Who are you now, Lady? Are you really my mommy?* Finally Noonie ran back into Watly Caiper's arms.

"Oh, Noonie, sweetie. Oh, no. I'm so sorry, baby!" Watly said as she hugged her child close.

The tickle in her nose and sinuses turned into a liquid burn and a great rush of tears overflowed from Noonie's eyes. She cried hard for a good two or three minutes before she could speak again. Finally, between gasps and sobs, she whispered into her mother's shoulder "Night Lady tried to kill me," and then the tears came back and drowned out any more talk.

Watly Caiper held her daughter and rocked her gently. "I know, I know," she said as the girl cried and held her tight. The child's grip was overhard and felt desperate. It even hurt some, but Watly let it be. The girl needed to hold hard. Watly held hard back. She hummed every soothing lullaby she could think of, every soft love song, and every silly little children's ditty. After a time, she leaned close to her daughter's ear and whispered, "I promise I'll try to keep the Night Lady away, my baby. I promise." She said a lot of soft, breathy "There-theres" and "I knows" and "Everything's gonna be all rights."

But the truth was, Watly Caiper didn't know if everything *was* going to be all right. She wasn't sure at all. The Night Lady was getting more and more powerful. The Night Lady was making more and more frequent appearances.

It was a relief to Watly when her daughter finally calmed down enough to fall asleep in her arms. It was nice to hear the child's breathing slow and become steady against Watly's breast, her body slack, her mouth half open. A little sleep-drool slid casually out of the girl's lips now, running onto Watly's left arm. The child was finally relaxed. But Watly herself was not relaxed. She was worried. She was hinkier than she'd been in a long time. This was all getting worse and worse. Turning into a very serious problem, this. Maybe the worst problem there could possibly be. And there was no use denying it anymore.

Sentiva Alvedine—the *real* Sentiva Alvedine—was trying to come back. It seemed to Watly that it might be just a matter of time. After ten years of mental prison, ten years of being trapped helplessly in her own body while Watly had control of it, Sentiva was making a break for it. She had gained power somehow, coming out more and more now as Watly slept. And sometimes,

Watly realized, sometimes coming out in little ways while she was awake. The woman wanted her body back. She wanted to evict Watly Caiper. She wanted to be back in charge of the vessel they shared. And on top of all that, Sentiva was, the evidence would seem to indicate, seriously pissed.

CHAPTER 2

There was a dead guy lying in a puddle of stale piss on the church stoop. His stone-cold forehead was wet with condensation like it was a glass full of iced soljuice. It almost seemed to be sweat. But it wasn't. The guy was dead, for sure. To Dr. Alysess Tollnismer, he looked to be dead about half a day or so. Old age, malnutrition, too much booze, too much of this heat, and definitely too many Soft pills. Somebody had already tagged the body for pickup and disposal. The lowtruck would be along for him any day now, for sure.

Dr. Tollnismer left the dead guy there and entered the building. She was late. If she'd had the time, she might have looked for something to cover the body with. Maybe it was silly, but that always made her feel better somehow, giving the dead their privacy. A little raping dignity in the end.

Passing into the building's filthy antechamber, the doctor approached the open doors where Cruda services were being held. It was a large, high-ceilinged auditorium, packed with people. The loud "Praise Cruda!" shouts vibrated the floor under Alysess's feet as she neared. She stopped for a moment, wiping greasy-feeling *real* sweat from her forehead and looking inside.

She herself had already gotten a first-warning ticket for missing one of her twice-weekly mandatory Enlightenment sermons. If she missed two more Cruda services, she'd be arrested. And then she'd be no good to anyone. Missing any services at all was a stupid, lazy chance to take. All it did was call attention to her, and that was one thing she didn't need.

Alysess made a mental note to attend tomorrow night's service at the church near her apartment. She had to keep up appearances. She had to play by the rules, no matter how unpleasant. She'd take an extra Soft pill tomorrow after dinner to make the whole thing go down easier. It seemed like each time she went, the services were harder to take, harder to sit through.

From where she stood outside the auditorium door, Alysess could see a side view of the shabby-looking congregation. Everyone there appeared sick to her. Every single one of them—each poverty-stricken, gaunt First Level face, staring and smiling glassy-eyed at the far end of the room—looked like they were in need of some serious medical attention. But then, wasn't everyone? The entire First Level of the country of Manhattan was like one big sickroom now. The Soft pills were out of control, there wasn't enough food, there wasn't enough water, there wasn't enough medicine, and there sure as rape weren't any healthy young folks cropping up to replace the dying ones.

On all of the First Level, no one she knew was younger than thirty-four years old. The prophy chemicals saturating every drop of water—what little water there was—were still doing their jobs. No one, but no one, on First Level was capable of conceiving children. And they sure weren't going to be able to get hold of antiprophies so that they *could* have children. That dream had died long ago. The dream of children. The lowerfolk were growing old. Growing old and dying off fast.

Alysess herself was a relatively fit thirty-eight, though she was sure the last ten years had aged her well beyond that—if not physically, then certainly mentally. Things had sure gone downhill.

The painfully loud "Praise Cruda!" screams from the congregation were fading some. Formal services were starting now. But the yelling was certain to return to punctuate the sermon at key points. And that yelling—that frenzied, religious bellowing—was, in a certain way, the whole reason Alysess was here in the first place. She leaned into the room, resting her medipak on her right foot, and turned to look down the central aisle at the shimmering CV image that floated above the auditorium's altar.

The cable vidsatt projection of the Cruda priestess was blurry in the weak CV mist. It was obviously an old CV set, in need of some major repair—or maybe in need of being trashed altogether. Nonetheless, Alysess could still make out the priestess's kind, wise, and trustworthy face, and her attractive pale-skinned naked form below. The white, full breasts rose up pleasingly with each broad, sweeping gesture. *No malnutrition or symptoms of disease or starvation on* that *body,* Alysess thought wryly.

The projected priestesses were always healthy and attractive. Every one of them. Beautiful, sexually appealing, and honest-looking. And young. Twenty-five or so. Younger than anyone on First. Well-kept, youthful, graceful Second Level bodies; soothing, high-cheekboned Second Level faces.

"The shawls of Cruda say that the meekest of the meat shall inherit the Ultimate," the priestess was saying with passion. The crowd shouted "Praise Cruda!" joyfully back at her.

"And so," she continued, her overamplified voice filling the hall, "we must be meek, for meekness is holiness. Hard work and suffering are holiness. Pain is holy. Serving is the holiest of all. We must *serve* the Second Level, we must serve, unquestioning, those above, those closer to the Ultimate. We must serve our Parents above, for we were made in the image of them. We are shadows, who toil in darkness, to be rewarded with the Ultimate at our ends. Our time will come with the sweet softness of our deaths."

Again the crowd roared, "Praise Cruda!"

Before she continued, the CV-projected priestess cupped her own bare breasts firmly in the traditional priestess "honesty gesture."

"Thou shalt not question the wisdom of the Parents above," she said. "They love us as only the rich can love. Those who have, cherish, nurture, and guide the have-nots. They love us. They are our Parents and wish us only the best. It has always been thus. It is the way of the rich, of those closer to the Ultimate."

Now she squeezed her breasts hard, proving her sincerity. "We say to you, Cruda, God of meat, of flesh, of rare sustenance, 'Thank you for the suffering. Our sins dwindle and are forgiven with each pain we feel, with each loss, with each hunger left unsated.'"

Alysess snorted quietly to herself and turned from the meeting room's doorway toward the hallway to the left, realizing she had just needlessly made herself even later than she'd already been. She took the metal stairs two at a time, spinning quickly around each of the four piss-smelling landings as she climbed to the fifth floor, trying to make up time. She felt sheets of sweat pouring down her back as she hopped up the flights. It was too raping hot to be moving this fast. "Praise Cruda!" She could still hear it all around her. The sermon and the chants reverberated throughout the entire building.

By the time she vaulted up to face the closed door at the top of the last stair, she was way out of breath and dripping wet. She rapped twice on the locked plasticore door, leaning into it for support. She waited a beat and then knocked quietly once more.

"Who?" a soft voice asked from somewhere close behind the barrier.

"Alysess," the doctor said, her breathing slowing now. Her white doctor-smock was totally drenched. "Alysess," she repeated, "and her little black bag. Open up."

The door opened and Alysess looked inside.

It was Tavis at the door. Tavis the unsexed. Tavis the wild, dangerous IT. Tavis with the stubbly face, crazed, dark eyes, and the serious penchant for hurting; standing there in a tight, filthy brown smock that showed the swell of two somehow intimidatingly masculine breasts.

"You're late!" Tavis giggled out in that unique voice that was too high and birdlike for a man, yet too low and gravelly for a woman. "Late, late, late!"

Alysess pushed past Tavis, brushing uncomfortably close to the creature's tattered smock and sour-smelling breath. She entered the room and looked around. It was dark and sweltering in there. Alysess felt instantly claustrophobic. The only light was from the four floating pinlamps that hovered in each corner near the ceiling. The floor was dark and lumpy and there were dusty boxes and crates looming in tall piles against each wall. There was a whole bunch of broken chairs dumped right in the center of the floor. It was obviously a storage room of some kind. It smelled like sweat in there. For a minute Alysess thought she was smelling her own perspiration, but this smell was of old, rancid sweat. Ancient, long-ago sweat. She couldn't help wishing she was up on Second—up in Watly's cool, clean, sweet-smelling world—sipping a drink and discussing politics.

"Praise Cruda!" The room shook.

Even in this small, cluttered chamber way above the meeting hall, the sounds of the service were clear and loud, echoing through the building's metal beams. That loudness was the whole idea, the reason they always picked a room near a church.

"Take your Soft pills, my people," the priestess was saying. "Never forget them. They soften the pain you must suffer to achieve the Ultimate. They help you to understand the pain. To welcome it openly. Never forget them."

"Praise Cruda!"

In the far left corner of the room, the Subkeeper and three other workers stood high on rickety placene ladders, fiddling with their equipment up by the room's ceiling. They had already prepared the ceiling's surface, chipped off the first layers of paint and cemeld, and were now positioning the heavy-duty I-cutter, balancing it between them. Alysess walked around the pile of chairs toward them.

"You're late," the Ragman said, glancing down at her. He looked tired. Old and tired. Even beneath the cloudy glass of his safety goggles, Alysess could make out dramatic dark circles under his eyes that reached from the bridge of his nose to his deep crow's-feet. The gray-red lips that were framed by his white beard appeared dry and chapped. His hair was disheveled and greasy-looking. A few thick clumps of it tangled down over his lined forehead. The Ragman robe, his signature outfit, was wrinkled and stained. It looked more threadbare and faded than ever. The brass-colored metal shavings woven into the fabric that were supposed to give it a magical wizard-of-authority effect had long since lost their gleam. Alysess wished he would throw the cloak out or replace it, or at least try to spruce it up a little. But no, for every important event he insisted on wearing it as is. For every meeting, every Revy planning session, and, of course, for each time they cut a portal, there that ugly robe was. *Have a little class, Ragface,* the doctor thought. *Wear something respectable if you want respect, already.*

"Late. Yeah, I know," Alysess finally answered him.

The Ragman looked back down sternly. The lines on his face showed barely concealed anger. He didn't usually show his anger, but lately it seemed he was always close to the edge. "Tardiness is unacceptable, Doctor," he said in a firm, level tone. "Building a portal is always dangerous work, you know that. We must have a doctor here at all times, every time." He grunted under the weight of the I-cutter.

"Yeah, yeah," Alysess said.

The Ragman stepped down a rung and pulled his goggles up, leaving the others to hold the machine. He leaned out from his perch and turned fully toward the doctor. "*No* 'Yeah, yeah,' " he snapped, his eyes full of frustration. "This is no game, here. You can't just stroll in when you feel like it. We're counting on you."

"*Praise Cruda!*" the crowd roared below.

"In case you hadn't noticed," Alysess said, feeling some heat- and fatigue-fueled anger rising in herself as well, "doctors are in a bit of demand lately. I wasn't exactly out shin-scrimming or diddling myself. I was trying to maybe save a few lives before I got here."

The Ragman shrugged, replaced his goggles, and turned back up to the ceiling, taking his share of the load back from his straining helpers. "Put your bag down and guard the door," he said blandly. "Tavis, get over here and steady the ladders."

"Join our army of goodness," the priestess's voice boomed out. "You are the chosen ones, the special ones, Cruda's favorite children. The god of meat smiles on you."

"*Praise Cruda!*"

Alysess went back toward the door, crossing on the other side of the chairs from the side Tavis passed by on. She ignored Tavis's giddy singsong whisper of "Naughty, naughty doc-*tor* . . ." and pushed the door closed. She leaned into it, looking back toward the Ragman and his helpers.

"The god of meat gave you life. The god of meat gave you sex, and hunger, and fear, and hope, and desire. Arms and legs and hands and faces and stomachs and penises and vaginas and ears and eyes. They are all gifts you can only repay with your suffering. With your suffering and your meekness and willingness to serve. Meek meat is the mightiest meat of all!"

"*Praise Cruda, god of meat!*"

Alysess watched the Ragman and his helpers—two women and one man, each wearing plastic safety goggles—push the I-cutter up against the ceiling's steel surface. Tavis ran around below them, pretending to steady all four ladders, but mostly just doing a bizarre little dance. "I'm helping, helping, helping . . ." he/she mumbled while skipping about.

One of the helpers was a tall, serious-faced woman who looked as though she'd never found anything in life worth even the slightest smile. Scowling seemed her natural state. The woman fiddled with the cutter's control ringlet, glowering at nothing in particular, and then her eyes fixed on the Ragman's stressed features. "Whenever," she said finally, her frown deepening.

The Ragman glanced at each of the other helpers. The portal cutters were all precariously balanced, their arms locked firmly above their heads, each gripping a side of the I-cutter's dull metal surface. From where Alysess stood, the I-cutter looked like some strange, four-legged metallic spider clinging to the ceiling between them.

"Wait for it," the Ragman said, and then it seemed that all of the room's occupants—including Alysess—had suddenly stopped breathing. Nobody moved.

"If you are angry," the priestess said loudly from far below, "there is an answer. If you are upset, there is an answer. If you feel frustrated, there is an answer. Cruda has given you all the answers. Cruda has given you Soft pills. Cruda has given you the CV. Cruda has given you sex. Cruda has given you the right to die and join the Ultimate, if you are ready."

And then, just as the congregation bellowed "Praise Cruda, god of meat!" again, the tall, frowning woman next to the Ragman pulled the ringlet and the I-cutter activated for a short three-second burst. There was a flash of blinding light from the cutter, instantly followed by a loud boom and then a shower of sparks and falling metal bits.

The noise of the I-cutter had been perfectly timed to coincide with the roaring Cruda chant.

"Fuck freely if you are angry, or frustrated, or feeling upset or restless. Cruda has given us fucking for just this purpose. Take the Soft pills. Watch the CV. If that is not enough, do all three: take the Soft pills, watch CV, and fuck freely and frequently. Do these simultaneously as necessary. Sex and the CV and the Soft pills are Cruda's medicine for a wandering and unhealthy heart. If these things do not work, if you still feel a restlessness, an anger, or a need to take action, then join the Ultimate. The feeling that you need to take action, to do something, is Cruda's way of saying, 'You are ready for me. You have suffered enough. You are ready for bliss.' That is your answer. Cruda gives you peace and perfection in the Ultimate. Cruda gives you an end to the suffering."

Again the crowd chanted, and again there was the loud explosion from the I-cutter as it blasted away a section of the ceiling. Alysess felt her heart pounding in her ears and head. She took a few steps forward into the room, watching them work, making sure her medipak was within easy reach.

Dr. Tollnismer had to admit it was exciting. Actually a kinda fuckable experience. Each time she'd aided during the cutting of a portal, she'd felt the strange exhilaration—the fever, the spirit of Revy. She didn't *want* to be excited by this. The Ragman was well aware of her feelings against preparing for a violent overthrow. She'd made it clear through all the years of cutting that she wanted them to hold off, to wait and see what Watly Caiper could accomplish peacefully from above. But still, it was a thrill to be here. To be in on it.

She knew it was dangerous; maybe that was part of its strange appeal. She knew they could get caught and executed, and she sure as hell knew they could get hurt. One time, one of the cutters had actually died while she watched. The man had gotten beaned by a big chunk of falling cemeld and died instantly. Many other times, her doctoring skills had been put to good use.

Portal cutting was not a safe venture, by any means. Alysess supposed that was why the Ragman always insisted on being involved personally. Oh, he claimed he did that because it was so important, so pivotal to the revolution, that he didn't trust anyone to do it correctly without him . . . but Alysess suspected he also wanted his "Revies" to know he was willing to take the physical risk himself, that he wouldn't ask them to do anything this dangerous unless he did it too. But how much of a risk was it really, for one who had the sight? *Hey, Rag-face, where is the danger if you can see the future?* Alysess thought to herself.

"Pra-" BA-BOO- *"-aise Cru-"* -OOOM! *"-da!"*

Again sparks and flying metal and cemeld shot downward. It would take a long time before they got through to the final layers of ceiling. They would have to stop and cut through pipes and cables, rerouting and redirecting all the wiring and tubing they encountered without ever interrupting services. The higher they cut, the slower and more careful their work would be. By the time they got up near the Second Level floor way above them, they would be toiling with painstaking care, as quietly as possible. Alysess knew it would take at least ten or fifteen more cutting sessions at this one portal alone to reach the flooring above. And, as tempting as it would be, the workers wouldn't go breaking through that final layer once they reached it. When they did get to that point, days or even weeks from now, they would stop and silently position the lines of string explosives all around the floorboards above their heads. Then they would cover their tracks: put up a false ceiling over the hole they had cut, and clean up all evidence of their activities.

It was a long, tedious process. Other doctors would be here to watch over the other cutting sessions. Other helpers would do the work at various stages. It all depended on who was available and who was on duty during the times when Cruda services were held. But the Ragman would be here through it all, beginning to end. He, Ragman-the-Subkeeper, was the only constant when the revolutionaries built a portal. He and his faithful companion, Tavis-the-wonder-IT.

"The shawls of Cruda say we find our salvation in lust. We find our salvation in the holy state of orgasm. We find our oneness with the Ultimate in the moment of glorious climax."

"*Praise*"—BOOOOOOOM!—"*Cruda!*"

Alysess knew from the sound of it that the service would be ending soon. The priestess would be bringing out her Fluffel, an equally young, healthy, and attractive naked man. Then, after she did a little more preaching, the two CV projections, priestess and Fluffel, would stand side by side and lead the congregation in the Massturb ceremony. Things would get nice and noisy then, for a little while, as the congregation all jerked and diddled off together. But after that the service would be over, the priestess would say a few final words, and then she and her Fluffel would fade slowly out, arms raised in salutation. The congregation would then all pull their respective pants up and go home. The cutting would have to stop at that point. Any portal work done after that would have to be silent work. They wouldn't need a doctor for that. If she rushed, Alysess could go up to Second then and be close to on time for her twice-weekly appointment with Watly Caiper. If she rushed. If she felt like rushing.

"*Praise*" BABOOO— "*Cruda!*" -OOOM!

"Join us now, good people, for The Massturb. Let my Fluffel and I arouse you. Let a holy lust build in this temple of Cruda, the god of meat, the god of goodness, the god of sex. We come together, as a people. We make a joyful cry of climax unto Cruda. Decant your organs now, my meek ones, let your genitals out to show the world how you love the god of meat. . . ."

Alysess heard a noise behind her. It wasn't part of the booming sermon, nor was it an echo from within the room. Someone was at the door behind her. She suddenly realized that all she'd done was lean against it. She hadn't bothered to lock it; she had just closed it. And now here she was, in the middle of the room. The Ragman turned to look down at her, his expression hinky and questioning. Tavis took a step toward her, crazy eyes blazing. Alysess swiveled around quickly and jumped forward to lock the door, but it was too late. Just as her hand reached the bolt, the door swung inward.

Alysess tried to push the plasticore door back closed, but somebody had already stuck a head in. She shoved hard, squeezing whoever's face it was between the door and the molding.

"Hey!" the face said.

Tavis was right behind Alysess now, shoving her aside. As she was pushed away, Alysess could see the confused look on the face of the person trying to get free of the doorjamb. It was a ratty old face, thin with hunger and streaked with dirt and grease. *Probably just some hapless, Softed-out bum looking for a place to take a pee,* Alysess thought.

Tavis yanked the door open, grabbed the bum by his ripped collar, and pulled him into the room.

"Hey!" the old guy said, glancing around. "What the rape is goin' on? I's just lookin' for—"

Alysess saw Tavis glance up at the Ragman and then saw the Ragman nodding somberly back. With that, Tavis pulled a tarnished blade from the sleeve of the smelly smock. It was a blade Alysess had seen many times before, long and curved on the tip, with a white plastic handle that was stained brown in spots. The blade itself had always reminded Alysess of its owner: thin, strange, dirty, and dangerous.

"Tavis, *don't!*" Alysess shouted, reaching forward.

"Yeah, don't!" the bum said, looking down at the knife.

Tavis giggled, smiled sweetly, and stuck the blade into the old man's chest, killing him instantly.

CHAPTER 3

Watly Caiper got some abrasion salve from the large selection of first-aid supplies in her curlicue-framed, gold-leaf bathroom cabinet. She sprayed some of the stuff behind her ears. It stung bad.

She resisted the urge to rub her wounds and walked slowly into the large sitting room of her bedroom suite. Crossing to the center of the room, she turned, her nightgown billowing gracefully, and sat on the overstuffed genuine leatherlike chair. Her arms were crossed tightly over her chest. The regulated air seemed cold to her now, and she was feeling incredibly tired, but she knew she'd never get back to sleep. Not tonight. In fact, she didn't *want* to get back to sleep. That felt too risky now. Sleeping was becoming a downright dangerous activity. No, tonight she had to think.

She looked around the opulent room. The walls were filled with expensive paintings, sensory-M drawings, photos, and chromells. Some were ancient, strange, dark, brooding works full of shadows and mystery and signed in blurry, indecipherable handwriting; but most were recent creations, passionless art by rich, passionless Second Level masters. The old paintings, the ones from prehistory, held the most intrigue. Strange, tender faces peered out from the faded canvases. They seemed like friendly faces: kind, gentle people who would have been nice to know. Other paintings spread out impossible landscapes and broad vistas of another time. These seemed to be beckoning to be entered. Whether they were imaginary places or places as real as the country of Manhattan was impossible to say. But there they were, real or not, looking warm, sunny, and inviting. Perhaps they were renderings of other UCA countries in the old days. Maybe Jesusland, or the drug zones, or parts of the Nuclear Nations. Watly didn't know. Maybe they were even representations of the Outerworld, way before Euroshima. Early Pre-Cedetime. Whatever they were, they looked like places one would want to be.

Below these paintings, the room's floor was covered with a plush, wire-heated air carpet, its rainbow of colors constantly shifting from one end of the room to the other as it cleaned itself. The furniture carefully positioned on that carpet was of all different styles, a Dillo sofa, a post-Cedetime chair and vanity, an antique rolltop writing desk, a state-of-the-art, gold-plated keyboard, a post-Lathone lamp and end table, and a brand-new cable vidsatt, hardly used.

This was home. This was comfortable. Familiar. Watly stared around the huge room for quite a while, wishing her head would stop throbbing so she could think clearly. The scrapes weren't deep, but they hurt like a rape and a half. It was obvious what Sentiva Alvedine had been going for. She'd been going for the wafers. She'd been trying to dig them out with her bare hands. That's probably why she kept calling for a short blade: to cut out the creosan. And the two creosan wafers, surgically embedded in the head on each side flanking the cerebrum, were all that was left of Watly Caiper.

Watly Caiper—the real Watly Caiper—was dead as a dung heap, killed ten years ago in this very house by that cop extraordinaire, Ogiv Fenlocki. Watly had been a male back then, but now she was definitely a female. And the wafers were all that was left of her self. Her personality, her emotions, her beliefs . . . all contained in two slim, fragile implants buried in the head of this unfriendly woman's body. And this unfriendly woman—maybe *raving sadist* was a more accurate, if melodramatic, term—was fighting for control.

Watly had always liked to believe that these many years might have mellowed Sentiva some. She liked to think that Sentiva, powerless but aware, had been changing and learning as she lived within Watly's life, watching how Watly behaved, experiencing what Watly saw, smelled, tasted, touched, heard, did, and said.

And Watly liked to believe that there was no such thing as an evil person. She'd always been sure of it—that everyone, deep inside, was good. That no matter what atrocities people did, they did them thinking they were doing the right thing. They did them thinking, in their own distorted way, that they were good people. They were *wrong,* but not evil. And so it was just a matter of informing people, educating them, opening their eyes. That would change them. No one was intrinsically evil. Intrinsically bad.

But maybe this wasn't the case. Maybe Sentiva *was* evil. Or was so set in her ways that it amounted to the same thing. Maybe Sentiva Alvedine had just gotten more and more enraged as time went on, more furious and determined as an imposter led her life for her. Maybe her powerlessness had fueled her anger. And maybe being locked impotently in her own body with no control over anything for so long had made her truly insane. That was a scary thought.

"Sentiva?" Watly whispered aloud, talking to the one within. She had done this often over the years, knowing that Sentiva could not answer, but had no choice but to hear. Watly kept her voice low. She didn't want to reawaken Noonie, whose room was across the hall, and who'd certainly been through enough for one night.

"Sentiva," Watly hissed again. "What the rape is your problem? Grow up, already. I'm not trying to hurt you. I'm not trying to destroy you or your people. You *know* what I'm doing. I'm raising my daughter and I'm trying to help the people below. I'm trying to help them nonviolently, from the inside—from up here where the power is. A nonviolent revolution is a good thing, Sentiva . . . you must realize that. After all this time with me, how could you still not understand what I'm fighting for? Have you spent ten years with me, seeing my every move, understanding my sincerity and my—my attempt to be . . . *good* . . . and been *snickering* to yourself in there the whole time? Have you maintained your condescending superiority through all that?"

Watly shook her head with disbelief. "The Second Level idea that the plurites below—the 'mixed-race' people on the First

Level—actually *deserve* to live like that, to suffer like that, is just plain wrong. It isn't *fair*. Come on, already. You must see that just because you Second Level people are pure of race—pure caucasoid, pure negroid, pure mongoloid, whatever—doesn't mean you are superior. Can't you see the obvious? We're all just *people*. *I* was a plurite before I died, remember? I was a mutt. Am I so horrible? Am I so different from you? Am I some inferior, subhuman creature who deserves to live in shit while you live in terradamn *gold*?"

Watly looked around again. She, herself, *was* living in gold. In fact, she had grown pretty darned *used* to living in gold. That sort of blew the bolehole out of *that* argument.

Ah, shit on toast! Watly thought to herself. *What the rape am I trying to do here, anyway? It's not like I haven't said all this catshit to her a million times before in the last ten years.*

Watly almost felt like running. Running away from everything. She almost wished she could take the elevator to the top floor, climb to her roof, hop in her personal Floobie-pod, and Floobie her way to some distant land. Floobie away from her job, her ambitions, her responsibilities, her whole life. But that wouldn't help. Because Sentiva would still be inside her. And that was what she really wanted to run from. She wanted to Floobie away from the beast within.

Watly stood up suddenly and began pacing the room, finally ending up in front of her full-length dressing mirror. She stopped and looked into her own green eyes—Sentiva's eyes. She tried to remember what she used to look like. She tried to remember the male Watly Caiper she had left long ago. She couldn't. She could only remember a dark blur of maleness—a vaguely high forehead, a vaguely crooked nose . . . broad shoulders . . . tallness . . . a penis . . . a sack of something behind it. . . . It was like a very old dream, that old life. It was like a book read long ago.

Watly looked at her face, the face she had now. The familiar, current one. It was still strikingly attractive: the pale skin, the high cheekbones, the full lips, the overly strong jawline, the symmetrical dimples that had gradually—with time—turned into the midpoints of two thin lines that ran from the edges of her nose to her chin. The long eyelashes, the fluffy mane of long, brown hair with the twin streaks of gray that pointed down toward her firm, trim body. And the body—the round curve of the softer, slightly sagging breasts, the narrow waist, and the little bit of a belly that had appeared after Noonie's birth. Then the lean, taut legs, the feet with their familiar map of delicate blue veins that crisscrossed the tops, the long, strong fingers—fingers that were now stained with blood around and under the short nails. . . .

"You want the body back, don't you?" Watly whispered to her reflection. "Maybe that's all you want. Maybe I read you wrong. Maybe you don't give a rape about politics anymore. Maybe you just want to be a whole person again. That's fine. I can deal with that. I don't blame you for wanting out. Maybe we can cut a deal. I need to raise my child and I need to see how I can help the revolution—particularly with this election thing coming up, and all. But those are the only two things I care about accomplishing. So when Noonie is old enough to take care of herself, and when I have done all I can to fix this insane system we live in, we might be able to work something out. You and me."

Watly took a deep breath, surprised at the sudden rage she saw in her own reflection. "Until then, you lay one hand on my daughter, I'll raping *kill* us. I'll raping kill us and you'll never get out. I'll do it too. So . . . so you stay put, Sentiva. Sit back and relax awhile." Now Watly's voice came out even louder than she expected. "Stay where you raping belong! You hear me?"

Watly stared at the beautiful woman in the mirror a while longer, hardly aware she was muttering "I'll raping *kill* us" over and over. She was too busy obsessing to really notice her own words. She was too busy wondering. Wondering how she could protect her own daughter from *herself*. Sometimes . . . sometimes it was hard to tell where Watly ended and Sentiva began. Sometimes it felt like they were merging, their shared mind becoming one obscene, monstrous composite.

Eventually Watly went back to the armchair and sat down. She was even more afraid to sleep now. She reached over and snapped on the CV, looking for a Music Hall pleat. The CV mist quickly filled the room.

Music would be nice right now. Music would be distracting. Something modern and sexual. Or old and dissonant. It might help her ignore that strange sensation in her head. Misdirect her from this feeling. This impossible feeling that, even though Watly couldn't read Sentiva's thoughts at all—and vice versa—it seemed as though Watly *was* picking something up. It was as if—faint and distant though it might be—Watly could sense something radiating from Sentiva's brain. Maybe it was just imagination, but it sure seemed like she was feeling something coming through. And it was a something she didn't want to feel.

Watly could feel Sentiva Alvedine laughing. Laughing calmly and quietly deep within Watly's own head.

CHAPTER 4

Noonie wasn't really asleep. She was pretending. She was used to pretending. She knew her mom had been upset by the latest Night Lady episode, and she knew it would make Mom feel better if her daughter seemed to have relaxed enough to go back to sleep.

So she had faked it. Taking care of Mommy. She had slowed her breathing, stopped her own crying, made her body go limp, and even let a little drool bubble out of her lips. And Mom had liked it. Noonie could tell.

After a few minutes, when Watly finally left the room and Noonie was sure her mom was back in her own suite across the hall, the child got out of bed. She felt no pain yet around her throat from the choking, just a strange echo-of-big-hands feeling.

She wished she had a cat to pet. She'd had one once, but not anymore.

Noonie pulled her drawing stuff out of the dresser drawer and went over to the night-light corner of the room. She sat cross-legged by the big-nosed glowing face and started to sketch. She felt dreamlike, as if her methodically drawing left hand were moving through thick, viscous fluid. She drew numbly for a period of time that might have been five minutes or might have been an hour.

There was still no pain around her bruised neck, but Noonie was beginning to feel the familiar secret ache a little lower. The secret ache was connected to the Big Secret. The secret ache was just at the base of her throat, in the little hollow right at the center of her collarbone and directly above her breastbone. That small indentation was the center of the secret. It was the valley where the secret ache always began. She had looked it up in an anatomy leaf once, but couldn't seem to find its name. On one chart in the leaf, arrows pointed out things in that area of the body like the thyroid gland, the esophagus, the clavicle, the sternocleidomastoid, and the larynx. No arrow seemed to point to and name the little neck hollow. The closest one said "Isthmus" on it. Maybe that was the place. It sounded right. The "Isthmus" place. That's what she'd call it.

So her secret sprang from the Isthmus. It hid in the Isthmus. It felt like it was buried in the Isthmus, like a creature hibernating for the winter. Sometimes the secret seemed to swell. Now was one of those times. It felt to Noonie like the secret had swelled so much this time that it was hard to even swallow past it.

But no matter how much it swelled, Noonie refused to think about it. It was too monstrous. Too wild to let loose. It was a secret about Noonie, about her very self, but it was also a secret about an event. A certain event two years ago. An occurrence from the distant past. The cause of her secret scar. A thing that Noonie had done once, long ago. Maybe two years, or maybe really a lifetime. A thing that Watly and Aunt Alysess knew all about but never spoke of. Ever. A deed of Noonie. An act of Noonie. A thing. A monstrous, unthinkable thing.

Noonie Caiper drew in the dim glow of the grinning night-light until she was tired enough to finally go back to sleep. Then she put her picture away and climbed in the bed. She wouldn't look at this picture again. She didn't need to. She knew what she'd drawn this time. She'd drawn lines. Hundreds and hundreds of little black lines, layered carefully, one above the other, until they filled the entire page. In the end the page was solid black.

And Noonie didn't need to look at the picture to see solid black. All she had to do was close her eyes.

CHAPTER 5

Alysess dragged the body down the four flights all by herself. It wasn't easy to move the bum's corpse down all those stairs, although the guy couldn't have weighed more than ninety pounds. The last two flights she'd just kicked at it hard and watched it tumble down by itself as she shouted "Look out below! Body fall!" to anyone who might be in the way.

She could've used help. She felt overheated and dizzy. But the Ragman had been adamant. Rules were rules. "You raped up," he had said. "Now you clean up your own mistake."

At the bottom of the stairs she pulled the body through the hall, across the antechamber—past a few straggling parishioners—and down the front steps. No one paid any attention to her efforts—to her grunts and groans or to the streaked trail of fresh blood the body left on the worn tile. Death was not unusual on First Level nowadays.

Alysess leaned the corpse up against the other dead body on the church stoop. She stretched over backward a little and twisted side to side to loosen her sore muscles. Slipping her medipak off her sweaty shoulder, she fished out a bright red body tag and stuck it on the bum's forehead. She hoped the death lowtruck would pick both bodies up at the same time. If not, someone else was sure to call in when the guy started to smell bad enough. She wiped her bloody hands on the bum's ripped shirtsleeve.

Rape, Alysess thought as she crossed Eighth Street and headed uptown on Second Avenue. *I hate all this shit. Why is every raping thing okay to do, as long as it's in the name of Revy?*

She walked fast, angrily remembering what the Ragman had said when she had yelled at him for letting Tavis kill the intruder.

"We cannot risk discovery at this point, Doctor," he had drawled calmly, trying to soothe her with his eyes. Suddenly she didn't buy the charismatic eyes deal anymore, and she'd just glared back at him, demanding a reason, an answer.

"Sacrifices must be made, my children," he'd continued, talking to everyone in the room now. "Some innocent people must die for the greater good." Now he looked directly at Alysess, as if warning her. "Everyone, my child, *everyone* is expendable when it comes to the success of the revolution."

And this is our fearless leader, Alysess thought as she walked rapidly up the street. *This is the kind soul who will set the world right.*

She stepped to the side of the street, letting a broken-down unmanned copper speed noisily past her from behind. Wasn't much police work for the copper to do, as far as Alysess could see. Scouting out dead bodies was about it. Breaking up a sunbean fight over by the rationing stations, maybe. A few rapes pretending to be fucks in the name of Cruda, perhaps. But the coppers didn't ever bother with those. No prob.

If there was trouble down here it usually came from Second Level anyway. Almost every host was a fade-out host now. When donors up on Second took control of their First Level hosts, anything went. They were wild. None of the rules were followed anymore because, apparently, nobody was punished for misbehaving.

Alysess pulled her hat out and smoothed it over her head. It was dripping pretty bad now, big dirty drops splashing all over the place, making her wetter than she already was. It also made walking very slippery work. That rancid, recycled liquid that fell constantly was, at least, water. People tried to use it, to filter it, to boil it, to clean it for drinking. It wasn't much good for that, but it was something. And fresh water was in short supply. This stuff sure wasn't fresh, and it would make you damned sick no matter what you did to it, but it just might keep you alive.

It was sure nice of the Second Level to keep the thirsty First Level constantly soaked. Of course, this wasn't for altruistic reasons. They just wanted First nice and moist, woodless, and paperless. Nothing flammable, everything wet—through and through. Cruda forbid a fire should break out down here and spread the five stories up to Second where the *real* human beings lived.

Alysess snorted quietly to herself, a habit she found unpleasant but that she seemed to be doing more and more lately. It was fast turning into one of those characteristic traits she found so annoying in others. She didn't like chronic eye rollers, head shakers, shoulder shruggers, or finger snappers . . . and here she was turning into a full-fledged snorter. That was worse than all of them. Alysess stifled the urge to snort again in response to her own thoughts.

The daylites cycled down to night setting, making it even harder for her to walk. Alysess sidestepped something that was either a pile of garbage, a sleeping bum, or yet another dead body.

The daylites' night setting was darker than ever. Nobody ever repaired the broken ones anymore, so night was getting darker and darker. The day setting was darker, as well. The First Level was turning into a place of shadows. Shadows, dirt, and death.

There was no evening setting for the daylites at all anymore. That would have at least added variety. But no, it was either day or night, as far as those huge, oblong lights way up on the First Level ceiling were concerned. And even *that* cycle was pretty arbitrary. There was now "Lower time" and "Upper time." Lower time was shifting daily. Upper time had to do with the sun. It'd been three or four years since the daylites were properly calibrated to actual day and night. They'd been slowly slipping around the whole clock, bearing no relation at all to the real sun.

Now First Levelers were lucky enough to have a time cycle all their own, wasn't that just dandy? Alysess felt fortunate that she was one of the few First Levelers left who actually got to go up to Second to see the sun. Everything was so raping automated up there now, there was hardly any call for workers to go above. A few-odd technicians, repairpeople, and specialized cleaners were all that was called for. Even deliveries were made without workers now. Goods manufactured or repaired in First Level factories traveled up by sealed factory lift. And those lifts were well guarded and continuously flooded with toxins—just as a good-natured precaution, should some misguided, overly ambitious plurite try to travel up one. Only a few other doctors still traveled up to Second like Alysess did. Even that age-old practice was on the wane. Alysess was the lucky one. Twice a week she got the privilege of witnessing Upper time in person. As Watly Caiper's personal physician—no mean feat, that—Alysess had a regular pass to go up and see the real sun biweekly. By her latest calculations, this First Level evening, seven P.M. or so, was actually a Second Level morning, five-thirty A.M. or so.

The doctor turned quickly, almost walking into one of the avenue's uprights. She had drifted to the side of the street and almost bashed her face into a terradamn cemeld girder. They were on either side, every thirty feet or so, holding up the ceiling. *A fine piece of work, those,* she thought. *I'd like to knock 'em all down right now. Every single one of them. Every raping five-story-tall girder that holds up the ceiling. Every raping one of the zillion uprights that separates the First Level from the Second.*

She found herself snorting again. *You and what deity, Alysess? You and what raping atomic bomb?*

She slipped once and fell on her hip. Didn't hurt too bad, but she got up quick. Fall down nowadays and stay long enough, some old Softed-out fart'll come along and try and rape you. "Fuck for Cruda," he'd say. Fortunately, most of them were so sick and hungry, all they'd need was a poke in the nose to knock them out of commission. She felt comforted by the fact she still wore her boot dagger. Thankfully, she'd never had to use it. Nor did she know if she'd ever be able to use it if the situation arose. But it still gave her some sense of security.

She looked behind her quickly as she started off again. There were a bunch of "young" people—middle to late thirties— gathering in front of an empty store. They were breaking out some cheap booze, getting ready to party. It was somewhat of a shock to Alysess. As a doctor, she saw mostly the older ones, the dying ones. Sometimes she forgot that there were still some relatively young, relatively healthy people about. It was nice to see.

Some of the men of the group were shirtless. Their thin, muscled chests looked good. Very male, very strong. As she glanced at them, Alysess was reminded of Watly's old, male body. Sometimes, especially recently, she missed it. She missed the man-ness of it. The smell, the size, the weight, the firm feel. She missed the whole penis thing.

But that was just silliness. Watly was Watly, and Alysess was just experiencing some kind of middle-aged sexual restlessness.

She took a last look back. Beyond the young ones was

something shiny working its way up the avenue. The gleam was from a hosting cuff. The cuff caught the dim light with each upward arm swing as its wearer walked nearer. The partyers split up quick, trotting off in all directions. But none went toward the host. Alysess picked up her pace as well, not wanting to be anywhere near a cuffer. That's where the real danger was. A host. That kind of rape, or beating, or murder attempt was not so easily pushed away. No matter how weak the host's body was, the power of a strong, thrill-seeking Second-Level donor's mind was in charge—and that was nothing to underestimate.

Alysess walked around a few tenters. Their tents were worn and ragged, but she could see lights inside. "Cuffer comin' up," she whispered, warning those within.

She was almost at the Fourteenth Street tubestop now. The tubestop was a dark shape up ahead, going from the street surface all the way up to the dank, mildewed ceiling. Alysess walked carefully toward it, wary of falling again. A couple of bums were sprawling in the center of the street in front of her, leaning in and gnawing on something. They glanced up defensively, looking worried that she had come to bother them. Alysess graciously gave them wide berth and continued. They'd probably caught a live cat somehow, and they sure as hell didn't want to share it with anyone.

"Cuffer approach," she said over her shoulder, and she could hear them scrambling away with a slurpy-sounding "Thanks!"

Dr. Tollnismer opened the tubestop's scal and stepped inside the tube. The circular blue light flickered and went on around her. She slipped her identicard and travel pass into the slots.

"Face forward, please," the mechanical female voice said.

"I *am* raping facing catshit forward!" Alysess snapped. Why did she feel so enraged suddenly?

"For what purpose do you wish to travel to the Second Level of Manhattan?" the machine asked blandly.

"Listen, bolehole breath, I gave you my raping pass, I gave you my raping ident, now you read them and send me up, subspawn! I'm in no mood for conversation today, okay? *Move* it!"

CHAPTER 6

It was early morning. The hazy sun was just now peering timidly over some of the Second Level buildings. It was cooler today, and the skies were relatively clear. As clear as they ever got.

Noonie Caiper was drawing pictures of huge monsters that ate people. She was lying on her bedroom floor, propped up on her elbows with her feet crossed in the air behind her and her tongue sticking absentmindedly out of the left side of her mouth.

She had already put her makeup on for the day. She had learned well. Her mother had taught her to apply it first thing in the morning, because you never knew when you were going to run into someone. Better to be prepared.

Noonie touched her neck absentmindedly as she worked. It still hurt, like a bad bruise all around the outside and a sore throat on the inside. *Major choke wound*, she thought for a brief second. *Battle scar. Monster-bite injury.*

She had actually gotten a little sleep after her middle-of-the-night drawing session. She couldn't remember her dreams, but when she'd woken up her left hand had been twisted across her body, stretched around as if trying to cover the scar that ran down the back of her shoulder and right arm. The entire left arm had been numb and tingly from lack of blood.

Noonie cleared her throat and ran her hands through her hair. She'd need another hair-straightening session from Mom soon. *That* was always a real pain. Noonie wished that just once she wouldn't have to straighten her hair or put on the skin-lightening makeup. But she always had to. Her skin was a little too dark and her hair was a little too kinky. She was, genetically, a plurite. She was the biological result of the joining of Watly Caiper's sperm with Sentiva Alvedine's egg. She was *supposed* to be the joining of Sentiva's egg and Corber Alvedine's sperm. So her whole life was an attempt to disguise the fact that Noonie was a plurite.

Noonie wasn't even sure what a plurite *was*. She knew it was what those below were. Her mother had spent hour after hour, year after year, explaining about First Level life, telling her what the people were like, what they did, how they acted. Telling her that she was really one of them. That she was a plurite. That she belonged there. But she'd never actually *been* below. The Second Level was where Noonie'd grown up. *It* was where she belonged. If she belonged anywhere.

Noonie pushed the hair out of her eyes as she colored in her picture. The monsters she drew were enormous. They were building-high, purple beasts with big fangs and sharp talons, and the people under them were tiny little multicolored creatures scampering about in a panic. At least that's what Noonie wanted them to be. The colors were smearing so that her crowd of frenzied citizens was rapidly turning into a big mess of yucky brown. The color-adjustable click-pen she was using smudged way too easily. It reminded her of something. The smudges. They reminded her of another secret. The big, big secret. The secret Noonie herself tried never to think about. The Isthmus secret. The worst secret of all. Noonie swallowed the thoughts down. Down deep.

She set the drawing roughly aside and was about to start another one when she heard voices coming from the hallway. She jumped up and ran to the door, opening it and leaning into the corridor. The voices were coming from down at the end of the hall where her mother's office was. Noonie tiptoed down the bright green carpeting until she was directly in front of the office doors. The doors were large, made of heavy inlaid wood, and sported shiny brass handles. Noonie carefully turned the right door's handle. She pushed the door open a crack and put her eye to the narrow opening.

There was a thin veil of CV mist covering the entire room. This room was Watly's office, an exact replica of the corporate boardroom at the Alvedine Building. Carefully aligned CV lenses and projectors were evenly spaced all around the top molding of the walls. Noonie knew that all the dimensions and fittings were exactly the same in both places. Here and at Alvedine, everything was identical and carefully positioned. Each item of furniture was bolted to the floor, except for the chairs.

When she moved her head from side to side, Noonie could see all of the large conference table in the center of the room, with the twelve tall-backed black chairs spread around it. The far end of the long, gray table flared out gradually and then abruptly rose up into an intimidatingly large semicircular desk that cradled a thronelike wooden chair.

Noonie's mother sat in that throne, holding court. She was wearing a power outfit—a bright green, skin-tight, two-piece business suit with orange accessories. Her hair was swept back into a severe little lump, which pulled all the skin of her face into a smooth mask. Her voice was shrill, her accent *very* Second Level, and she was speaking corptalk like a real pro. She spouted the Missers, Mams, Charticles, Re-ebbs, Voldowns, and Graphups like she had invented the language.

She was also the only real person in the room. All the shimmering forms of her top corporate executives were projections. The twelve men and women sitting around the table, listening intently and nervously to Watly, were in actuality back at the Alvedine Building. Some of them looked like they were sitting *inside* the material of the chairs instead of *on* them. It was kind of a spaf effect. Since the chairs in both locations weren't bolted in place, the alignment of the projections with their supposed seats was always at least a little bit off. Noonie figured her mother probably looked the same to them. To the real executives sitting there in that huge office building some sixteen blocks away, the CV projection of Mom's head probably looked halfway embedded in her duplicate throne's top spires.

Noonie was annoyed she hadn't arrived sooner. She'd secretly spied on her mom's CV board meetings many times before, and the best part was always the beginning, when all the glowing executives slowly materialized around the desk. It was a max spaf thing. Peaky prone.

". . . which is totally unacceptable," Watly Caiper was saying. "The reports were required two days ago. You've all screen-flowed me badly. I am not a pleased pres, here. We were supposed to upsize the forpushing on conpros. I needed the profit-and-loss on the expanded hosting program, I needed the Soft pill production schedule, and I needed, people, the buyout figures on those three CV pleats." Noonie's mother took a long, dramatic inhale, and then let it out very slowly, glaring at every face in the room. She stared at each person in turn, just long enough to force his or her eyes to turn away.

A dark-skinned bald man sitting on the opposite end of the table coughed and timidly raised his head. The hand trembled as he spoke. "I'm sorry, Mam Alvedine, but we were working on your political campaign as well. In the time we had—"

"Not good enough," Watly interrupted. She leaned forward and shuffled some of the plastic sanifiles around in front of her. "I don't expect a hundred percent from my people, Misser Woage. That is unacceptable. A hundred and twenty-five percent is also unacceptable. I expect a full two hundred percent from everyone in this room. Nothing less. I need twice what is humanly possible from each of you. If I don't get it, you are out."

The short, pale woman sitting to the right of Woage kept her eyes downward and said, "We apologize, Mam Sentiva."

"*What*, Mam Celdene?" Watly Caiper asked, leaning farther forward and raising her eyebrows. "*What?*"

"I said, we apologize," the woman repeated, almost whispering.

"Mam Celdene, you and Misser Woage are, as of this very moment, and effective immediately, *budgeted out*. Misser Woage, for insubordination; Mam Celdene, for interrupting me. I will not be interrupted during my meetings. You spoke without being recognized."

Woage and Celdene stared blankly at Watly for a moment.

"Was I not clear? You are both budgeted out. Do I have to repeat myself?"

Noonie watched the projections of the man and the woman slowly rise, walk silently across the room, open a nonexistent door, and disappear into the wall. It was a spaf effect. Aside from the chairs, the doors to the two respective conference rooms were the only things that didn't match up, so watching the CV people leaving was always fun.

"Try and get a job over at Gavy, would you?" Watly yelled after her ex-employees. "They could use a few more cretins."

Noonie was used to seeing her mother act like this in public. This was the Sentiva persona. This was Mommy's public role in life. The part she played every day. It was always weird to watch, though. It always made Noonie feel slightly uneasy, a tad hinky. It made her feel funny, and maybe, she thought, for all the wrong reasons.

Other than when Mommy was alone or was with Alysess, she was this other woman. This backstabbing, overly ambitious, cruel businesswoman, the president of Alvedine Industries. Mommy would spend hours alone with Noonie explaining why this behavior was necessary, why it had to be. And explaining how this "Sentiva Alvedine act" was just a mask she used to gain needed power and prevent suspicions from arising. "Always remember that I don't really believe the things I say when I'm like that, Noonie," Watly often said. "That kind of attitude and behavior is exactly what I'm fighting *against*, my baby. But I've got to pretend. We've got to play make-believe until we have enough power to change things."

Noonie had grown up with these two women as her mother. The make-believe woman and the kind, compassionate, patient, concerned Watly Caiper. The weird thing was—and Noonie would never confess this to her mom—the weird thing was that Noonie sometimes liked the make-believe lady better. That woman got respect. There was something strong, charismatic, and hypnotic about her. And, the girl suspected, Watly sometimes actually enjoyed being Sentiva too. Noonie sensed that it wasn't all an act, that—though Watly'd never admit it—this ten-year-old Sentiva Alvedine behavior was drawn in good part from elements within Watly's own personality. Maybe it had started as totally fake, but over the years more and more of that side of Mommy's own personality had come out into use. Noonie thought of *both* creatures, both her mothers, as a little bit of a lie, and a little bit of the truth. And lately, the nine-year-old Noonie had felt more in common with the public Sentiva persona than the private Watly one. *That's* what made her hinky.

"Well," Watly said, standing up and walking slowly around the entire conference table, "on to business. But remember, do right by me, people. I have no compunction about budgeting out anyone—or everyone—at this table. You're *all* incompetent." She stopped walking when she was directly behind her seated assistant, Roullic Neets. "Roullic, what's the story with the campaign?"

The projected Misser Neets shuffled through his monitor's screens, looking more annoyed than fearful. He was the only one at the table who didn't seem afraid of Watly. He was a very good-looking man, with shoulder-length, bright red hair. Almost *too* good-looking. He appeared to be a broad caricature of handsomeness. "Well, Mam Sentiva," he said, his voice strong and resonant, "things look good. Your announcement about how you'll increase the Soft pill dosages down below if you're elected went over well. It's a smart business move profit-wise, and a smart political move First-Level-solutions-wise. And the voters know it. They respect the profit motive and they like the politics. You're up ten points in the polls."

"I want to be up another ten by tomorrow," Watly said without emotion.

"Could be tough. Gavy's going to announce something today. Something about promising to push for an increase in references to suicide in the Cooda services, if he wins."

"*Cruda* services," Watly corrected.

"Whatever," Roullic continued. "Anyway, that should increase his popularity by an estimated three to six points."

Watly bent over Roullic's left shoulder and stared him down. "Then I'll just have to announce something better, won't I?" she spat. "What about the food situation? I hear they're hungry on First. Hunger makes people dangerous. What if I announce plans to increase supplies of food down there if I win? Calm those hungry vermin down."

"No good, public relations-wise. Doesn't read right. Anyway, they've got plenty of food. They're just hoarding it. We already give them enough." He fiddled with his screen for a minute. "If you announce a plan to give them more food below, I figure . . . you'll get a drop of two and a half points. Maybe more."

"So think up something good and release it, Roullic. I insist on those ten additional points. Give me a good, solid campaign announcement and release it at once. Something really fuckable. I want it out on CV by noon." She straightened and resumed striding confidently around the table.

"People," she said, "I've a little more than a week before the elections, and I intend to win. If I do, that's good for our business, good for our country, and good for all of you. Everyone here gets a bonus, and since I'll be running the country as well as the company, there will be more responsibility for each of you, and along with it, a higher salary. However, if I should lose—"

Watly stopped abruptly and stepped forward. She stretched her arms right through two of the projected executives so she could lean in and spread her hands on the table between them. Their ghostly images flickered as her body invaded theirs. Watly's teeth flashed. She looked like she was about to pounce down and eat the table's gray placene surface. "If I should lose, people, I'll budget you all out. The whole gang. No question."

She stood up tall again and walked casually back to the end-desk, easing herself into its throne. "Now," she said finally, "the reports. Misser Pallig, why aren't I seeing more money from the Hosting Department? I want to know why it's fallen off. If stats aren't up soon, I'll cancel the whole raping system. And don't give me catshit about how many of the plurites are too sick to host. I don't buy that. They're not *all* sick. We pay big. So what's the story, Pallig? Make this good. And give me *solutions*, here. . . ."

Noonie heard the sound of the front door buzzing behind her. She quickly pulled Watly's office door closed, careful that it didn't click too loudly, and ran down the hall. She hopped the entire hallway in three seconds flat and then slid down the wooden bird-wing banister to the downstairs living room. The door buzzed again as Noonie trotted across the foyer towards it. *Spaf*, she was thinking, *Peaky prone. Aunt Alysess is here for her appointment! She's even early! More time for me! Playtime!*

It wasn't Alysess.

CHAPTER 7

Roullic Neets swept back some of the long, red hair that fell in front of his face and poured himself a tall glass of water. He played with his left eyebrow for a few minutes, looking at his two new aides. They both wore dark gray one-piece business jump-suits. The woman had short-cropped blondish hair and the man had a stylish laser-cut and the beginnings of a thin mustache. They were both very young. Nicely young. Roullic took a long, refreshing drink from the glass, his eyes never leaving his two helpers.

The board meeting had ended ten minutes ago. Sentiva's image had flickered out after she'd spouted one of her more vivid patented obnoxiousnesses, and then all the executives had filed quietly out of the room. Back to their cages. Show over. *Back to the sunbean mines, folks.* Roullic alone had remained behind, summoning Kness and Volder. Now his aides stood in front of him, patiently awaiting his instructions.

Roullic put his glass down—it was empty now—and his hand went back up to fiddle with the eyebrow hairs. He liked the way Mam Kness and Misser Volder were looking at him. There was admiration there, and respect. And not just a little lust.

Roullic knew he was attractive. He'd paid good money over many years to become attractive. He'd thinned the nose, thickened the lips, sharpened the jaw, lowered the hairline, brightened the eyelashes and died the irises a pale yellow, lightened the skin tone drastically, broadened the chest, narrowed the waist, added two inches to the legs, and more than tripled the size of the lump in his pants. Being attractive and desirable was a very useful thing in the business world. As long as one was careful that the attractiveness was corporate in nature.

"Mam Kness. Misser Volder." He nodded to each. They both smiled endearingly at him, more at ease now that he'd spoken. Roullic counted three times Kness had so far glanced down at his prominent crotch bulge—and two for Volder. This was good. He could trust these two. Lust was the strongest tool of loyalty.

"Things are a little out of hand here, situation-wise," he said very softly. Unlike Sentiva, Roullic believed that the more power one wielded or wanted to wield, the quieter one's voice should be. Both Kness and Volder stepped in closer so they could hear. This was good. Roullic had applied even more illegal pheromone-augmenter than usual this morning. *Breathe deeply, my little faithful assistants.*

Roullic switched hands, playing with the other eyebrow now. It felt good, like petting and pulling on a tiny furry animal. "The Sentiva Alvedine situation is way too sticky, control-wise. I'm doing all I can to help her, to work for her, to get her elected and run her business properly. That's what I get paid for, and I always do my job. Always. But she is not a good executive. She has no poovus, which is a bad image decision. Company presidents should always have mates. Corporate parties don't work properly otherwise. She has no control of her temper, which is also bad. She makes enemies—which is good—but she makes *personal* enemies, which is not. She is, quite frankly, a major bolehole. Which is very bad. She's not a nice person. Not . . ." he consciously tensed his sphincter muscles hard suddenly, making the prominent mass within his pants twitch and expand for his aides' viewing enjoyment, "not like me. And I am next in line here at Alvedine, corporate-progression-wise. I deserve the job. I've certainly earned it. If I were, hypothetical-wise, head of the company, this could be very good for both of you."

Both Kness's and Volder's eyes were now riveted on Roullic's crotch. He made it dance once again for their benefit. And his own. He had to be careful not to be too blatant with Volder,

though. Even a hint of overt homotending could, if it got out, ruin
his career. That kind of stuff was very First Level. The only
acceptable Second Level outlet for *that* behavior was to be a
donor. You could do any damn thing you wanted when you were
vacationing inside a plurite. Roullic would have to set up a hosting
appointment soon, if he wanted to scratch *that* particular itch. He
made a mental note to do some multilusty donoring in the next day
or so.

"What I need from you two, help-wise," he continued, "is
your intelligence, your ingenuity, your discretion, and your
complete and utter silence." He smiled charmingly at them, aware
that his expensive, prefab dimples were deepening perfectly with
the grin. "We have ten days until the election. I need you to find
something, instigate something, or fabricate something. Something big. Something that will blow her out of the water. A
startling epiphany of epic proportions. Something no one can
blame on me."

Roullic took a quick look around the room to double-check that
all the surveillance lenses were off. "I need a revelation," he
murmured slowly, "that will ruin her—and not just politically,
that's not enough. I don't give a rape about politics, though I
certainly don't particularly want her running the country."

This last statement was a bit of a happy fib on Roullic's part.
He did indeed give a rape about politics. In point of fact he hoped
to become Chancellor himself one day. Perhaps in the election
after this one. And the best way to get political power was to start
with corporate power. But his two assistants didn't need to know
all that.

"The point is," he continued, "Sentiva's got to be ruined,
corporate-image-wise as well as politically. Both at once. Enough
to lose her the Manhattan election, and enough to get her instantly
budgeted out as Alvedine's president because her reputation
makes her useless to the company. She's got to be stopped cold.
If she just loses the Chancellorship but keeps her job, then I'm
out. We're all out. Budgeted right the subs out. That won't do. I
need to move up into her chair, my friends. And if we can do that,
if we can accomplish that one simple task, I will pull both of you
right along with me"—he patted his upper thigh—"to sit on my
proverbial corporately presidential lap."

Roullic slowly poured himself another tall glass of water,
holding the pitcher over his lap. He pretended to lose grip a little
on the pitcher, and let a good deal of the liquid spill directly on his

crotch. He focused for a moment on the mental image of both his assistants in the nude, staring, awestruck, just as they were now. Then he glanced down and observed with pride as the clearly apparent shape within the wet pants swelled up some and shifted a little to the left, looking for egress. Volder and Kness appeared hypnotized by the growing, moving bulge.

"Over the years," Roullic said calmly, "I've let Sentiva be. I've done my job and nothing else. I was certain she would choke herself, bring herself down. But she hasn't. I was wrong. I seldom am. But . . . I did misjudge her. She is a shrewd one. She doesn't rape up when it counts. Yet everyone—trust me on this one—*everyone* has something to hide, something deeply rotten under the surface. If you look hard enough, there is a scandal to be found in the life of every human being. And now, with her power base growing and the election for Manhattan Chancellorship virtually in the bag, things are out of control. A scandal must be found—about her, about someone close to her. I don't care. Find something about her home life, her family, or her raping hairdresser if you have to. It doesn't matter. Something must be done. And you, dear friends, are the ones to do it. You are the maulers and breakers in this scenario."

The glassy-eyed Kness and Volder smiled widely and nodded like obedient, eager servants. Roullic reached up and firmly grasped Kness's right shoulder and Volder's left. He thought he heard a mild gasp of arousal from each of them at this unprecedented direct body contact. "If you can't uncover anything potent enough," Roullic whispered, "and you can't whip up something impressive in time"—he pulled them both in closer—"then Mam Sentiva Alvedine is going to have to have an accident, that Misser Roullic Neets had nothing to do with. Understand? I have nothing to do with it. Knowledge-wise, culpability-wise, *any-which-wise*-wise. Am I being clear, here?"

Roullic's two assistants nodded vigorously again. "Then we're done here," he said. "Keep me posted—discreetly, of course. I'm counting on the both of you."

Roullic turned to Kness and squeezed her shoulder. As he pinched it repeatedly through her thin jumpsuit, he tried to lift the skin of the shoulder slightly each time, hoping that he indirectly succeeded in rubbing her breast against the fabric of her suit. He looked straight in her wide eyes.

"One day, Mam Kness," he said without undue emotion, "I

would be quite delighted to fuck you heartily and at length, if you'd be at all interested."

Kness turned bright red and looked at the floor, smiling shyly. She twitched, shuddered, and closed her eyes for a moment. Roullic could've been wrong, but he suspected that Kness had just had a small orgasm, right then and there. It was a delightful concept.

"And you, Misser Volder," Roullic said delicately, turning his attention to the man. He squeezed and twisted Volder's shoulder hard, as if it were some other portion of the anatomy, and watched as small beads of sweat broke out on the man's forehead. He chose his words very carefully. "You, my young friend . . . you are quite welcome to watch any or all of our activities at very close range, should this proposed sexual event ever actually occur, reality-wise."

Roullic smiled warmly and compassionately at both the red faces before him. "That is all," he said, dismissing them. He thought he saw a brand-new, small stain on Misser Volder's jumpsuit as the two left. *Let's say there is and enjoy the feeling of power, shall we?* he thought.

CHAPTER 8

Noonie opened the front door, giggling gleefully. But Alysess Tollnismer wasn't standing there calling out "Nooner-face!" with her arms open, bracing for a big hug. Standing there at the top step was, instead, the man who had murdered Watly Caiper ten years ago. It was Ogiv Fenlocki, Mommy's executioner.

Noonie liked him instantly.

Chief of Police Ogiv Fenlocki was in high official regalia: knee-high leatherlike cop boots; bright blue pocket-jacket splattered with gleaming medals and highlighted with prominent police insignias crowning the epaulets on each shoulder and the elbows; polished silver chip pistol on his customized buzbelt; blue placene sun visor tilted way back on his high forehead; and sharply pressed dark blue veneer pants with gold buttons down each leg, from hip to boot top. He looked serious spaf.

Fenlocki smiled sweetly down at Noonie. He had a kind, thoughtful, weathered face. The features looked rubbery, accustomed to smiling a lot. All the strong lines in his cheeks pointed downward—ready to fold aside at any time for a broad grin. The deep creases across his forehead seemed to indicate that his bushy eyebrows had been raised in pleasant surprise one time too many.

"Hello, little girl," he said.

"I'm not little," Noonie said back, trying to look serious and businesslike. "I'm nine, going on ten. And I know who you are. You're Chief Fenlocki. I've seen you on CV."

"Good for you. You're absolutely right." Fenlocki stepped in the doorway, but Noonie Caiper was standing in his way, preventing him from coming farther into the foyer without pushing her aside. "Nine years old, huh? No kidding? That's just spaf. You're right. You're a big girl."

"Don't patronize me, mister," Noonie said, holding her head up high and standing her ground.

"Okay. You win. I lied. I still think you're a little girl. Nothing wrong with being a little girl, in my opinion." He put his hands on his hips and looked down at her expectantly.

Noonie put her hands on her hips also and looked up at the chief. They stood like that for a moment. "Well?" she said finally.

"Well, is your mom home?" Ogiv asked politely.

"Why?"

"Because . . ." Fenlocki thought for a second before going on. "Well, because I used to *know* Mother Sentiva Alvedine years ago and I'd like to have a little chat with her. *Possible?*"

"My mom's a busy woman," Noonie said, trying hard to scowl up at the chief. "A very, very busy, important woman."

Fenlocki squatted down in front of Noonie so that they were eye-to-eye. She noticed little flecks of light gray in his blue irises.

"Are you going to give the chief of police of the entire Country of Manhattan a hard time, little kid?" he asked softly. "Huh?"

"She's finishing up a CV meeting upstairs," Noonie replied. Then she added, "And you have long nose hairs. You ought to trim them."

"Touché."

"She should be down soon. Want me to check?"

Fenlocki reached over and took her hand. "We'll wait here for her, okay? I wouldn't mind talking to you for a moment, huh? Let me . . . let me ask you something, little girl. I have a question I'd like answered, okay? Honest answer? Just between you and me?"

"What?"

"Your name's Noonie, right?"

"Yeah. It's a contraction of 'no one.' "

Fenlocki smiled again and all the face wrinkles deepened. He squeezed her hand playfully. "It is not. Don't patronize *me*, little girl."

"That's not patronizing. That's condescension. And outright lying," Noonie said. She couldn't help but smile back at the man. "So? The question?"

"You have another name?"

"Alvedine. Noonie Alvedine," she answered, feeling hinky suddenly. "Want me to spell it? How'd you get this job, anyway? You're a little thick, it seems to me."

"You have a secret name?" Fenlocki asked, his eyes intense yet still vulnerable and kind-looking.

Noonie felt her hand stiffen in his. Even that word *secret* alone had such brutal power, such weight. "What?" she said.

"What is your secret name, Noonie? You have a secret one? A name nobody knows?" The chief's grip wasn't hard, but he wouldn't let Noonie pull her hand away.

"I don't know what you mean," Noonie said, her heart pounding heavily in her chest.

"You can tell me. I may be a little thick, but I'm an okay guy. 'Peaky prone,' as you kids say. Maybe even what you call 'spaf.' So what's your secret name, Noonie?"

"You're crazy."

Fenlocki pulled her gently forward a little and spoke very tenderly. "Is it . . . Caiper? Is that your secret name? Noonie Caiper?"

Noonie finally managed to jerk her hand free and jump back from the chief. She could hardly breathe, suddenly. "I'll . . . I'll go see if my mom's done," she blurted. The child spun around and ran down the foyer. She jumped quickly up the wide bird-wing staircase and turned back at the top, way, way out of breath and a little dizzy. "You can have a seat in the living room if you want," she gasped, trying to sound composed and in control of herself. "I'm . . . I'm sure my mom'll be down soon."

Fenlocki had moved in to stand right at the foot of the shiny wooden staircase. He looked up with genuine compassion. "Hey. Don't bust your power ringlets, little girl. I was just curious."

CHAPTER 9

The Ragman was exhausted. His arms were aching and his robe was too damned hot. And his butt itched. Another raping heat rash.

He let the cutters finish cleaning and installing a temporary ceiling. They had only gotten up to the first layer of CV cables and sewage pipes before calling it quits. The Ragman would be back tomorrow during morning services to continue the work with a new team. This was enough for one day.

The Ragman and Tavis climbed down the steps and exited the Cruda building. Three bums stood before them next to the dead bodies at the bottom of the stoop. Each beggar had a hand out.

"Spare a dollar, my friend?"

"Got an extra Soft pill, brother?"

"Food token? Want to pass on one little food token to a starving old woman?"

The Ragman pushed past them, muttering "Go rape your-selves" under his breath. Tavis laughed heartily.

They walked a few blocks in silence. Tavis kept a steady two paces ahead of the Ragman, partly as a bodyguard, partly as a lookout, and partly just out of that strange one's need to dance about in front. They passed by a food rationing station, ignoring the crowd of people who were yelling angrily. The station had apparently exhausted its sunbean supplies and was only dispensing small pieces of hardloaf for each food token inserted. The mob was furious.

Farther down the avenue, the amount of tenters thickened. The Ragman cursed under his breath every time he had to walk any distance out of his way to sidestep another tent. A few bicyclists rode their rusty vehicles noisily past, and then both Tavis and the Ragman had to move toward the uprights to let a couple of pullers pass by, dragging their overloaded lowtruck.

A bus was coming up the avenue toward them. The Ragman watched it approach. This was an unusual sight. Buses were a rarity now, only a few left, most of them long ago having succumbed to lack of supplies and maintenance. This one listed badly to one side, its left cylinders almost dragging along the road surface. As it limped slowly by, the Ragman could see it was overflowing with passengers, some hanging on to the outside, unprepared for the rigors of shin-scrimming.

When the bus was gone and they had started walking down the center of the street again, Tavis finally spoke. "Subkeeper. Subkeeper—can I have an *evening* tonight? Can I?"

"Oh, Tavis, Tavis, Tavis. Didn't the bum do anything for you, my child? Didn't that killing give you any pleasure?"

Tavis jumped up and down as they walked. "Too fast! Too fast! Nothing for me there. Please, please, *please.*"

The Ragman smiled. It was almost painful, as if the muscles of his lips had atrophied, as if they had gone dry and brittle and would crack from the effort. "Okay, Tavis, okay. You did well today. You acted swiftly and surely and properly, helping Revy."

"Yes, yes, Tavis *did*. Tavis was good!" the genderless creature shouted.

"You may have an evening tonight. After we eat, you can find your friends and go to sexsentral. Get yourself a fade-out host and have an evening. But *Tavis*—"

"Yes, Subkeeper?"

"Make sure it's a *fade-out* this time. You hear me? No torturing and killing *regular* hosts, okay, my child? Remember, fade-out hosts get lots of money to die. That's the idea. They've signed a contract and they expect it. They want money to leave to someone. *Regular* hosts are just trying to make a living. A dangerous and *stupid* living, but a living. No killing the regular ones, Tavis."

Tavis jumped up and down five times in quick succession. "Oh, yes! Yes, yes, yes!"

"Ta-*vis*! Do you hear what I'm saying?" The Ragman stopped walking and glared at his companion. "A regular host is a person just like you or me. They need money so they decide it's worth taking the risk of letting a Second Leveler vacation inside their body for a few hours. They're not doing it because they want to die. You already know that, my child. I've told you this before, and you're not stupid."

"I'm having an *evening*! I'm having an *evening*!" Tavis sang as they walked.

"Are you listening to me? I'll take it back and you'll have to stay in the subs tonight if you don't listen to me, my child."

"Yes, yes, *yesss*! Tavis listen good!"

"Okay," the Ragman said. "Then you find a good fade-out to kill for your evening. They get paid quite well, and they expect it."

The two of them turned down a dark alley and approached its dead end. In the dim light, all the heaping piles of garbage looked threatening—as if ready to spring to life and attack them. There were mounds of shattered cemeld with rusty cables poking from them, great lumps of shredded plastic and broken placene, and huge hills of smelly rags and twisted wire. The Ragman and Tavis stopped in front of one of the smallish piles. The Ragman glanced around to be sure they were alone, and then moved various pieces of the artificial garbage in careful sequence. The pile clicked and then slid aside, revealing the opening to this particular subs-access ladder.

Climbing down the sub tube was not easy for the Ragman. His muscles ached and his bolehole rash chafed with each slow step downward. His eyes were heavy. He needed a bath. His beard itched. He felt completely drained and very hungry. A good dinner would be very welcome. He could hardly wait. After dinner he might even take a spin at his starwet machine. It had been a while since he'd done that, and it usually refreshed him. Maybe part of his fatigue was old-fashioned sexual frustration. Sex might perk him up. He needed to regain his strength. Right now he felt so exhausted, all he wanted to do was give up and live in the subs forever. At least the subs were safe, comparatively clean, and dry. At least they had food and water and private starwet machines down there for the revolutionaries. Sometimes everything seemed too raping hard. Sometimes the Ragman wondered why he even bothered. Why he was so obsessed even after all these years. Why he didn't just quit entirely, find a poovus, and retire from leading the revolution. Retire from the responsibility, the disappointments, the endless waiting, the frustration.

The last ten years had not been happy ones for the Ragman. His Revy plans had been quashed at every turn. Second Level's powers-that-be were smarter and more perceptive than he had imagined.

The one thing he'd always known was that, if the revolution was to be successful, the First Levelers would have to be behind him. It was all well and good that he had a team of trained revolutionaries and rooms full of weapons down there in the secret subs below First Level's streets—down where "subways" used to be in ancient pre-Cedetime days. The point was he needed more than that. He needed the people. He needed their minds.

At one stage, ten years ago, he'd had them. The groundwork had been laid and everything was ready to go. The Ragman and his cohorts had been carefully spreading California rumors. Stories soon abounded all over First Level that a successful revolution had occurred way out in the Republic of California. The Ragman had watched hope grow in the people, spreading like a benign disease. Hope spread desire, desire fed rebelliousness. Spirits were raised, and unrest was in the air.

What the Ragman hadn't counted on was the Second Level. They had apparently watched carefully as those below became more restless. Though they didn't know about the subs, they saw the danger in the rumors. The danger of unrest. And they took countermeasures. Those up above started their *own* rumors, paying off money-desperate plurites to spread them.

"The California Revy has failed," these new rumor mongers said. "Anyone involved in the revolt was brutally executed by nerve gun. Crowds of people—thousands upon thousands—were murdered and tortured. Now things are worse than ever over there. The far-off country of California is now a living nightmare: curfews, constant surveillance, no minor freedoms, and no CV."

And the plurites—the Ragman's people—they believed these new stories. They became afraid. They became cautious. With no battles and no bloodshed at all, Second Level had won the first skirmish.

And so the Ragman had fought back. The next years became a

continuous war between the Revies and the Second Level for
control of the most valuable weapon of all: the spirit of the First
Levelers. And the Ragman was now uncomfortably aware
that—so far, at least—those above had won that war. Won it
completely. They had, in fact, beaten the raping shit out of him.
They had the money, and they had the resources.

The strongest and most lingering defeat had been the latest.
When, four years ago, the Second Level quietly introduced Soft
pills and the religion of Cruda to this formally atheistic country,
things had changed drastically. These mind-control strategies
quashed the feelings of revolt, turned the people into sheep. The
Ragman had respected, almost admired, this ingenious tactic.

But the Ragman—the Subkeeper—was not done yet. It was *his*
turn to make a move—and this move was to be the biggest of all.
It would be a different kind of move—no more the slow, gradual
rumors that built a mood of rebellion. That was too easily
sabotaged. He had learned his lesson. The foundation was in place
for a swift, radical change. The seeds had been planted. Secret,
ingenious seeds. He was prepared. He and his Revies still had
their resources. They still had the underground subs complex. At
least he had managed to keep that a guarded secret over all these
very difficult times. He had over eleven hundred people working,
living, and preparing down there now. And he had others, like
Alysess, who lived in First Level squalor, but were part of
the sub's extended family. Part of the Revy's army.

He also had the portals now, doorways to the revolution. There
were fifty-four of them at this point, finished and waiting to
be used. He had the technology ready and in place to override the
seven tubestops to Second, as well as the thirty-eight factory lifts.
This gave him a total of ninety-nine usable doorways. Ninety-nine
holes in Second Level's armor, waiting to be used.

The Ragman wasn't worried about neighboring countries.
Come the revolution, they were not likely to make trouble.
Pennyork and Jersey and Longeye were too weak and disorga-
nized to even try. The Noreast Commonwealth was far too busy
with its internal squabbles. In fact, none of the Outerworld would
be apt to get involved. In spite of all the various trade agreements,
treaties, alliances, and countless protection promises, each of the
individual governments of the United Countries of America was
too deep into isolationism to mess with a Manhattan revolution.
That's why they all split up in the first place back during

Cedetime. They wanted to be separate, uninvolved in each other's problems.

The Ragman had no fear of them. His only concern was making Revy succeed. He had the portals, which was good.

And he had other things. Big things. Things only those who lived with him down in the subs knew of. Things people like Alysess could not know of. Particularly not Alysess. She traveled to Second. This was good, because she could gather information. But it was a danger, because she was constantly at risk. She couldn't know too much. So the Ragman kept her in the dark as much as he could. She was not permitted down into the subs, and he only told her what she had to know. She was a messenger. She found out what she could by herself or from Watly Caiper, and relayed it all back. And she was the sole go-between for the Ragman and Watly. Watly Caiper—Revy's Second Level mole.

Tavis was using that same well-worn, curved killing blade as a key now to unlock the sealed hatch at the bottom of the sub tube. It was dark down there, now that the garbage pile had slid back into place above their heads. The Ragman tapped his foot impatiently. When the hatch finally swung open, they both stepped in and quickly crossed the red-tiled sub platform. The platform was crowded with crates and barrels, leaving only a narrow path between the tall stacks of containers. Every spare inch of the subs was storage now. Where it used to be spacious and clean, it was now crowded, claustrophobic, and dirty. No time was wasted on cleaning now.

A rather rotund-looking cockroach ran over the Ragman's left foot. He crushed it, enjoying the satisfying crunch. Roaches were coming back lately. They'd somehow rebounded after years of being well controlled. And he had no love for the little beasts. No love at all.

Tavis set up the unicarriage and they both climbed aboard, feeling it wobble and adjust for their weight. They sat side by side in the carriage's cab, riding the one-wheeled vehicle along the right-hand silver rail toward the Ragman's quarters. The Ragman leaned back in his seat and closed his eyes as they sped along. Tavis would know not to disturb him now. He could think in peace. He thought about Alysess and Watly again. That situation worried him.

The Ragman had little hope for Watly. He didn't trust her anymore. Perhaps he never really had. How could he rely on someone who inhabited the body of the revolution's worst enemy?

Where was the guarantee that Sentiva was forever silenced? Could the Ragman be expected to entrust vital secrets to someone who had an anti-Revy brain within, hearing and learning everything? Watly already knew way too much, and therefore the Sentiva inside knew it also.

And even if that wasn't a factor, there was the problem of the inherent corrupting influence of the Second Level. Who knew what living in luxury for ten years had done to Watly? The Ragman often wondered about that. He also wondered, even if she *was* still trustworthy, could she do any real good anyway? So far she hadn't exactly supplied an abundance of priceless information as a spy, and her plan of "revolution without death" —to change the system from within—was a long, excruciating uncertainty. The Ragman had little patience or hope left for the idea. His way was better. Fast. Surgical.

Alysess often pleaded with him to give Watly's way a chance, to see what she could accomplish before they had to resort to bloodshed.

Well, he might do that. If Watly won the Chancellorship he might give her a month or two. But no more. He had waited long enough. And if she *lost* the election . . . that was another story.

"Before you go, Tavis," the Ragman said after they had reached their destination and hopped off the unicarriage—the Ragman's quarters were a short walk from this sub platform— "you have to check on a few things for me. Run a few errands. Go to the print shop and check on how the signs are coming. Make them work faster. Check out the distribution planning centers. Also drop in on the lab. The chemicals must be ready in time. We have to get moving. I want the Man-With-Hat-On misdirection ready to go and I want those signs ready to go up and the distribution ready to start. It all has to run smoothly and simultaneously. We've got three days. We need to get all the Revies working harder to meet the deadline. I will not veer from the deadline, tell them that. The plurites have to be ready and ripe by election day. We need a full week to do that—no more and no less. I want this whole lower country—every raping person, cat, and insect—to be ready to explode on the day of the elections."

The Ragman put his hands on Tavis's shoulders. He knew, as he always knew, that this strange being before him understood a lot more than he/she let on. "If Watly wins, we'll back off a little, my child. We'll cool down for a short while. But I want to be ready. If she loses, it's time for the big one." *Maybe*, he thought, *it'll be time for the big one even if she wins.*

Tavis's wild eyes seemed to glow with excitement. "What does the *sight* tell you, Subkeeper? What does the sight say?"

The Ragman looked into those shiny eyes—his partner's eyes, his loyal companion's eyes. He let his hands drop and felt the blood drain from his face. Then the Ragman closed his eyes tightly and let his whole body go limp and relaxed. The only thing keeping him from falling was the stack of crates at his back. "The sight tells me, my little friend," the Subkeeper said softly, "the sight tells me—shows me—that this little island country of ours is going to split wide open like a crushed sunbean. Yes, my child."

CHAPTER 10

Watly Caiper snap-ignited an expensive cigel with her left thumb and forefinger and took a long drag from it. She tried to appear calm and even-tempered, watching the curls of pink smoke rise and obscure Ogiv Fenlocki's face in swirling sections. Cigels were still illegal, but Watly thought smoking one now was a nice touch—something the real Sentiva Alvedine would do in front of the chief of police without hesitation. The smoke made her a little lightheaded, and there was the beginnings of a distinctly queasy sensation growing in her lower abdomen. She smiled slightly—trying to make it a cold, superior smile—and settled into the bent-wood rocker, feeling it tip back perhaps a bit too far.

"My daughter said you wanted to speak to me, Sergeant," Watly said placidly.

"And a delightful child she is, too," Ogiv said. He grinned boyishly. "But it's 'Chief' now, if you don't mind."

Watly had to admit that Fenlocki was charming—looking all dressed up in his cute soldier suit, his older, lined face now somewhat reminiscent of Watly's late uncle, Narcolo Caiper. Fenlocki had aged well; he looked even wiser and kinder than she remembered him.

"Oh, yes," she said. "One promotion after another through these years, so I hear. Congratulations. Now running things, are you?"

"I have that old case to thank for it, in a way. That old case *you* were wrapped up in, Sen-tiva. Catching and killing that notorious murderer, Watly Caiper, did wonders for my reputation and my career. Forgive me for saying it, but Watly killing your famous poovus, and then me killing *him,* was the best thing that ever happened to me."

Watly scowled.

"Sorry," Fenlocki said. "Didn't mean to open old wounds."

Watly detected something sarcastic and mocking in the chief's tone. Even in the way he said "Sentiva." Sen-*tiva.* It was as though he were making fun of her name. She wasn't sure if the sarcasm was really there, or if her hinkiness was making her paranoid. Noonie *had* looked seriously shaken when she'd dashed in to inform Watly of the unexpected visitor. The girl had blurted out "Fenlocki's here!" and then run into her room, slamming the door shut. Watly wondered if something strange had passed between them. She took another long draw from the cigel and let the smoke drift slowly out of her nose.

"To what," she said, as if impatient, "do I owe the honor of this reunion?"

"Well . . ." Fenlocki said, sitting back in the wicker love seat and crossing his legs. He rested his left boot across the spotless fabric over his right knee. Both sharp pants creases held firm. "Well, the funny thing is, it happens to be related to that Watly Caiper mess. And to the— Can I have one of those?" He motioned to the silver cigel case on the table between them.

"Help yourself," Watly said, still inhaling her own. The wooziness seemed to be increasing.

The chief fumbled to snap-ignite one. Finally he managed to clumsily pop the flame capsule on its tip. It looked as though he might have singed his thumb a little in the process. He winced. "I never could get the hang of these things," he said, taking a short puff. He wasn't inhaling, just filling his cheeks with the smoke and blowing it out. Pretend smoking.

"Mr. Fenlocki, I don't have all day to sit here and reminisce—"

"Then I'll try to get right to it. Bear with me for just a moment . . . Sen-tiva." The chief looked at Watly with what seemed to be genuine affection. He took another half-assed puff, instantly expelling a great ball of pinkness, and then continued. "If you remember, I got out of your hair pretty quick after all that trouble back then. I didn't hound you, I didn't harass you, and I didn't poke too deeply. I closed the book on that Caiper incident quickly, in spite of all the loose ends and unanswered questions. Did you ever wonder why?"

Watly looked down at her blunt fingernails. She felt a lot like biting what was left of them, but decided it wouldn't look good. "There's nothing to wonder," she answered. "It was over. A man killed Corber Alvedine, my mate . . . then he lured me down to that retched lower level and tried to kill me . . . then he came up here and tried to rob my house, and then you killed him. It was painfully simple."

"Painful, maybe. Simple? No." Fenlocki coughed a little from what looked like an unintentional lungful of cigel smoke. "But I didn't pursue it. I didn't investigate. I didn't question the donor plates we found in the bed where Watly died—*your* bed, incidentally. I didn't ponder too deeply over why the rich and powerful Sentiva Alvedine should subsequently take on Dr. Alysess Tollnismer as her personal physician—a low-class, *very* First Level doctor who also happened to have been Watly's suspected accomplice *and* possible poovus at one point—"

"That's catshit," Watly interrupted. "That doctor saved my life. She *protected* me from Watly. She saved me from him after he lured me—"

"So you said. So you said. I remember the story well. And I never bothered to dig deeper. I never bothered to delve into the meaning of a certain note I got from Caiper's bag. I also never bothered to think too hard on the coincidence that Watly's reported ambition was to have a child . . . and after he dies, suddenly you're pregnant."

Watly closed her eyes and sighed deeply. "What a remarkable and earth-shattering coincidence, Mr. Chief of Police. Arrest me immediately on the charge of motherhood."

"And, perhaps *most* important, I never bothered to delve into Watly's side of the story. I never once formally investigated the veracity of his frame-up claim. I never investigated the possibility that he was telling the truth about his innocence."

"And you were correct not to," Watly said angrily. "Are you going to believe every wild story a fugitive murderer makes up?"

Fenlocki freed another round cloud of smoke that dissipated just before it reached Watly's face. "Do you know *why* I didn't scrounge around any further? Do you know *why* I closed the case and walked away?"

"I have the feeling you're going to tell me," Watly said, trying her best to look bored and annoyed as she pushed out her cigel butt. What she really wanted to do, what she really felt like doing, was crying. She wasn't sure why this should be her reaction to the situation, but that's what she felt like. Just raping crying like crazy.

"There are three reasons, really. The first I'm not all that proud of. The first was, frankly, selfishness. The capture and murder of Watly was, as you can see"—he gestured down toward his impressive uniform—"good for me. I knew it would be. I didn't particularly want to jeopardize that by finding any uncomfortable loose ends or contradictions. And so here I am, actually *living* on Second Level, hobnobbing with all you important folks and running the entire police department. My lack of professional curiosity was the wisest career move I've ever made."

"I'm so happy for your good fortune," Watly said, shifting in her seat to try to ease the rising nausea. She cleared her throat quietly. *Be a woman, Watly. Don't cry.*

"The second reason is the obvious one. All was as it seemed to be; why push it? 'Don't overthink, Fenlocki. Take things at face value!' I said to myself. A murderer everyone was looking for was disposed of. Calm is restored. A peace officer has done his job. Business as usual on the island country. Anyway, there's no such thing as a complicated murder case and personhunt that isn't followed by a few unanswered questions. It's the way of the world. There are more important things to worry about."

"I fail to see . . ." Watly started slowly. Then she stopped, trying to relax. She gazed off at the view of the quiet street beyond her enormous living room windows, hoping the serenity would calm her. The hazy sunshine looked inviting. "I fail to see . . . what any of this has to do with—"

"The *final* reason," Fenlocki said, uncrossing his legs and bending forward over the table, "is the one I think you'd be most interested in. And that reason has to do with Watly Caiper himself. It has to do with the last few minutes of his life."

Fenlocki almost whispered now. "The man spared me, Sentiva," he said. "Watly had every chance in the world to kill me, and he didn't. He couldn't do it. He stopped cold, looking at me with pity and empathy, lowered his weapon, and waited for *me* to kill *him*. Sometimes I'm sorry I did. Truly. I sensed something at the end. I sensed that this was a good man. Whether he killed Corber or not, this was a good man. And he must have had a good reason for what he did or did not do."

"Fabulous," Watly said, looking back from the windows and glaring at the chief. "So you came here to tell me that you hold forgiveness in your heart for the man who killed my poovus. I'm delighted to hear it. You've made my day."

"I'm not finished. The point is, I got to thinking that—even if something weird *was* going on—I'd leave it alone. Even if the donor plates and the Alysess thing and the letter and all sorts of other little clues indicated the possibility of . . . of *something* . . . of—oh, I don't know—of Watly still being *alive* in some form, I still wasn't going to touch it. Why should I? Everything was back to normal, everyone was happy, and I had no desire to continue tracking a man . . . a man I have . . . respect for. A man I owe my life to."

"This whole conversation," Watly spat out, "is preposterous! Your insinuations are outrageous, Mr. Ogiv. I have no idea why you're here or what the rape you want from me . . . but I have every intention of filing an official complaint as soon as—"

"The reason why I'm here, Sentiva," Fenlocki said firmly, "is the polls."

"What?"

"You're doing very well in the polls. I've been following them."

Watly stared at Fenlocki incredulously. "I'm so damn glad you care," she said.

"As of yesterday, it appears not unlikely that you'll actually win."

"You don't know how much that means to me, coming from you," she said, shaking her head. She wanted to appear as aloof and above-all-this-catshit as possible.

"Bear with me for another moment, Sen-tiva. Humor a harmless old man. Let's just say, for sake of argument, that my guess is right. Let's say Watly is alive. Has been for ten years. Let's say, just for fun, that he's been in your body. 'No problem,' the spry young Fenlocki says. 'Watly lives the good life on Second now. He has a beautiful daughter and a great job.' The youthful cop's gut says the guy just may deserve it. A quiet, peaceful, luxurious life. Maybe the Watly fellow might even find some ways to help those below, ease the suffering a little. Give them a hand from above. I'm all for that. They're my people. I haven't forgotten. The system's hard on them."

Fenlocki squashed out his own cigel and stood up. He strolled slowly around the furniture as he talked. "Well, the sergeant—he's still a sergeant—watches quietly from the wings. He keeps track, and his theory doesn't pan out well. This sake-of-argument Watly doesn't do diddly to help those below. If anything, his corporate catshit makes life tougher for them. Either the sergeant is wrong about Watly still living, or the guy's alive but doesn't give a rape about helping the people he came from, *or* he's just damned scared and therefore damned good at playing the part to the hilt. Fine. Still no problem."

Watly watched the chief as he wandered around the room. The sense of teariness had passed, but her stomach felt really bad now, like she might vomit any minute. She was afraid to do much with her hands, afraid they would tremble so violently her fear would be obvious. She kept them in her lap and tried rocking a little in the chair. "Is there, by any chance, some bizarre point to this whole thing?" she asked, perhaps a little too loudly.

Fenlocki ignored her comment and continued. "So this Fenlocki gets promoted and promoted again. The Second Levelers trust him. And they should. He's trustworthy. He's a good cop. Sure, he cares about First Level and fairness, and all. He cares about improvements, but he has no interest in destroying all of Manhattan while trying to save it. There are other ways. He's a part of the system. And the system has been good to him. He works with it. In it. So, eventually, he gets promoted right to the top, in charge of everything. Quite an accomplishment for a First Leveler, if I do say so myself. Virtually unheard of. 'Course I am light-skinned, and mild-featured enough to pass for pure caucasoid, and I suppose that was a factor. . . ."

Fenlocki paused for a moment to stroke his face lightly—top to bottom—as if double-checking to see if what he'd just said was true. He crossed over to the windows and looked out at the street, appearing deep in thought. Watly saw the chief fish in his left-hand pants pocket absentmindedly. He pulled something small out and popped it in his mouth, chewing loudly. Was that a sunbean he was eating?

"Anyway," he said while crunching, "there he is: Fenlocki, chief of police. He's the boss. And he's privy, suddenly, to Second Level's most important and vital secrets. Defense secrets. Counter-Revy secrets. All the emergency plans, special equipment, and secret strategies and techniques we have ready to stop uprisings. This Fenlocki may not agree with all the methods planned, but he understands the need. Should people go crazy one day and resort to violence, they must be stopped. And so he's happy to be a part of it, happy to be a peacekeeper—what he's always been. Knowing these secrets is quite a responsibility. Only the chief of police, the high district officials, the cabinet . . . and the Chancellor of Manhattan him- or herself, are privy to the entire picture."

"Is all this babbling supposed to mean something to me?" Watly asked. She snap-ignited yet another cigel—something her tummy really didn't need, but her hands and mouth did. She tried to slow her rhythmic body movements, realizing she was rocking the chair far too frenetically.

"What all this means," Fenlocki replied, turning back to face her, "is that I started to get a major attack of hinkiness as soon as I realized you might win. That's when it occurred to me that there was *another* explanation for your perfect Second Level behavior over the years. That Watly was indeed in there, but was biding his time, waiting for just the right opportunity. That concept makes me mucho hinky. When it was a matter of me turning my back on someone who was living a simple Second Level life, raising a sweet daughter, and all, that was one thing. It's another story for me to ignore the possibility of revealing vital secrets to someone who might use them against us. I will not do that. My job is to prevent that."

Watly stopped rocking altogether. She wondered for a moment if she should come clean. Confess everything. Get Fenlocki on her side; help him to see it her way. She wanted desperately to tell someone . . . anyone. Alysess and little Noonie weren't enough. What a relief it would be to bare all. This seemed the perfect time. Ogiv Fenlocki seemed to have guessed almost everything anyway. But he was wrong about one thing. Watly did not want a violent upheaval any more than he did.

Watly Caiper just wanted a chance to change the system from within. She was confident she could do it as Chancellor: slowly, gracefully, and comfortably for all. It had been hard to do much of anything as head of Alvedine without raising suspicions. In truth, she'd *had* to do bad things to maintain her cover. She didn't like to think about that. It'd been necessary. But if she failed even as Chancellor, and that *was* a possibility, the truth was she *would* probably help the Ragman. She had promised him. If she failed, she would have to pass any new defense secrets along to help Revy. She'd made that deal long ago. And so the chief was right. She was a danger to him, to his job. But perhaps he would understand. This man was a wise and thoughtful person. This man had lived below once. He was a plurite.

Watly watched the chief pop another something into his mouth and chew.

Could she trust him? What did he really want? Perhaps this was all a bluff. Perhaps he was just following a hunch, trying to trick Watly into confessing who she really was. That way Ogiv Fenlocki could kill Watly Caiper once again—for good this time. Finish what he had started—doling out state justice. Close the Caiper case forever.

Watly was confused. And when confusion set in, it was always best to play it safe. "You are a deranged bolehole of a sergeant," she said coolly.

"Deranged bolehole of a *chief of police*, if you please," Fenlocki said. "I could be wrong about everything. In which case, I do apologize, but if that's the case it should make no difference to you, Sen-tiva. You go ahead and try to be Chancellor, you've got nothing to fear. If I'm wrong, I can't hurt you. The truth can't hurt you. I don't like your politics, but I'll work with you. And for you."

Fenlocki walked around the table until he was right in front of Watly, looming over her, brass buttons and medals gleaming. Watly found herself rocking rhythmically again.

"However," the chief said, "if my little fanciful, farfetched scenario is *correct*, I suggest you gracefully back out of the race. Immediately. Because, unless you quickly pull your name from the ballot, I'm reopening the Watly Caiper case as of tomorrow and starting a thorough investigation. I'll find out the truth and, if the truth is what I guess it is, it'll ruin you. It'll be ten years ago, all over again."

He took a step even closer and continued speaking. "If you keep running for Chancellor—and if the woman I'm talking to right now is Sentiva Alvedine—then she is looking at her loyal chief of police. But if you continue running—and that's my good friend Watly peering out from those beautiful green eyes—then she is looking at her worst enemy. Understand? *Worst enemy.*"

Watly suddenly had an embarrassing coughing fit from her own smoking. The chief bent toward her as if to help, but she angrily waved him away. "Open any case you like," Watly said when the coughing subsided. "I have nothing to hide. And you'll have a *lot* of explaining to do next week when I'm elected your direct superior!"

"I'll give you till tomorrow noon to pull out."

Watly stood up. They were face-to-face. His weathered features were only inches from her eyes. She could smell Fenlocki's cigel breath. She also detected the distinctive odor of dried sunbean coming from his mouth. She wondered absurdly if her own breath was as embarrassingly acrid. "I am not pulling out! I have no intention of pulling out! And you, Mr. Fenlocki, are leaving my premises!"

Fenlocki smiled again—that charming, boyish smile—and slowly turned toward the door. "You have until tomorrow to decide. I owe Watly that much. I owe him an opening, a chance, a way out. He gave me one once. A big one."

"Get the rape out of here, now!" she yelled.

Fenlocki started sauntering down the foyer toward the front door. "It's been a pleasure," he said as he walked. He motioned back toward the wooden stairway. "Say good-bye to your daughter for me, would you? Sweet kid." He indicated something with a precise, upward point of the finger.

Watly's eyes followed the direction of the point and saw what he was motioning to. At the top of the banister, where the carved wings were widest, she could see the crown of Noonie's brown-haired head. The child had been watching all of this.

When the chief got to the door, he turned back and looked Watly over. His eyes seemed to pause for just a brief flash at breast level. "Forgive my candor," he said quietly enough for Noonie to miss from her distant vantage, "but if you *are* Watly Caiper in there, you make a damn gorgeous woman. As a man you were a bit gawky. So long, now."

And he left.

CHAPTER 11

Watly thought back. Talking with Fenlocki had spawned a rush of memories she couldn't stifle. The old days. Ten years ago. Her death. Her rebirth as a woman. There were things about being a female human being she had not expected at all.

Right from the start, Watly had been surprised. When the consciousness transfer occurred all those years ago, Alysess and Watly had gone straight down to the subs. There they met the Subkeeper to explain what had happened. They both related the bizarre story, Watly doing most of the talking near the end.

"So you see, I've been killed," Watly had told the Ragman. "The plan didn't work, and I've been killed. But what's left of me is here, in this body. It's *me*, Watly Caiper. And I'm ready to stay down here and work for the revolution. I am ready to help you revolt without death. Without violence." Watly looked at Alysess and gripped her hand tightly, saying, "We both are."

The Ragman thought for a moment, stroking his beard. His face went very pale and Watly wondered if maybe he was using the sight to see into the future. He must have been. His body trembled slightly, looking weak and vulnerable. Watly was sure he was witnessing some unseen future event, peeking into what would be.

"No," the Ragman said finally, looking strong again. His eyes were hard. "You will not stay in the subs, my child. You are Sentiva Alvedine now. You will go up to Second and live as her. We can use you better up there."

Then came the arguing. There was a huge, seemingly endless fight over this new plan. Watly didn't want to be a spy. Alysess didn't want Watly to risk it. Neither wanted to be separated from the other.

But even as they fought, the Big Idea was taking shape in Watly's mind; the Great Plan to Change the World from Within the System *as* Sentiva. She fought less vehemently as the plan took form. Eventually she began to agree with the Subkeeper and present her new proposals. Alysess continued to protest. But even her protests grew less strident. It didn't seem that the doctor was being convinced; it just seemed she was slowly giving up.

"Yeah," Alysess began to say as they talked. "Yeah. I see. That makes sense. I see your point. Yeah. Well, whatever you think is best. No prob."

All through that meeting in the subs—the explaining, the fight, the discussions that followed—Watly felt a strangeness coming from the Ragman. It was as if she were suddenly a frightening thing to him. It was as if she were a different kind of creature now. The Ragman acted a touch more condescending, made a touch less eye contact, seemed slightly more fearful, a smidgen more uncomfortable, seemed to listen to her just a little less, to interrupt her just a touch more, and acted just a tad as though Watly were now slightly less than human.

At the time, Watly thought the Ragman's shift in attitude was due to him not trusting the Sentiva Alvedine within. Only later did she realize that this was not it. Aside from Alysess, *everyone* treated her slightly different now. Not because she was no longer a plurite, not because she was to live among the elite, not because her "self" was only a projection, not because she was a spy now, and not because she shared her body with the suppressed mind of a very dangerous person. *Everyone* treated her different. People who hadn't known her former self treated her different. People who didn't know anything about her situation treated her different. It was as though she had somehow dropped a rung or two in humanness. Particularly with men.

She had dropped a rung or two in humanness because she was a woman.

Watly had thought that kind of attitude was an extinct, ancient thing. She thought it had died somewhere in early prehistory, way before Euroshima, way before Cedetime. But it was still very real. As a man, Watly had not seen it, had not noticed it, *could* not see it. The thing was apparently invisible to men—even supposedly sensitive men. It was a look, a nonlook, a choice of word, a tone of voice, a pattern of speech, and an overall shift in attitude.

In autorestaurants, in stores, at parties, on the streets, at the Daviti games, with her coworkers at Alvedine . . . it was always there. She had to talk just a little louder to be listened to, act just a little more serious to be taken seriously, appear just a little less childlike to be treated as an adult, and behave just a little more intelligent to be taken as smart.

As the time passed, she realized just how lucky she was to be in such a powerful business position. If she hadn't had the weapon of her corporate clout, she suspected everything would be much more difficult for her. It was a strange new world. She couldn't help wondering if she herself had treated women this way when she was a man. She finally reached the conclusion that she had—unconsciously and unintentionally. It was woven into the fabric of society, stitched deeply into the culture.

She resented it. It was stupid. Unless she flexed her corporate powers with men, she sensed that she was always just a little bit condescended to, always just a little bit ignored . . . and—whether she flexed her powers or not—always, always, always just a little bit frightening. Women, she concluded, were apparently very intimidating things to men. Scary things. Foreign things. Somewhere along the line, men had gotten it into their heads that these creatures were not like them. That they were mysterious, dangerous beings of a whole different species. Kind of funny, that. It was as if it were unconsciously believed that with breasts and a vagina came an unfathomable, incomprehensibly different brain.

Foreign creatures, these things with ovaries and breasts.

Ah, breasts.

That downward "flash of assessment" that men's gaze often took within the first few seconds of meeting.

How surprising it had been to Watly to discover how many men seemed more comfortable talking to her breasts than to her face.

"Hey, Misser Neets," Watly said one day during a board

meeting. "Pardon the interruption, but what the rape are you staring at?"

Roullic Neets squinted, looking confused. "I was looking at you, Mam Sentiva." He pulled at his left eyebrow and continued with his report. "As I was saying, production-wise, the Soft pill situation—"

"Excuse me. . . . *Yoohoo!*" Watly jumped in. "Excuse me, but my tits are not going to reply to you. *I* might, but they won't. Most assuredly. They're just tits, Misser Neets. Just tits. *I'm* up here."

It was a strange phenomenon. Being beautiful may have made that problem even more pronounced. Sentiva Alvedine did have a beautiful body, and Watly saw that this made men even more uncomfortable, more fearful, and more convinced of her slightly less than human status than they already were. She thought someday she might learn to use that to her advantage, but the whole situation was very weird and made her feel hinky. She was both less than human and more than human because of it. Never just plain human.

Sometimes men stared at her as though she were a kind of abstract religious icon. As though she were a god. There was something approaching worship in their eyes. Worship hinged with . . . what? Resentment? Maybe even anger. She was a thing, an object, a divine being, whose beauty was a slap in their faces.

"No," Watly wanted to say, so many times. "I'm just a person. Just like you. As impossible as it is for you to comprehend, I am *just like you.*"

But the male part of her understood. The old Watly guiltily sympathized. She *was* gorgeous. She had a gorgeous face, gorgeous eyes, gorgeous hair, gorgeous hands, and arms, and legs, and ass, and feet, and hips, and waist . . . and yes, world-class tits.

In fact, Watly Caiper spent most of her first months in Sentiva's body masturbating any chance she got. She really turned herself on in a major way. She had *become* the icon, the god. She had transformed into the achingly beautiful, mysterious object of desire. This male self had turned into the thing most ached for. She was instantly madly in love with herself.

Of course, she didn't grab herself right from the very start. There were other things to deal with then.

After working out the plan with the Ragman, bidding an unpleasant farewell to Alysess, and returning to Second Level,

Watly got rid of all the cops as fast as she could. They were swarming in and around the Alvedine residence in huge numbers. Watly went inside and hurriedly gave Sergeant Fenlocki the story she, the Ragman, and Alysess had worked out to explain away everything. After a moment, she watched the cops carry her own male dead body down the wooden bird-wing staircase and toward the door. Now, *that* was a weird feeling. She watched the limp, lifeless Watly Caiper, the tall man with the high forehead and the crooked nose—and the serious need of a shave—being carried toward her like a sack of stale sunbeans. A stiffness seemed to be setting into the limbs of that dead thing. The arms were rigid-looking, the legs partly locked. Watly was glad the eyes were closed. She hadn't remembered closing them at the end. Maybe Fenlocki had closed them for her.

It still smelled like her, that old shell. It still had that Watly Caiper sweat smell. A very male, musky smell. She could smell it strongly even from across the room.

That thing had been her body a few short hours before. The only body she'd ever known till then. For twenty-seven years it had been home. She had grown up in it. And there it was, empty and lifeless and slowly stiffening. Her old face, cheeks, lips, nearing her, but no longer any part of her. Just a dead animal. A heavy pile of cooling flesh.

As Akral and another cop lugged the body by her, Sergeant Fenlocki stared at Watly as if searching for some significant reaction. She didn't want to give him one. She closed her eyes for a moment and recited her old chant silently:

> *The me is not the body.*
> *The me is not the body.*
> *The me is neither hand nor face nor sex.*
> *The me is Watly Caiper, I.*
> *(A sense of self.)*
> *The body is an it.*
> *The body is a that.*
> *It could belong to another.*
> *For the me is a movable thing.*
> *The me is a movable thing.*

Then Watly opened her eyes just in time to spit on her old body as it passed. It was not an easy thing to do, but Watly did it, numbly, feeling like a bad actress on CV.

The spitting reaction seemed to satisfy Fenlocki and he left shortly thereafter, saying he would return soon to clear up more questions.

When she was finally alone, Watly climbed the wide bird-wing staircase to the second floor. She went into the master bedroom and touched the large bed she had been killed on that very night. The sheets were cold. She looked at the pillows, trying to remember the pain of the horrible nerve-gun death. The pain was all gone. And the memory of it was vague, as if it had happened long ago. Watly found herself choking up some, her hand tracing the wrinkles in the sheet that ran from one end of the bed to the other. The hand was unfamiliar. The whole body was unfamiliar.

She lay slowly on the bed, feeling the lightness of her new body, the smallness, the thinness. The legs still felt strong, maybe even stronger than her old ones, but the arms and upper body seemed nowhere near as powerful. She felt weak. Vulnerable.

Watly stretched out on the bed, spreading her slender limbs as far as they would go. They felt good. They felt . . . maybe not as strong—but tough. Wiry. Agile. Quick. Lithe. Limber. There was a different kind of strength here. But strength nonetheless. Not brute power—but flexibility, looseness, speed, dexterity, and tremendous agility.

After a while Watly began to play with herself, masturbating for the very first time in her female body. Masturbating in the bed she had died on recently. It seemed the right thing to do.

She loved the new body. It was a great thing. Everything was different, yet somehow the same. For many days to come she would stare at her reflection, totally naked, playing with all the new toys. The breasts were so fun, the nipples so much more sensitive than her old ones. Each was almost like a little penis, and yet they seemed to have some kind of direct hotline straight to her groin when she touched them. All the body's skin was so soft and smooth and sensitive, more pliant and alive than her old skin.

And the other stuff! Wow! What great stuff there was down there. Soft hair, lips and lips, and a wonderful achy channel that went up inside, and . . . oh . . . that incredible, amazing, electrical little cosmic button. And the great creamy wetness that appeared anytime she looked at herself, touched herself.

Coming was different. It was better. And it seemed so much easier and quicker, even. It was a whole body thing, and there were bright colors in her head—purples and reds and oranges— and the coming seemed to last forever. It made her head buzz and her hands and feet tingle with non-numbness. Every muscle tightened, red splotches popped up on her face and chest, and every square inch of skin burned and trembled.

And then she could do it again, right away, if she wanted. And again. Sometimes it was the same and sometimes it was a lesser thing. A simple, crotch-centered type thing that was similar to the old male orgasms. Those were fun, too, but the big ones were better. Fiery explosions that enveloped her whole self and made the colors appear.

The first few times she came, she cried afterward, long and hard. It was a great kind of crying. A glorious crying. Later, she would not cry so much, but be overwhelmed with thoughts each time. *This is why women are threatening to men,* she would think. *Because women are made better.*

Sometimes she wondered if she would be having the same reaction had the switch been reversed—had she gone from woman to man. Maybe she would. Maybe she would be thinking the *male* body was superior. She didn't know. She didn't care. She was enjoying herself.

By the time Alysess made her first personal-physician-to-Sentiva-Alvedine visit, about two weeks into Watly's womanhood, Watly was well versed at coming. And all Watly wanted to do was play. And come. Alysess seemed shy at first but warmed up fast. It seemed Watly's excitement was contagious. Her delight over this thing called sex, over the newness of it, the intoxicating *wonder* of it, was a wonderfully infectious disease.

They tried everything. They wore each other out. Watly discovered new things. There was more that two could do than one. Much more. And surprises. Games. Things to be done with tongues and lips and hands. Wondrous experiments.

Watly discovered that she sometimes liked the feeling of fullness, of something being inside her. She particularly liked the first, intense, thrilling moment of entry each time. They used some secret toys for that stuff. The fullness thing was fun, different, but never made her come in and of itself. It didn't affect the button enough. Not nearly. The button was the main thing, the button was the funnest part, and everything else was merely a nice addition.

But it got Watly to wondering, even in those first few weeks, what it would be like to fuck. Heterosexually speaking, she was a virgin in this body. The idea of sex with a man was kind of repulsive, kind of intriguing, and kind of scary all at the same time.

Ten years and one daughter later, in spite of her curiosity on the subject, Watly Caiper was still a heterosexual virgin. For all she knew, she would die a virgin mother. That seemed a wrong thing.

As she watched Chief of Police Ogiv Fenlocki walk now down the front steps of her opulent home and out onto the white-topped street, Watly couldn't help but think about all this. Fenlocki cut a severe, stark figure as he marched up the empty Second Level street in his fancy dress duds. Maybe it had been that sexual comment the chief had made at the end. "You make a damn gorgeous woman," he'd said, eyeing her. Or maybe it was that typically, obnoxiously male breast assessment thing he'd done. Kind of nasty, that.

Rape you, Watly thought. *Rape you and all your catshit threats and the penis you rode in on.*

Watly looked up to see Noonie scampering from her hiding place on the balcony and back to her room. The child slammed the door roughly behind her. The sound echoed. That noise snapped Watly out of her memory drift, whipped her back into the present. Back to her current life, her work, her campaign, her Sentiva-beast within, and her disturbed daughter. She should go to her, talk to her. But she was afraid. Afraid of what she might do. Afraid of what *Sentiva* might do. She couldn't even trust herself to be alone with her daughter anymore.

And Watly thought for the first time in maybe two years (when that unthinkable thing had happened) that perhaps her whole world was about to fall apart.

CHAPTER 12

After leaving the Ragman at his quarters, Tavis-the-IT ate dinner in a sub dining hall. Then IT ran all of ITs annoying little Subkeeper errands—the lab, the print shop, the planning centers—changed ITs clothing, put on ITs own signature masklike makeup, took a unicarriage to a sub platform under Forty-second and Broadway, and climbed out into sexsentral for an evening.

The night was rape warm, like all of them had been recently. Tavis liked the heat. Nicely stifling. The heat was comfy. The heat made people cranky. The heat made people hinky. Cranky and hinky. Hinky and cranky.

The heat made the air feel charged with violence, thick with the violence mucus. The violence bile.

Tavis walked through sexsentral looking for ITs friends. They were sure to be around somewhere. They were always somewhere. Everyone was always somewhere. Ha.

Sexsentral was different now. Funner. Lots funner. More dangerous. A place of bad sex, good violence, and *fabulous* music.

Tavis took ITs blade out of ITs deep cloak pocket and tested the point on a fingertip, drawing blood. IT would need to sharpen the

knife soon. But for tonight, IT would leave the curved one alone.
The blade would do as is. Sharp enough to kill good. Sharp
enough to slice up good. Pain and blood and laughter. Ha.

Tavis walked past the booze bars and sex clubs and orgy cafés,
dodging the drifting floaters. Some of the floaters were anchored,
some not. The ones that weren't were probably signs from an
entirely different street—orphaned, lost signs, far away from the
fuck palaces they advertised. The floaters showed repetitious,
explicit moving images of all kinds of sexual adventures. Different genders doing different things to different genders. Hand jobs,
blow jobs, tongue jobs, fuck jobs, rub jobs, pit jobs, knob jobs,
diddle jobs, rim jobs, bolehole-bugger jobs, squeeze jobs, pinch-
and-twist   jobs,   high-tech   chipfuck   jobs,   no-touch   pop
jobs . . . every kind of job. All kinds of jobs.

These floaters, Tavis thought, were inaccurate. None showed
hurt. None showed pain and the dark, ripe redness of open
arteries. Many showed only the starwet sign—the universal
symbol for orgasm. Ha. All of this was catshit. Any man or
woman who wanted job sex wouldn't go to sexsentral anymore.
No way. There was plenty of normal sex to be had elsewhere.
Cruda made simple, boring sex something you could find anywhere. Job sex was all over Manhattan. Lots of jobs to be had.
Sexsentral wasn't for sex anymore. Sexsentral was for danger. For
real excitement. Sure, there was plenty of sex there still, but it
wasn't job sex. It was mostly pain sex. Sexsentral was for
strangeness. For fear. A home for the pain-freaks. For the infinite
pleasure of the hurt. Ha.

Tavis walked west, toward the darker districts. IT could hear
pain sounds coming from some of the doorways and alleys IT
passed. But they were minor pain sounds. Silly sounds. Little hurt
sounds. ITs friends would not be found there. This was not pro
stuff.

Tavis skirted some of the naked bodies that were entangled on
the sidewalk. Men and women and mixes, moaning and wrestling.
They were doing job sex with biting and chewing thrown in. Not
much blood or real pain at all. "Amateurs!" Tavis snapped at
them, kicking any body parts that happened to stick out in ITs
direction.

Where was an *evening* to be had in this place? Tavis heard
music coming from an open doorway now. Good, angry music
blaring loudly from a strip bar called Tequilla Carmells. IT would
have liked to go in and listen. IT liked the sound. No words, just

screams. A melody that rose constantly. The sensory-M tingle of good piellna playing. The rhythm unpredictable, sharp, and loud. A wild, blood-filled, erratic-heartbeat rhythm. But Tavis kept walking. Strip bars were boring. They did nothing for IT. The strippers never stripped farther than the first layer of muscle. And the skin was treated somehow to come off easily in huge sheets. To top it off, the strippers nowadays were so Softed-out they felt nothing. Where was the funness in that?

There was a severed arm in the middle of the street, still twitching. Tavis laughed. Yes. This was good. Pro stuff. Tavis knew ITs dear friends were near.

Then Tavis saw a cuffer up way ahead. Raping great. *Please, please, please let it be a fade-out!* Tavis thought, skipping quickly toward the cuffer. The light was very dim and Tavis had to be careful not to trip as IT danced down the puddly street.

There were a few others gathering around the host now. They all had brightly painted faces and all wore long cloaks that were shredded at the lower hem. Tavis's friends at last. Ha.

Tavis approached the crowd—four of ITs dear friends surrounding the one host.

"Tavis!" one of the color-splashed faces said.

"Yes, yes, *yesss*! Out for an *evening*!" Tavis shrieked gleefully. "Hello Nibba, and Flahv. Hello Beniseat. Hello Eunaw."

Tavis's friends nodded back.

"What have we here?" Tavis asked, looking at the host. IT was the leader of this group. These dear friends were *Tavis's* personal army. No kowtowing to the Subkeeper here. IT was in charge. IT wasn't an underling, a second-in-command, here.

Tavis enjoyed how the others were looking at IT for leadership. "What *do* we have here?" IT said again, jumping in place a few times.

The shriveled old man in the hosting cuff was not a fade-out. His elbow-to-knuckle cuff had large yellow numbers on it, but no telltale *FO*. He was wearing faded anklepants, a ripped pocketvest, and scuffed-up slip-ons. He had a khaki green bag slung over one shoulder. The donor's bag, no doubt. His eyes were not afraid.

"Well, well, well, well, *well*!" Tavis sang. "A cuffer with a bag!"

The cuffer looked around at the ones surrounding him. Tavis liked the man's eyes. They were Second Level eyes. Superior.

Confident. Invincible. Ha. Tavis would like to have those eyes in ITs pocket. Something to toy with when ITs hands got fidgety.

Why couldn't this be a fade-out? The old host sure looked deathable, in Tavis's opinion. He'd lived enough. He'd probably had *someone* to leave the scads of fade-out pay to. Friends. Family. Ha. *Someone* he wanted to make rich with his death. Why was he only a regular host?

"You a fade-out, cuffer?" Tavis asked, already knowing the answer was no.

"Don't be idiotic," the man said. The accent was thick with Second Level snobbishness. "I've no interest in experiencing death. I'm here for fun. I'm looking for a male."

Tavis giggled. "Nibba is a male. Aren't you, Nibba? Beniseat here is also a male. Right, Beniseat?"

"I've got the standard equipment somewhere under here," Beniseat said, laughing.

"You want to poke one of them? That what you went donor for? Huh? Poke, poke, poke? Want to poke *me*? I'm not sure I qualify. Want to take a chance I do?" Tavis took the blade out and spun it deftly between two fingers.

"I'm going to a sex bar. I'm not interested in any of you." The cuffer tried to pass by Tavis, but IT pushed him back into the center of the circle. Tavis's friends laughed heartily.

"But we," Tavis said softly, "are interested in *you*."

"I think not," the donor said indignantly, trying to back away. Those behind blocked him. "This old man's body may be nothing," he blustered, "but my *real* dick would bust you wide open, subspawn!"

Like that made a difference.

Tavis lashed out sideways with the blade, expertly taking off the very tip of the old host's wrinkled nose. "Not interested in that kind of sick sex stuff," Tavis remarked, twirling the knife again.

"Hey—*ow*!" the cuffer cried out, holding the bleeding nose wound with both hands.

"Take that bag from him. We split the money later. Now . . . now it's time to have an *evening*. An *evening*!" Tavis felt the familiar tingle in ITs groinal area. Blood was rushing down there, even as it escaped up here. *This* was excitement. *This* was sex. Ha.

"Back off, you boleholes!" the cuffer whined out nasally, fingers red with thick, dripping fun.

Tavis and ITs dear friends drew in closer. Nibba, Flahv,

Beniseat, and Eunaw all pulled blades out. None of the knives was as beautiful as Tavis's.

"Sorry, hosty in there," Tavis said, addressing the poor helpless little plurite whose body was being controlled by this Second Level, catbreath donor. "Sorry, sorry, sorry. You should've signed up for fade-out pay. Tough luck, there." Tavis lashed out again with the blade, nodding to the others that it was okay for them to join in. They would all start slowly and build gradually, making it last. Looking to see what was inside the guy. Looking at the blood and bile flowering outward. Looking at what the host was made of. Making an *evening* of it.

"I'll remember this, you catshit subspawn," the donor said angrily as they started to do some serious cutting on him. "This is *not—OW!*—a fade-out. And you obviously intend to kill this body. *Hey! OW!* You're breaking the law here! And I'll remember. *Hey!*"

Sometime before Tavis took the eyes out, the donor stared straight at IT, bleeding and breathless with pain. "I . . . I know your face, you rapehead," he said. "I'll . . . I'll remember it, too. Recognition-wise, revenge-wise, *any-which-wise-wise!*"

CHAPTER 13

"I need your help, Alysess," Watly said. Her face looked very somber.

Alysess sat back on the large bed's fluffy comforter, sipping her drink. She reveled for a moment in the cool, regulated air, thinking of nothing else. *Damn, but it's nice up here.*

As usual, she'd been too caught up in playing with Noonie to relax and appreciate the luxurious surroundings. Now that the girl had gone off to interactive social school, Alysess could lie back and take in the environment. Even here, in Watly's bedroom, the contrasts were apparent. The worse things got down below, the more extreme the comfort and opulence felt up here. There was, Alysess felt more and more, something obscene in it.

"Why didn't you tell me about this earlier, when it first started?" the doctor asked. The truth was, she had already heard about this latest, and the other, Sentiva incidents from Noonie. She just wanted to make Watly feel guilty.

Watly smiled sheepishly. She put on that self-deprecating, I-can-be-so-stupid-sometimes expression that Alysess found so annoying lately. "I thought it might go away. I thought it might stop all by itself—that it was just a temporary thing." Watly sat down gingerly on the bed next to Alysess. "But it's not. It's getting worse." She sighed. She looked like she hadn't slept in a while. Her eyes were a bit sunken and droopy on the sides. There were small, puffy bags under each one. "I was also a little afraid to tell you," she said. "I don't want the Ragman to know. He can't know Sentiva's trying to come back. He'll tell me to forget the whole election thing, after all this work."

"And you didn't trust me to keep a secret?" Alysess asked, feeling rather hurt at the idea. Secrets were her raping specialty.

"I don't know. I guess I didn't want to put you in the position of *having* to. I didn't want to put you in the middle."

I'm already in the terradamn middle, Watly, Alysess thought. *More than you know.*

"What do you want me to do about it?" Alysess asked. "I can't boost the power of the wafers. The best I could do is remove the raping things and put them in a new body. You got a new body in mind?"

Watly grunted. "Be serious, Aly. I can't do that now. I need to be Sentiva. No . . . I want you to help me another way. I want you to do something. For Noonie. I've already told her to lock her bedroom door at night. But she needs more protection than that. I need you to give her something. I need you to give her something I don't know about."

"Give her what?"

Watly looked into Alysess's eyes. The doctor could see Watly's pain and fear now, and she felt for her. The knot of frustration in Alysess's stomach loosened some. She felt pity for her lover.

"A weapon, Aly," Watly said haltingly. "Some secret weapon. Something she can always have with her. I can't know what it is."

"You want me to arm your nine-year-old daughter with something she can use against *you*?"

"I don't want Sentiva hurting her again, Aly. I won't have that. Sentiva could kill her next time. I'd rather Noonie kills me."

Alysess set her drink on the bedside table and lay back on the bed. She stared up at the ornate tin ceiling that was a good twelve feet above her head. The tin was inlaid with elaborately detailed orange-colored patterns made up of diamonds, ovals, triangles, circles, and tiny teardrop and heart shapes.

Alysess thought for a moment about suggesting that she herself take Noonie down to live with *her* for a while. That would be nice. For both of them. The doctor and the child. Real nice. And Noonie would be safe from Sentiva. But Alysess didn't say anything. She knew the idea would not go over well. When it came to Noonie, Watly wasn't going to give up proximity that easily.

Watly pulled one leg up on the bed and leaned over Alysess. Her expression was desperate. "She's the most important thing in the world to me, Aly."

"All right. All *right*," Alysess said. "I'll get something from the Ragman's lab and bring it up next visit to give to her."

"As soon as you can," Watly said, looking relieved. "I'll fake a stomach virus or something tomorrow, so you'll have an excuse to make an extra visit up here."

"Okay, okay."

Watly lay down next to Alysess and they both stared at the patterns on the ceiling together. "Thanks," Watly said softly.

"No problem."

And then neither spoke.

Alysess felt an anger rising in herself. A taut tangle of knotted cables in her esophagus, and a steel ball in her intestines replacing the lump of frustration she'd felt earlier. Anger. This was anger now. She was mad. As usual, she wasn't sure why.

She was only sure she was tired of all the deception. She was tired of having to keep the Ragman's violent plans a secret from her lover. Tired of feigning ignorance. Tired of lying. She resented now having to keep *Watly's* problems with Sentiva a secret from the *Ragman*. And having to keep Noonie's hidden weapon a secret from Watly. She was angry that earlier, when she approached Watly's house, she'd seen someone leave. She'd seen good old Ogiv Fenlocki walking out of the Alvedine residence. And Watly had said nothing about it. More deception? Everywhere she turned, there were secrets. And lies and more lies. It was hard to tell what the truth *was* anymore.

She was also tired of herself. She was tired of this knot of cables and this steel ball. She was tired of her own anger and jealousy over Watly's life-style. She was tired of her own ambivalence and doubts about Watly, her poovus, the woman she supposedly loved. Where was that love now? Sometimes it felt like the love words and the love actions were just habit.

Watly always tried to include Alysess in her luxurious life— often faking an illness for herself or Noonie so that the doctor could spend extra time on Second—but it didn't help. This was still Watly's privileged world. Alysess was a visitor, no matter what. An outsider.

And every time Watly asked Alysess if it bothered her, Alysess said no. Another lie. She always said she understood: it was part of the plan, the grand scheme. Watly had to have this cushy life-style, this fabulous home, and wonderful food. Alysess had to live on First to maintain appearances. And Watly had to pretend in public to hate the First Level—hate the plurites—to even do them small harms when necessary in order to maintain her cover. No, it didn't bother Alysess. Sure, Alysess understood.

Sometimes Watly reminded Alysess of the Ragman. They were two of a kind, in a way. Both were willing to do bad things in order to do good things eventually. And Alysess, the good sport, the team player . . . Alysess understood. Alysess always understood.

It was Watly, Alysess felt, who didn't understand much. She didn't understand how bad things really were down below. How painful it was for Alysess to stuff her face with fresh, exotic gourmet foods twice a week and not be allowed—*too raping risky!*—to bring any of it down to her hungry neighbors.

Watly didn't understand how much it hurt Alysess that Alvedine was the company that manufactured and distributed the Soft pills and that ran the hosting business.

And Watly didn't understand how Alysess felt about Noonie. How Alysess thought of the girl as *her* child, as well. How she hated it when Watly referred to her as "Aunt Alysess." How much she really loved the girl, cared about her, wanted to spend more time with her. And how she worried about what was happening to the child—this privileged, pampered child who could never be herself, who could never let her guard down. There was something warped and sad about the girl. Alysess wanted to hold her more often, to talk with her. Watly didn't seem to understand that the thing that had happened with Noonie two years ago hadn't just disappeared merely because they'd stopped talking about it. It hadn't vanished; it was just buried. And things that were buried sometimes sprouted thick roots and grew large.

And Watly didn't understand how Alysess had doubts. Doubts about the revolution. Doubts, even, about Watly. Watly didn't understand what it felt like to wake up in the middle of the night in a cold sweat, panicked with the idea that your lover might be turning into what she was supposed to be fighting against.

Watly didn't understand.

Watly didn't understand because Alysess never told her. In ten years, Alysess had never explained any of it. "No problem, my love," she would say. "I understand." And the anger and frustration and resentment would build. She loved Watly—yes, she did. But in a way, she also hated her more than anyone in the world. Alysess still blamed Watly for getting her wrapped up in all this stuff to begin with. The doctor's old pre–Watly Caiper days seemed so much simpler. Calmer. Happier, even. She loved Watly, yes, yes, yes, of *course* she did. But things were so much easier before they had met. She'd had her practice, a few short-lived love affairs, a nice salary. . . . Things had been uncomplicated. *If I'd never met you* . . . Alysess thought.

But that was silly. All these thoughts and feelings and negative emotions were silly. Childish. Immature. Better to quash them. Hide them away.

Where they festered. And grew roots. Like Noonie's secret.

Watly turned to face Alysess there on the bed. She reached over and tenderly stroked Alysess's cheek.

Ah, yes.

It would be sex again, then. Loving, gentle, heated . . . yet somehow empty sex. Habitual, mechanical sex. It was hard for Alysess to feel sexual toward Watly when she had such a wiry knot and metal globe inside her torso. Their sex life had felt routine and hollow lately, something they did because it was something they did. So many lies, hurts, and angers smothered the lust.

Maybe that's what would've happened anyway, after a time, no matter who it had been. Maybe that was normal. Maybe good sex was something that couldn't be maintained under the best of circumstances. Alysess had always bowed gracefully out of any relationship that had lasted too long, demanded too much of her time. The longest she'd ever had a particular poovus was three years. And even then, didn't the sex get a little stale by the end? It was hard to remember. And this one was a decade-long relationship. Perhaps making love was something that dwindled in pleasure the longer you were with the same person. Maybe it was a fact of life. Maybe that was why she had lustily eyed those young men on the street earlier.

Or not.

Watly was progressing now. The same moves, the same kisses, the same strokes as always. Variations on a theme. They knew each other's bodies well. They knew just what to do. They knew what the other liked and didn't like. They were both experts on the other's body, the other's preferences. And they did it the same way each time. But where was the surprise in that? The passion?

Watly continued. And Alysess began to play her well-rehearsed part.

It would feel good, Alysess knew, and she would come. Like always. But it would not be intimate. It used to be intimate in the old days. Wonderfully, intensely, humorously, passionately, spontaneously intimate. But there were too many securely placed masks for any intimacy now. There was too much unspoken anger for any genuine closeness. And that fact just made Alysess feel angrier, and that anger just made her feel more closed off. And she knew that didn't help matters any, and that made her angrier still.

She tried to relax as Watly slowly, lovingly undressed and gently caressed each part of her. She even tried to caress back with something approaching genuine feeling. She felt empty. Vacant.

Alysess wished she at least felt comfortable and secure enough to ask Watly to close the curtains and turn off the lights. But that wasn't in the script. That wasn't part of the sex plan. The plan, the habit, was to have plenty of light. Alysess wanted it dark this time, though. She wanted it pitch-black. She just didn't feel like seeing the contrasts today. She didn't want to witness her own dark brown skin against Watly's pale, pink flesh. Today it just reminded her of their separateness, of their differences. Of Watly's other-ness to her.

And, if she was really honest with herself, she had yet another, even sillier reason for wanting to close the drapes. Privacy. Paranoia.

Yes, truth was, Alysess felt a little like someone was watching them through the window. Pretty raping silly.

CHAPTER 14

Sentiva Alvedine would have permitted herself a momentary smile if she were indeed capable. She did manage, much to her satisfaction, to elevate the corner of Watly's right lip just a slight fraction. It seemed apparent that Watly did not even note this barely perceptible activity. Presumably, Watly was entirely too preoccupied with the endeavor of bathing that absurdly grotesque physician's inner thighs with her acrimonious saliva. This was a singularly unpleasant activity, in Sentiva's conviction.

But Sentiva had accomplished that one meager task—she had propelled the lip in question a few millimeters, discharging this assignment of her very own volition. And Watly was not even somnolent. Watly was irrefutably awake and cognizant.

This was an agreeable development. Things were progressing well. Sentiva could perceive her potency expanding, her domination escalating. She could sense Watly swiftly weakening. It was delightful. Invigorating. Watly Caiper was foreordained to fall. And Sentiva was unquestionably destined to win. Sentiva would terminate Watly's ambitions. She would, further, terminate Watly. And quite naturally, she would terminate Noonie as well. She might even slay the doctor woman, though it scarcely mattered.

Additionally, she was entirely willing to annul herself if the act were obligatory. That was nary a dilemma. If events dictated that suicide was the only way to obliterate Watly, then so be it. It was the rational, reasonable thing to do. And, if Sentiva was anything at all, she was irreproachably rational. She was extraordinarily sound-minded and clearheaded. She discerned herself to be intensely, drastically sane.

There was, Sentiva Alvedine unyieldingly surmised, no individual in the absolute cosmos who was the least hair's breadth saner than she.

CHAPTER 15

The sex was not too bad, after all. Pretty nice, actually. Maybe things were improving. And the "afterward" was very nice. Alysess felt a lot of the tension leave her body. She felt liquid inside, soft and comfortable. Watly's body was nice and warm beside her. Her pale skin was smooth and comforting. Her beauty was real and solid and no longer twisted into ugliness. They looked at each other, kissed, and smiled.

Watly's eyes appeared clear for the first time in a long time. Honest and aware. Alysess loved those eyes. Those uncloaked, truthful, sensitive Watly eyes. There was no difference—in spite of the fact Watly was now in a new body—between those eyes and the eyes Watly used to have as a man. They were a different color, a different shape, and a different size, but they had the same *feel* right now.

They stared at each other, unblinking eyes locked, for a few moments. It was as if they were trying to communicate directly, without words, trying to say all the things that couldn't be expressed with something as confining and limited as language.

Alysess caught some sideways movement with her peripheral vision. Something had flashed by the window. She turned to look.

Nothing. Maybe she hadn't seen anything after all. She was still a little jumpy. She wondered if maybe this sense of relative calm was the eye of a hurricane, a false lull. She wondered if maybe both she and Watly were pretending. Faking the love they both needed right now. Or maybe, Alysess thought, maybe this was farewell sex. Maybe, on some level, they both believed this might be the last time they'd be with each other. So they'd make it good.

"Everything's going to be all right, Aly," Watly was saying. "Everything's going to work out, my poovus." Alysess felt Watly's arms cradling her as if she were a child. She let the arms hold her. She rested her face between the softness of Watly's breasts and felt Watly's thin fingers stroking her hair. "Everything'll be fine."

It seemed to Alysess, as she lay in the warmth of her lover's arms, that Watly wasn't really talking to her. Watly was talking to herself. Watly was actually trying to convince herself that everything was okay. Watly was mothering, calming, pacifying herself.

And that was all right. That was fine. Because it was also soothing Alysess. And Alysess felt she needed the soothing. She would have to part with Watly soon, part from these safe arms. She'd have to get up, get dressed, and leave the Second Level. She would have to go back down to the dangerous streets below. Down, in fact, to the most dangerous of the dangerous streets.

She had to get Noonie a weapon. She had a mission now. A plan. A task to complete. It was sort of nice to have a mission. Whether she agreed with the task or not, it was nice to have a goal to work toward. And this particular goal wouldn't be easy. When she dressed, she'd make sure her boot dagger was easily accessible. She just might need it.

"Everything will work out okay in the end," Watly said now. And Alysess, for her own sake, pretended to believe it.

CHAPTER 16

The eyeballs didn't roll around in Tavis's pocket as IT had hoped. Tavis hadn't been able to get all the stringy stuff off of one of them, and the other had been accidentally punctured. They slid into a mushy, slippery wet mess when IT played with them. But squeezing them was something to do. Something to keep ITs right hand busy as Tavis and Beniseat sat in a booze bar called the Quivering Quim on the outskirts of sexsentral. The two of them were winding down together after the *evening*. It was a nice, satisfying feeling. Thumpy nice. Ooh-ooh nice. Nice. Ha.

Tavis sipped the tiny glass of booze slowly, savoring the bitter bite. No matter how cold the glass, cheap booze always felt warm going down. Like blood or piss or come. Like any fresh body fluid. Warm and biting. Ha.

The floor show had ended long ago. Tavis and Beniseat had missed it, but there were still some telltale fresh puddles of red fun on the small stage indicating it might have been a good one. But Tavis knew it couldn't have been any funner than the show they had created themselves. Live, up close, and personal. Intimate. Lovingly violent.

The bar's swinging doors flew open and that doctor lady

walked in. Tollnismer. She looked a real mess. A real nice mess.
Doctor smock filthy and bloodstained, hair all crazy (up on
one side in a big lump of weirdness), face real hinkified and a little
scratched up—but set firm. She was mucho disheveled. De-
sheveled. Mal-sheveled. Ex-sheveled. Not sheveled at all. No.
Ha.

She walked right over to the table where Tavis and Beniseat
were enjoying their wind-down. "*Lovely* neighborhood, Tavis,"
she said loudly. Some of the other people at the bar looked over
to see what was going on.

"You want to die, lady?" Beniseat asked, voice lilting with
what seemed honest curiosity. Good old Beniseat. Tavis knew the
doctor was a stranger to 'seat. But could be she did want to die.
Why not? Why else was she hanging out in sexsentral? Maybe she
was coming to have it done right. Have it done by Tavis, master
cutter. Ha. Be a nice change of pace—killing someone familiar.

Alysess turned to Beniseat and raised her fist. "Rape off,
bolehole. I want to talk to Tavis."

Beniseat rose to cut the woman's head off, but Tavis grabbed
a sleeve and held him back. "Go," Tavis said quietly.

Beniseat smiled and walked around the table, passing by the
doctor silently. Then he backtracked a bit to reach around and grab
a big handful of Tollnismer's left tit from behind before making
his exit. Alysess brushed his hand away, looking too distracted to
be genuinely annoyed. She sat on the metal folding chair directly
opposite Tavis. "You're not an easy person to find," she said.

"Tavis finds Tavis just fine, every morning," Tavis said, and
then laughed heartily. Good joke. Yes.

"Yeah," the doctor said, snorting. She took a swig of Beniseat's orphaned drink. "You just follow the trail of blood and
bodies. That's what I did."

Tavis smiled at the compliment and looked Tollnismer's body
over. "Tavis cuts good," IT said, scanning what was visible of her
figure. Tavis didn't like the doctor, never did like the doctor, never
would like the doctor . . . but liked the doctor. From the first,
Tavis would have liked to do something to that smooth brown
skin. Break it up a little. See what's under it. Inside it. Maybe
she'd have something different in there. Something new. Maybe
she'd be the one. "What do you want from Tavis? Cut cut cut?"

Alysess brought her voice down real low, so that Tavis could
barely hear her. "I need to see the Ragman. I need you to let me
into the subs."

"Ha. Not allowed, you know that. Naughty, naughty doc-*tor*! I'm telling."

"I'm not kidding, Tavis. All you have to do is open a sub tube, unlock the hatch below, and then you can leave. I need to see him."

"See him tomorrow," Tavis whispered back. "Same Cruda portal as before."

"No good. I need to see him now."

Tavis tried to roll the eyeballs around each other within the pocket. They weren't rolling. They seemed to be sticking together at this point. Whatever had leaked out of the ruptured one was congealing on them both. "No," Tavis said simply.

"I didn't go through all the shit I had to go through to find you just to hear that. I didn't just spend an hour and a half in the worst section of First Level just to hear no!" Alysess said angrily.

Tavis wondered what exactly she *had* gone through, and how she had survived sexsentral. The blood, the messed hair, the scratches. She must've had a weapon on her, since she was still living. Maybe the doctor was more resourceful than IT had imagined. Kind of amazing she was breathing and in one piece, when you thought about it.

Tavis let the silence linger just a tad—let her think he was pondering the situation—and then, when the timing was just perfect, said no again, but this time with a giggle.

Alysess looked around the room like she was deciding something. Tavis looked too, seeing nothing in particular except a typical bunch of indifferent bar patrons who had lost interest in their whispered conversation long ago. Some old woman was sitting on a stool near the stage, plucking her own hairs out one by one, and talking a little to each gray strand before letting it glide to the floor. Someone had passed out on the floor by the booze machines. Or maybe that person was dead. Another waste of a death. A naked couple was arguing heatedly at one table and another couple was fucking on top of their triangular corner one. *Yick. Job sex. Straight, ordinary job sex. Always job sex*. They were jostling and spilling their drinks all over the place as they jobbed each other. That reminded Tavis of ITs own drink, which IT picked up and took a tiny sip of.

Alysess turned back to Tavis. "You know how I finally found you? You left your calling card—a host all cut to pieces down on Forty-third. Then I just had to ask around."

"Tavis cuts good. Ha," Tavis said proudly, and sipped a little more booze. Piss warm still.

Alysess leaned in real close and Tavis was sorely tempted to clip off the tip of her broad dark nose. It was a pretty nose. Would be prettier still with the end missing. And something thick and dark running from the new hole. . . . Or maybe something different. Maybe she had something different inside. . . .

"I saw the guy's cuff, Tavis," Alysess said. She raised her eyebrows and her eyes twinkled.

Tavis took a big gulp from the glass this time, almost choking on the hot booze as it burned down ITs gut. *Twinkling* eyes might roll better in one's pocket. Ha. "So? So so so so *so*?" Tavis said, singsonging.

"*So,* I don't think the Ragman will be very pleased to hear the host wasn't a fade-out."

Tavis squirmed a little in the hard metal seat. Suddenly IT felt a little feverish. A little hinky crinkly stinky. It was as if the heat from the booze was boiling up into Tavis's forehead. Yicky. "I could cut those little titties of yours off and fry them up in a pan with oil," Tavis said quietly. "Some salt, maybe. Splatter, splatter. If you fry them enough, they shrink down and aren't so spongy. You do it just right, they're very tender. Moist. Ha. They're *fattening,* mind you, but Tavis could use a little weight."

Alysess didn't bat an eye. She hadn't cringed or flinched once during the tit speech. It was most disappointing. Tavis didn't like being ignored.

"Do you *want* me to tell the Ragman—the Subkeeper—about that host?" she asked.

Tavis felt a touch whoopsy weepy woozy. No good, this. No no good. "My tits are bigger than yours, though," IT said, trying to gain control of the subject. "Even if I *am* skinny. Your tits are barely an appetizer."

"Tavis," the doctor said firmly, "you help me get down to the subs and the Ragman will never hear from me that you helped me, *or* that you killed another regular host. You understand?"

Tavis fidgeted in the pocket for a moment and then pulled out one of the gooey eyeballs, holding it up. It was hard to grip on to. "Want an eye?" Tavis asked in a little baby voice.

Alysess seemed to cringe just a little at this—not much of a cringe, but a cringe-pleasant nonetheless. Sadly, it passed very quickly. The doctor kept her chin raised and her eyes fixed directly on Tavis's face, ignoring the goopy stuff slipping around ITs fingers. "No," she said. "I don't want an eye. I want to be taken to the subs."

Tavis put the eyeball back in with its mate and stood up, sighing. "A tour guide I'm *not*, you know. . . ."

CHAPTER 17

The Ragman looked up from the monitors strewn across his small desk. His expression was all at once startled, amazed, and furious.

"What the rape are you doing down here?" he asked.

Alysess folded the doors to the Ragman's quarters closed behind her. She did it as quietly as she had opened them. "Sneaking around," she said breezily. "Spying. Gathering secrets for your enemies."

"How did you get down?" he demanded. The veins in his forehead stood out thickly. Some of them looked ready to bust out entirely.

"Magic," Alysess said, waving her arms dramatically. "I popped in. Don't worry. No one else could do it but me."

The Ragman obviously had no patience for wisecracks. He looked seriously disturbed at this breach of his supposedly impenetrable fortress. "You're not supposed to be down here, Doctor. Ever. I should kill you right now."

"Maybe later," Alysess said, crossing farther into the room. "Right now I need something from your lab. It's important. I need a weapon. Something concealed."

The Ragman's mouth was open. He appeared absolutely

dumbfounded by her audacity. It looked as if someone had severed the connection between his brain and his vocal cords. "What?" he said finally. "What for?"

"A secret."

"A secret," the Ragman echoed, as if it would make more sense to him if he said it himself. He straightened up in his seat now, regaining some of his composure, replacing his mask of authority. "There are no secrets down here, my child."

"Tell me about it," Alysess said, and leaned into the boxes that were piled high against the wall of the Ragman's small quarters. The containers filled every corner of the room. Terradamned things were everywhere down here. Alysess must've seen thousands of the sealed placene containers on her short trip through this one small area of the subs. Every spare inch, empty corner, or bare wall was piled high with assorted cases—barrel-shaped, box-shaped, tube-shaped, pyramid-shaped, spherical . . . all different kinds. Each one had some kind of code number stamped on its side. The entire third level of Manhattan—this incredible, secret Revy country beneath the country beneath the country—seemed to have been turned into a raping warehouse in the nine years since she'd last been down.

"What the rape is in all these boxes and barrels and crates?" the doctor asked, rapping one with the back of her hand. It thumped hollowly, as though filled with something half solid. She was suddenly overcome with the irrational fear that the things were full of dead bodies. Thousand upon thousands of dead, rotting bodies, sealed up tight. "What's in 'em?" she asked again, a little less cocky this time.

"Why do you need a weapon so badly?" the Subkeeper asked, ignoring her question, his eyes cold.

Alysess found herself snorting again—a great catchall response. "Why don't you use the sight to find out? Why don't you read my future?"

The Ragman leaned back in his chair and crossed his hands over his chest. His head rested against one of the crates balanced in the middle of a tall stack behind his desk. He looked suddenly elfin. A pixie leaning against a tree. "You're not worth it, Doctor," he said icily, and then smiled just a little. When the smile was gone, it left no residue.

"What's in the boxes?" she asked again.

"Supplies for Revy," he said, as if that dismissed the question forever. "What do you need a concealed weapon for?"

"Protection," Alysess said, as if that dismissed *that* question forever. They both stared at one another. *We sure are two raping stubborn bolehole subspawns,* Alysess thought to herself, almost breaking the tense mood by smiling. She didn't.

"How did you get down here?" the Ragman's voice boomed. There was some dangerous-sounding anger seeping into his tone now.

Alysess walked closer to him down the narrow path between the crates. She watched a small cockroach run from one pile of boxes to another. "How come you didn't know I was coming down here ahead of time?" she asked, trying to sound young and naive. "How come the sight didn't tell you that?"

"You know very well that the sight doesn't tell me everything." The Ragman closed his eyes for a moment. He seemed to be thinking. Alysess wondered if maybe he was trying to use the sight right now. Maybe he was sneaking a surreptitious peek at her future even as they spoke. That thought gave the doctor the shivers.

"What's in the crates, Ragman?" Alysess asked yet again, nearing his desk.

"None of your business."

"I'm part of Revy, Ragman." She leaned her hip on the thin edge of the desk. "How come I'm not supposed to know? How come I'm not allowed down here?"

The Ragman opened his eyes again. "It's too dangerous," he said slowly.

"For *who*?" Alysess asked, raising her eyebrows to emphasize the question.

"For *you*. For you to know too much." The Ragman rubbed the back of his hand across his beard and almost panted. He looked scared and vulnerable now. *"How* did you get down into the subs?" He asked it very, very softly this time, like a child asking for nourishment.

Alysess shrugged and turned to look at the looming boxes. On the left there was a narrow opening between them that led to a small cot. It was the Subkeeper's royal bed, no doubt. "Someone helped me," she said. "Someone . . . anonymous. A Revy person. Not their fault. I forced them. Don't bust your power ringlets, Rag-face. Your secret hideout is still safe." She turned back to him. "So what's in the crates and barrels. Weapons?"

"Yeah. Sure." He seemed relieved to hear her explanation.

Now he appeared to be virtually ignoring her, dismissing her presence now that he knew his secret level was safe.

Alysess looked carefully at the fatigued, white-bearded face before her. "I don't believe you," she said.

"I don't *care*."

The doctor sighed and shrugged again. Maybe she would try to force open one of the boxes when she left this room. Right now she needed to get Noonie's defense. "Will you please get me the weapon?" she asked, very politely this time.

"Will you tell me why you need it?"

"No."

The Ragman stared coldly at the doctor for a long while. He slowly unclasped his hands, stretched his arms back over his head, and rubbed his face vigorously. Then he burst out laughing. The laughter was real and jolly and continued ringing through the cramped room until tears were dripping into the Subkeeper's beard hairs. "Okay, Doctor—aheh. Sure thing. Hahum. I trust you. I do."

Alysess snorted—that nasty habit again. "Why would you want to do that?" she asked, punctuating the sentence with one more disbelieving snort for good measure.

"I trust you, Doctor. Leave it at that," the Ragman said, wiping the laugh tears away. He missed a few that clung to the lower, more straggly hairs. He stretched again, stood up, and walked around the desk, appearing shorter than ever. "You can go down to the munitions lab in this quadrant and have them make up whatever you want. Tell them I said so."

Alysess was amazed the Subkeeper had given in so easily. Much as she appreciated it, she didn't buy it. "You trust me because the sight tells you I'm on your side? Is that it? The sight says I'll remain faithful to Revy?"

"I trust you, Alysess, because I trust you," he answered cryptically, still giggling a little.

The doctor suddenly felt defensive. Angry, even—that familiar knot and ball. The Ragman was treating her like a child. He was being condescending. "And I suppose," she said, "that being able to see snatches of the future has no bearing on that?"

"Not at all," he said simply, as if it were obvious.

"Yeah? So what *does* your crystal ball say, O great one? What does the future have in store, Mr. Soothsayer?"

The Ragman stopped giggling and merely smiled broadly. He motioned for Alysess to step around his table, to take his command chair. "Sit a minute. I feel like talking to you. I do. You're a neat person to talk to, I must say. Been a long time since you and I really talked. There's no one down here who's much fun to talk with. Plus I've got to keep my 'Commander-of-Revy' distance from these folks. Better for discipline." His smile seemed genuine enough. "Please." He motioned toward his seat again, bowing slightly.

Alysess sat down in the Ragman's soft armchair. It made a flatulent noise as she settled into it, but neither of them acted like they'd heard. The Ragman sat on the edge of the desk opposite her, still smiling. Somehow, they had managed to totally swap positions.

"So," Alysess asked, "am I about to die some horrible death?" She now had to look upward to face this short old leader of the revolution. "Is that what the sight says? Is that why you trust me? Because I'm about to fall on a knife?" From where she was sitting now, she could see the far corner of the Ragman's royal cot. There stood a female starwet machine, hovering waist high, its plastic orifice wet and drippy-looking and its power ringlets cycling down. Suddenly Alysess was embarrassed—embarrassed to be in the Subkeeper's private chambers, and embarrassed for the Subkeeper himself. There was the leader of the revolution's masturbation machine, floating by his bed, looking recently used. It seemed wrong that Alysess had seen it. It seemed too private, too sad and lonely and pathetic and intimate a sight to witness about the powerful wizard. Alysess looked away quickly, trying to pretend she hadn't noticed the thing. She tried to remember what she'd been saying. "So, uh, what does the sight tell you?"

If the Ragman picked up on Alysess catching sight of his personal orgasm machine, he didn't let on. He leaned forward, still grinning from ear to ear, and whispered conspiratorially, "The sight, my dear child, is catshit."

"What the rape is *that* supposed to mean?"

"I am not a wizard, my child," he said tenderly. "I am not some magical guru. That is an act that serves my purpose. I am a *scientist*. But I have found, over the years, that the people's desire for the supernatural—for *religion*—is a useful tool. Religion is in the business of answers. Rational science is in the business of *questions*."

Alysess recognized the Ragman's tone. She hadn't heard him speak like this for years. He was in his teacher mode. His face was animated and his hands relaxed and expressive. He looked two decades younger.

"Science is a process," the Ragman continued, "and part of the process is admitting ignorance. Admitting that the pure, scientific search for answers is really just a search for more questions. It is a never-ending, arduous, humbling, exciting process."

The Ragman stroked his beard thoughtfully and the focus of his eyes drifted upward. Alysess wondered what this speech had to do with the sight. But she didn't interrupt. In truth, it was refreshing to see the man like this. The Ragman was enjoying himself. It was as if he hadn't talked—really talked—in years. Alysess figured she had the time to watch him play around a little until he got to his point.

"But most people don't like that," he went on. "They want answers. All superstitions, religions, and pseudosciences are based on providing answers and alleviating basic fears. *Fears.*" He said the word carefully, as if Alysess were a favorite student and he were waiting for her to write it down, spelling it correctly.

"And not just fears," he said, "but specifically the fear of being afraid. Take the death fear, for example. The fear of death—of death as what it obviously is: the end of one's existence—is only natural. You'd be crazy not to fear it. In fact, I'm convinced it is impossible for one to comprehend one's own death for what it really is. It is beyond our species' capability. I can imagine what it would be like for *you* to no longer exist. But—with this little brain of mine—I cannot really imagine, I cannot truly comprehend, or anywhere near accurately fantasize about what it will be like when this very brain turns off. Because the imagining, the comprehending, and the fantasizing are all intrinsic to that brain being *on.*"

The Ragman's eyes brightly reflected the room's three corner pinlights. The reflections looked like a trio of stars orbiting his irises. "So death is naturally fearful. But human beings don't want to feel that fear, to own it, to embrace it. And so they invent an afterlife, the eternal soul."

Alysess was starting to get impatient. *Time's up, teacher.* She hadn't come here for a lecture on religion. She had given him enough playtime. She was tired and had a lot to do. And where the rape was the lecture leading, already? What was the point? She suddenly had a vivid, embarrassing image-flash of this same old man pathetically pumping his withered organ in and out of the metal orgasm box that floated by his bed. "Ragman," she said, "I appreciate what you're saying, but—"

"The fear of growing up," the Ragman interrupted, running right over Alysess's words, "is another healthy fear. The fear of not having a parent anymore, not having someone wise and strong and powerful looking over one's shoulder, punishing us, rewarding us, guiding us . . . this is a normal fear. But people don't want to feel *that* fear either. They invent eternal parents—gods—so that they never have to grow up and face that fear."

The Ragman held up a finger, indicating Alysess should wait just a few minutes, that he was winding down, coming to some conclusion. "The fear of the unknown," he said, "the fear of ambiguity, the fear of unanswered questions, the fear of experiencing that vulnerable, human feeling you have when you admit you just don't know—the fear of the wonder of life, the mystery, the unfathomable beauty of nature—all these fears are soothed by religion. Religion gives people blacks and whites, villains and heroes, bads and goods; pat, simple answers so they can sleep at night. Pat, simple monsters to be afraid of in the darkness."

Now the raised finger was joined by four others, turning into part of a spread-open hand. Alysess leaned forward in her chair, wanting to jump in again, but the spread-fingered hand somehow stopped her.

"Don't misunderstand me," the Ragman said earnestly. "I am not judging or condemning people for inventing answers, for constructing elaborate mythologies, rituals, inventive stories, and traditions to deal with fear. Homo sapiens have been doing this since the beginning of time. I am convinced that, as a species, we will grow out of it eventually, if we survive long enough. But in the meantime, I have used it to my advantage."

The Ragman slid off the edge of the desk and stood up. He rubbed his upper thigh for a moment and then pressed both his hands into his lower back, massaging in a firm side-to-side motion. Again Alysess thought of the man with his lonely starwet machine.

"One of the biggest of all human fears is the fear of the future," he said, grunting a little as he worked out his muscle kinks. "People are naturally afraid of the future. Yet, like all the other basic fears, they don't want to *feel* the fear, to own it. And so . . . I invented the sight. A little logic, a little common sense, a little deductive reasoning, a little guesswork, a little extrapolation, some finely honed people-reading abilities, and a healthy dollop of theatrics. That's all it is, my child. And it doesn't really matter if my forecasts are right or wrong. If I'm vague enough, people will bend and squeeze what I've said to fit what happens. They want someone to believe. They want a leader. They want someone with the answers. And I have given that to them."

This time the Ragman's raised hand didn't stop Alysess from speaking. "And what if I just go tell everyone what you've just told me?" she asked defiantly.

The Ragman chuckled. "Would I be saying all this if I was worried about their reaction? I take no risk in revealing this to you, my child. You cannot unmask me. They want to believe. They *need* to believe. They will not listen, even if you show them proof otherwise. Did you notice how fast Cruda caught on when it was introduced? Here comes a ridiculous, unreasonable religion, thrust upon the First Level by law. A state-created superstition— brilliant move, I must say. It was just what the people wanted. It gave them answers, it gave them the meaning of life."

Now the Ragman smiled warmly once again, the same kind smile he had led Alysess to the farting chair with. "I'll tell you a secret, my child," he said sweetly. "The *real* meaning of life—both intoxicatingly comforting and overwhelmingly terrifying—is that there *is* no meaning of life."

There was silence for a time. "And why are you telling me all this?" Alysess asked.

"I like you, Dr. Alysess Tollnismer. I like talking to you. You do not follow blindly. As I said before, I trust you. You're intelligent, resourceful, pretty terradamned honest—if not downright impudent—and not a bad doctor, to boot. And I need you. One of the reasons I feel all this about you—this trust and need—is because it's quite obvious that you don't like me. That is refreshing. I appreciate that. I need that."

"You *need* someone who doesn't like you?" Alysess asked, shaking her head and throwing forth a major snort.

"I need that perspective, yes. Keeps me honest. Keeps me on my toes."

"Do you know *why* I don't like you, Mr. Ragman? You want to know why?"

"Because I have sex with a machine instead of a person?" the Ragman asked with a smile.

Alysess felt herself flush. He *had* noticed her looking. She ignored his comment and repeated the question louder. "Want to know why?"

"I think I can guess."

"Because," Alysess said, pushing the chair back and standing up, "you have no morals. All that catshit you spewed about religion may be true, but it doesn't mean you shouldn't have morals. In fact, it makes morals and ethics and . . . being *good* . . . all the more important."

"I have no morals?" The Ragman looked wounded. "I who am trying to free my people have no morals?"

"But you don't care how you do it," Alysess said, almost yelling. "Any means are acceptable as long as you get what you want in the end. Any terradamned obscenity is fine, if done in the name of Revy!" She was going to add *Sometimes I think Watly is the same way,* but then she thought better of it.

"You don't think the compromises I make *hurt* me, my child?" the Ragman asked, his eyes sad. "You don't think it pains me deeply every time I have to do a little bad for the greater good? These are rough times, my child. These are hard times. War times. Painfully sacrificing one's morals when absolutely necessary doesn't mean you don't *have* any. The decisions I make *every single day,* my child, tear me apart inside."

What Alysess asked the Ragman next was not something she had pondered over. It seemed so obvious a question, but it had never occurred to her before. It just hit her like a mountainous chunk of steel-reinforced cemeld. "And who, Mr. Martyr Sub-keeper," she started, her voice shaking, "do you plan to put in charge if you win? Huh? Who is going to run this island country after Revy succeeds?"

"You ask the good questions, my child. You see why I need you?"

"This whole thing is a power trip for you, isn't it?" she spat, anger building again in her belly. "You want to 'free' your people and then be their king. Am I right?"

"It's certainly something to think on. A good, biting question, that."

Alysess was starting to feel really hinky now. "And what, O wise and powerful Ragman," she said, "is in all those thousands upon thousands of crates and barrels? What highly moral ventures are *they* connected with?"

The Ragman turned away, facing his tiny cot. "You don't want to know," he said. "Especially considering our current topic of conversation."

"I *do* want to know." She reached across the desk and grabbed the tattered sleeve of his robe. "You say you need me? You want me to keep you honest?"

"Believe me," the small, bearded man said, "you'll find out soon enough."

"I want to know *now*—or I'll go over and rip one of them open with my bare hands. You'll have to kill me if you want to stop me."

The Ragman actually looked ashamed. He turned his eyes away again, this time looking up and down at all hundred or so crates that were just in his quarters alone. "It was something that was necessary to do," he said softly.

Alysess shook the fabric she held hard, pulling on the Ragman's arm. "Don't justify, don't qualify, don't excuse—just tell me what the rape is in all those zillions of containers that are clogging the place!"

The Ragman looked back into Alysess's eyes. "Food," he said, appearing close to tears. "Food, water, and medicine."

CHAPTER 18

Watly was in her small private keyboard office on the third floor of her home. Something was wrong with her.

She had been sitting for over an hour, staring at the thin haze of the CV mist that was flowing from the back of her brass keyboard. Intensely bright sunshine hit her eyes from the room's open-shuttered windows. The office had a parquet wooden floor, paneled wooden walls, and a wooden ceiling patterned with interlocking wooden hexagons. The wood was perfectly pure and unblemished everywhere but under her chair. Down there in Watly's shadow were twin grooves caused by years of back-and-forth scraping as the chair was pulled in and out.

But Watly wasn't looking at those scrapes now. She was staring at the mist, her hands poised over the keyboard's light-keys. She hadn't moved in ages. The last sleep she'd gotten had been three hours long, and that had been over a day and a half ago. She felt dizzy and her stomach had a sour, toxic, acidic feel to it. Her eyes felt heavy and all her joints throbbed, particularly her knees. She couldn't remember ever feeling this tired before. Sleep was the enemy now, and the lack of it was turning her catatonic. She felt distanced from reality, groggy, unable to think. The world was turning dreamlike around her. And something was wrong. Something was very wrong.

Someone was there. Someone was pushing, pushing, pushing hard for freedom. Someone was slamming into an invisible mental wall, scraping at it, chewing on it, trying to tear it down.

There was a war raging in Watly's skull.

It wasn't nighttime, she wasn't asleep, she wasn't unconscious, and yet . . . something was very wrong. Her hands twitched and trembled uncontrollably as they hovered over the light-keys.

"Go!" Watly whispered. The word fell flat and echoless in the dead, soundproof room.

Sentiva was there. Pushing, pushing, pushing hard. Watly felt frozen in position, totally immobilized by hinkiness, fatigue, and that pushing, pushing, pushing.

Watly felt the left corner of her lips raise up. And she didn't make it happen. It happened by itself.

A singsong, nursery-rhyme voice came from her own mouth. "*Whaaat*-leeee?"

"*No!*" Watly shouted, breaking the paralysis enough to raise her hands up and hold her face. Her lips began to move, opening and closing in soundless conversation. Then a hissing sound erupted from her.

"*Shhhh* . . ." Watly heard herself say softly. "Shhhort blade. I . . . need . . . short blade. . . ."

Watly stood up, knocking her chair over with a loud bang, and actually pulled her right hand back and slapped herself hard in the face. "Go away!"

"Whaaa . . . Whaaat . . . leeee?"

"I'm busy!" Watly cried. "Call back later!"

"Whaa . . . *Shhhh*—"

"I'm very busy. Get out of my head. I have to use the keyboard. Leave me the rape alone, Sentiva." Watly began jabbering a nonstop monologue, trying to overwhelm and block out Sentiva with pauseless speech. "I have things to do here. I have work to do. Communications to make. Many, many, many keyboard-CV calls to make. I came in here to do just that. That's why I came in here. That's what this room is for. It's my private keyboard office. I am a busy, busy, busy woman, and I don't have time for any of your foolishness. There's work to be done. Now, I'm going to sit back down—where's the chair? Oh. There we are. There it is. I'll just set it back, and . . . and . . . and now I'm sitting. There we are. I'm sitting. I sat . . . and . . .

and . . . I'm going to do some work here. Lots of important work on the keyboard. On this keyboard right here. And . . . and . . . if you think I'm going to go get a little knife just so you can cut me out of your head, then—"

The keyboard suddenly beeped loudly and the CV mist above it flickered. Silver words appeared and floated in the center of the gray haze.

> INCOMING COMMUNICATION
> SENDER CODE: WELTER, WELTER, NIE,
>   ONE, SIX
> CALLER: CHIEF O. FENLOCKI
> AUD/VIS REQUEST
> PAYMENT GUARANTEED BY SENDER
> PARTY TO PARTY: S. ALVEDINE
> RECEIVER CODE: THREE, WELTER,
>   THREE

Watly stared numbly at the message. After a few seconds, this call indicator disappeared and was replaced by the blinking acknowledgment query.

ACCEPT COMMUNICATION?

Watly impulsively pulled the keyboard's left ringlet and hit the access/send-&-receive light-key. She'd take anything as a distraction at this point.

Suddenly there was Ogiv Fenlocki's jolly head and torso, floating two feet in front of Watly's face. He was chewing on something.

"Hello there, Sen-tiva! How're things?" the chief said, smiling broadly.

"Fine," Watly said, trying to smile calmly back. Underneath the desk, she pinched her own left thigh real hard. "And how are things in the peace business, Mr. Peaceman?"

"Oh, I was just sitting here wondering if you'd made up your mind about running for Chancellor," he said, sounding as though he were discussing the warm weather. "As you know, the time I gave you to decide is up."

Watly felt an abrupt, painful headache rise up from the back of her neck. It felt like someone was slowly sticking needles in her, starting near the top of her spine and then working higher. Her

mouth started moving again without her control. *Sentiva again.*
"Whh . . . whaaat—"

"What do you *mean,* 'what'?" Fenlocki asked, his expression
rapidly souring. "You know what I'm talking about, Sen-tiva.
You remember my deal. You've had plenty of time to think—"

"*Shhhh . . .*" Watly's mouth began.

"Shhhush, your*self*! I want an answer. If you don't give me a
straight one, I'll assume the answer is no, and I'll start my
investigation anyway."

Watly bit down hard on her own tongue, tasting blood almost
instantly. "My . . . answer *is* no," she said, forcing the words
out. "I . . . have . . . nothing to hide." The headache was
growing worse. Spreading into her temples and throbbing with the
rhythm of her rapid pulse. "I'm . . . still . . . running . . .
for . . . You can . . . invest— . . . all . . . you . . ."

"Hey, are you okay?" Fenlocki's shimmering projection asked.
"You don't look so good, Sen-tiva."

"My doctor . . . is . . . here." Watly squeezed the words
out, trying to overpower the vocal constipation fast creeping in. "I
have . . . a virus. Stomach. My doctor . . ."

"You mean Tollnismer?" Fenlocki asked. "She sure spends a
lot of time up here with—"

"Shhh . . . shhhort blade!"

Watly reached over and snapped off the keyboard, breaking the
communication, but not before she had caught a glimpse of
Fenlocki's startled and bewildered expression. She collapsed into
the chair's firm back, gasping for breath.

And then the stress and pain in her head suddenly eased.
The war ebbed. It was as if Sentiva had been as exhausted by the
effort to emerge as Watly had been by trying to contain her. The
Night Lady had apparently found it necessary to retreat again. At
least for a while.

There was a sharp knock on the office door. Watly groggily
turned toward it. "Yeah?"

The door opened. It was Alysess. She too looked tired. And
upset.

"Okay," the doctor said, all business. "I just gave her the spaf
secret weapon and a starter lesson on how to use it. You happy?"

"Thanks. Appreciate it."

Alysess stayed in the doorway, gripping her little doctor case
with both hands. Her knuckles appeared clenched tight. "You
look like shit," she said. "What's the deal?"

"I need sleep, Aly."

"So sleep."

"Do you . . . have something in your bag?" Watly asked somewhat timidly. "A drug to put me out? Keep me out? And Sentiva?"

"I've got some Chortium pills," Alysess answered, rummaging in the case. Her voice was cold. "Send you right to Chortyland for ten or fifteen hours. It's more like a coma than sleep, though. You won't get much REM."

"They'll do," Watly said wearily.

Alysess looked hard at Watly's face. She frowned. Watly could see her lover assessing her, judging, pondering.

"She's coming out while you're awake now, isn't she," Alysess said. It was a statement, not a question, but Watly responded with a nod anyway.

"Bad news," Alysess added, tossing the plastic pill bottle to Watly. Watly missed it, and the bottle bounced around the shiny wooden floor, finally coming to rest in one of the chair legs' scars.

"Thanks," Watly said, feeling miserable. She swiveled the chair a little and bent over her aching knees to scoop up the drugs.

"I want you to answer some questions for me, Watly," Alysess said. Her face looked set in hard cemeld. She still hadn't set foot into the room yet. When she'd arrived that morning, she'd gone straight to Noonie's room without a word.

"Sure. Ask away," Watly said, trying to sound close and friendly. Trying to loosen up her tense poovus.

"What are the Revy countermeasures they have prepared up here?" the doctor asked coolly.

Even in her debilitated state, Watly was surprised enough by the question to turn the chair the rest of the way around and face Alysess head-on. Watly leaned forward toward the doctor, squinting. "You already *know* everything I know about that, Aly," Watly said. "For years I've been passing every scrap of information I could find to you so you could tell the Ragman."

Alysess didn't move. "Tell me again," she said somberly.

"Well . . . I don't know . . ." Watly tried to recall. "There's that thing about there being some kind of well-protected secret command center up here. And, as I've said, there's supposedly a whole bunch of fancy new fighting machines hidden away someplace. Rumor is they're either heat-seeking or movement-sensitive, or both—You *know* all this stuff, Aly!"

"Keep going," Alysess said, her tone still even.

"Okay, okay. Let's see. There was all that stuff about missing or kidnapped First Levelers a few years back. Between five hundred and a thousand were supposedly taken up here for some reason. For questioning, as recruits, as future spies—I don't know. Nobody ever saw them again. They might've been killed. You know all that. And there's the escape one-shot Floobie-pods some people have on their roofs up here so they can Floobie out fast if they need to. But you know about *that*, too. You know everything I know. And I won't learn any more until I'm Chancellor. Then I'll know everything. Then I'll be able to tell you more."

"Is that all you know?" Alysess asked, looking skeptical.

Watly examined her lover's face carefully, trying to read her. "Suddenly you don't trust me?"

Alysess inhaled through her nose abruptly, in something that resembled a weak snort. Watly found snorting obnoxious, and it seemed the doctor was doing it more and more. Probably just to bug her. "You don't trust *me*?" Watly repeated. What had happened to the doctor? What was making her act this way? She looked almost numbed into shock, as if she'd seen something that changed everything, blew her world apart.

"What about Fenlocki?" Alysess asked now, her eyes fixed on Watly's.

"What *about* Fenlocki? He's in charge of the whole thing. He knows everything about anti-Revy."

"And why," Alysess said, taking her first step beyond the threshold, "did I see him leaving here yesterday morning?"

"Oh, Aly." Watly sighed, feeling both lost and sad somehow. "You think I've sold out and joined forces with him or something?"

Alysess stepped closer to Watly. "I don't know what to think."

Watly began to laugh. It was a sad, ironic laugh. She didn't feel any humor behind it, just the physical spasms. It was almost painful. "He's trying to unmask me," she said. "He thinks I may be Watly Caiper. Imagine that. And he doesn't want Watly Caiper to win the election and learn about all of Second Level's defenses."

Alysess stood right in front of Watly now, looking down at her. Watly felt naked and embarrassed under her watchful brown eyes.

"So why didn't you tell me?" Alysess asked.

Watly swiveled the chair to the side, looking off at the paneling. She could see her own blurry reflection in the polished wood. She wasn't sure she liked what she saw there. "I don't know," she said finally. "I didn't know if I should or not. It didn't seem necessary."

"You were afraid I was going to tell the Ragman," Alysess said, grabbing the chair arms and turning Watly back toward her. "*That's* why."

"I don't know if that's—"

"You don't trust *me* either," Alysess said with conviction, letting go of the chair.

"Aly—"

"I'm so tired of all this. I'm tired of this catshit. I'm tired of keeping secrets *from* you and *for* you. I'm tired of you keeping secrets from me. I'm tired of the Ragman's secrets. Noonie's secrets. Your secrets. My secrets. All we *have* is secrets. It's all there is left."

Watly saw that Aly's whole body was trembling. She seemed to be shaking with rage, or fear, or hate, or something. "That's not true, Aly." Watly reached up to touch Alysess's warm brown cheek with the palm of her hand. "I *love* you."

"No, you don't. Not anymore. You don't even know me anymore. Nobody knows anybody. Everybody I *know* is a fake. There isn't one raping person who isn't pretending to be something other than themselves. You, me, Noonie . . . the Ragman. . . . I'm tired of it." Alysess looked angrily down at Watly, ignoring the gentle hand on her face. "You don't love me. You just want me for sex. Well, I'm tried of *that*, too. I don't like it anymore. I don't want it. I can hardly remember the last time I did it because I wanted it. I've been doing it because I thought it was the thing to do. Well, I don't like it at all anymore. I may never like it again."

Watly withdrew her hand. She felt stepped on. Squashed under an angry foot. She felt so hurt she wanted to hurt back. But she didn't. She couldn't. "Alysess, don't do this to me," she pleaded. "Not now. I need you with me now."

"No, you don't!" Alysess yelled. Her voice was full of rage. It was as if some dam had burst within her and a flood of anger was pouring wildly out. "You need somebody to tell you you're a good person! You need somebody to say everything you do is okay!" Alysess straightened up and for a moment Watly actually thought she was going to hit her. "Well, it's *not* okay! It's a raping mess! For ten raping years you've been keeping your cover by hurting people. By drugging people, by making people hosts, by controlling people, by preaching lies. It's all your raping company! It's all you. I don't give a rape if it's for the best in the end—if you'll make it all better one day. Doesn't matter. It's raping disgusting. The way you live. What you do."

Watly felt like she was drowning, smothering under the tidal wave of anger that was crashing down on her. "Aly," she said softly. "Aly, why didn't you say something? Why didn't you tell me you thought—"

"I'm saying it *now*! I didn't say it before because I'm a raping bolehole, okay? I'm as bad as you. But not anymore. I'm through with it."

"Aly, poovus, I need you with me now—"

"Well, I need this to *end* now!" Alysess shouted. She closed her eyes tightly for a moment. When she opened them, her expression was a little calmer. "Maybe when everything's blown over we can work things out. Maybe we can. But I can't take it now. I can't take any more of this."

"Aly, this is the worst possible time for—"

"There's no such thing as a *good* time for this." The doctor's eyes flashed. "If I waited for a 'good' time, I'd be miserable forever."

Watly took a deep breath, feeling it catch at the end. She felt like crying, but she knew it would just make things worse. She held it in, letting her nose and sinuses burn without relief. "I'm sorry, Aly," she said sincerely. "I'm sorry if things haven't been great lately. I've been going through a lot. You have, too—I know that. It's a rough time, now. Stress. Pressure. And I'm sorry. I apologize."

"I'm sorry too," Alysess said. "I'm sorry I just can't take it." She turned to the door. "At least, I can't take it right now."

Watly stood up and put a hand on Alysess's shoulder. Alysess didn't turn around to face her.

"Aly. Poovus—"

"Say goodbye to the kid for me," Alysess whispered. "I love that kid. You don't know how much. That messed-up kid is the only trustworthy one of all of us. 'The Face.' Nooner-face. Noonie." The doctor pulled out of Watly's weak grip and started slowly for the door. "I wish you well, Watly Caiper," she said. "I hope you win. Because if you don't, I'll tell you something—one more big secret you're not supposed to know. . . . If you don't win, the entrails are really gonna hit the fan." She continued walking straight through the threshold.

"Aly, I *love* you!"

"Yeah. Me too," her voice came from the hallway. "See you around, Watt."

And she was gone.

And there was no need for Watly to keep the tears inside anymore.

CHAPTER 19

Heavy, heavy, heavy stuff.

Eiter Eimsler was carrying a bunch of it. But Tavis-the-IT still had a heavy load. Rupture city. Ha. No way they weren't going to have to stop and rest a few times. Most of the equipment was lightweight, but the chemicals sloshing around—four three-gallon, metal-handled jugs of them—were weighty indeed. And unwieldy. Not wieldy at all. Nonwieldy. Not even semi-wieldy. Ha. Hard on the hands and arms and shoulders and the lower back. Should've had a lowtruck for this stuff. Much easier. *Really* should've had a 'nother whole helper. Should've insisted to the Subkeeper that two was not enough for this super-duper, extra-special, major mission. The misdirection mission. Delicate diversionary duties.

Why Subkeeper hadn't come along himself was a mystery of mysteries. The guy had seemed weird to Tavis lately. Ever since Tavis had snuck that bolehole doctor down to him, the Subkeeper had acted strange. Strange and distant. Maybe sad, even. All holed up in his quarters for hours at a time. Like he didn't want to directly partake in his plans. His *own* plans. Guilt or shame or something.

Tavis knew the Ragman's moodiness wasn't because he was mad at Tavis, although the thought had struck IT at first. But if the doctor-head had spilled the sunbeans about how she'd gotten into the subs, IT would know. If she'd done that, Tavis would've heard from Subkeeper. Tavis would've heard right away, and been punished severely. Blade confiscation, revoked *evening* privileges, or worse. Bad stuff.

No, the Subkeeper was just going through a thing or something. Some kind of thing, maybe. He'd snap out.

Rape! Heaviness! Tavis had to rest awhile.

"Eiter? Stop here. You look to need a rest," Tavis said, and IT put ITs load down on the pitted road surface, stretching. *A mule I am not!* IT thought angrily to ITself.

A half hour later they had finally made it down Varick to the Man-With-Hat-On, on Worth Street and West Broadway. It was not a pleasant trip at all. It was dripping bad the whole way, it was hot as a body-melt vat, the streets were crowded with boleholes, the jugs were heavy, and Tavis was not a mule.

The Man-With-Hat-On building was in a relatively desolate district. It was downtown, three blocks from the west Riverwall, and not much was around it. The building itself was sealed up and vacant here on the First Level floors. Up above on Second, it was undoubtedly occupied. When Tavis and Eiter reached the steps of the building, Tavis said it looked like Eiter needed another break, so they set their burdens down and took one. This time Tavis actually sat on the chemical jugs for a while. Portable stools. Ha.

It was going to be slow, hot, hard work. Pain in the bolehole work. They'd set up the spraying equipment, hook it up to the jugs, and then split up. Tavis would start on the outside of the building, while Eiter Eimsler broke inside to work there. Later, Tavis would join him. They would have to spray every exposed portion of plasticore wallboard they could. Their job was to apply the chemicals to as much of the building as possible. If anyone happened by to ask what they were up to, they were to say they were exterminating a roach infestation. If the person or people didn't buy that—which they probably wouldn't—Tavis and Eiter were to kill them. *At least there's a possibility of* some *fun happening here*, Tavis thought. *A kill or two while we work. Pleasure with business.*

When they were done spraying and had used up every last drop of the chemicals, they were to leave. Then it was up to the special formula to do the rest. If this secret sauce worked the way the sub chemists said it would, it would start changing the composition of the plasticore. By tomorrow night the structure would be ready for phase two. By tomorrow night, all the plasticore in and on the lower level of this building would have changed drastically. It would be, if the scrotum-headed chemists were right, unlike any plasticore in all of the country of Manhattan. It would be flammable. *Highly* flammable.

Fire. Ha.

CHAPTER 20

Two days later Fenlocki was in his office, poring over the Watly Caiper case. That was where the horrible news reached him.

Things had been busy lately, and this was the first chance he'd gotten to buckle down over the Caiper mess. He had pulled all fourteen sealed sanifiles, twenty-six keyboard tubes, a dusty metal box full of recorder-lens tapes, and even all his own barely decipherable noteleaf scrawlings—anything and everything that pertained to the ten-year-old homicide case.

He was smiling absentmindedly and humming a little made-up tune to himself, happy and secure in the knowledge that somewhere in this pile of catshit was evidence—or something that could *lead* to evidence—that would bring Sentiva/Watly down. He *knew* Sentiva was really Watly, knew it deep in his gut the same way a throbbing toe could tell him the rain was coming. Maybe he'd known it from the beginning, but, like he'd told her, if he had, he'd chosen to ignore it. The guy had been okay, this Watly guy. The woman-Watly was too. Pretty damn cute, actually. But this Chancellor thing was too much.

The chief had a hand-painted antique tin box full of salted, dried sunbeans on his desk. Every few minutes he would pop one into his mouth and chew noisily on it. Fenlocki liked sunbeans. He was probably one of the only people in all of the country of Manhattan who ate them by choice. Now that he was on Second, he could have anything he wanted: fresh spiced weeders; pickled or marinated birdmeat; raw, untainted farleymeat; and even pseudopeanut butter on orange hardcrackers—but Fenlocki still liked the occasional sunbean. He had them shipped up special once a week to his apartment. Every bitter, enamel-shattering bite of a 'bean was a reminder of the past. The face-puckering taste was a First Level taste, a carryover from the old days, a reminder of his roots. Even the unmistakable look of them held nostalgia. Their little oblong kidney shapes cradling the lumpy brown acidic heart, the speckled tan surface—so like some long-extinct, thick-skinned desert lizard—and the salty, earthy, almost sexual smell of them. . . . The chief popped another one in his mouth and crunched happily on it.

Fenlocki flipped through some of the old police-report screens—nothing too interesting there—and powered up his keyboard to check out some of the old tapes. He was still humming and smiling as he chewed. Most peace officers didn't like this kind of methodical, plodding deskwork, but Fenlocki was different. You could take fieldwork any day; *this* was a challenge, a puzzle to be solved. This was the kind of thing he liked about being a cop. The brainwork of it. The art of it. And the comfort. It was organized, there were rules, and you knew just where you stood.

Fenlocki liked knowing where he stood. He liked rules and regulations. They made life livable. He'd made it his mission to always live by the book. In fact, the one time he hadn't, the one very *long* time he hadn't, had been this Caiper thing. He'd thrown the book out for ten years. Totally ignored it. Turned his official back on it. And, frankly, it felt damn good to be back playing by the rules again.

"Chief? Chief! We got a major problem down here, Chief!"

It was Akral's voice screaming out of the emergency squawker. He sounded near panic, if not entirely over the edge already.

Good old Akral, the chief thought, tossing a sunbean up and catching it deftly in his mouth. Akral was now commander of First Level's police force. He was still under Fenlocki's country-wide/country-deep jurisdiction, but Fenlocki let him handle most things down there on his own. Akral wasn't too bad at it, even if he still was, as he'd always been, more than a tad thick. But being a little stupid wasn't necessarily such a bad thing when it came to police work. Stupid people don't overthink. They look at the obvious.

"Steady your sockets, Akral," the chief said calmly, the loud sunbean crunch ringing pleasantly in his ears. He was having some difficulty opening the recorder-lens tape box. "What's the sitch?"

"Fire!" the hyperventilating voice came back.

"*What?*" Fenlocki dropped the box. A piece of 'bean flew out of his mouth and stuck to the top of one of the sanifiles.

"Major, major fire at Man-With-Hat-On. Everything's going. Can't stop it! And it's spreading up."

"Are the unmanneds there?" Fenlocki asked, leaning forward toward the squawker. His elbows sent some of the files and tubes clattering to the floor.

"They're spraying CO_2 on it like crazy, but it's not doing much good."

"You got water on it?" The chief's booted feet were twitching uncontrollably under his desk. He swallowed the whole lump of unchewed sunbean still in his mouth. It felt like a handful of sharp pebbles going down his throat.

"What water?" Akral's hysterical voice said. "We got CO_2 like crazy. It's still burning, though. It's like it's making it *worse*. Don't make *sense*! The *plasticore* is burning like crazy!"

"Plasticore doesn't burn, Akral." Fenlocki wiped his hand up over his forehead and through the thin hair behind it. "Get every cop you have over there. *Every one*, you hear?"

"*Every*one?" Akral asked.

"*Yes*, dammit. Everyone. Listen to me. Give them extinguishers. Cartridges. C-bombs. Pass buckets of raping soljuice if you have to. *Any* liquid. Have them raping *piss* on it. And get all the unmanned coppers—every single one—over there hitting that building with CO_2. Have someone climb up in an exhaust-fan cleaning basket and bust open the ceiling nearby to tap into a drip pipe."

Akral sounded more afraid than ever. "You coming down to help me, Chief? It's crazy down here—"

"*You* do it, Akral. Put the raping thing *out*. I'm going to go over and try to handle it on *this* end. I've got to keep your raping fire from spreading up *here*, you idiot. That building's over a hundred and fifty stories high up here! Full of people."

"Yes, sir," Akral's shaky voice responded.

Fenlocki didn't say goodbye. He grabbed his hat and left his office—and his heap of Watly/Sentiva material—without looking back. He had to get downtown fast.

If he hadn't been such a competent, smart cop, he would've thought of the obvious. If he'd been more than a little thick *himself*—or even just plain stupid—then instead of acting swiftly and surely and doing exactly what the situation called for, he would've stopped, chewed a few more sunbeans, and wasted precious seconds wondering. Wondering if maybe putting every single First Level police resource into the same small area wasn't just what somebody wanted.

CHAPTER 21

Eiter Eimsler almost died in the fire. He was almost roasted alive while he and Tavis were starting it. It was not an intentional thing—just one of those freaky accidents that tend to happen when you do freaky things. Setting fire to the First Level of a structure was definitely high on the freaky thing list.

Eiter was to start inside of the Man-With-Hat-On, while Tavis did the outside. They had returned to the chemical-saturated building twenty-four hours after spraying it. They were on a strict time schedule, everything had to be done just so, just then. Eiter took his lasertorch inside, preparing to go for the baseboards, and Tavis circled around the building's "feet," ready to go for the lower part of the exterior walls. They started right on schedule: seven P.M. Lower time exactly.

They were only at it five minutes when Tavis heard the screams and ran inside. Eiter had apparently flamed himself into a corner somehow. Very careless. The smoke had blinded him so he couldn't see a way out and the edge of his clothing had caught. No one had thought to equip them with flamesuits—it was supposed to be a simple in-and-out job.

Tavis kind of liked Eiter. Eiter was a quiet, serious fellow. He never said much, and never complained. Except now. Now he was yelling "Help, Tavis! Help me!" over and over. Now Tavis saw messy emotions bubbling up in him like in some of the others. That was a disappointment. But Tavis certainly didn't want the guy dead. In fact, it was important that all the Revies stayed alive right now. Tavis understood that. The more, the merrier. Strength in numbers, and all. More than that, the Ragman would kill Tavis if Eiter turned up dead during a simple misdirect excursion. Yet it would've been nice to just stand there and watch him burn. A big part of Tavis wanted to stand back and enjoy the show. What else was there to do? No reason to let a good, gruesome death go to waste. Fun to be had.

Yes, yes, yes, it would've been most entertaining. A joy to watch; quite a feast for the eyes. And Tavis would've gotten a certain pleasure—beyond the mere aesthetic—in realizing that the guy broiling quite spectacularly was Watly Caiper's biological father. There was a good deal of fun to be had in that thought. Watly's daddy toasting.

Tavis had never liked that Watly Caiper fellow. Tavis hadn't seen Watly in ten years, but IT still didn't like the fellow. IT could hold a grudge as well as anyone. Tavis remembered well not liking Watly way back then, so IT held on to that dislike quite faithfully and loyally, no matter how much time had passed.

Watly Caiper had stolen an evening. Way back then, Tavis had been tricked out of slicing up Watly. That was annoying. Very. So it really would've been kind of fun to watch Watly's father's skin bubble off and hear Watly's father's mellifluous death screams. Ha.

But Tavis did what IT was supposed to. Reluctantly, but efficiently. Tavis whipped off ITs cloak, tossed it over the flames between them, and dashed in to the burning room. "You are very, very silly," Tavis said, patting Eiter's burning shirt down, hoisting the guy up and rushing him through the burning transom. The flames were spreading fast and the smoke was making it hard to see and real hard to breath. Tavis got them to the outside of the Man-With-Hat-On, tripping only once or twice, and parked Eiter on the stoop. Then Tavis finished up at the base of the building with the lasertorch and backed off, coughing rather violently. Ick. Throat sore and eyes tearing up something fierce. No "ha" in that.

The building was really going now. There was an acrid, burning-plasticky chemical smell. The angry flames' noise grew—first a few snaps and pops and then, finally, a constant baritone roar. Though the fire was spreading and growing, it appeared dimmer and dimmer as the smoke filled the street. The thick gray clouds flowing out were contained by the First Level's ceiling. Tavis and Eiter would have to leave the area quickly if they didn't want to drop dead as catshit from smoke inhalation.

Somehow Tavis hadn't expected all that foul-smelling smoke. IT had imagined only clean, crisp, beautiful yellow and blue flames gracefully consuming more and more. This wasn't like the fantasy. This was messy. Messy and very, very smoky. Inelegant. Un-elegant. Non-elegant. Not even quasi-elegant.

But it was a job well done. Well done and right on time. Misdirection mission completed. Silly Eiter saved in one coughing piece. Ragman would like that fact. Tavis had done good.

Tavis grabbed Eiter, slinging him over ITs right shoulder like a sack of soggy hardloaf, and took off up West Broadway at a half trot. There was a slowly growing grin on ITs face as IT jogged casually along.

Saved a life and set a fire. Ha. Burn. Ha. Revy is on the way. Ha.

CHAPTER 22

Nine-and-a-half years ago, Watly wanted a parent. She wanted her mommy.

Watly wanted her family. *A* family.

She wanted to share this pregnancy thing. She wanted family support, shoulders to lean on. She wanted to have relatives then . . . now that a baby was on the way. Her baby. Noonie.

Uncle Narcolo Caiper was dead. He had given his life for Watly's almost a year ago. Pepajer Caiper, Watly's mother, was dead too. Long dead. She had died back in a time that seemed like ancient history now. She had died, in her own way, for Revy. Her personal Revy. Maybe personal Revys were the way to go.

So Watly had no family left. And it was a family time. A strange time.

What a weirdness, this.

Being pregnant.

Strange enough to be a different sex than before, but to have all the bizarre changes thrown in . . . Sometimes it was downright scary.

Watly had Alysess with her frequently. The company was nice, but it did little to soothe her reactions to the unexpected transformations. Alysess knew nothing of pregnancy. She was a doctor, yes, but a First Level doctor. She'd never had a pregnant patient, never delivered a baby, never had any schooling in the subject. And sure Alysess was family. She was the only family Watly had. But that didn't seem enough.

Watly knew Alysess was trying. Trying to help. Trying to be both doctor and lover. She knew Alysess was using whatever little spare moments she had to seek out reference materials, to track down older First Level doctors still alive who'd been around during the pre-prophy baby times.

But Watly still felt a void. And she was still worried. She wished she could have consulted with someone close who had been through all this. She wished she could at least have talked with a Second Level babier. But that would've looked funny. Here she had pulled all the strings she could—absolutely insisting that Dr. Alysess Tollnsmer be granted passes to become her personal physician—and now she would consult *another* doctor for the pregnancy? No, that wouldn't appear right. They would have to muddle through.

"Look at this! What is this, Aly? What is happening to me?"

"Don't worry, Watly."

"My breasts are huge. I know they were way smaller before. And they tingle. Everything feels so fragile and sensitive. I can hardly touch them."

"I'm sure it's normal, Watly."

"And why is that dark now? Why is that part around the nipples brown and so much more lumpy? It's spotted. It used to be pink. And I'm all veiny, Aly. I've got a road map of blue veins all over my breasts and down on my tummy."

"I've heard of that."

"It's ugly."

"It's supposed to happen."

"I'm supposed to get *sick* is what's supposed to happen. Everybody knows you're supposed to get sick if you're pregnant. How come I never feel sick? I'm *supposed* to feel sick. I'm supposed to be nauseous. All *I* ever feel is tired. So raping tired. Something's wrong. I *know* something's really wrong."

"Nothing's wrong. You're pregnant."

"I want a family."

"You're making a family. You're manufacturing one as we speak, Watly."

"More than that."

"What am I? A broken Floobie-pod? *I'm* your raping family, beanhead!"

"Aly, Aly, Aly—there's a little squeezing thing that happens down there every so often, Aly. All by itself. I'm not doing it. Why is that? It's really weird-feeling."

"I'll find out."

"I'm so tired."

"So rest, Watly. Rest."

"I have to pee again."

And Alysess would go home, shaking her head, trying to find answers, and Watly would worry, worry, worry as her belly grew. Where was Mommy? Where was family?

"I can't stop peeing, Aly. All the time. And right after I pee I have to pee again. And look at this, now. Look at these purple lines on my thighs. I think I'm dying."

"You're not dying, Watly. You're pregnant."

"I have *pimples*. I haven't had pimples since I was an adolescent boy. I've got pimples all over the place."

"That's okay."

"I'm ugly. I'm fat. I'm pimply. There are blue lines everywhere, I have gas all the time, and my body's going crazy on me. I'm a monster."

"You're not a monster. You're pregnant."

"Aly?"

"Yes?"

"I have to pee again."

Eventually Alysess found a doctor on First Level who remembered some of the birthing stuff. She studied with her every chance she could. And went back up to Watly between times.

"Can you get me some sweetened sunbeans, Aly? Nobody has sweetened sunbeans up here. You can't get any kind of sunbeans on Second."

"I'll make you another nutri-gruel and some juice."

"I don't *want* a nutri-gruel. I want sunbeans. Sweet."

"You're already constipated. You said you have cramps. It'll make it worse."

A pause.

"I love you."

"I love you too, Watly."

"Can I have a hug?"

"Sure."

"Will you make love to me?"

"You horny?"

"I've never been hornier."

"Okay."

"Wait. I have to pee."

"So pee."

And the belly got bigger and bigger with little pink, scarlike stretching streaks all around it. And Alysess kept visiting as often as she could. But Watly had an image in her head of other people gathering around her. She had a fantasy of her dead mother and her dead uncle coming back to join Alysess—and sometimes even the Ragman himself—at her side. In the vision, the group would warm and protect her in a soft quilt of wisdom and comfort and a sense of togetherness.

"Something's wrong."

"What's wrong, Watly?"

"I don't have to pee as much anymore."

"That's okay."

"And my breasts don't hurt so much."

"So?"

"But look, Aly. Look at my feet. They're all swollen and they ache like crazy. Painey bloats. I get leg cramps in the middle of the night. Bad ones. And there are so many blue veins now, Aly. All I am is blue veins. My hands are swollen too. I'm all puffy. I think my face is even puffy too. I think I'm dying."

"It's edema. It's normal."

"And I can't concentrate. I'm dizzy. I get headaches. I raped up a remote board meeting 'cause I couldn't think straight. I can't think anymore. And I'm leaking down below."

"You're leaking?"

"Something milky keeps dripping out of me. It smells funny. And I'm all sore-feeling down there, Aly. Achy. I think I'm infected inside. The baby's infected. The baby is dying."

"It's discharge. It's normal."

"*Every* raping thing is normal? Every raping thing I say is normal?"

"It's okay, Watly."

"I hate you."

"Try to relax, Watly."

"Oh! Oooh!"

"What?"

"Something moved! Something moved in me!"

"The baby."

"The baby?"

"The baby moved."

"Oh, my. Oh, my. I felt it. Feel it? Oh, my. The baby. I love you, Alysess."

"I know. You want a hug?"

"Don't touch me."

Alysess spent more time below digging up old books, leafs, and records about birthing. She needed to know as much as she could find out. Meanwhile, Watly spent more time worrying. Only occasionally did Watly take a break from worrying.

"How's the pre-mama doing today, Watly?"

"I'm fine."

"You're fine?"

"My back hurts a lot, and I get these bad pains and cramps in my tummy and sides. I'm growing hair where I didn't have it, my palms are all red, I've got these spots on my face—see?—and there's a dark line from my belly button downward. My gums bleed, my nose is stopped up, my ears are stuffed up, my stomach is incredibly itchy—itchy like raping *crazy*—I leak that white stuff all the time, I'm hungry every second, I've got indigestion and gas, my feet keep falling asleep and tingling, and the damn kid kicks me in the ribs and stomach all night long."

"And you're fine?"

"Yeah. I'm fine. I am. I'm pregnant, Aly. I'm going to have a baby, don't you understand?"

During the last months of Watly's pregnancy, Alysess started spending more and more time on Second. It wasn't easy, but Watly really needed her. Watly cut down on her work and rested a lot. Sometimes excited . . . but mostly just worried, as always.

"I'm sweating like crazy. It's hot in here, Aly."

"I'll turn down the heat."

"I think I'm going crazy. I have crazy dreams. I have crazy thoughts. Someone is haunting me. A shadow figure. A person I don't know. I can't sleep. I'm scared."

"I know. It's okay to be scared, Watly."

"Everything hurts. Everything's painful. My back, my legs, my feet, my . . . Everything. And the squeezing thing hurts lots too."

"I know. Did you do the exercises?"

"Everything still hurts."

"I'm sorry."

"I look funny. I feel funny. I feel funny all over. I'm huge. I'm all heavy. I'm grotesque. My thighs are like tree trunks. I'm clumsy. I don't get horny anymore. I've lost it. I've no sex drive. And . . . and I can't even come anymore when I try, Aly."

"You came the other day."

"It wasn't the same. It felt funny. It's different. And . . Aly?"

"What?"

"Want to hear something weird?"

"What?"

"My breasts are leaking."

"That's good."

Watly's eyes went wide with wonder. "Women . . . women go through all this catshit every time? Women have been going through this stuff forever?"

"Yeah, Watly. Yeah. You got it."

And as the big day neared, Watly let the haunting dreams solidify. She came to learn that they were not nightmares at all, but wishes. The figure in the dream was only frightening because it was unknown. But the wish was for the shadow figure to be known. To become family.

"Alysess?" Watly cried out, running into the downstairs kitchen. She knocked over a pile of medical leafs crossing into the room. "Alysess? Can you get a personal message to the Ragman? Tell him I want to arrange something. I want him to find some excuse to have someone who works in the subs come up here."

Alysess looked up from her cooking. She was making Watly a hot weeder salad with boiled sunbean sauce. "Come up *here*? Watly, it was hard enough for us to arrange for *my* visits, let alone—"

"Just a one-time thing, Aly." Watly wrapped her arms around Alysess from behind. She felt her huge belly press into her lover's lower back. "I promise," she said. "Have the Ragman figure a plan. Tell him he's got to."

"What do you want now, beanhead?" Alysess asked, putting her spoon down to clasp Watly's hands and press them affectionately into her own crotch. "What earth-shattering need requires filling today?"

Watly tickled Aly's mound teasingly. "I want the cleaner. The tile cleaner. The older man with the high forehead and the crooked nose."

Alysess turned around and frowned. "The one you think was your mother's poovus?"

"Yeah. Him."

"The one you think might be your biological, paternal father?"

"Uh-huh."

Alysess sighed. "*Watly*—"

"Please?"

"Yeah, sure," Aly said, turning back to the stove. "No problem."

No problem. Messages were exchanged. The Ragman resisted. Watly kept insisting. For weeks Alysess was the means of communication between these two stubborn beings. Now she was not only rushing around researching pregnancy, doctoring her poovus, and spying for the revolution, but she was also playing negotiator between the Subkeeper and Watly Caiper.

Finally the Ragman gave in. Finally it was agreed. A one-shot deal. A date was arranged. An excuse was made.

Watly reported a broken toilet that would not clean itself and could not be removed and factory-lifted down for repair. The man with the crooked nose and the high forehead took the temporary identity of a First Level loo maintenance person. Ragman's shop made up false travel papers and identicards for him. Word came that he was all set to go. Soon the shadow man would come up, for one single afternoon.

And Watly learned through Alysess, just weeks before the visit was scheduled to occur, what the man's name was. Her father's name.

Eiter Eimsler.

Her mom's poovus. Eiter. Not a bad name.

And then came the pain. Real pain. Bad pain. The contractions. The fluid. The pain. Blood. Pain. More pain. More blood. Breathing. Pushing and pushing and pushing. Breathing through the pain. Pushing through the pain. Blood and breathing and pushing and pain. And pain, pain, pain, pain.

And, after a relatively short labor, Noonie Caiper came into the world.

And she was just perfect. Absolutely perfect in every way. And her granddaddy was going to come calling.

CHAPTER 23

Alysess quit Revy. She quit the revolution entirely.

It was a big, impulsive, unplanned move. But it didn't come as a surprise to her when she did it. It seemed the natural progression. She'd broken up with Watly; now she was breaking off with the revolution. She was severing her ties. She had had enough of everything. She'd done her time. Now she wanted nothing more than to go back to an unfettered, unambiguous life of a simple First Level doctor. Heal the sick. Ease the sufferings. Tend the wounds. No more confusing lovers, no more messy "great" causes. No more complications.

She hadn't known she was going to quit ahead of time. It just happened naturally, quite comfortably.

She'd been attending her local Cruda church to catch up on her enlightenment services. As she sat there, two Soft pills calmer, she felt herself getting caught up in the atmosphere.

What the Ragman overlooked, she thought to herself as she shouted "Praise Cruda!" along with the rest of the jovial congregation, *was the group spirit. In all his talk of religion and superstition and people's "needs," he forgot the most important need of all. The need for camaraderie, for togetherness.* That *is more the foundation of religion than anything.*

Alysess shouted "Praise Cruda!" joyfully right along with the rest of the folk. She turned and smiled at the old woman sitting next to her.

People need to belong to something, she thought. *That something could be a religion, a political drive, a form of music, art, philosophy, whatever. It could even be—get this, Ragface—a revolutionary movement. We all need a sense of community—it is a nice sense. And is that really such a bad thing?*

The priestess and her Fluffel were about to begin the Massturb ceremony. Group sex for Cruda. Jerk and diddle for the god of meat. Somehow this made Alysess think of Watly, and she felt a gray, heavy something fall over her.

She desperately wanted to talk about her loss, about the breakup. But there was no one to talk to. The one person she could talk to about such things—the one person in her life who she could open up to at least a little—was the person she had pushed away. Watly.

Maybe she'd made a mistake. Maybe she'd blown it. The tangle of steel and the solid sphere had begun to evaporate from her stomach as soon as she'd told Watly how crappy she'd felt. Maybe complaining was all she'd really needed to do. Maybe she should've stopped there.

No. Watly was an addiction she was well rid of. No addict could expect to give up her drug without experiencing pain and second thoughts. It was only natural. But what about Noonie? What did that make the child? Some secondary, peripheral addiction? Noonie was not a drug. Noonie was a glorious, magical, somewhat damaged child. Noonie was a sweet, wonderful, confused little girl who . . . And there was a really bad missing feeling there too. A *really* bad missing of the talks, the games, the drawing together, the laughter. . . .

As Alysess reached down to undo her pants along with the rest of the congregation, she noticed her hands were wet. Something clear had dripped on them. Some thin, transparent fluid, like water or expensive booze or a clean weeder broth. She reached up and realized the fluid was coming from her eyes. Alysess wiped the stuff on her waistband.

Suddenly there was a loud commotion from outside the church—the whoosh of cruisers, the clicking noise of many rapid footfalls, and the loud screams of emergency back-off beepers howling from what sounded like hundreds of unmanned coppers zipping by.

"What the rape is that?" someone said.

"Do you hear that noise? What the—"

There was an anxious tumble of conversation from the congregation. It sounded to Alysess like a room full of folks mumbling "What-rape-noise?" over and over. People pulled their pants back up and started for the door. The projected image of the priestess and her Fluffel continued the service, oblivious to the crowd's growing indifference to them. By now the priestess was pumping her Cruda wand in and out of her vagina rapidly, while her faithful Fluffel flexed his well-toned muscles in the standard poses and pulled roughly on his holy penis.

"Praise the God of Sex," both projections said breathlessly.

"Praise her yourself," one of the parishioners said, abandoning the church to investigate the ruckus. More followed right behind. Alysess yanked up her pants and ran after them.

There was a flood of cops, coppers, and cruisers streaming down the street at top speed, lights flashing blindingly. The parade of police was heading downtown. To Alysess, all the blinking lights looked hazy. Even their reflections on the wet road, the nearby walls, and the shiny ceiling way above seemed to be fuzzy and streaked. Every bright point of light was like a little smudged four-pointed star. Alysess closed her eyes for a second, thinking they were blurry from that wetness, from those tears. No, the fading flood of cops and coppers still looked foggy to her. On top of that, the avenue itself had a faint nasty smell to it, like burned hardloaf or overfried sunbean.

The doctor joined the crowd that was cautiously making its way downtown toward the source of the excitement. The air seemed thick and old. It now had a closed-in, closety feel to it. It was the smell ancient, decomposing plastic would have . . . if plastic could rot.

Alysess was walking down the center of the street with the group for fifteen minutes before they came upon the first crowd of near-rioters gathered around one of the Subkeeper's food dumps. At first she had no idea what was going on. She pushed her way into the frenzied mob with difficulty. When she got near to the center of it, she started to be able to make out the busted-open crates and containers between the bodies still blocking her way. She could also see some of the bright red and white signs plastered to the sides of the boxes and all across the nearby buildings.

THIS FOOD SHOULD'VE BEEN YOURS LONG AGO!
THE 2ND LEVEL KEPT IT FROM US!
THEY'RE TRYING TO STARVE US!

Some of the signs carried the same basic message about water and medicine. Others just had a few words on them.

C.V. LIES!
or
CRUDA BRAINWASHES!
or
SOFT PILLS KILL!

or more wordy ones like:

THEY WILL NOT LET US REPRODUCE!
THEY FORCE US PROPHIES SO WE
PLURITES WILL DIE OFF CHILDLESS!

But as Alysess backed away from the dangerous feeding frenzy that was now going full tilt, she saw that many of the signs stuck high on the walls around the food dump had only one word on them, repeated over and over.

GENOCIDE
GENOCIDE
GENOCIDE

Alysess stepped back farther so that she was closer to the center of the street and could see down it. There were red and white signs everywhere, off into blurry infinity in both directions. It was as if they had magically cropped up in the blink of an eye. Farther down the avenue in either direction, she saw other swarming mobs of people at what must have been other food dumps. Fights were breaking out. People were grabbing handfuls of food, armfuls of food, even whole boxes of food and trying to run off with them. Barrels were hacked open. Water spilled out on the pocked road surface. Some slipped and fell in it, only to be stepped on or kicked aside. The air was even thicker than before, cloudy with throat-itching grayness.

To the left, one of the ceiling's daylites shattered and sparks flew down on the struggling bodies. Someone must have thrown

something very well aimed up at the light to break it like that. Fists
flew in the shadows. Bodies tumbled and grappled. The noise of
screams and yelling was incredible—it sounded like it was coming
from everywhere. One body was actually tossed violently up in
the air and landed behind some smashed crates. Alysess flinched.
Clothing was ripped and shredded. Blood flowed. People ran
frantically in all directions.

The entire First Level seemed to have been turned into a
madhouse in a few short minutes: food, medical supplies, and
fresh water barrels on almost every street corner, revolutionary
slogans emblazoning every empty surface, and crazed people
trying to kill each other over a chunk of hardloaf. Alysess watched
the violence building. She felt as if it were unreal, as if it couldn't
be happening—right here, right now, right in front of her. The
entire country was just a bad nightmare, a horrible dream. Men
and women, youngish and old, battling viciously for scraps of
food and drops of water. Hurting each other. Killing each other.
Genocide.

Yes, Alysess thought numbly, standing well clear of the nearest
mini-riot. *Yes, that is not a lie. They are not letting us reproduce.
What else can you call that? And they are, perhaps, even trying to
quietly kill us off with Soft pills and Cruda suicide doctrine, and
all. But mostly with indifference and neglect. They were not trying
to starve us. That was the Subkeeper's doing. That was just his
little extra-special technique for driving his point home—for
shaking up the plurites. For making them sick, hungry, and angry.*

"Lovely move," Alysess said aloud to no one. "Works
wonderfully." Her eyes stung from the smoke that was filling the
street. To her left, she saw someone with a tattered patchwork
cloak and brightly painted face doing something behind an
upright. She walked over, staying near the sidewalk, away from
the madness around her.

It was a man she didn't know, wearing Tavis-like warpaint and
carrying a large bundle under his left arm.

"Putting some more signs up?" she asked the man loudly. "Not
done yet? You must be behind schedule."

The man flinched just a little, and then tried to move around
her. She stopped him.

"Smooth job you-all have done, I must say. Well choreo-
graphed. Fast and accurate. Looks like you've got some kind of
literal smokescreen going too. Mucho kudos. And no cops around
to stop you either. Where'd you send them?"

The man's face was blank under his thick makeup.

"You *do* work for Revy, don't you?" she asked, wondering why her hands hurt so much. She looked down and saw that her fists were clenched so tightly that her fingernails had drawn blood from her palms.

"I don't know what you're talking about," the man said softly, trying to sidestep the doctor.

She blocked him again. "I have a message for the Subkeeper. I want you to deliver it for me."

"Hey, lady—"

"Tell him . . . tell him *Dr. Alysess Tollnismer hereby tenders her resignation from the revolution*," she shouted. Everyone on the street was too busy screaming and fighting over food to notice her meager yells. "Understand? *Tell him that*. Tell him I *quit!*"

The man finally pushed by her, still giving no indication he'd heard anything. As she watched him work his way up the avenue she saw that he was indeed slapping more signs to the walls and uprights he passed beside.

"Good," Alysess said. She felt better. *This* breakup held none of the ambiguity of her Watly split. This one felt raping *great*.

No more Revy for me, Ragface, she thought, scanning the avenue. Now there was just simple doctoring to do. And it looked like there would be a lot of it. There were riot injuries all around her, plus—if the thickening smoke was any indication—there would be other injuries too. That smoke tasted none too healthful. And it had nowhere to dissipate.

It was only after that thought that it finally occurred to Alysess that the Subkeeper had somehow started a fire somewhere. A real honest-to-Cruda fire.

"Brilliant," she said aloud. "Raping genius misdirection."

And then she snorted heartily. And it felt good.

CHAPTER 24

Alysess remembered the meeting between Watly and her father. Somehow the memory of that day seemed important. Pivotal. It seemed to signify something, something just beyond her grasp.

Noonie was fresh and new. Just born. Alysess loved her dearly. The child had been born bald, her smooth little head as tender and soft as a ripe fruit. She barely cried at all. To Alysess, it was almost as if the newborn infant could sense how unhappy her mother would be if she cried a lot. It was as though this tiny baby was already deferring her own needs, suppressing her urges, for the sake of others.

Watly was nursing the baby when Eiter arrived. Alysess was reading a medical leaf. At first Alysess had politely declined Watly's invitation to join the reunion. But Watly had insisted. Watly needed her poovus there. She needed support. So Watly was with her child, feeding Noonie breakfast, and Alysess was sitting next to them. One of her hands was holding the leaf, the other cradled Noonie's little left foot.

The nursing was better now. It had finally become a pleasant thing. At first it had been clumsy and fumbling. Difficult. Everything was wrong. This perfectly natural thing was not

coming naturally at all. There were many tears on both sides—
Noonie's and Watly's both. It seemed to Alysess they would never
work it out, never be in sync as mother and child. And when they
did begin to work it out . . . then came the pain and discomfort.
Watly's breasts seemed a full three times larger than they had
started out, and she complained constantly about how sore and
achy they were. They did not want to be sucked on. They
apparently did not want to be touched at all. The nipples were little
flaming points of pain, dry and cracked. Sometimes they even
bled rawly. But that too passed.

And nursing became a wonderful thing. A time when the small
creature and the large creature became one. Alysess watched this
happen, feeling both touched and a little jealous at the same time.
Watly would smile and whisper quietly, "Drink of me, my perfect
little child. I feed you. I nourish. You feed me. You need me."

It became a special, magical ritual.

"I wish I could do that."

It was a man's voice, a voice very much like Watly's own used
to be. Alysess looked up. She was looking into an enchanted CV
projection. A distorted, bewitched mirror that reflected Watly's
former self. There before her, leaning into the wooden column at
the far end of the foyer by the living room, was an older version
of the male Watly Caiper. He wore Second Level worker
clothes—a black jumpsuit, yellow workervest, and short yellow
boots. A buzbelt with dirty tools hung from his slightly paunchy
waist.

The face was Watly's face; Alysess's lover's old face plus
twenty years. The crooked nose was more bulbous and reached
farther to the south, the forehead was higher and the hair thinner,
the eyebrows bushier and highlighted with fine gray hairs, the chin
a tad longer and with a little bag of soft-looking flesh hanging just
behind it . . . but it was still Watly's face. A kind, near-to-
handsome face. A wise, strong plurite face. Alysess glanced to the
side to see Watly was staring just as she had been. Watly's eyes
looked hypnotized, her mouth half open, as if she'd stopped
midword while trying to say something. Maybe trying to say
"Daddy."

The man brushed back his little bit of hair and scratched his
scalp. His hands were like Watly's hands had been, large and
wide, with long, sensitive fingers. Hard-worker hands. Fatherly
hands. Family hands. Alysess remembered how Watly always

used to quote her old Uncle Narcolo Caiper: "Ain't hardly such a thing as family anymore, Watly."

"Maybe I should go," Alysess said, starting to rise.

"No," Watly hissed, pressing Alysess back into her seat with one hand. Watly again looked over at the man in the doorway. "Wish you could do what?" she asked, sounding shy, excited, and just a little hinky.

"Nurse," Eiter said, smiling.

Watly smiled back. Alysess noted that this man even had her old smile.

"One of the many benefits of being female," Watly said. Her voice sounded kind of proud suddenly.

"Oh, I wasn't talking about being a woman. I was referring to the baby."

It took Alysess, and probably Watly too, a moment to realize what he meant. Alysess glanced at Watly and thought that she looked like she might throw up. *Finally some morning sickness,* the doctor thought absurdly. Something was wrong here. Something wasn't as Watly'd planned it. The way he looked at her. What he'd said. His tone of voice. Alysess was uncomfortable. She watched Watly pull Noonie from her nipple and lay the child back in the crib, closing her shirt. The child began to cry instantly. Noonie wasn't done with breakfast yet.

"Noisy kid," Eiter said, and stepped farther into the room.

Alysess stood up and walked toward the man, holding her hand out. "I'm Alysess. Watly's . . . uh . . . doctor." Eiter shook her hand lightly. Watly walked over as well, her footsteps timid. She too held out her hand. "And this here is Watly," Alysess said, letting Eiter's hand drop.

"How do you do," Watly said.

Eiter took the hand, raised it up, and kissed it softly. "We met before. Briefly, when you were a guy."

"Yes, I know." Watly pulled her hand back. "That's how I knew of you. That's why you're here. Were you my mother's poovus?"

"For a short time," he said, sounding a touch bored.

Alysess noticed that Eiter was not looking at Watly's eyes. He was looking lower.

"Yes?" Watly prompted.

"She was pretty hot. We had a fling."

"I think you might be my father."

Eiter shrugged. "It's certainly possible. Does that kid always cry like that?"

"You look a lot like I did. I'm pretty sure you're my father."

"Could be." He put his hands on Watly's shoulders. Alysess could tell that Watly didn't like the feel of them. They made her squirmy. "So what's the deal here? Why'd you want to see me?"

Suddenly Watly didn't seem sure why. Her eyes appeared to cloud over with confusion. "I . . . I wanted . . ." she said haltingly. "I wanted . . . with the baby, and all . . . I wanted to—you know—have a sense of family. I wanted a sense of family, and all. And I thought . . . you being my father—I mean you *maybe* being my father—"

Alysess stepped in. "Watly wanted to connect with you. You were her mom's poovus before Watly was born, and you look remarkably like Watly did when she was a guy. You're probably her father. And Watly's looking for a sense of family, right?"

Watly smiled, appearing grateful for the clarification.

Eiter slid his hands up and stroked Watly's neck. Alysess could see his fingers playing with Watly's ears. The touch did not look parental. His hands rose to her hair, caressing, fondling. Watly froze. She seemed removed from herself, as if in some confused dream. She looked powerless. Powerless and dead. Withdrawn from the world as if she were hosting again.

Noonie wailed.

For a moment Alysess was so taken by surprise at the scene before her that she too felt frozen in place. Finally she reached in and tried to gently push Eiter's hands away. "Hey! What's the deal here?"

"You want to fuck me?" Eiter asked Watly softly.

That broke Watly's trance. She slapped his hands away, looking close to tears suddenly. "I'm your *daughter*!" she cried out.

Eiter smiled jovially, reaching for her again. Watly stepped back. Alysess moved in, blocking the man's path.

"I have no daughter," the man said, pushing in closer. "If I had anything, I had a son. And we're not even sure of that." He tried to move past Alysess, his hands reaching toward Watly again.

"*Stop* it!" Alysess yelled, shoving him away.

"You've got a great body, Watly."

"Hey, hey, hey," Alysess said. "What is your *problem*?"

"Get the rape out of my house!" Watly yelled.

Alysess realized this whole thing was not working out very

well. "Hold it just a sec, Watly—" she said, standing firmly between the two of them. Noonie's crying was louder than ever.

"Get the rape out of my house, you *bolehole*!"

"Hey," Eiter said, his voice relaxed and level. "I went through an awful lot of trouble coming up here just to get kicked out, lady. Is that why you called me up to Second? To kick me out?"

"This is not what I wanted at all," Watly said breathlessly. Her face was flushed and her arms were crossed severely over her chest. "Now, get the rape out before I call the cops." Watly was crying now. Alysess saw the tears flowing down her cheeks and running into the collar of her nursing blouse. The crying seemed to just make her madder.

"Okay, okay," Alysess said, grabbing up both Watly's and Eiter's right hands. "Let's just start over, here. This thing got raped up from the start. Let's just take it easy."

Watly looked intensely at Alysess, her eyes pleading. "I want him to leave," she said very softly.

"Suit yourself," Eiter said. Then he muttered "Crazy woman!" and Alysess had to hold on really hard to keep him from walking back out the door.

"Sit down, guys," Alysess ordered, pulling Eiter's strong body toward the wicker couch with one swift twist of her wrist. "Just sit down and don't bust your power ringlets. What've you got to lose? You're up here already."

Eiter stared angrily at Watly as he sat, but his words were directed at the doctor. "What the rape is her problem?"

Alysess eased Watly back down next to Noonie. Watly picked the child up again, hugging her, and Noonie's crying lessened instantly. "What the rape is *your* problem, guy?" Alysess asked.

Though Noonie's crying had subsided, Watly still had streams of tears working down her face. "I *have* a family," she was muttering, perhaps to herself. "I have Noonie, and myself, and I have Alysess. And I have the memory of my mother. And my uncle. That is my family now. And that's all the raping family I need!"

"I don't know what the rape you're talking about," Eiter said.

Alysess sat down on the coffee table between them. "What the subs is the deal with touching her like that? What is that all about?" Even as she said that, sitting between these two people, a small part of her was wondering how she always managed to end up in the middle. Why, in every situation, did she always seem to wind up as the diplomat, the negotiator, as the reasonable one who tried to help everyone get along?

Alysess looked over at Watly, who was hugging Little Noonie maybe a little too hard. The child had stopped crying entirely, as if she sensed how much it disturbed Watly. She was a remarkable baby. Watly didn't just appear angry at Eiter Eimsler, she looked like she despised him with every fiber of her being. She looked like she loathed him from her toenails to the beginnings of her hair's gray streaks.

"What was I supposed to think? Huh?" Eiter said coolly. His high, man-Watly-like forehead crinkled up into little exasperated lines. "This lady I don't even know pulls all sorts of strings to get me up here for one afternoon. I show up and she's got one tit out, flashing me. What am I supposed to think? I figure she wants to fuck. Is that so crazy?"

"She's your *daughter*!"

"So you say. I don't know what she is."

Alysess took a deep breath. "Watly wanted to see you. To get to know you. This was an important meeting to her."

"Meeting?" Watly said suddenly. "Meeting? You mean this conjugal visit from my father? You mean this delightful rendezvous with the incestuous bolehole who wanted to fuck me? Fuck his own *daughter?*—son?—whatever the subs I am to him? Is that what you mean? Is that the delightful visit you're referring to?" Now Watly started crying real hard. Her tears ran down her own face and onto Noonie's little swollen cheeks. Watly looked so hurt, so pained, so deeply wounded that Alysess didn't know what to do or say.

"All right," Eiter said slowly. He seemed moved by Watly now. Something in her words or tears had touched him. "Don't make me into the bad guy, here. Why do women always make you into the bad guy?" He leaned forward a little in his seat. He looked pained now, attacked and harassed, as if Watly's crying were some unfair, conscious tactic, some intentional manipulation. "Look, I'm not the most educated man. I never had much schooling. So I'll say this as best I can, and just bear with me, please. I feel bad if there was a misunderstanding. I'm sorry. I'm real sorry about everything. I really am. Okay?"

Alysess turned to see if Watly had any reaction. The mother held her child and rocked slightly from side to side, her eyes focused at some middle distance between them. "Look, Eiter, here's the deal," Alysess said finally. "You hurt Watly bad just now. All she wanted was a sense of 'parent' from you, a sense of family. I think Watly hoped you two might become friends, develop some kind of special bond. A father/daughter bond." Alysess gestured toward her lover. "This woman here just had a kid, see? She misses her mom and her uncle and some sense of family togetherness, family history—you know—generations getting together. All she wanted was a circle of people she loved to gather around and celebrate this new addition, this new life."

Alysess could've gone on like this, speaking for Watly, but she didn't. She could have talked about how lonely she suspected Watly was. About how Watly had no one but Alysess to talk to, no one to share things with day to day. But Alysess didn't say any of this. She already felt as if she had betrayed Watly's confidence. Watly had not given her permission to say these things to this man. Here Alysess was, talking about some of Watly's intimate feelings right in front of her as if she weren't there. But it was as if she really *wasn't* there. She looked drugged.

"Okay," Eiter said, sighing. He sounded like he was giving in to something. It was as if, to him, a conversation was something a person won or lost, and he had just lost. He was defeated, squashed. "Look, sometimes I can be a real jerk. I'm not perfect. I do stupid things. I don't think sometimes." Eiter sounded more genuine now, more honest. He directed his words at Watly's blank face. "I know I messed up. I know it, okay? I do that a lot. That's why your mom dumped me, actually. We broke up because I was being stupid. I understand that now. It took me a lot of years to."

Eiter rubbed the side of his nose with his finger. He seemed embarrassed and young. He looked a lot like the twenty-seven-year-old male Watly Caiper Alysess had known. "She was a good person, your mom," he said. "We spent a lot of time together. She was very smart, very passionate, and very 'right there.' You know what I mean? We loved each other for a while, I think. We had lots of sex. Good lusty sex. So it is possible you were my offspring, genetically. You did look a lot like me when you were a man." Now he just looked confused. "But what is that supposed to mean?"

"It means," Watly said abruptly, "that you're my raping father. My raping parent trying to fuck me!"

"Just a sec, Watt," Alysess said, feeling unrestrained fury radiating from Watly's very pores. Watly's unusually huge anger scared her. "A parent is the one who mothers the child, Watly, you've said it yourself. That's why we call them mothers whether they are male or female. They mother. If Eiter did anything, all he did was father you. A man or a woman who only fathers a child is not a mother. They are not a parent. They are nothing. They are genetic contributors and nothing else. Maybe you want too much from this guy."

Watly's eyes blazed. "Whose side are you on?"

"I am sorry," Eiter said before Alysess could respond. "I saw you there and I got mixed up. You were this beautiful woman with a nice tit hanging in my face, okay? You were sexy and attractive. How'm I supposed to make the connection to you being my son? Or being my daughter, or whatever? Before I even got here I had in my head how you asked me up so I could make sex with you. I don't know why. Sometimes I act really stupid and don't really know why. This was one of those times. I guess it means I'm human and as messed up as anyone. I apologize."

"And that makes everything just fine?" Watly yelled, spittle flying from her mouth. "That excuses everything?"

"Hey, Watly, take it easy, the guy is trying," Alysess said. She tried to touch Watly's arm, but Watly pulled it—and the child it held—angrily out of reach. Alysess felt a pang of annoyance and protectiveness that Watly had moved Noonie so roughly. "He said he messed up, Watly. We all mess up. He's human, Watly. We're all raped up, you know, in our own way. Everybody's crippled somehow." How had she managed to suddenly find herself in the position of defending Eiter's behavior?

Eiter didn't look thrilled with that last remark. He stood up and sighed deeply. "You say you want a parent, huh? I don't know if I can be that for you. I was never your parent. I didn't raise you. I just met you a little while ago. I feel no connection. Nothing real. You are a stranger to me. Maybe that explains part of what happened when I came in."

Watly seemed to be calming some. She looked directly at Eiter's eyes. Alysess wondered if Watly could see her former self in them, in the whole body, in the voice . . . maybe even in the attitudes. "I made a mistake," Watly said quietly.

"Look, Watly," Eiter said. "I don't know if I'm up for anything more than nothing else, you know? I can try. I will try if you want me to. What I do know is I am sorry for hurting you, okay? You are a good person, just like your mother was a good person. I can see that, I guess. I hope someday I get to talk to you about her. If not, that's okay, I'll understand." He began walking toward the door.

Alysess raised her eyebrows to Watly. *Come on, beanhead, last chance to make something good of this mess. Come on!*

"Wait!" Watly said. "Wait."

"Wait what?" Eiter said from the transom.

"I hate your guts," Watly said.

"Hey," Alysess jumped in, smiling a little at Eiter. "It's a start. Right?"

"Look," Eiter said, "if you want to try again, I will, and I promise it won't be like before. I'm really sorry that happened like that. I'm sorry about what I did. I hope you are okay. And the little kid, too. This kid is kind of cute, I think."

"Alysess," Watly said without taking her eyes off Eiter. Alysess, will you leave us alone for a few minutes? I want to try to talk to this guy."

"Sure," Alysess said cheerfully. She felt instantly furious. Furious and unappreciated. *I spend all this effort with you two boleholes, trying to help you make some kind of peace, and what happens? You kick me out.* "Want me to take Noonie?" she said calmly.

"I'll keep her with me," Watly answered.

And Alysess left the room, alone and resentful. She left the father and daughter to try to hash it by themselves. *If they were going to do that*, she thought, *why the subs couldn't they do that from the beginning?*

CHAPTER 25

It was the day of the elections.

Fenlocki was in the huge auditorium of the Lathone Civic Building on Fifty-seventh and Eighth. Everyone who was anyone was there. Even some people who *weren't* anyone were there. The chief was in the first row, right near the center. He had diplomatically shifted aside a few important types in order to sit directly beside Noonie Caiper.

The child ignored him. Her clothes were all black: long-sleeved black shirt, black ankle-pants, and small black shoes. She sat with her head bent over, drawing strange dark pictures on a pad with tight little lines from her click-pen. Her tongue was sticking out. In spite of this childlike, hunched pose, it struck Fenlocki how incredibly adult this kid seemed. There was something disturbing in the jaded grown-upness that radiated from this small nine-year-old with the slight overbite.

Fenlocki had always had a personal guide-rule for judging the mental health of fellow adults. If, as he got to know them, he could see the infant within, they were okay. If he could easily picture them wailing because they wanted to be nursed, or because they'd made a big poop in their pants, or because they were afraid of the dark, or picture them giggling joyously over a light tummy-tickle—baby food splattered all over their face—then they still had a healthy connection with the child they were, with the baby still inside us all. This nine-year-old sitting beside him—this girl who was barely more than an infant herself—revealed none of those qualities. This child was not a child at all. In some ways, she appeared more grown-up than he himself felt.

Fenlocki turned away from Noonie, feeling a shudder of sadness pass through his chest. He looked around the room. The auditorium pinlights shone brightly from all directions, making the cavernous hall glary and shadowless. In the exact front center, above the stage, there was an enormous master clock which read 12:45. Instead of being lit up, the numbers on the clock readout were darked so as to be easily read in the strong lights. Fenlocki knew this was one damned expensive timepiece. Each large numeral was a solid, light-absorbing, negative black void, in sharp contrast to everything else in the room. No expense too great for the elections.

On the stage below the clock, there were two wooden podiums. Far upstage from those were a row of leatherlike armchairs. The chairs were packed solid with well-dressed assistants, aides, and assorted political types—two to a seat. They looked cramped, thighs mashed against thighs. They also looked bored. All their different-colored faces—brown ones, pink ones, olive ones, yellowish ones, reddish ones, and one particularly striking pale one topped with long red hair—were frowning glumly. This row of dignitaries was more than ready for things to start. And so was the audience. Even Fenlocki's security cops, flanking each alternate audience row, looked restless. Fenlocki was glad they were there. He wasn't going to take any chances with a room full of Second Level's M.I.P.s (most important powerhouses).

Everyone waited. The packed hall was making distinctly impatient noises, harrumphing regularly. As always, there were technical problems. On either side of the auditorium there were two enormous CVs. The top ones were to project, live, the debate as it actually happened. The bottom ones were to show the altered, pre-recorded version of the debate as it was shown on First Level. Beside the CVs were tally graphs that would indicate how the voting progressed during the ceremony.

Second Levelers, watching the proceedings on their home CVs, would continuously vote by keyboard until the time was up. First Levelers would do the same, sitting in Cruda churches and operating individual voting ringlets. But, of course, *their* votes were not counted. Fenlocki did not particularly like that fact, but that's the way it worked. The way of the world.

He too was getting impatient. It seemed like, every election, there were last-minute bugs no one had bothered to smooth out. A crew of technicians was scampering around from one piece of equipment to another, down into the narrow control pit and then out onto the apron and into the wings. They looked increasingly harried and desperate.

Fenlocki fished in his jacket pocket for a sunbean. He found a whole handful. "Sunbean?" he asked Noonie, picking some clumps of lint from the pile.

Noonie kept drawing what looked like a huge, mutating chained bat and said nothing.

The chief shrugged and popped one into his mouth. He looked back up just in time to see Sentiva Alvedine and her opponent, Zephy Gavy, enter from opposite wings of the stage. Gavy, a descendant of the famous Walker Gavy, stood at the right-hand podium. Sentiva took the left-hand one.

Gavy was Fenlocki's boss. He had been Chancellor for the last two years. He was a short, round-faced man with a long bedlock. His head was shaven clean except for the one two-foot-long curl of blond hair that started at the top center of his forehead. It ran down the left side of his face to dangle in front of his shirt. The thing was very stylish, but Fenlocki always had to resist the compulsion to reach over and push the bedlock away from the man's eye. He found it distracting and annoying to look at.

But there was something even harder to look at. Sentiva. Fenlocki got a sense of instant indigestion seeing Sentiva up there like that. He hadn't had any chance to investigate her at all. The week since the fire had been crazy. They'd gotten it put out before it spread to Second, but that was the least of it. The smoke still wasn't all cleared out down there, in spite of increasing every exhaust fan's output . . . and, in a way, the fire itself was still burning. An emotional fire.

All that crazy rioting, the sudden food supplies, those provocative, anonymous signs. It had taken most of the week just for Fenlocki's cops to get all those posters removed. And the mood down there was something else. Fenlocki had ordered all the tubestops sealed up right away. He'd also shut down every factory lift. He wasn't going to take any risks. If ever it looked like people were on the verge of revolution, it was now. It felt like they'd come swarming right up, if they got the chance. Fenlocki had even posted cops on all the exhaust vents on Second. He didn't want anyone to do the impossible and climb up like Watly Caiper had all those years ago. And though he'd sealed off all known means of access to the Second Level, he still felt hinky.

Things were real scary right now. Akral had recently reported that Soft pill usage was waning and that church attendance was down—even though both were mandatory. The whole First Level was acting like one big violent, rebellious, wounded animal, and Fenlocki didn't want to mess with it. He'd set a daylite-night-setting curfew, telling Akral to have curfew breakers jailed. That didn't seem to be doing much to calm things, though.

Two days after the fire, the chief had put all his anti-Revy forces on alert, just to be safe. All countermeasures were in a state of readiness. The plurites had no way to get up to Second, but Fenlocki wanted to be careful anyway. Things were way out of control down there. The mood was nasty.

Fenlocki hoped the election might calm things. At the very least, having all the plurites sit quietly in the churches to watch the ceremony and vote might calm them down some.

The master clock read 12:55. CV mist poured out from the large machines that flanked the stage. The technicians seemed to have solved their problem. They scampered buglike off the apron and into the pit just as all four CV images flickered on. Sentiva and Gavy were both motionless during all this, smiling vacantly. Their smiles were now echoed in the large CV projections to each side.

To Fenlocki, even that little empty grin of Sentiva's looked like a Watly Caiper grin. He was convinced Sentiva was indeed Watly. *Damn*. There'd been no time to find proof, what with all the catshit below. Now he'd just have to hope she'd lose. And if she did win, he'd have to secretly pick up the Caiper investigation and stall her on the anti-Revy secrets until he had the goods to dethrone her. Not an easy task.

"Settle down, folks. Sorry for the delay."

Some tube-necked bolehole of a moderator was standing between the two candidates, his squeaky voice overamplified to a point just barely below the pain threshold.

"We're starting in thirty seconds. Settle down."

The THUNDEROUS APPLAUSE, PLEASE sign blinked darkly from just below the large clock, and the bolehole began his countdown from twenty. By the time he hit zero, his arms were

spread, his smile enormous, and the audience—Fenlocki included—
was roaring and clapping frenetically. The sign flicked off. So did the
audience.

"Thank you! Thank you! Good afternoon, people of our great
country of Manhattan, and welcome to the *elections*!"

Now the sign said MODERATE APPLAUSE, PLEASE, and the
crowd complied readily.

"Oh, you're all just delightful. Very fuckable, indeed! I'd like
to make you *all* my poovuses. Each and every fun-loving one of
you! Or should I say Poovi? Poovum?"

MEDIUM LAUGHTER, PLEASE.

"Without further adoration, I'd like to bring out our two teams
of competing Chancellor Dancers. The women represent Sentiva
Alvedine, and the men represent our incumbent, Zephy Gavy.
You viewers may each start voting at any time, and continue
voting right up until two P.M. sharp. Remember, you can change
your vote as often as you want, but when that clock-erini hits
two-ee-osity, the winner is the winner. Now, please welcome the
fabulous *Chancellor Dancers*!"

The THUNDEROUS sign went on again and the moderator
backed over to stand by the row of upstage chairs as the dancers
trotted in from the wings.

The vertical tally graphs lit up—the red Alvedine line starting
at exactly equal length to the green Gavy line.

Loud piellna vamping music came up as the Chancellor
Dancers took their positions. Sentiva's five female dancers lined
up in front of her podium and Zephy's five male dancers stood in
front of his. Both Sentiva and Zephy held absolutely still, the only
indication that they were not statues being the occasional blink.

The teams of dancers bowed to each other as the music built.
They'd start with the duel dance.

The women began twirling in sync—their yellow node hats
flopping and bobbing to the music as they spun. They each wore
stiff casement shirts and loose yellow skirts with golden tassels
that flared and glowed as they turned.

It was strange to see women in skirts. Fenlocki couldn't
remember seeing a skirt or dress in ages. The last time he'd seen
anything like that had been on some old CV history program. It'd
been a boring educational that droned endlessly about how this
kind of clothing was originally designed for women back in
pre-Cedetime patriarchal days. The purpose apparently had been
to connote female availability, to imply easy sexual access. The

history program theorized that the principle behind putting women in skirts and dresses—with their open, loose underside—had been to create the impression that the outfit could be flipped upward at a moment's notice should the male desire arise. "Rape attire." Well, perhaps the fashion was returning. Fenlocki didn't keep up on current styles very much.

The five women dancers stopped swirling, raised their arms, and did a complicated thumping dance on the wooden stage floor. Their heavy black boots clomped in intricate syncopation as they tilted their heads up and smiled. The music sped up to a frenzied crescendo and somehow their blurred feet kept up with it, smiles never wavering, hands pointed up like stiff flesh antennae looking for a signal. They finished with a breathless formal bow and turned to their competitors.

Fenlocki glanced over and noted that Sentiva's red tally rod was raising up a good twenty points above Gavy's now. He popped another sunbean in his mouth and chewed without tasting it.

It was Gavy's dancers' turn. They started with the traditional twirl. Unlike the women, they wore visor caps, no shirts, and veneer pants with large, bulging codpieces. After their spin, they began an elaborate, very athletic dance which involved acrobatic jumping, tossing one another, and one-handed cartwheels and flips—all timed perfectly to the recorded piellna music. When they were done, they bowed as well, looking even more winded than the women had.

Now Gavy's green rod was well above Sentiva's. The clock said 1:08.

The music shifted to a simple clean melody riding on a soft, slow beat, and all the Chancellor Dancers started their strip.

When Sentiva's dancers finally exposed all ten of their mammaries, the red tally indicator jumped a good twenty-five points. But when Gavy's men threw their codpieces into the audience, revealing five identical erections, there was spontaneous applause and the green Gavy rod edged well above the red.

Fenlocki was sure those erections had to be either totally artificial prostheses or seriously augmented natural ones. The females' body parts looked to be equally synthetic or enhanced. Fenlocki shifted slightly as he looked at the women, feeling his own quite natural member thicken a little in his pants.

By the time the dancers were totally naked except for their hats, the voting indicators looked about even. The performers swayed with the music, wholesome grins shining from their faces. They all began caressing themselves to the beat just as the females started their campaign verse.

> *"Sentiva is a true believ-a.*
> *Sentiva's not the dregs.*
> *Sentiva A. will never leave ya.*
> *Sentiva's got brass eggs."*

Now the man sang in close harmony.

> *"Cast your vote for Zephy Gavy,*
> *His ears are never deaf.*
> *You'll note his hair is straight, not wavy*
> *—so's his sexual pref."*

Then the women squeezed their breasts—almost like Cruda priestesses—and sang again.

> *"Don't take chances with your Chancellor,*
> *Vote for one with legs.*
> *Mam Sentiva is your answer*
> *When the question begs."*

Now the men grabbed their respective bobbing penises in five two-fisted salutes as they sang.

> *"In Gavy's name we stand erect.*
> *No games, no lies, no tricks.*
> *He's the one you should elect,*
> *We swear this on our dicks!"*

The music rose and the two teams sang with each other, overlapping in perfect counterpoint.

> *"Vote Sentiva!"*
> *"Zephy Gavy!"*
> *"She will lead ya!"*
> *"He's your baby!"*
> *"Vote, vote, vote, vote, vote, vote, vote . . ."*
> *"He's the Zeph-man!"*
> *"She's Sent-triffic!"*

"Got a great plan!"
"She's specific!"
"Vote, vote, vote, vote, vote, vote, vote . . ."

The piellna slowed for the big finale.

"Zeph's the one . . ."
"Sent's the one . . ."
"He's for you . . ."
"She's for you . . ."
"Gavy gives . . ."
" 'tiva tries . . ."
"Yes, he's the one . . ."
"No, she's the one . . ."
"FOR YOOOOOOOU!"   *"FOR YOOOOOOOOOOOOOOU!"*

The sign flashed ENORMOUS OVATION, PLEASE just as the women turned and bent over, doffing their node hats and plunging them up inside themselves. Meanwhile, the men were ejaculating in perfect sequence—left to right—in a synchronized ballet of arcing fluid.

The crowd went wild. "Bravo! Brava!" somebody yelled from the back. Both tally bars climbed sharply, Zephy's a little ahead of Sentiva's. The Chancellor Dancers grabbed up their clothes as they danced off. The moderator stepped forward again, arms outstretched, being careful not to slip on the wet spots.

"Thank you so much. What a wonderful citizenry you all are!"

He grinned and looked over at the tally bars. "Keep those votes coming in! It's going to be a close one! And now, the moment you've all been waiting for . . . the great debate! We'll start with the incumbent's opening words and then go to the challenger."

He did a quick spin around and pointed his finger dramatically outward. "Take it away, *candidates*!"

Fenlocki looked up at the master clock. Its dark numbers read 1:21. In exactly thirty-nine minutes the country of Manhattan would elect its next Chancellor. And it better not be Watly Caiper.

He popped another sunbean in his mouth and then spat it out. It was covered with lint.

CHAPTER 26

Noonie Caiper drew a picture of a little girl with no face. Behind the figure, she drew a single line across the pad with her click-pen, to indicate a horizon. If she hadn't drawn that line, her color sketch would have appeared to be just of a faceless girl on a blank page. Putting the line in gave the girl a location. And that location was No place. A flat, lonely plain with nothing on it. An empty white sky. Empty white earth.

She had only stopped drawing for a few minutes to watch the silly dance number. Yeah, the live sex stuff at the end had been kind of gross; she saw enough of that mushy stuff on CV. But the dancing and singing had at least been somewhat entertaining. Mildly peaky prone. Borderline spaf. Then the Gavy guy had started droning on. The guy with that long thing dangling down his face.

"Ladies and gentlemen, citizens, constituents, people of the First and Second Levels, distinguished colleagues, officers of the law, honored guests, and my small-breasted, wide-vaginaed opponent . . . I stand before you—"

Noonie stopped paying attention at that point. She was both bored and nervous at the same time. And her surefire cure for both conditions was to retreat into the world of her pictures. For as far back as she remembered, the insulated land of her drawing was the place she ran to when things got rough.

And things were rough now.

Truth was, she was really hinky. Not even just hinky—downright scared. Mommy had been really weird this past week. The Night Lady seemed to be popping up in her real often. It was as though, at any given moment, the stranger was just below the surface, ready to push through if Mommy let her guard down. It was like living with a mother who kept slipping into weird trances and having strange seizures without warning.

And here was the election. After all that waiting. The raping election.

Noonie didn't want her mom to win. But she didn't want her to lose, either. She just wanted this whole Chancellor business to fade quietly away. If Watly won, she'd be even busier than before. Noonie would never see her mother. If she lost, Noonie had a feeling that the shock and disappointment would be just enough of an opening for the Night Lady to take over the weakened Watly's brain entirely. And then Noonie would *really* never see her mother. Ever again.

But who *was* her mother anyway?

Was her mother really the Night Lady? The Watly that Noonie liked best lately—the strong, protective, assertive, corporate mama—seemed to be an awful lot like the woman who was trying to break out. It sure matched the description of the real Sentiva Alvedine she'd heard her whole life.

Noonie was so confused. She wished she had someone to talk to about it. She didn't. She didn't have Alysess anymore. Aunt Alysess was gone. The girl hadn't seen her in days.

Alysess hated Noonie. It was obvious. Noonie had apparently done something horrible and now Alysess wanted no part of the child. Mommy had tried to explain it away—to say Alysess's absence had nothing whatsoever to do with Noonie—but that was just lies and excuses. Noonie saw the pain and sadness in her mommy's eyes when she spoke of her ex, and Noonie knew it was all her fault.

Alysess just didn't love Noonie anymore. The girl was bad. If she had just *done* bad, Alysess would have forgiven and returned. But she *was* bad. And Alysess was gone forever.

Maybe her badness was why Mommy had tried to choke her

back then. Maybe that wasn't the Night Lady at all. Maybe it was Mommy, trying to get rid of a bad child.

She was a bad child. She had bad thoughts. She didn't care about things she was supposed to. She didn't care about Revy. She didn't care about the people—"*her* people"—down below. She'd seen a lot of special news reports on CV recently about them. They were acting crazy. They were wild, murderous monsters. They were dirty. They were ugly. And they looked like they smelled bad, as well. Noonie knew she was bad not to care about them, not to feel some connection to them.

And she was bad to like her hard, phony mommy better than her soft, real one. And to wonder if the Night Lady would be better than both. And she was bad to want to be—want to *really be*—what she pretended to be. She was bad to dream of a day when her face would need no makeup to be pale and pure, and her hair would need no treatments to be smooth and straight.

And she was really, really, *really* bad to kind of like the man who was sitting next to her. She was afraid of him. He was the enemy. She wouldn't talk to him. He made her heart pound. But . . . but she liked his face. And his honest smile. She liked the chief.

And she was really, really, really, really, really, really, *really* bad because of the Big Secret. The thing she had done two years ago. The feelings from the Isthmus place.

Noonie looked up from her drawing to steal a sideways glance at Fenlocki. He was chewing nervously on his sunbeans, totally focused on the stage. But he wasn't looking at Gavy, who was still babbling loudly. He was staring at her mommy, his expression both curious and slightly wounded-looking. There might've even been some lust in that look, or something like it. It *was* a nice face. Noonie looked away before Fenlocki could notice. She saw Gavy's tally rod climb way up above her mother's.

Then she looked at the CV projections to the left of the stage. The top one was live—an exact three-dimensional reproduction of what was happening on stage right at that moment. The bottom one was different. It showed the same puffy-looking face, the same shiny head, the same single long yellow lock of hair obscuring the same left eye. It too showed Gavy making a speech, but it wasn't synced up with reality. This lower Gavy's mouth was moving in its own pattern. There was no sound coming from the image, but it was apparent that this lower Gavy was saying something entirely different from the real live Gavy.

Noonie knew that the lower CVs were monitoring what was being shown to the First Level. She wondered what kind of speech *they* were hearing. She supposed that they too were being told things they wanted to hear. They too were being made empty promises. If only she could read lips. . . .

"*Sure* you don't want a sunbean?" Fenlocki whispered suddenly in Noonie's ear, making her jump. He smiled. "Laaast *one*. . . ."

"Nuh-uh," she answered, pulling away a little in her seat. "Thanks, though." She looked back to the stage. Zephy Gavy was just finishing up.

"And so, good people, I am the only choice. I have done you well these last years, and I will do you even better in the years to come if you elect me. As I have indicated, I shall solve the nasty, troublesome plurite problem, I shall better all our life-styles, and I shall protect our values, our beliefs, our educational system, our international trade system, our corporate structures, and, in particular, our good relations with Longeye, Pennyork, the Noreast Commonwealth, and Jersey; as well as our security treaties with the Nuclear Alliance and Arizonia, and our civil policy toward Jesusland. But, most importantly, I shall protect the integrity of our property, our standard of living, and—without question—our wealth. These things I promise on my honor both as a human being—pure of race and pure of thought—and as a corporate president—very rich and very powerful. I thank you."

Noonie was certain that the thunderous applause that followed would've happened even without the darkly flashing sign. The green tally rod was now twice the length of the red.

Noonie glanced at her mother—it would be Mom's turn to talk now. Then she looked at the black numbers on the clock. They said 1:34. The child swallowed hard. Twenty-six minutes and counting.

CHAPTER 27

"Gentlemen and Ladies, people of the great country of Manhattan, wise voters, unwise voters, respected dignitaries, friends, enemies, honored guests, and my forever limp- and tiny-penised opponent . . . I am thrilled to have this moment to speak with you all," Watly Caiper said, trying to keep her smile firmly in place.

In spite of the conditioned air, it was raping boiling under the hot lights, and Watly had been standing motionless for what seemed like hours upon hours. Her legs were sore and wobbly. What felt like a large search party of insects was climbing in groups of two and three down the inside of her loose blouse—from the back of her neck all the way down to her butt. It wasn't really a group of bug scouts, it was just sweat—sweat dripping its way down her back in little tickling rivers.

She was sure the makeup they'd applied to her face had by now all run down into a little orangy-pink grease pool at her collarbone. Foolish as it sounded, she felt she wouldn't be anywhere near as sweaty and nervous if only Alysess were here. Or if only she knew Alysess were at least with her in spirit. She needed that moral support. Watly wiped her hand across her forehead, glanced at her notes, and continued.

"My people. Let me say this as plainly as I can. I am your answer. I am all your dreams come true. I am the best. If you have half a brain—or even a quarter or an eighth of a brain—you will vote for me. You'd be just plain stupid not to. I'll be the best Chancellor ever. I'll work hard. I won't take catshit. I will *give* catshit—and plenty of it—when necessary. I will get this sorry excuse for a country back in shape. I am tough. I am smart. And I am honest. I won't lie to you. Ever. One truth I'll tell you right now: I hate plurites. I can't be more straightforward than that. As you know, it is *my* company that manufactures the Soft pills to quiet them down, and it has been during *Gavy's* administration that the recent unrest has occurred. There's been violence down there, rioting, rebelliousness, and talk of revolution. *There has even been a fire.* A *fire*, of all things. During—I say again—the Zephy administration. Well, none of these kinds of outrages will happen when I'm in charge. I simply will not tolerate it. I have no patience for the mutts. There are too many of them, and they all—without exception—have an attitude problem . . . each and every dirty mongrel subspawn down there!"

During the spontaneous applause that followed, Watly looked down at the podium's built-in gauge lights to see that her tally rod was now thirty-seven points higher than Gavy's and climbing fast. This was good. If she could keep this up through the speech, gain the advantage, then she could coast through the short point-counterpoint debate afterward to a sure win.

"These plurites," she continued when the clapping began to ebb, "these . . . creatures . . . are not like us. And it is time we stopped coddling them. If you've seen how they live, you know that no self-respecting human being could exist under those conditions. Therefore, I propose to you that they are *not* human beings, at least not human as we know it. What we have below us, good people, is a dangerous infestation problem. And you're looking at the solution."

There was more unplanned applause. The crowd was really getting into her speech. Watly smiled broader, feeling a little dizzy and headachy suddenly. Maybe another Chortium hangover. She'd been visiting Chortyland an awful lot lately.

"Oh, I could focus on the other issues, just as my unjustifiably esteemed and clinically impotent opponent did. I could talk about bettering our economy; our international relations; our investments in other countries economies, real estate, and businesses; our schooling systems; our construction projects; and so on, and so on, et cetera, et cetera, blah-blah-blah-*blah*, ad infinitum. I *will* improve all those things. You *know* I will. It goes without saying. And unless you're brain-dead, you take it as a given that I'll handle all those issues a *rape* of a lot better than Zephy Gavy."

There was a wave of surprised muttering at Sentiva Alvedine's use of a bad curse word in public. But the crowd actually seemed to like it. Cursing showed a spark of angry passion Gavy had not exhibited at all.

"But these are all side issues, my intelligent friends and bolehole enemies. Focusing on them is just a smokescreen. *I* know what's most important to you. *I* know where your concerns really lie. You want somebody to deal, quickly and surely, with the raping rug-rats below us. *Well, I am that someone!*"

Cheers rang through the auditorium. Watly took a deep breath and held on to the podium for support. The red tally rod was now over three times longer than the green. Her head was throbbing bad, though, and her vision was blurring up awful. It was harder and harder to continue. She took a quick sip from the water glass next to her notes and then pulled herself back up as tall as she could.

"You *don't* elect me?" she shouted angrily. "Let it be on your heads, then! What ensues will be your own raping faults—and it will be too late to come running to Sentiva for help. You *do* elect me . . . and I . . . I . . . and I . . . I . . . uh . . . I . . . need . . . shhhhort . . ."

Watly felt like she was about to pass out. It took all her strength just to remain upright. Sentiva was trying to . . . *Rape*, her head felt like it was being squeezed into a bloody mass by a huge vise.

"You *do* elect me," she started again, "and I will . . . You *do elect me* . . . and . . . I . . . short blade. Need short blade . . ."

There was a confused buzz from the crowd.

"Uh, *yes!*" Watly said, curling her toes up hard inside her shoes. "Yes! I need a short blade to, uh, cut through the political catshit! Yes!"

The audience seemed to relax a bit.

"Uh . . . yes. I need to slice that blade through all the past administration's . . . uh . . . I . . . need a shhh . . . short . . . Whhhh . . . Whhhat . . . leeeee!"

Suddenly two people burst through the doors at the back of the auditorium and headed down the center aisle toward the stage.

Watly slumped against the podium. She was relieved at the interruption. The arrival of these two trespassers gave her a chance to compose herself, the distraction bought her time to push Sentiva back down. She'd almost lost it. Sentiva was pushing real hard again. Harder than ever. *Leave me the rape alone!* Watly thought.

She raised her head a little and watched the two figures, a young man and woman, climb over the pit and up onto the stage. They crossed the apron toward her. Watly's eyes were so clouded over now that she couldn't make out their faces. She smiled weakly at them. To her surprise, instead of coming up to her, the pair crossed right past her and over to the row of chairs behind.

Watly turned to watch, still leaning against the podium. Through her blurred eyes, she watched as the two leaned in and whispered to someone. Someone who seemed to glow. *A lot of bright red there—is that Roullic Neets they're speaking to?*

Then the young woman handed the red blur something small.

CHAPTER 28

Roullic Neets took the CV tube from Mam Kness and tossed it from hand to hand for a second, smiling up at her and at Misser Volder. The timing of his two young assistants could not have been more perfect. Right on the proverbial button.

"Excellent, my darlings," he whispered quickly. "You must meet me later in my home for your . . . rewards." Kness smiled shyly and shuddered a little, and Volder looked down at his feet, blushing.

Roullic's promise of a reward was actually pretty empty at this point. He was rapidly loosing sexual interest in the both of them. They were too familiar now—too human. At first they had been this young, slender, thick-lipped, and large-chested mysterious girl/woman . . . and this young, muscular, mustached, and broad-shouldered, mysterious boy/man. A perfect pretty face and a perfect handsome face—both of which Roullic could happily picture wrapped around his mighty member. Now they were just Kness and Volder, two people he knew. They had become specific.

Roullic brushed some of his bright hair out of his eyes, stood up, and strode regally down to center stage. He knew he cut a striking, charismatic figure. The stage was his. Anywhere he went, in fact, the stage was *always* his. He casually pushed the moderator aside and faced the bewildered-looking audience and the rear bank of CV lenses. "I apologize for the interruption, surprise-wise," he said, his deep, well-modulated voice filling the hall. The audience seemed to calm some at this confident, attractive voice of authority. Roullic cheated his face and body slightly to the right, showing his best side and letting the audience get a better, three-quarters view of his expensive pant bulge.

"But folks, this is an emergency. As some of you know, I am Roullic Neets, Sentiva Alvedine's faithful and loyal assistant." He nodded toward Sentiva. She looked tired and confused, but managed a smile back. This was good. A nice touch. It was show time.

Roullic reached up with his free hand to pet his left eyebrow lovingly and then continued. "I've just been handed some information, the source of which is unclear. And, painful as it is for me, Roullic Neets—two *L*s—to do this, I feel it is my duty to make this material available to you, the voting public. It is my heartbreaking and deeply unhappy responsibility—civic-duty-wise, societal-obligation-wise, morality-wise, *any-which-wise*-wise—to show you this new material for you to judge it for yourselves."

Roullic expertly tossed the small CV recording tube into the control pit. He knelt down to look at the technicians as they scrambled to pick it up from the black floor of the pit. "*Play that now,*" he hissed down at them, and then stood up to smile sadly again at the murmuring crowd. The audience was ripe. Ripe and ready, mood-wise and curiosity-wise. Roullic craned his neck to look at the clock above him. It said 1:51. Perfect.

At the two sides of the apron, the CV recording flicked on from the higher machines, replacing Roullic, Sentiva, Gavy, and the angry-looking usurped moderator. The lower mists still showed the pre-recorded Sentiva continuing to preach her platitudes to the plurites below.

But now the upper ones presented a sunny outdoor Second Level street scene. At first these images were just of the outside of a building. The projections dipped and swayed some, obviously recorded from an illegal floater lens. Then they closed in on one window. After the lens compensated for the lighting contrasts, the room within the window became clearly visible. There was a large white fluffy-looking bed right in the center of the images. On the bed was Sentiva Alvedine. She was nude, pale and beautiful, her eyes closed. Her head slowly lowered—so slowly that it almost seemed the tape was running at the wrong speed—and then her face was hidden between the brown thighs of another naked woman.

The audience gasped in unison. "That darker woman," Roullic said loudly, "is a *First Leveler*! Now you understand why I had no choice but to show this to you. Not *only* is Sentiva Alvedine—my longtime employer whom I have never had an unkind word for—not *only* is she clearly seen engaged in the abomination of *homotending*—yes, blatant irrefutable *homotending*—but she is engaging in this obscenity with a *plurite*!"

The crowd gasped in horror again, even louder this time. Outraged chatter washed from the audience in waves, even as all eyes were still glued to the tender ministrations occurring on the tape. They seemed hypnotized by the gentle love scene. It was not like regular CV porn. There was a pure and real quality to it totally unlike normal sex tapes. The participants were *people* somehow, real humans and not just pretty fucking objects.

Roullic knew this made the tape that much more offensive to the crowd. And to him. He turned to his left and noticed that Sentiva's tally rod had dropped down to near zero. Then he shifted his eyes slightly to catch Gavy smiling jovially at him, long bedlock swinging happily against his nose. Roullic knew that he was using up all Gavy's point-counterpoint debate time with this little dramatic revelation, but *Gavy* certainly didn't seem at all disappointed at the interruption.

"People, *please*!" It was Sentiva talking.

Roullic turned back to face her. She looked different somehow. She was flushed like she used to flush with anger during a board meeting, but there was no anger there now. There was pain, shock, and desperation. She looked soft and vulnerable. In all the years of working for her, he'd never seen her like this. He almost felt sorry for her. He almost felt genuine pity for this strange un-Sentiva-like woman. Almost, but not really.

"Please, *listen* to me!"

The crowd did not silence. There was still loud mumbling, gasping, and even the occasional shout of *"Homotender!"* and *"Plurite-Lover!"* But Sentiva's voice was still so well amplified that she could speak above all the noise.

"*Listen!* It's not what you think. I mean, it *is* what you think, but . . . I *love* her. That's my poovus up there. And, yes, that's me. And I love her. I really *do*. What can be wrong with love? *People, what can be wrong with love?*"

To Roullic, it seemed—in a pathetic sort of way—that Sentiva was just now understanding, realizing, and believing what she herself said as the words came out of her.

"I *do* love her. I love her more than anyone in the world except my own daughter! She's my poovus. And . . . and . . . I haven't done right by her . . . and . . . but . . ."

Roullic looked back at the clock. Four minutes to go. He looked at the tally rods. Sentiva Alvedine's rod was now nonexistent. There was only Gavy's tall, green column, climbing up and up like an excited phallus.

"Listen . . ." Sentiva continued, her voice cracking. Roullic could see tears welling up in her eyes. He smiled, knowing she would get no sympathy from the audience with cheap, weepy theatrics. "Please . . . I haven't done right by you either. Everything I said . . . it's not true. I lied. I'm sorry. I was trying to . . . Please listen to me. The plurites are not our enemies. They are us and we are them. We're all humans. We're all the same. To help them is to help us. If you'll please just give me a chance, I'll do my best to help us all—slowly, carefully, and with . . . with kindness. Just give me that chance. Our whole system is messed up bad. You must feel that. You must sense that inside yourselves. It hurts us all. If you'll just let me try . . . I'll work to straighten it out."

Reflected light glittered brightly from Sentiva's tear-streaked face as Roullic watched her deliver this silly monologue. He looked at the audience to see their reaction. They sure weren't buying this new approach. They seemed even more outraged and angry than before. People booed and screamed obscenities. Someone threw a shoe at the stage. It hit Sentiva's podium and bounced back into the pit.

Roullic tried not to smile too broadly. It was difficult. He was looking out at a beautiful sea of fabulously furious faces. Everyone in the room seemed uniformly ready to kill Sentiva now. Every expression Roullic could catch spread out before him was full of anger and hate. Every face was contorted in outrage. Well . . . every face but two. Roullic saw two nonoutraged faces right in the first row. One of them he recognized as the chief of police's face. Fenlocki. On Ogiv Fenlocki's old, wrinkled face, Roullic could only read what seemed to be some kind of forlorn, wounded sympathy. And next to the chief was the other nonoutraged face. A small face. A girl. She was crying heartily right along with Sentiva. Crying with apparent hurt and fear.

Ah, well, Roullic thought, *two dissenters out of the entire Second Level isn't bad—odds-wise, statistics-wise, unity-wise, and almost-unanimous-wise.*

The moderator was trying to push his way back into Roullic's center-stage position. Roullic would let him, but first he stepped farther down onto the apron, turned, and looked up at the dark clock. 1:59. One minute to go.

CHAPTER 29

Alysess Tollnismer had almost decided not to vote at all. It was not required and she certainly didn't have any driving desire to do it. In fact, she had heard long ago from both Watly and the Ragman that First Level votes didn't even register. And that what the plurites saw was a largely artificial, pre-recorded version of the event.

But she was curious.

She was very curious. She did want to know what happened. She wanted to know how things would turn out. And most of all, she wanted to see what it would feel like to see Watly again after over a week—even if it would just be a projection.

It had been a hard week. A busy, crazy, nearly sleepless week. A week full of overflowing death lowtrucks. Almost three hundred people had been killed in the food riots, and over a hundred had died of smoke inhalation downtown. The seriously injured had numbered ten times that. And the bump, bruise, fracture, and minor laceration cases were still turning up. Every doctor, nurse, and medition had pulled triple shifts through the week.

It was hard, good work. It made Alysess feel worthwhile. And exhausted. She was so exhausted, in fact, that she seriously considered going home to rest instead of voting. But she knew that wasn't the real choice. Much as she wanted to, she realized she *wouldn't* rest if she didn't vote. She knew herself better than that. She'd end up working. There was an endless supply of patients needing doctoring. So, at the last minute, she went to vote.

Her local Cruda church on Seventy-ninth and Amsterdam was standing room only for the elections, but there were enough voting ringlets for everyone. Alysess let hers drop to the floor right after the cop handed it to her. There were two cops in church during the election, supposedly keeping things orderly. There was probably a police presence in every church that day.

Alysess watched the dance number with growing boredom. Maybe she should have worked after all. This did not seem worth wasting a morning on. But when the singing and dancing ended, the speeches started. Alysess saw an obvious, badly matched cut as the live feed stopped and the tape started. There was Gavy speaking of "the wondrous Cruda-fearing plurites" who are "sons and daughters of us all." There was occasional scattered applause from the congregation.

Then Gavy's image seemed to get overwhelmed by the CV mist. He got very fat suddenly, then very thin, then all fuzzy. His blond bedlock seemed to stretch longer and longer, looking like a string more than a thick curl of hair. Finally he popped out of existence entirely. The two cops ran down the aisle to the CV projector, trying to figure out what was interfering with the signal.

Alysess had a guess.

Gavy's image popped back for a second and then faded slowly out again. For a while, they could still hear his speech without seeing him. Then the sound faded too. Slowly, what looked like an aerial view of a huge landmass—maybe an island—began to appear in the mist. It was white and shaped like an upside down blurry letter A, but had a curved bottom where the point of the A should have been. It looked familiar.

The landmass grew more solid, slowly gaining definition. Its white edges were uneven and asymmetrical—millions of tiny, thin peninsulas curling outward from every side. The lake below the A's cross-line became reddish, and the bay above turned slowly pink. Near the mouth of the bay, the shape of two black ships took form. They seemed to be anchored on a perfect horizontal line, parallel to the line of the inverted A. The image resolved. They weren't black ships, after all. They were eyes. And the white, upside down A was not a landmass, not some strange island; it was a beard. This was a face. The face of the Ragman.

". . . boost the . . . yes . . . yes . . . that's got it . . . oh. *People of the First Level,* I am the Subkeeper! I am electronically taking control of these transmissions. Would you like to hear what these politicians are *really* saying? Would you like me to tap into the *live* feed without their knowledge, so you don't have to watch these fabricated speeches they have taped in advance to trick us? *Watch,* my children. . . ."

And so that was how Alysess—and the rest of the First Level—came to see the *real* elections. She found it fascinating. And frightening. By the time Watly was halfway through her angry, plurite-hating speech, the congregation was like one rageful creature bellowing back at the CV mist all the things they had read on the walls a week ago. "CV lies!" and "They're trying to kill us off!" and "Genocide!"

Alysess found herself yelling too. Caught up in the infectious energy of the room. It was impossible not to become one with the group spirit.

She wondered, even as she chanted "Genocide, Genocide, Genocide!" with the rest, if this mob energy was ever a good thing. It was the dark side of that religious "feeling of community" she had thought was so warm and wonderful days ago.

"Genocide! Genocide! Genocide!"

Alysess found she could not stop, even if she tried. Was rallying the emotions of a large group of people into a frenzy ever a positive force? Be it a music performance, a sporting event, a political demonstration, a lynch mob, a revolutionary rally, a religious ceremony, or any such thing? No matter what the cause, good or bad, righteous or villainous, harmless or earthshaking, was this powerful people-force ever positive?

"Genocide! Genocide! Genocide!"

The doctor realized it was a very specific thing—the mob mentality. Individualism was lost. Dissent was lost. Each part of the group became a cell in the brain of an irrational, unthinking, yet single-minded brain. There was a group loss of the ability to discuss, to negotiate, to reason, to analyze, to reevaluate, to stop and think things through. Actions people could never take as individuals—good, bad, or in between—they could take easily when hypnotized by the power of mass anger, mass joy, mass celebration, or mass hatred.

This is a dangerous thing, Alysess decided. *This is always a dangerous, bad thing. Good may have come of it in the past, and good may come of it in the future, but that does not excuse it. It is inherently a badness. It is just as bad as a mind-shattering drug.*

The cops were frantically trying to figure out what was wrong with the CV, as though it were just this one machine that was acting up. Alysess knew it wasn't. The Ragman's sub technicians and scientists had somehow tapped into the entire cable vidsatt system and were piping this to every church on the First Level. She suspected that the whole lower population of Manhattan was now a part of this raging, out of control mob spirit.

Ragface must be thrilled, she thought to herself, her fist raised up and her lips still mouthing "Genocide!" over and over.

People settled down a little to watch Roullic play his sex tape. Alysess's jaw dropped. She saw her naked self up there over the church's altar. There was laughter and jeers all around her. Snide comments flew. Someone tossed an empty booze bottle and it appeared to pass right through Alysess's enormous-looking projected pubic hair before shattering against the CV projector's casing.

Alysess shrank back against the rear wall of the church. She felt humiliated. Exposed. Raped by the recorder lens. Raped— right now—by the entire country of Manhattan. Why hadn't she trusted that instinct to close the shades that day?

The pain of seeing herself displayed like that was enough to pull her away from the power of the crowd. She felt herself slipping aside, differentiating, no longer a tiny piece of gray matter in the hulking First Level brain. She was an individual again.

A man beside her glanced in her direction, as if wondering for a second if Alysess was the same brown woman they all watched writhing, larger than life, above the holy Cruda altar. He might have recognized her, too, if her hands hadn't already been clasped firmly over her mouth, covering half her face. Alysess wondered for a brief moment if the room would have turned on her if the guy *had* made the visual connection. Would they have torn her apart to vent some of their rage?

Now Watly was talking again. The real Watly. The Watly Alysess had met and fallen in love with way against her better judgment all those years ago. This was her poovus.

And Watly was speaking of love. She was speaking of her love for Alysess. And she was saying, to unhearing ears, what she truly

felt about the world. She was saying she cared about *all* people.
And that she had lied. And that she was sorry. Really sorry.

The strange, shuddering sob that burst, unbidden, from the
back of Alysess's throat was so loud it would probably have drawn
attention had the room not been ringing with the sounds of boos,
hisses, and cynical laughter. She leaned her whole weight against
the wall and felt a rush of tears pour out of her. It felt like they
were retroactive tears. Tears collected and kept in for a decade;
tears hoarded and protected like Ragface had hoarded all that food
and medicine.

She was not crying like an adult usually cries. She was not
standing stoically, arms at her side, mouth turned downward,
water welling up in her eyes. Her hands gripped her face, her head
was tilted back, pushing into the hard wall, her shoulders shaking
violently . . . and she was wailing. Wailing like a baby.

The congregation threw their voting ringlets at the CV mist,
chanting "Revolution!" and "Genocide!" and "Kill Sentiva!" The
cops had given up toying with the projector and now scrambled for
cover to each side, pulling their chip pistols out and looking truly
scared for their lives.

As her crying calmed some, Alysess wondered if the Ragman
had ever really planned to give Watly a chance to do it her way.
She wondered if, all along, the Ragman hadn't planned a violent
overthrow whether Watly won or lost. She couldn't imagine him
trying to soothe this frenzy should Watly be elected. No, he had
lied once again. He had planned to use the election as a
springboard for the revolt, whatever the outcome. He was
impatient and power hungry. He wanted a swift change. He
wanted to be king.

But the question was apparently a moot one. There was only a
minute to go, and Watly had lost. Lost big. On the CV, the
moderator was back center stage, his projection being pelted by
the remaining voting ringlets.

"Well, folks. It's been quite an exciting afternoon, has it not?
I'm afraid we don't have time for any back-and-forth debating.
We're up against the wall now! Cast your final votes. This is it,
good people! Let's all count the seconds down together! Forty-
five! Forty-four! Forty-three! . . ."

The tears finally stopped for Alysess. She felt better. She felt
emotionally cleansed. Renewed. Reborn. She was ready for
whatever might come next.

"Thirty-seven! Thirty-six! Thirty-five! . . ."

Alysess stared raptly at the projection. The CV lens cut quickly between Watly, Gavy, and the counting-down crowd. On one particular pan of the audience, Alysess caught a glimpse of Noonie Caiper's tear-streaked face passing rapidly by. Then the lens cut back to an exhausted, desperate-looking Watly Caiper, clutching her podium as if her life depended on it.

My loves, Alysess thought.

CHAPTER 30

A burst of strident music blared that old campaign tune "Winning Is the Only Answer," and the technicians released the party pins.

Thousands of bright pinlights fell from the flies of the stage. They fell everywhere, bounced everywhere, and looked more like a shower of hot sparks from some enormous, godlike welding operation than a political victory celebration. A lot of them rolled into the control pit, but quite a few bounced clear of it and scattered into the audience. The glow of them was blinding.

Watly had to keep brushing them from her hair. She could barely make out the glary form of the moderator as he held Gavy's left arm high. Gavy was smiling and twirling his fat face vigorously—making his one long lock of hair spin in circles. The crowd bellowed. Many of them were standing and cheering, hugging and kissing one another.

Well, at least my headache is gone, she thought to herself. *Rape of a way to cure a headache. . . .*

Because a whole pile of bright party pins was collecting in huge drifts at the feet of the first audience row, Watly could now see that row clearly. Her daughter and Fenlocki were sitting side by side. Their faces were lit up from the pinlights below them,

PETER R. EMSHWILLER

looked disturbed. Watly would've expected him to look happy.
She was glad he did not. It was nice of him not to look happy.
Noonie was crying. Mommy's baby was crying hard. Her little
face stood out starkly in sharp contrast to her all-black clothing.
Watly watched through the storm of descending pinlights as the
chief put his right arm around Noonie, apparently trying to soothe
and comfort her. The girl accepted the arm, and Watly felt a flash
of her protective instinct. Or maybe jealousy.

"Okay! Okay!" the moderator screamed, his voice barely
audible above the commotion. "Folks, it's time for the rejectance
and acceptance speeches. Folks?"

The crowd was not settling down. People were loudly singing
along with the song, some even dancing in the aisles.

> ". . . begin again . . . to win again!
> *Bash the villains into jelly,*
> *Where pain's concerned, be the inflictor!*
> *Hit them in the underbelly!*
> *All the spoils go to the victor!*
> The only sin . . . that's genuine . . . is not to win.
> To live again . . . begin again . . . to win again!
> *Mash* this *in the loser's face:*
> *To lose a race is most abhor-ious*
> *Defeat's the ultimate disgrace!*
> *The* only *side's the one victorious.*
> *Glorious! Glorious! Glorious!*
> The only sin . . . that's genuine . . . is not to win . . ."

Through the continuous blizzard of pinlights, Watly saw the
moderator signal with one broadly waving arm to the control pit.
The music stopped abruptly, and there was an eyeball-bursting
blast from a warning horn. The audience finally quieted some.

"Now," the moderator said, brushing some party pins from his
shoulders, "Sentiva Alvedine's few words of rejectance."

The crowd booed with obvious relish.

Watly coughed. She had not planned a rejectance speech. She
had somehow felt writing one would be bad luck, like she was
asking to lose. Now she wondered what the rape she should say.
And why she should even bother. What was the point? Everything
was over. Everything was hopeless now. She'd lost the Chancellorship, and she would no doubt lose her job. She'd be budgeted

out instantly. And if she'd understood Alysess's comment about the entrails, soon the Ragman would be making some major, messy move. Everything was over. What the rape was the point in a speech?

"I . . . uh . . ."

In one enormous flash, the headache was back, full force. It was so sudden, for a moment Watly thought someone had come up behind and clobbered her with a three-hundred-pound leatherlike armchair. She leaned forward, elbows on the podium, her hands holding the sides of her face. Her water glass fell and shattered.

"I . . ."

And then Sentiva Alvedine stepped through the pain. The pain was a doorway, and Sentiva walked smoothly through it, hardly pushing at all this time. Watly felt powerless to stop her. Perhaps she was not truly powerless, but she certainly felt emotionally powerless. All Watly could think, over and over, was *What's the point?* And with that thought was the loss of the will to fight.

Watly was buried under the weight of Sentiva's mind now, and there was almost relief in that, a release of responsibility. There was almost joy in not fighting anymore. The pain was gone, the pushing was gone, the tiredness was gone, and Watly felt that she, herself, was gone. The falling pinlights made the world look surreal and unimportant. A distant, fairy-tale fantasy. A land where the falling snow glowed.

"People. People of Manhattan," Sentiva said, her voice powerful and strong. "You have made the appropriate choice!"

Now the crowd's boos turned to cheers.

"I . . . am . . . not who I appear to be. I am not Sentiva Alvedine. I have appropriated her body using a revised, cuffless hosting procedure. I am, in reality, *Watly Caiper:* malevolent revolutionary, unscrupulous First Leveler, and the cold-blooded assassin of Corber Alvedine!"

The whole audience gasped as one.

"Do you grasp my meaning? The person upon whom you gaze is *Watly Caiper,* world-famous, priority-one, death-imperative criminal. It is I, Watly, still functioning, still *alive!*"

Deep within the body of this woman—this woman orating in an awkwardly erudite manner to a suddenly hushed audience—Watly Caiper actually felt like laughing. She saw the exquisite irony of the real Sentiva Alvedine saying she was Watly Caiper, after the actual Watly Caiper had spent so many years saying that she was Sentiva Alvedine. There was something really raping funny in that. *Maybe I'm finally going mad,* Watly thought, sinking deeper within the body, trying to close it in around herself like a cozy blanket.

All the security cops in the room were edging toward the stage. Some were looking at Fenlocki for a signal or an order; others just stared at Sentiva as they cautiously approached.

"I yearned to win so that I could conduct a First Level revolution against all of you. I am the paramount threat to your way of life. I wish you all dead. You made the clearly correct choice in not selecting me. But the danger is still substantive. I have assimilated that, if I should *lose,* the 'entrails will hit the fan.' You must ready yourselves. You must fortify. They are coming. And I am to convey them. You must dislodge the hosting wafers from my head and obliterate them so that I may help you. If not, you must kill me—for I shall try to kill you otherwise. Additionally, I must tell you that the child—"

One of the officers, parallel now to Fenlocki's row, did not wait for a signal. He raised his chip pistol, aimed, and fired. Someone in the audience screamed. The slug shattered the upper portion of Sentiva's podium and ricocheted off. Sawdust flew.

Inside the body, Watly Caiper felt the stiff wind of the near-hit like a cold slap in the face. Her desire to survive kicked in strong. And her mother instinct—that more than anything. *My child,* Watly thought. *What about my child?* She pushed hard against Sentiva's mind. *Let me back, you crazy rapehead!*

Sentiva calmly stepped aside from the wide podium and spread her arms apart, palms outward. She was the perfect target. "Ah. So be it," she said. "Then kill me. Kill me *well.*" Then her voice dipped to a whisper. "Mea culpa, Watly Caiper."

Watly pushed.

She pushed hard.

Nothing.

Watly could hear all the dignitaries behind her scrambling for cover as the cops drew closer to the stage. The policepeople walked forward slowly and raised their weapons, ready to cut Watly down in a shower of slugs as soon as the stage was relatively clear. She heard panicked shouts and the sound of a door slamming from the control pit before her—"Hold it! Don't shoot yet!" The pit technicians each obviously wanted a chance to exit through some hatch under the stage before the shooting started. The cops all cocked their weapons.

Watly pushed. And pushed and pushed. It sounded like the

people onstage behind her had all cleared out by now. The police officers aimed.

She pushed.

Something gave.

"No!" Watly shouted and dove down behind the podium just as some of the cops let loose. The sounds of their shots echoed loudly through the hall. Watly crouched low, hearing the podium above her being torn apart by slug blasts. Slivers of wood flew into her hair. She stuck her head out the right side of the podium.

People in the audience were scrambling in a stampede, climbing over each other to get to the rear doors. Fenlocki was not moving. He was standing in place, his arm still around Noonie, his polished silver pistol drawn. Watly's eyes met the chief's and then the chief's eyebrows turned up in an expression of apology. He turned his gun, pressed it to Noonie's left temple, and mouthed the words *Give up*.

"Mommy!" Noonie cried.

Another volley of shots rang out, and the floor beside Watly's face exploded open from the slugs. From the sides of the almost demolished podium, Watly could see the legs of the police moving forward, closing in, vaulting over the pit, and climbing up onto the apron toward her.

"Noonie!" Watly cried out.

I'd give the rape up if you'd tell them to stop shooting at me! she thought.

To her left, Watly could see that the moderator had been hit in the stomach by a stray slug and lay moaning and bleeding near the wings. His twitching body was slowly being covered by the falling party pins. Everyone else behind Watly had fled into the wings.

Another loud burst of chip pistol shots blasted out, ripping more of the wooden podium apart. Watly turned to see one of the front cops stepping out on the apron, only a few feet away from her. The officer aimed, and Watly suddenly realized she had nowhere to duck from this guy. The cop took one more step forward, about to get a clear shot, but his foot landed directly on a puddle of Chancellor Dancer semen, and he slid comically sideways, flipping over so his head collided against the stage-left side of the proscenium arch.

More shots rang out. Something white-hot hit Watly in the right shoulder. *Ow!*

She thought she heard Fenlocki crying out "Stop firing!" but the voice was faint and the cops were in a deaf killing frenzy now.

They closed in on Watly from both sides. She tried to crouch down farther and push herself deeper into the small recessed area at the podium's base. There was a slight noise—a squeak. Watly looked left to see the barrel of a pistol pointed right down at her face, inches away. The officer holding it smiled sweetly, about to blow her head off.

BOOOOOOOOOOM!

Suddenly the whole building rocked from a tremendous explosion. The stage shook violently. Everyone standing was knocked over from the earthquakelike force of the blast. It felt like it'd come from one of the floors below. Watly took the opportunity to reach up and grab the gun as the startled cop tried to steady himself. She ripped it from his grasp and shoved the guy back hard, watching him fall backward, his head thumping to the stage. Watly peered over the broken podium, her shoulder throbbing painfully.

All the police on the stage with her—and the ones still in the aisle—were on their hands and knees, looking around the room for the source of the explosion. Everyone seemed frozen with confusion and surprise. Fenlocki was holding Noonie up in both his arms, leaning into his chair to steady himself. Now there was the sound of other explosions, farther away.

BOOOOM! BOOOM! BOOM!

It seemed like whole sections of the country of Manhattan were blowing up in quick succession.

The huge CVs flickered. A gigantic furry face appeared in the mist.

"Surrender, Second Level!" the Ragman's voice boomed out. *"The Rug-Rats have risen!"*

Watly stood up. She dropped the pistol.

Fenlocki glanced at her angrily and then headed up the aisle toward the auditorium's doors. Noonie's small legs flopped against his thighs as the girl struggled to look back toward the stage, her eyes flooded with tears.

"Mommy!" the child's voice rang out.

"Noooooooonie!" Watly cried, and then the cops around her broke their frozen poses and aimed again. Watly felt herself instinctively leaping forward as they opened fired. She could feel the shots whiz by all around her body with little blasts of hot air as she soared in a twisting somersault. She flew over the short apron and landed hard on her back deep in the control pit.

Pinlights scattered everywhere. Shards of wood flew all around her from the pounding slugs. Wood dust blasted into her eyes and down her blouse. She scrambled to find the pit's exit door—*It has to be somewhere down here!*—as more slugs tore into the wood above her head. Splinters flew down on her. Watly scampered to the left side of the narrow control pit, knocking over pieces of equipment as she went. Some of the equipment exploded from slug blasts as the cops drew closer to aim down into the pit. Watly rolled across the dark floor, still looking for the escape hatch.

All the while she was screaming *"Noonie! Noonie!"* and *"They have my baby!"* at the top of her heaving lungs.

PART TWO

BLOODY SHOW

Yicky icky sticky mess. Ha.

TAVIS

CHAPTER 31

"Nursing a baby is *not* a seduction technique," Watly said, cradling the newborn Noonie in her arms. Alysess had left the room moments before.

"Hey, look. I didn't know what to think, okay?" Eiter said. He looked exasperated again. Harassed. "I'm not an expert on women. I'm the first to admit I don't know how women think."

"Do you know how *you* think?"

"What's that supposed to mean?"

"Think of it as a clue. If you get some idea how you think, you'll be able to figure out how women think." Watly leaned forward on the couch a little, feeling as though she were talking to a child. "I've been a man and I've been a women, Eiter, and I'll tell you a big secret. The basic difference between the sexes is not in how they think or behave, it's in how they're treated."

"You lost me."

"Forget it."

"What the subs do you want? What the subs do you want from me anyway?"

"An apology would be nice."

"I did that."

"A real one."

Eiter shook his head. "I'm *sorry,* okay? I'm sorry that an attractive woman I don't know pulled all sorts of strings to get me up to her house for one afternoon. I'm sorry that when I came in she was half naked right in front of me. I'm sorry I assumed maybe she wanted to fuck."

"That's one great apology."

"What do you want me to apologize for?"

"For being an idiot. For being an unfeeling, disgusting, warped, inconsiderate, beanheaded bolehole!"

Eiter took a deep breath, staring straight at Watly's eyes. He seemed about to argue, about to lash out defensively. But he just exhaled slowly, appearing deep in thought. "Yeah," he said finally. "I'm sorry for that."

Watly smiled just a little. "Good. That's a start." Noonie squirmed slightly in her lap, gurgling contentedly.

"Hey," Eiter said suddenly. "Hey. Can I hold the kid?"

Watly just gripped her baby more firmly. "Her name is *Noonie,* not 'kid.'"

"Can I hold her?"

"Why? You want to try to have sex with her too?"

Eiter scowled. "Gimme a break. She's supposed to maybe be my granddaughter, right? Can I hold her a sec?" He held his arms out.

Watly looked at him, this older version of her male self. He seemed right then to be just a weak, simpleminded, confused old man. An ignorant, empty-headed oaf. "Crippled," Alysess had said earlier. "Everybody's crippled somehow." Maybe that was true. Watly didn't know anyone who wasn't pretty messed up in one way or another. In fact, it often seemed that the healthier a person appeared on the outside, the more raped up that person turned out to be when you got to know him or her. *The only normal people,* Watly thought to herself, *are the ones you don't know very well.* The idea made her smile.

Eiter stood and stretched his hands toward Noonie timidly. "Can I?"

"She doesn't like strangers," Watly said, but she let Eiter gently lift the baby into his arms.

Noonie didn't cry. She made a little gurgle-giggle sound and wiggled her toes. "I don't have to be a stranger," Eiter said, staring down at the baby. He seemed nervous and gawky with Noonie. But he also looked like he'd rather die than drop her. His expression appeared full of awe and delight with the child, as if he were hypnotized by her angelic features and tiny bald head. Maybe under the awkwardness there *was* something grandfatherly in the way he held her. "Hey, little girl. Hey there," he said.

And Watly wondered if there wasn't a little hope. A little hope that there could be something like a family here. But Eiter would be going back down soon. And this was a one-shot deal. They could have no more contact. No meetings, no messages. That was the bargain she'd made with the Ragman.

So if there was to be any family here, it was only a one-afternoon family. And then it would be over forever.

CHAPTER 32

Alysess was the last one left in the room.

She was the only one in the church who had not gone up yet to join the revolution "party." The festivities.

Right after the congregation had watched Sentiva Alvedine lose by an absolute landslide, two strangely garbed people entered the room, strode up the center aisle, and faced the rowdy parishioners. They wore what looked like outer-space wear. Highly reflective silver outfits topped with phallic-looking darkly tinted helmets. On each of their backs was a trio of identical gas and fluid canisters, and strung over their shoulders were large, mean-looking rifles. Their silver belts were heavy with other complicated weapons.

Alysess recognized what they were wearing. It was not hard for her to figure out. They were in Subkeeper-issued battle togs. Revy was on.

The entrails were indeed about to hit the fan.

"Good people," a metallic-sounding female voice issued from one of the space suits. "We are going to take the Second Level. We are going to liberate the sun together."

The two church cops stepped cautiously forward from the

sides, chip pistols raised. The Revies in the battle togs pointed their rifles at the police. The cops pointed their guns at the Revies. It was a standoff, police on the outside, Revies in the middle.

"Are you with us or against us?" a male voice came from the other space suit. He was speaking to the officers.

One of the cops lifted his gun just a fraction higher and the Revy man casually fired at him. The cop flew clear across the room and slammed into the CV machine, a jagged red hole in the exact center of his uniform. He twitched for a moment and then was still.

The crowd cheered loudly, stamping their feet and clapping.

"Are you with us or against us?" the Revy man repeated mechanically to the remaining cop.

The woman cop glanced at the frenzied crowd and then back at the two anonymous spacepeople. After a second, she lowered her gun.

"With," she said, her lips moving only slightly. Or maybe she whispered aloud. Either way, it was impossible to hear over the crowd's loud bellows.

"We go up, then!" Over the noise, the female voice boomed from her battle-tog squawker. "Join us. We are breaking through. Follow us up and take what is your right! We have weapons waiting for all of you!"

The crowd cheered again, and Alysess felt that mindless mob energy blooming wildly all around her. The room vibrated with it. The sweaty air reeked of it. The doctor leaned back into the wall and tried to shrink into its hard material.

"Are you with us?"

"Yes!"

Are you with us?"

"YES!"

"ARE . . . YOU . . . WITH . . . US?"

"YEEEEEEEEESSSSSSSSSSSSSSSSS!"

The Revies marched regally down the center of the aisle, fists raised in some kind of salute. These two surreal-looking silver creatures chanted a rallying cry as they passed through the throng.

"Genocide! Genocide! Genocide!"

The congregation quickly joined in.

"GENOCIDE! GENOCIDE! GENOCIDE!"

Everyone in the room fell in behind the two Revies and raised their fists and screamed the chant. Everyone but Alysess. She watched them all yell their way out of the room—the hungry, hot, angry faces of her neighbors—and she slumped down to the floor.

She could hear the boom of their voices as they climbed up the stairs toward the top floor of the building. The noise echoed all around her.

"Are you with us?"

"Yes!"

"Genocide! Genocide! . . ."

"GENOCIDE! GENOCIDE! GENOCIDE!"

Only Alysess was left to watch the rest of the CV election program. She looked up between her bent knees and saw Watly's rejectance speech. She saw Sentiva come out. She saw the cops shooting at her poovus. She saw the election image rock and grow blurry from some tremendous explosion. Then she heard one herself, nearby. And then another, blocks away. Alysess held her ears and braced herself just as she felt the building around her shake violently as the Revies from her own church ignited their string explosives, blowing open the final layers of the Second Level flooring, opening this particular church's Revy portal.

She could hear other explosions continuing now, farther off. On the shaky CV she could make out Watly dodging more slugs, and Fenlocki running off with Noonie in his arms. Then the image flickered out abruptly.

And she was alone in an empty church, sitting on her butt, head against the wall, her knees pointed up toward the altar. She was crying.

The floor around her was littered with discarded voting ringlets, and there was the dead body of a cop on the far side of the room.

And she cried.

She cried for Watly, and Noonie, for the Revies, for the plurites, and for the Second Level. She cried for all the people who had died and were about to die. She cried for the entrails that were, even now, hitting the fan. She cried for the fact that nothing was ever going to be the same, no matter what happened. She cried for her poovus, who she really did love—she really, really *did*—and who probably was dead by now. Probably.

But most of all, she cried for herself. For there was something she had to do now. She couldn't just sit here and wait. She couldn't just curl up on the Cruda church floor in a tiny fetal position and wait for everything to be over. She couldn't sit out the raging storm, let it all sort itself out. She wanted to, but she couldn't.

She had to go up. She had to go *into* it. Not to fight for Revy. Not to fight *against* Revy. Not to doctor and heal the wounded on either side. Not to try to stop the bloodshed. No. She had to go and help Noonie. She had to find her. She had to rescue her. Who else would, now? And she had to save Watly too—if that was still possible, if Watly was still alive. She had to find her two loves. Rape Revy, rape the people, rape the whole raping country—it was the only thing that mattered anymore.

The doctor rolled to her knees and stood up. Yeah. There was something she had to do. Alysess had to save her poovus. And Alysess had to save her daughter. Her daughter, yes. Watly and Aly's daughter. Little Noonie.

Not a niece, not a friend, not a lover's child—the girl was her raping daughter too, dammit. And she was going to find her.

"If I don't die in the first thirty seconds up there," she said aloud. She wiped her eyes with her shirtsleeve and then she snorted and headed for the door.

CHAPTER 33

It was not nice to look at. Even for a doctor.

The portal had cut through into some Second Level family room. The string explosives had made a perfectly round hole in the wooden floor—about six feet in diameter. All around the hole was a dark ring—the burn mark left by the explosives.

Little tendrils of smoke rose from the edges of the portal and Alysess could still smell the unpleasant metallic smell of the explosive mixed with the pleasant burned-wood odor from the parquet floor.

And another smell. Death.

The doctor stood on the top rung of the placene ladder and peered over the edge of the hole up into the room. The frenzied mob of revolutionaries had certainly done a job in there. Scattered around the large family room—on the colorful rugs, on the expensive, soft-looking couches, the polished wood tables—were pieces of people. A large CV still played in the middle of the room. It was still set on the election pleat, and now the only image it projected was a standard written notice reading:

> SORRY. SOME PROBS. PLEASE RELAX
> WHILE WE SORT THEM OUT. HAVE A
> DRINK.

There was no one alive in the room to read the notice, though. It appeared to Alysess, as she stared at the carnage, that it had been a family of four. A woman, a man, and two children. They had been watching the elections together. On one brass-fitted end table was a crystal pitcher partially filled with some bright blue, ice-filled liquid—mayjuice, perhaps—and surrounding it were four half-filled glasses. On the floor near the portal was a small homework monitor, a stuffed doll, and a toy police cruiser.

The rest of the room was filled with meat. Human meat. Blood and great thick running chunks of steaming people parts—some still half wrapped in their expensive clothing. A child's leg, the foot still clad in a small leatherlike shoe. A tangle of intestines somehow knotted up in a silken scarf. A head. An arm—the flesh jagged and ripped right along with its orange shirtsleeve. Blood everywhere.

This one small Second Level family—relaxing in the playroom for an afternoon of voting—had been literally torn apart by the Revies. Their floor had suddenly exploded and fallen open in a great, perfect circle, and hundreds of angry people had begun climbing out of it. Some had been wearing the battle togs, but others had probably been wearing their First Level rags. Alysess doubted that the Ragman had manufactured enough battle togs for every First Leveler. So some would have climbed up in their usual clothing—a ragtag bunch of dirty, hungry, messy-looking people—carrying new and unfamiliar Revy weapons, wanting to start venting their fury on the first evil upperfolk they came across.

And they'd done it. They were probably doing it all over Manhattan. How must they have looked to this quiet family when they'd first burst up into this lazy, quiet room? What terror the four of them must have felt.

Alysess hoped with all her being that they'd been shot right away—killed quick before the mob had begun tossing them about, ripping apart their fragile bodies. She tried not to think about it. She tried not to look. She tried not to throw up. She was a doctor. She was used to blood and body parts. But not like this. Nothing like this. Suddenly she wanted a Soft pill really badly.

She climbed the rest of the way out of the portal, crawled into a clean corner, and vomited.

She wiped her mouth on a lace tablecloth and stood slowly. She felt trembly all over. Hinky to the max. From outside the building—even through the thick, insulated walls—she could hear gunfire, shouts, explosions, and screams.

She had no battle togs. She had no guns. She was wearing her white doctor suit and had a small doctor bag slung over her shoulder. She'd half expected to find some extra uniforms and weapons lying about in the portal room below her. There had been none. The Revies had apparently distributed everything they'd had to the people as the ascension began, handing stuff out as the congregation climbed up the ladder.

So she would have to make do. She would have to make do, basically, with nothing. A little boot dagger.

All she could do was the best she could do.

Alysess walked carefully around the bloody mess, stepping gingerly over the pieces. She was looking for a door. She had to get out in the war. Into the battle.

And there was nothing on earth she would rather avoid more.

CHAPTER 34

Noonie Caiper looked at the little motes of dust that hung in the air and kept her tears in. There were no windows in the interrogation room, but the crisscrossed beams from the high pinspots lit up the air flecks nicely. She watched them move slightly in little eddies and currents from the air-conditioning.

It was, she imagined, almost like being underwater. Or in a big vat of clear broth. The tiny dust flecks flowed in and out of the yellow beams in slow, soupy waves, and Noonie was just a small fish among them. When she closed her eyes, the motes were still there, it seemed. They were imprinted on her lids or something. Only, with her eyes closed, the dust and the room became reddish and thick.

She kept her eyes open. It was easier not to cry that way. Early in her trip here, she had decided crying was not the thing to do. She'd swallowed it down, feeling a tightness in her throat that still lingered. Her nose tickled and itched with unwept tears, and the back of her eyeballs, just behind the sockets, felt as though they were filling up and becoming achy and swollen with liquid that she would not allow to escape. She was lonely. She was scared.

She had entered the room smiling, but now all she felt was yuckiness.

"I will not cry," she whispered to herself. She had whispered the same thing—very quietly—during the cruiser ride over.

Fenlocki had rushed her out to his private police vehicle—a blue-gray lumpy-looking cruiser with overlarge cylinders on each side. Noonie and Fenlocki sat on the plush orange cushions in the back while the driver rushed them down the city streets. The muffled sound of explosions came from every direction as they sped east along Fifty-seventh.

"You know where to go!" the chief yelled to the driver. As the vehicle banked sharply to turn down Fifth Avenue, Fenlocki gripped Noonie's hand. "It's gonna be all right, kid," he said tenderly.

She snatched her hand back and stuck it under her left armpit, remembering the vivid sensation of the chief's pistol barrel pressed into her temple back at the auditorium. She pulled her sketch pad and click-pen up with the other hand. She pressed these over her chest and held them tightly, as if for protection. She hadn't let go of them the whole time. They were her armor. Her sword and shield.

This was when she first mouthed *I will not cry* to herself. The cruiser turned right on Thirty-fourth, speeding past the original Empire State Building. Something blew up loudly nearby. Noonie looked upward through the blue-tinted plastic, staring at the duo of gleaming connecting bridges that spanned the gap between Empire State One and Two. The bridges looked like twin lacy, gilded spider webs, one above the other. They were now passing by a tall stone wall that stood between the buildings, shielding a tree-filled courtyard within.

The cruiser tilted into a sharp left turn over the whitetop. Its driver yammered something cryptic into his dash squawker just as another loud explosion came from the right.

"Chief P . . . Welter. Nie. Nie. Nie. Access. One. Control. Admit."

"Yes," the squawker squawked loudly.

The driver was headed right toward the base of the newer Empire State Building. He didn't even slow down. They were just off Herald Square, at Thirty-fourth street near Sixth, turning into the cul-de-sac at the base of State Two. Noonie felt her heart quicken as the cruiser hurled straight at solid stone wall. A suicide mission, it seemed. Some crazy suicide mission. She grabbed

Fenlocki's hand just as the stone slid up suddenly, revealing a large door. Without braking, the driver whisked them right into the Second Level base of Empire State Building Two.

The cruiser stopped on a New York dollar and the huge stone door closed behind them. It was suddenly dark. Noonie blinked and squinted.

Fenlocki grabbed her up gently and rushed her out of the vehicle. Either his eyes adjusted a whole lot better than hers, or he'd been here many times before. Noonie caught vague glimpses of huge dark machines to either side—endless row after endless row of them. They were definitely not cruisers or coppers. They were too big for either. They were some kind of hulking metal monsters, giving off a sense of huge power even in the darkness of this vast room. The room seemed to be some kind of enormous high-ceilinged garage. Noonie wished she could stop and let her eyes adjust to the darkness. That way she might be able to make out all the infinite black shapes in the room better. But the chief kept rushing her along, lifting her up higher to brace her against his right hip.

She was bounced through an open doorway and down a bright corridor. Fenlocki was running now, and Noonie could feel his lungs heaving in and out against her stomach. They reached the end of the corridor quickly. Two guards flanked a small doorway at the end of the hall.

Fenlocki stuck a card in the door's orifice. She could feel his whole body vibrate with impatience as he tapped his foot nervously, waiting for the door to admit them. Finally it folded open.

And there was wicker.

Wicker and caning and rattan and wood everywhere. It was some kind of high-tech state-of-the-science control room. There were a dozen people bent intently over individual wicker stations, operating polished wooden ringlets, dark-grained keyboards, and artificial mahogany diotes. The room was filled with CV projections and wicker-rimmed monitors showing images of a zillion Second Level streets, as well as several views of the outside of the building. It was all double spaf-looking. There were flashing inlights moving about in complicated patterns overhead, panels covered with pieces of self-rotating wood, brown and tan ringlets flying up and down and twisting gracefully on their wires, and hundreds of wicker-covered cables being coupled and uncoupled faster than Noonie could keep track of. Spaf. Peaky, peaky, peaky prone!

Fenlocki put Noonie down by the door. He strode to the middle of the room and up onto a central high-gloss wood platform. He was fumbling in his pockets for something as he shouted, "Sitch? Sitch?"

None of the technicians looked up. The chief stared at them, one after the other, trying another pocket in his jacket. He apparently didn't find what he was looking for there. He tore off the jacket and hung it over the rattan rail. He looked annoyed—out of sunbeams, Noonie guessed—and leaned into the railing next to his jacket. "Somebody?" he yelled even louder. "Anybody? What's the raping sitch, people?"

A woman wearing funny-looking complicated metal goggles looked up from the tiny CV image that floated in front of her and frowned at the chief. "Not good," she said flatly, pointing to one of the larger monitors.

Noonie looked over at it just in time to see the image of a group of strange, silver-suited creatures pouring out of a building and onto a white street. They carried nasty-looking weapons and they were followed by others who wore what looked like scraps of garbage. People, tons of people, crowding up onto Second.

The other monitors and CVs now showed similar scenes. Silver suits and then messy, smelly-looking weirdos. Guns, rifles, clubs, knives, and fists raised. It seemed the streets of all of Manhattan were suddenly full of angry-looking wild folk with weapons.

Noonie felt excitement building within her. This was it. This was the revolution. Revy. This was what Mommy had talked about for all those years. The big one.

"Where's Gavy?" Fenlocki snapped, his face contorted with stress. Again nobody answered. "Get him here! I don't care how. He's Chancellor—he gets to get hooked up."

A man in the far corner leaned forward and started whispering into his squawker. Fenlocki began pacing back and forth on the central platform, leaning into the ornate rattan railings on each side for just a split second before moving on. Each time he leaned, his right knee would press into the light tan caning below the rattan rail, almost busting through. He fiddled in his pants pocket now—then seemed to remember something. "Okay. Get the raping fighting machines out there. *Immediately*. All of them. Raise up the shielding. Turn on the anxiety field in the courtyard. And prepare the hosts. I want them ready in fifteen minutes.

Scramble all the cops we have and arm them with everything. Put them on standby—we may need them. And get those nerve cannons out here. *Now*. I don't want them"—he pointed at the monitors—"getting anywhere *near* here."

Noonie watched the monitors and CV projections. Something different was happening on each of them, yet it was all somehow the same: movement, chaos. On one large CV display Noonie saw a wide-angle shot of the stone base of the very building she was in. Holes appeared in the foundation, opening wider and wider like stone apertures. Then enormous silver cannons began to slide out of the building. With no frame of reference it was hard to say, but the cannons looked like they were about twenty feet long each, the barrel holes at the end big enough for Noonie to sit comfortably in. Huge weapons, these. Then there was more movement. Between some of the cannons, vast slabs of the stone were sliding upward—opening doorways like the one Noonie had entered the building through. There was a pause, and then the giant unmanned machines began coming out. The fighting machines.

They floated about three or four feet above the ground like coppers, and they moved pretty damned fast. Each one was solid black: they had two black cylinders on each side for lift and three big black ones in the back for thrust. Above each machine's swollen-looking saucer base was a ringed half-sphere section. Out of that grew dozens of serious-looking gun turrets like branches on some leafless, bulbous-trunked tree. Some of the weapons were chip guns, some nerve guns, and others Noonie couldn't recognize at all. Above that killing stuff was what looked like each machine's head: various sensors and lenses on a thick black pole covered with cables. If these things had been people and not machines, they wouldn't have looked very friendly.

The huge, flat-black monsters kept zipping out of the garage. One after another. Dozens and dozens poured out of the openings in endless streams. There sure were a lot of them. It looked like hundreds altogether.

"Gavy's on the way," one of the workers shouted.

"Good," Fenlocki said. "Make sure you keep the machines away from his cruiser. I don't want him killed on the way here. And move them outside of this sector. I don't want any machines near the command center. We need room for phase two." He glanced over and noticed Noonie as if for the first time. His lips curled up in a weak smile and then he turned to one of the workers. "Leeta, take the child to one of the interrogation rooms. She doesn't need to see all this."

Leeta was the woman with the funny-looking headgear. She stood up, her right eye looking absurdly tiny through the monitor lens of her goggles. "Standard body search, Chief?"

"Yeah, sure. Why not?" He smiled at Noonie again. "Let her have her pen and pad, though. Kid's gotta have something to do."

Noonie couldn't help but smile back at Fenlocki. She took Leeta's hand and let the woman lead her toward the door.

"I'll be in to talk to you in a while, Noonie," the chief added, his tone obviously an attempt to be soothing and motherly. He was still breathing far too heavily for it to be affective, though. "Sit tight till I get this stuff running, kid."

Before the two guards closed the door on the soundproof control room behind them, Noonie heard the chief's voice raise up again, barking out orders rapidly.

"Spread the machines out, Celna. One to each area of the grid. You know the drill. Somebody . . . will somebody— And get the cannons charged up, terradammit. I want them ready *now*, in case anyone gets through. And somebody get me . . . What's happening with the hosts, already? Are they prepped? I want them ready to go the second Gavy arrives. And . . . will *somebody please get me some raping sunbeans?*"

And then the door closed and Noonie was politely searched and then led toward the empty room full of dust motes. She smiled all the way, clutching her click-pen and her pad.

She was happy she could keep her drawing stuff. She wasn't in the mood to draw, but she was happy anyway.

The click-pen had been a gift from Alysess. Yeah, it streaked a bit, and yeah, the colors tended to mix and run a lot, but Noonie didn't mind. Alysess had shown her how to use it.

It only held two slugs, and Aunt Alysess had warned it would only work effectively at close range, but—what the subs? It was peaky prone anyway. A spaf secret weapon.

Who knows? Noonie thought. *It just might come in handy at some point.*

CHAPTER 35

Once she got through, Watly blocked the control pit hatch with a large table, five sandbags, some cable crates, and three relatively heavy boxes labeled COSTUMES.

The makeshift barricade wouldn't stop the security cops, but it might slow them down some. She was under the stage of the election auditorium now, in a low-ceilinged room painted all black. There were wires and cables tangled everywhere, and a whole forest of silver vertical poles that looked like hydraulic lifts used for lowering and raising sections of the stage door. No one was around. At least not at the moment. The technicians had all fled from the gunfire and explosions.

Watly headed toward the staircase at the far left corner under the stage.

Her shoulder hurt. But it could've been worse. It was a relatively minor slug graze as slug grazes went. She'd been shot before—maybe not in this exact body, but she *had* been shot—and this wasn't too bad. A small bandage would fix it fine.

Her head, on the other hand, still felt like shit. Breaking back into the driver's seat had been painful indeed. Right now it felt like someone was drilling a hole with a blunt, slow-moving bit down the center of her skull. The pain started at a sharply focused point on the top of her head and then seemed to burrow its way down into the meaty nucleus of her brain.

But there was no time to convalesce. Watly continued for the staircase, navigating around the hydraulics and hopping over the cables. Just before she reached the foot of the scuffed wooden stairs, she stopped, turning, and ran all the way back to the hatch barricade. There were already loud noises coming from the other side of it. The auditorium cops were in the control pit now, trying to force the hatch open. But Watly had an idea. She might be able to use something from one of the costume boxes.

A few very short minutes later, when Watly climbed the stairs to peer out into a backstage hallway, she looked different. Hopefully, very different.

She was wearing a Chancellor Dancer outfit: red wig, floppy node hat, stiff casement shirt, heavy white "stomping" boots, and bright yellow skirt with glowing tassels.

Behind Watly the hatch door thudded noisily, and finally there was a loud crash as all her carefully balanced weights were knocked over. The cops were through the barricade. And right behind her.

Watly stepped quickly into the corridor, closing the door behind her with an unintentional slam. It didn't have a lock.

The hallway before her was crowded with people rushing up and down in a panic. No one backstage knew where to go, it seemed. Distant explosions continued rumbling from every direction, shaking the floorboards, bringing down showers of placene dust, and further widening the eyes of all the frenzied people in the corridor.

Watly joined the crowd, following one group that was heading toward the rear of the building. She hoped she was blending in okay. Everyone looked scared shitless. It wasn't hard for Watly to look scared shitless like the rest—she *was* scared shitless.

Where was Noonie? Where had they taken her daughter? Fenlocki would be going to the anti-Revy command center, wherever the rape *that* was. He'd probably taken Noonie with him.

Watly had to get there somehow.

The crowd she was with hit the back of the building, pushing through the small stage door exit and down a short flight of outside stairs. Watly squeezed by with the rest of them, wincing as her wounded shoulder was mashed against the casement shirt by the doorframe. Maybe it wasn't so minor an injury after all.

The crowd poured out the door and down the staircase, shoving and yelling. Watly almost fell twice. She made it down to the pristine white surface of the alley and stepped aside, watching the people scatter in both directions.

There were more explosions and then a loud crackle of static from the outdoor speakers. The speakers were floaters, spread out all over Second Level Manhattan.

> "People of Second. There is no need for alarm. Stay inside. Lock your doors and windows. Go to your upper floors and remain calm. The authorities will handle this inconvenience. Repeat: Remain calm and stay on the upper floors of your homes and offices. Have a drink."

Then the speakers began playing soft music. People-relaxing music. It was gentle piellna playing—soothing chords, a bland melody, and a dainty little sensory-M rhythm.

It didn't calm Watly any. She stepped farther to the side of the stairs, still watching the crazed crowd clamber down it, and wondered which direction to go. Now the staircase crowd was really getting wild, trying to move in both directions at the same time. Some people had heard the announcement and wanted to climb back inside, swimming upstream. Others were still struggling out. The stage door and its narrow staircase was becoming a huge bottleneck of angry bodies. Watly could just make out two blue visor-hats near the top. Two of the security cops were trying to work their way through the mess toward her.

Watly turned to the right and ran. Better a wrong decision than no decision at all. Better to make a choice than to get shot at again. The glowing shirt tassels danced annoyingly against her thighs as she ran, and the casement shirt chafed all over—particularly irritating her wounded shoulder.

At the end of the alley, on Fifty-seventh itself, a large, wood-covered cruiser pulled up suddenly, blocking the way. Its shiny brown body hovered high on powerful artificial-wicker cylinders. Watly stepped to the shady side of the alley, flattening herself against the wall. There was a small recessed area there.

The door to the vehicle slid up.

"'Bout time you got here," a voice came from just around the corner from Watly. She recognized its bass snob timbre. It was

Gavy's voice. Zephy Gavy, newly reelected Chancellor of the island country of Manhattan.

The driver of the vehicle leaned back and stuck her head out of the open door. "We goin' home?" she said, sounding pretty hinky. "Tell me we're taking you home."

"Shit, no," Gavy said, stepping into Watly's view and climbing into the cruiser. She could see his gleaming bald dome and the side of his dangling bedlock. The lock sprouted thickly from where his widow's peak would've been, like some long yellow leech feeding on his brain. "Just got word from that bolehole chief of police. 'Misser Chancellor is needed at State Two.' Raping duty calls. That beanhead can't even handle—"

But the passenger door had slid closed now. The rear cylinders revved and flared and the vehicle took off quickly.

Now it was riding a little lower. Gavy's weight—probably close to two hundred pounds—would account for some of that. He alone should've changed the cruiser's riding height by about three inches. But the machine was sagging a bit lower than that, even. Four or maybe five inches. There was at least another hundred pounds worth of sag now as the wood-veneered vehicle sped west on Fifty-seventh and turned onto Ninth Avenue.

Watly Caiper held on to the underside of Gavy's speeding cruiser for dear life. It wasn't easy. Not just because it was so difficult to get a grip on the greasy pipes of the undercarriage, and not just because the machine's rapid swerves kept threatening to toss her off, but also because someone was following close behind.

And that someone was trying to shoot her off the raping thing.

CHAPTER 36

Roullic Neets killed Kness and Volder in a very offhand manner, emotion-wise. After the three of them had run off the stage during that crazy cop shooting of Sentiva, he'd led them to the Missers' room backstage.

Roullic could still hear the gunfire clearly and there was one really enormous explosion that shook the whole building violently, but he didn't let any of it phase him. He had each of his two loyal assistants sit on the edges of the same toilet seat in one of the ornate brass stalls.

"Time for your rewards," he said, playfully pulling on his eyebrow hairs. Then he shot the two of them in the head with his gold-plated antique chip pistol. Volder first and then Kness.

He'd hoped to get them both with one slug, just for fun. It would've been elegant that way. But he'd ended up needing two. The first one had splattered Misser Volder's limited brain matter on Mam Kness's face and neck and shoulders, but done her little or no actual harm. The second one had done her the necessary harm, death-wise.

They'd served their purpose well. Roullic didn't want any loose ends. No matter what kind of stupid mess was happening out there, he didn't want these two technicalities ever leading back to him. Everyone in this world had sordid secrets to hide, and Roullic wanted to make sure his secrets were as well hidden as possible. He had ambition. He had his dreams. Head of Alvedine. And then Chancellor himself, next election.

"Thanks," he said to the dead bodies. Then he checked himself in the large mirror—he looked just wonderful, as usual—and headed for the hall.

The hall was crazy, pandemonium-wise. Lots of running boleholes, arms flapping and mouths open.

Some of them were cute. There were a few panicked male and female Chancellor Dancers scrambling about in their skimpy outfits, looking very fuckable in the midst of all that chaos.

Roullic had liked the Chancellor Dancing. It had been the best part of the whole ceremony, next to his exquisite speech. He would've liked to take all ten of them on at once, as the hub of an enormous wheel of adoring bodies. That would've been great fun, orgasm-wise. They were each just nondescriptly, nonspecifically beautiful enough to be very attractive.

One of the particularly cute female dancers came out of the doorway down the hall from him. *Lovely strong legs on that one. And a very blowjobby kind of mouth, fellatio-wise.* Roullic felt a little tickle in his trouser-meat. *Nice tight ass, too.*

The dancer took off down the hall and then the same door she'd come out of burst open a few seconds later. Four very pissed-looking cops jumped out, scanning the corridor.

Rape! That dancer had been Sentiva in disguise! She was still alive! Yes, that'd been *her* little nasty face under the wig.

Roullic ran down the hall after her, shoving everyone aside. He even pushed right past the cops as they tried to figure which way to go or how to split up. *Beanheads!* He pulled out his beautiful gun again as he rushed through the boleholes in his way.

If *he* could kill Sentiva, what a feather that would be! He'd have no trouble getting anything he wanted when things finally settled down. He'd be a terradamned hero. Chancellor material. It was perfect. And it looked like it was going to be pretty raping easy.

What more could I ask, he thought, *than to be the man who executed this crazy women—reputation-wise, notoriety-wise . . .* any-*which-wise-wise!*

CHAPTER 37

The Ragman's bolehole rash itched.

It was impossible to scratch at it while he was wearing the heavy battlesuit. He'd have to suffer and hope the thing eased up by itself.

It was, actually, better than the problem he'd had earlier. Right after finishing his "Rising Rug-Rats" announcement from the subs' improvised CV studio, he'd quickly donned the warsuit. He dressed fast, sealing the thing up nice and tight, and when he was finally done he realized a cockroach had somehow gotten in there with him. It must have climbed inside the suit before he'd put the damn thing on. And suddenly he could feel the roach's grimy little legs scampering up his left thigh, making him very hinky indeed.

This is the kind of thing that shouldn't bother me, he thought, but the truth was he felt near panic. The little insect was in his sealed outfit, climbing around on his leg. He slapped at his thigh, trying to crush the raping bug with the heavy fabric. After a few hard smacks, the thing stopped wriggling and the Ragman felt it fall down to the nonslip boot part of the suit.

Better. That was better. He could deal with a dead roach sharing the battlesuit with him, but not a live one.

And now, he supposed as he scanned the Second Level street before him, *I can deal with a little itch in my nether regions.*

He had ascended to Second through a Cruda church on Forty-second and Third Avenue. He'd wanted to arrive somewhere midtown, figuring the anti-Revy headquarters had to be someplace central. The Ragman had let the layplurites with him vent some of their rage when they'd first climbed up. He stepped aside and turned his back while his mob killed the two lovers they'd found in the room. The couple had apparently been fucking in front of the CV elections when their floor had blown open. Tough break they never got to finish. Nasty business. But couldn't be helped. This was war.

There were five suited-up Revies with the Ragman, as well as about a hundred and fifty layfolk. Nice-sized little battalion.

The Ragman led the group west across Forty-second, communicating with the Revies through his suit's mike. He didn't like the suits. Didn't, in truth, trust them, even though he'd helped design them. The visor readout was distracting, movement was awkward, and though the cold layer was not supposed to affect the temperature within, it damn well did—it was freezing inside. On top of all that, the Ragman knew that the shiny material of the outfit would only deflect a nerve gun bolt if it was hit on an angle. He also knew the likelihood of a direct, exactly perpendicular nerve hit was small, yes, but still . . . if it happened, that was it. Not a pleasant thought.

And what about chip guns? Damn suit wouldn't stop a high-powered slug at all. Might keep a weak slug from going too deep, but that just meant he'd die slower. The expensive automedipak catshit they'd built in hardly seemed worth it. And the suit's defense against a movement sensor was almost as dangerous as doing without, particularly for someone the Ragman's age. He wasn't sure his heart would hold up for even one dose of the fancy outfit's "anti-movement-sensor" option.

To top it all off, all of the controls for the suit were tongue-operated. That was an awkward design feature if there ever was one. But the Revy scientists had insisted that tongue controls kept the hands and feet free, could be easily contained within the helmet, didn't require much movement, and could be learned quickly after only a little practice. So if the Ragman wanted to do anything, operate any of the controls, he had to stick his tongue out into the little tabs that rested just in front of his lips.

All in all, it was a pretty stupid suit.

But still, he'd rather have the silly, bulky, unwieldy thing than not. It did provide for *some* feeling of protection.

Why do I have to be up front? he thought to himself. *Why don't I just have the layfolk wave their little sticks up front, followed by the few better-armed layfolk, followed by my heavily armed Revies, followed—a few blocks behind—by little old me? Why should the general lead the charge? Who the subs invented that stupid concept?*

There were still a few string explosions going on in the distance. Others were coming up all around the country. The sound of new portals opening was music to the Ragman's ears. There actually *was* some kind of music in the Ragman's ears. The damn level was full of it, blaring from every floater-speaker around. It was distracting. It was damn annoying. And for some reason, the serene, tranquil tones of canned piellna made him feel pretty damn hinky.

Forty-second Street itself was empty right now. Earlier, there'd been a few coppers dashing around on it before them, but the Revy to Ragman's left, Uuriz, had taken them out easily. She had a I-bazooka on her shoulder, and those puny little coppers were no match for that. KAPOW!—two burning hunks of metal and wire and cable.

He had expected Uuriz to use a scrambler rifle—a simple, unspectacular way of stopping a copper cold—but it had actually been nice to see the things demolished in huge fireballs. Fireworks could do wonders for morale.

They kept walking. And the Ragman kept leading, in spite of himself. He talked to the leaders of some of the other battalions.

"Where are you, Maikin?"

"We're moving down West End, near Eighty-first. All clear."

"Tavis?"

"Yes yes yes yes!"

"Tavis? How's it going?"

"Tavis's having fun, Subkeeper. Lots of fun to be had up here!"

"Be careful, Tavis."

"Tavis is always careful, Subkeeper!"

"Heevad? How's the progress."

"We're down on— Oh, shit. What the rape is that?"

"What's the problem, Heevad?"

"Shit, that's big. We got a problem here Ragma—"

"Heevad?"

The Ragman had lost Heevad's signal. He couldn't even see the guy's purple indicator on his visor readout.

The Ragman kept walking across Forty-second, slowing his pace just a little. Better to be cautious at this point. Better not to take too many chances right from the start.

Now the Ragman *did* see something moving up ahead. Whatever it was, it had come up Park Avenue South and was turning right on Forty-second. It was big. It looked maybe twelve or fifteen feet tall and twenty feet long. It was a strange, nonreflective black. Even from the block-long distance he could see a whole bunch of things sticking out of it. And it was coming nearer. Really fast. Impossibly fast.

Uuriz aimed the I-bazooka without even being asked. *That's a good soldier*, the Ragman thought, raising his hand to hold up the troops. She fired expertly, the disk streaking straight at the large black thing. The I-disk exploded on contact in a big bursting envelope of smoke and flames. Yellow sparks flew up in a great glowing blossom and then faded.

The breeze cleared the smoke pretty quickly. The thing was still coming, riding smoothly through the remaining smoke, its black surface not even dented from the direct hit of an I-bazooka. The sticklike things jutting out of it were moving around now, and the long "neck" and flat "head" on its top bent and twisted in all directions.

Uuriz's face exploded from a chip slug. It went clean through the helmet shielding with no problem at all. She was dead before she hit the ground.

Someone on the other side of the Ragman shot a scrambler rifle at the huge machine, but the projectile grapple-blade on the end of the wire just bounced right off it harmlessly, clattering to the street surface. And the huge black fighting machine kept coming. Straight for the four remaining Revies, straight for the battalion of inexperienced laypeople, and straight for the Ragman, who was in front of everyone.

Shit, the Ragman thought. *An itchy bolehole, some irritating music, and a dead roach in my boot are the least of my problems.*

CHAPTER 38

While little Noonie was growing from a newborn to an infant to a baby to a toddler to a child to a pre-pubescent, Alysess watched. She watched Noonie, and she watched Mommy-Watly. Sometimes what she saw worried her.

It wasn't that Watly didn't love the girl. Watly loved the girl more than anyone ever loved anyone. That wasn't the problem. Watly had wanted to have a child, to be a mother—a parent—ever since she had been a child herself. Ever since she had been a little boy, actually. Alysess had heard all about it. There had always been a great need in Watly. A need to parent. But maybe that was part of what felt wrong.

When Alysess watched the two together she saw what looked like too much need in the wrong direction. Watly seemed to need Noonie desperately. Watly seemed to need Noonie almost more than Noonie needed Watly. That didn't seem right. The child should need the parent. The child should depend on the parent, rely on the parent to fulfill the *child's* needs. That's what parents are for.

Maybe Watly missed having a parent herself. Maybe that strange, difficult meeting with Eiter Eimsler had been a bad idea.

It seemed Watly felt she might have gotten what she wanted from Eiter, at least eventually. If only they could have kept up contact. But that wasn't possible. So she had only herself now. And Alysess. And Noonie.

When Alysess watched this mother and child over the years, sometimes it seemed difficult to tell which was the mother and which was the child.

Watly obviously wanted to be a good mother. She was caring and attentive and considerate and patient and knew when to discipline and draw the line, when to give hugs and when to scold. . . .

But Alysess saw that the need in Watly to feel like a good mother was an almost desperate one. She needed Noonie to validate her, reassure her. She needed the child to acknowledge how wonderful a woman she was, what a great mommy she was. She needed, it seemed, for her child to give her a sense of self. She needed the child to be her friend, to take care of her emotionally.

That was not something a child should do. That was Watly's own job to do for herself—maybe it was even *Alysess's* job to help her with it—but it certainly shouldn't have been Noonie's.

"Alysess?" Noonie asked one day when Watly was in the CV boardroom for a meeting. The girl was five. This was two years before the secret thing happened. Two years before the event no one spoke of. Noonie was just a kid. A pretty little kid. She seemed scared, all fetaled-up in a ball on the bed. It was nap time but she wasn't sleeping. Alysess had gone through two story monitors with no luck.

"Yeah, Face?" Alysess answered. Sometimes she called the kid "Face." Noonie liked that.

"Am I doing okay?"

The child looked up at Alysess, her little features strained. She looked far more stressed than a little kid should look. Far more stressed than *anyone* should look.

"What?"

"Am I doing everything okay?"

Alysess forced out a little laugh, stroking Noonie's forehead with her hand. "You're not supposed to *do* anything, Face. You're a child. You're supposed to grow and learn. You're just supposed to *be*, Nooner-face. We don't love you for what you *do*. We love you for who you *are*. We love Noonie. And we love her for being

Noonie. That's plenty. It's *our* job to *do* right now, Nooner. *You* just have to be."

Noonie reached her little arms up for a hug and Alysess gave her a big one.

And Alysess felt read bad for the kid. The kid had to pretend every single day to be someone she wasn't. The kid had to smear her face with makeup and have her hair straightened. The kid had to deal with having a mommy who acted nice in private and really shitty in public. The kid had to live in a world where she didn't trust anyone.

And now it seemed to Alysess that on top of everything else, the poor kid had to take care of her own mom. That stunk.

Sometimes all Alysess wanted to do was rescue the girl. Rescue her from everything. Steal her away and save her. But she didn't. She didn't even try. Life down on First would've been even worse for the kid, and a damn sight more dangerous. And, in truth, Alysess had no confidence she'd be any better at parenting than Watly. Subs knew, she had her own problems. She might not make the same mistakes Watly did, but she'd sure as rape make her own.

And there was one thing she was sure of. Whatever faults Watly had as a mother, it didn't mean she wasn't a damn good one. She was doing the best that she could.

And that's all anyone can do. Alysess knew that. All anyone can do is the best they can do.

CHAPTER 39

All I'm going to do is the best I can, Alysess said to herself, stepping out onto the street. There was little comfort in that thought, but it was the only thought that had the slightest hint of real optimism in it. *I've got no gun, no battle togs, no game plan. I'll just do the best I can.*

There was no one nearby on Amsterdam Avenue. There was what looked like a whole pile of well-dressed but very dead Second Levelers heaped on the sidewalk near the corner of Seventy-eighth. A couple of expensive-looking private cruisers were parked on the street. Other vehicles were there, but certainly not parked. One was halfway up on the cream-colored sidewalk, its windscreen and passenger windows shattered and its occupants a bloody mess. Another was tipped up on its side, its right cylinder on fire. Still another was totally upside down, every part of its frame dented as if a hundred steel fists had pounded on it over and over.

On the far side of the street from Alysess, near the curb, what was left of an unmanned copper smoldered. A few hundred feet away was another one. And then another. They looked like enormous crushed toys, smashed by some angry giant child during a temper tantrum.

To her right was another dead copper, but this one looked in perfect condition. All that was wrong with it was it had a grapple-blade stuck in its surface, the ridged wire from the blade extending way down the street. It had been hit by a scrambler rifle, knocked out completely. One of the well-armed Revies had shot it at a distance, hitting it with the grappler, then pulled its wire taut, and engaging the rifle's scrambler. The copper's control chips were probably a gob of melted placene now.

Even the machines are dead here, Alysess thought.

The sun hung low and orange in the sky. Long shadows of buildings darkened the avenue's whitetop. Alysess glanced up at the ornately carved building in front of her. It was all stone, and each stone had been chiseled into a little winged cherub. Something caught Alysess's eye from one of the upper windows. There were two faces peering out at her. There were two people up there, peeking timidly from around long, gold-embroidered curtains. Their eyes seemed to say, *Please don't hurt us.*

Alysess smiled wryly up at them and turned to her right. She couldn't hear any more string explosions going off. All the portals must've been opened by now. She *did* still hear gunfire everywhere. And music. Really tacky, old-fashioned music, echoing everywhere as if intended to soothe the revolutionary spirit or something. But the gunfire was much louder than the annoying tunes.

Five blocks to the south, she could see many tiny figures running around—shooting, falling, diving, screaming. It reminded her a little of the food riots she'd witnessed a week ago on the streets that were five stories directly below her now.

Alysess heard what sounded like a wooden door creaking open behind her. She twisted her head to see two people coming out of the same building she herself had just exited. They were First Levelers, a ragged-looking pair of old, gray-haired women carrying metal pipes. They looked full of energy but confused. Apparently, they had not been unduly fazed by the carnage within the building. *They must have stronger stomachs than I do,* Alysess thought.

"Which way to the revolution?" one of them asked nervously.

Alysess snorted. "You got me."

"Is it over?" the other wrinkled First Leveler asked, looking very disappointed.

Alysess felt like laughing but held it back. "I don't think so," she said.

Now one of the women saw the commotion going on down the street and nudged her friend in the ribs. "There!" she said. And the two of them grinned and trotted off toward the melee.

Late arrivals, Alysess thought. *The more cautious ones.* It hadn't occurred to her till then that people were still coming up through the holes. People would probably *keep* coming up as long as there *were* holes. She wondered how many people there were up here by now. About a thousand Ragman Revies and—who knows?—maybe fifteen thousand or twenty thousand plurites in that first frenetic wave. Plus however many more were still dribbling up.

She was starting to seriously consider following the jolly wanna-be Revies—safety in numbers, and all—when another door burst open just up the street from her.

Alysess spun around. Three disheveled-looking plurites dragged someone out of a brightly painted brownstone about ten yards from her. It was a naked woman they yanked out with them, and she looked badly beaten up, but alive. Two of the plurites were male and one was female, and each was armed with Ragman chip rifles.

They pulled the struggling figure toward the center of the street, screaming "Genocide! Genocide!" in her tear-streaked face as she tried to resist their strong grips and violent shoves.

They dumped her trembling form midstreet. The plurite woman grabbed their captive's flailing arms and pinned them to the whitetop. She held them down with her knees. One of the men went for his frayed belt cord, undoing his pants. It looked like they were about to rape this bruised, terrified woman.

"Hey!" Alysess shouted without even thinking. "Don't *do* that!"

The man with his pants half down turned to stare at Alysess. His penis was exposed—erect and reddish purple. To Alysess, it looked like a weapon, an angry tool of violence. The man's eyes were wild and furious. His dirt-smeared face broke into a small, twitching grin and he licked his upper lip.

"Okay," he said simply.

Then he lifted his rifle, turned, and shot the pinned woman in the center of the forehead. She stopped struggling instantly.

All three plurites exploded into hysterical laughter. They apparently found this one of the funniest sight gags ever. A veritable masterpiece of comic timing. The man pulled his pants back up, almost falling over from laughter as he did it.

Then there was a flash of movement just behind them. They all turned, still guffawing heartily. A barefoot man in a red silk robe had apparently been hiding behind one of the crushed coppers. He took off in a rapid, desperate sprint up the street.

The plurites gave chase, quickly disappearing around the corner of Eightieth Street. They were out of sight now, these heroic revolutionaries. But Alysess couldn't wipe them from her mind. She stared at the dead woman and then back at the corner.

Way beyond where they'd turned, Alysess now saw a crowd of revolutionaries running in all directions. A huge black thing was in the middle of them, its turrets flying in rapid circles, firing chip slugs and nerve gun bolts quickly and with loud, percussive cracks. Some of the revolutionaries were shooting back, but most were trying to get away fast. They were all dropping one by one.

Alysess could see body parts—heads, torsos, limbs— shattering in bloody messes, one after the other. Some of the fighters literally flew across the street and into side buildings from the force of the high-powered slugs. Others were glowing— screaming out in agony as nerve gun bolts burned their way up their nervous systems toward their brains.

Alysess took off in the other direction fast, not wanting to be anywhere near one of those gigantic fighting machines. She turned left on Seventy-seventh, sidestepping Second Levelers' bodies every few yards.

Ahead was a whole bunch of dead Revies. Most were in First Level rags, but there were a few wearing bloody, slug-ridden battle togs. And all around the bodies were all manner of weapons.

Alysess stopped running. The warsuits and the guns obviously hadn't made much difference against the machines. But they were something. They were the best she could do. And all she could do was the best she could do. That she knew.

And she figured maybe it was time for this particular rescue warrior to get suited up and armed.

CHAPTER 40

Tavis-the-IT didn't even mind the constant music. It was kind of catchy. Background for the killing. Tavis-the-IT was having fun. Fun, fun, fun. IT had realized one wonderful thing. IT was a great soldier. And all it really took to be a great soldier was knowing how to stay alive, and knowing how to kill real good. Ha.

IT was doing both.

The main tricks Tavis learned to staying alive were to always remain alert, always keep your gun up, and—most important—always make sure there was at least one person directly between you and the enemy.

Right now Tavis was holding up dead Beniseat—old pal Beniseat—as a shield between IT and one of those ugly black things. 'Seat's body was being hit over and over again with blasts from the machine's chip guns. But Beniseat was long dead. At this point the slugs were redundant. Overdundant. Extradundant Dundant once again.

Tavis's troop was a mess. Yicky icky sticky mess. Ha. Tavis might've enjoyed the mess much more—lots and lots of running red fun and people pieces—had they not been ITs people. It was not as much fun if it wasn't the enemy. *Enemy* blood was

humorous and exciting and good. All around Tavis was revolutionary blood. ITs own troop's blood. Not so good.

They'd been ambushed by the fighting machine as they turned
the corner of Eleventh Avenue and Twenty-eighth Street. Some of
the crowd—Revies and layfighters—had made it into the safety of
nearby buildings. They'd blasted open doors with their weapons
instead of trying to fight the thing with them. But most of the
battalion was dead.

Tavis wasn't. Tavis was smart. Tavis had his evening buddy,
Beniseat, to protect IT.

None of the slugs was making it through the body yet, but
some were sure to soon. The corpse was riddled with them.
Falling to pieces in ITs hands. Fortunately, the machine's high-
powered slug barrel was on the far side from Tavis. *That* weapon
could shoot through the two of them like a knife through piss. But
there *were* nerve guns on this side. And if the black thing started
using them . . . well, that would be really nasty. A big nasti-
ness. A very yicky perdicky.

Tavis held the body up with one arm and aimed ITs chip pistol
at the machine with the other. The black monster was pretty close.
Four or five yards away. Its rapidly recoiling barrels were
pumping in and out, firing all around the area. It was repeatedly
shooting any of the revolutionaries who still twitched, any who
still had any warmth radiating from them.

The only ones it wasn't hitting much were those in the suits. If
the suits were still sealed, and the cold layer still functioning, no
heat should escape. And if the suits were still fully operational, the
movement-sensor-defense should work. But only for sixty-five
seconds. Not a great defense.

When engaged, the suit would, in effect, *kill* the wearer for a
little over a minute. Then it would revive the wearer. That way the
Revy would be dead and totally motionless for a while. No
heartbeat. No breathing. No nose scratching. And as soon as those
sixty-five seconds of deceasedness were up, the suit would
automatically jump-start its charge. If some of those bodies lying
around the black fighting machine were in suit-death, the black
machine would assuredly blast them the moment they came out of
it.

Tavis figured maybe two or three of the fourteen silver-suited
bodies surrounding the machine weren't dead yet. They were out
in suit-suspension-land, but they'd be up and about shortly. Up

and about and dead a second later. Ha. His comrades. Not too nice for them. Yicky business.

Tavis took a few shots at the metal beast. The slugs bounced right off, not even making little scratches in the black surface. IT shot more, aiming for the turrets and the gun barrels, then the headlike sensor platform, then the cylinders on the machine's bottom.

Nothing.

The machine swiveled its nerve gun barrel toward Tavis. *Shit*. Without so much as a pause, it shot Beniseat's body with a bolt. The streak of the nerve bolt's tail blazed out, hitting 'Seat's ripped-open torso dead center and dancing brightly there. Tavis felt the body heat up as the fiery bolt climbed up the dead man's nervous system.

Tavis knew IT would have to let go of ITs old friend soon. The nerve bolt might go through Beniseat's back and get into ITs suit. These warsuits could reflect just-fired bolts that came in at an angle, but they had no defense against touching a nerve-burning body. With 'Seat's body pressed right up against Tavis's suit, the bolt-stuff could surely climb right through the fabric. Right to Tavis-the-IT. Not a goodly thing to happen. No, no.

Tavis took some more shots at the monster, aiming over Beniseat's bloody right shoulder. "Die, you rapehead! Tavis *says* so!"

It seemed like the thing was unstoppable. No part of its surface appeared affected by ITs slugs. It was impenetrable. Even the razor-sharp blades of a scrambler rifle would undoubtedly bounced right off. If Tavis had a scrambler rifle. Which Tavis didn't.

Where was the weak point? *Every* damned thing has a weak point. Every, every, *every* thing. Tavis tried to see up into the area where the neck of the thing—the black pole—joined the rotating sensor pod on top. IT couldn't see. IT wasn't close enough. There were overlapping flaps of solid black metal shielding material there. Tavis couldn't see up under them. The little shields were hanging down in a circle from the thing's "head." Protecting that area. Protecting the area where neck met swivel pod.

Protecting it? Why protect something if it ain't vulnerable?

Beniseat was almost too hot to hold now. Tavis could see the bolt burning brightly under the skin on the back of the guy's neck. It showed right through 'Seat's shattered, dripping helmet. Getting awful warm. The whole guy was awful warm. The back of his suit, right between the shoulder blades, was starting to glow. The bolt was looking for more nerve, unsatisfied with the dead stuff.

More chip slugs pounded into Beniseat's body. To Tavis, it felt like his friend was still alive, twitching, jumping, convulsing, and bouncing against him. The dead body was slamming into Tavis like it was spasming from some incredible afterlife orgasm.

'Seat's head fell off. Thump.

Better do something, Tavis. Better think fast. . . .

Someone on the ground moved. One of the suited Revies was coming out of it, shocked and adrenalined awake by the outfit. Five of the black beast's turrets turned to the right, barrels blazing. The machine began blowing Mr. Sleepyhead into little pieces. Poor subspawn would never get a chance to come all the way back to life.

Tavis seized the moment. IT threw Beniseat's body hard, launching it a good four yards to the left with a grunt. Now some of the machine's turrets turned *that* way, already firing. Tavis dove forward—straight at the metal thing—and landed hard on the front cylinder, breasts mashed into the metal, legs splayed out behind. A slug tore painfully into ITs right calf. Tavis raised the gun straight up, aiming for the slit between the shielding and the post. There was a thin gap there, beyond which Tavis could just make out some cables and wires.

Tavis fired, over and over, arm locked straight above ITs head. *Crack-crack-crack-crack-crack-crack-crack-crack!* ITs finger cramped up on the trigger, so Tavis switched to the middle one. *Crack-crack-crack-crack-crack!* All the turrets were turning toward Tavis now, bending down at him.

"Die, you piece of catshit!" Tavis screamed. Another slug hit Tavis, this time in the upper thigh. *Yick!* Tavis kept firing.

Something popped and sizzled from above. The sensor head was spinning wildly now. The turrets were still shooting, but they didn't seemed aimed at anything in particular. The machine started to move—first left, then right, then forward, then back. It couldn't see anymore. Tavis had gotten its eyes. Tavis had severed the sensors from the rest of it. It was blind.

Tavis was good at going for the eyes.

"Yes! Yes yes yes yes *yes*! Tavis is a hero! Tavis found the weak point!" IT yelled. Then Tavis dropped off the machine's front and leapt for cover under some of the mangled bodies. *Ow! Hurt leg!*

The black thing careened down Twenty-eighth Street in a crazy

zigzag, still firing aimlessly in all directions. It was slowly
moving itself out of range.

"Dumb machine," Tavis said, giggling a little.

Two of the remaining warsuited Revies were waking up now,
and Tavis helped them to their knees. They still all had to be
careful not to be easy targets for some lucky stray slug. But that
was becoming less and less likely as the fighting machine moved
farther and farther off.

"I *did* it!" Tavis laughed at his two groggy comrades, ignoring
the pain from ITs two slug wounds. The automedipak would be
kicking in soon to take care of that. "Tavis *did* it! Just wait till I
tell the Ragman! Just wait! I'll call him right now. Yes yes *yes*!"

Tavis got no answer on the Ragman's frequency.

CHAPTER 41

Another Revy right next to the Ragman dropped, shot in the chest. He could hear others falling behind him to both sides. And the sound of panicked running. The fighting machine was approaching rapidly, shooting the whole time. The Ragman could clearly see one of the front gun barrels pointing straight at his face now. He stuck out his tongue, pointing it stiffly, and pressed his suit's NOMOVE tab.

He went down flat on his back. The rear of his helmet slammed loudly into the whitetop. He was dead. No breathing. No heartbeat. Nothing.

He could still hear screams and shots and running footsteps, but they were growing dimmer and dimmer. More and more vague and echoey and undefined. Shouts sounded like explosions. Footsteps sounded like gunfire. He felt himself slipping, slipping away. Little black and gray specks filled the corners of his eyes, closing off his peripheral vision. More and more spots came in from each side, closing what he could see down like some narrowing diaphragm. The circle of vision within the flecks got smaller and smaller until it was only a tiny dot. Then it blinked out.

And there was nothingness. Total and complete nothingness. There was no sense of self, no sense of time passing. No sense of anything. A second could've been an hour could've been a year could've been forever.

And then there was pain. Pain in the heart. In the lungs. In the arms and legs and neck. Everywhere, there was pain. The little dot of vision came back and widened like a slowly opening mouth. The Ragman was coming out of a tunnel. The tunnel's end got bigger until it filled the world, and the Ragman could see again. And what he could see was darkness. It was dark now. Like night. The Ragman was on his back, staring up at darkness. There was still the sound of chip slugs firing, but it was even louder now. Incredibly loud. It was so loud, the sound distorted painfully in his suit's speakers, which were made to handle just that kind of noise. The speakers whistled agonizingly noisy feedback squeals right in his ears.

There were some moans from nearby, and the sound of more shots. Then the unmistakable sound of a nerve gun firing: the whooshing, zipping, air-burning noise of the bolt flashing out. But it was so loud it seemed to the Ragman like he was *inside* the barrel of a nerve gun.

He moved his eyes for the first time since waking up. Now he understood. A few feet above him was an enormous piece of seamless dark metal. It filled the sky. To the left and right the metal bulged downward some, and there were holes in it on the apex of the bulges that blazed with blue fire. Cylinder fire. Lift fire.

The Ragman was underneath the fighting machine. It had been coming right at him. When he'd engaged the NOMOVE tab, he must've fallen right in its path. Since he was "dead," the machine must have stopped seeing him and driven right over his body. Now it hovered there, shooting at the remaining revolutionaries around him. Turning his head slightly, the Ragman could see how thorough the thing was. It shot at the movement of scraps of cloth that flew by. It shot at the warmth of a burning cruiser that had crashed just up the street. It was even still shooting the suitless dead people repeatedly, still sensing their body heat. That part was not pleasant to look at.

None of this was what the Ragman had expected. He'd have to think. He'd have to reevaluate. He'd have to figure other tactics to win this revolution. It wasn't going to be anywhere near as easy as he'd expected.

After a few more moments of eardrum-shattering firing, the fighting machine seemed satisfied. The shooting stopped. The Ragman saw the black metal above him slowly slide forward. He would be out in the open any second. He figured as soon as the machine was clear of his body, it would sense his movement. And it would stop and turn to kill him.

He'd have to engage the suit again just as it passed over. He'd have to hope it would be far enough away by the time he woke up that he would be well out of sensor range.

He'd also have to hope that his raping old heart would hold up for another leisurely sixty-five-second stop.

The edge of the orange sky became visible under the back end of the machine. The black metal was almost clear of the Ragman now. He was almost uncovered.

He stuck his tongue out and hit the tab again.

Here goes nothin'. . . .

CHAPTER 42

Why do I always end up in these situations? Watly thought to herself.

She was losing her grip around the greasy support poles on the undercarriage of Gavy's cruiser. She'd managed to get her feet above the bottom lip of the rear cylinder's casing—which kept them from dragging, but that didn't help hold her up any.

The machine she was clutching was speeding rapidly down the streets. The road was a blur beneath her. She felt as if she were trying to hold on to the underbelly of a rampaging dinosaur.

When she twisted her head down and looked back under her left shoulder, she could see the bottom of a cruiser following her as her node hat scraped along the rough road surface. Whoever was following was shooting at her. And they were quite good. Quite ingenious, actually. They must've lowered their windscreen and were shooting down from the driver's seat. The angle was bad, so it seemed to Watly they were aiming for the whitetop below her, hoping a ricochet would hit her. And they were getting damned expert at it. One slug thudded into the metal just next to her head. Another bounced up and pinged loudly off the pole she was gripping, making it vibrate even more than it already was.

Watly had no idea where she was or how close she was to the command center. Gavy had told the driver that they were going to see Fenlocki at State Two. Noonie should be there. Watly was counting on it. And if she could just hold on and keep from getting shot . . .

Gavy's cruiser swerved hard to the right. Watly figured the driver above her had heard the shooting. The woman had probably thought the cruiser following was trying to shoot *them:* Gavy and the driver. They were taking evasive action to avoid getting assassinated. Swell.

They're not trying to get you, *you idiots! They're trying to get* me! *Why else would they be aiming* under *your cruiser? Use your tiny heads, already! They're trying to get the little cockroach hanging on to the damn thing's bottom.*

But the driver kept swerving hard. And the cruiser chasing them kept shooting. And Watly's clinging body was tossed back and forth, slugs bouncing up all around her. She was having some serious trouble holding on now. She tried to swing her arms up higher and hook her elbows over the pipe. They kept slipping off the greasy thing.

The cruiser veered right and then made an abrupt left turn, banking sharply. Watly's fingers scrabbled to keep their hold through the turn. The machine tipped up and the driver sped up even as they hit the center of the curve's arc. Holding on was useless. Watly flew off the thing, her body completely airborne. She landed brutally on her butt and then rolled sideways. Finally her hip slammed into the curb and she stopped tumbling.

She was bruised all over, but in one piece. Nothing felt broken. She tried to sit up. It wasn't easy. She didn't feel like moving. *I'll just lie here for the rest of the afternoon on—what is this?—Ninth and Thirty-third? Yeah. I'll just relax here and listen to all this lovely music they keep playing, thank you.* Her shoulder was killing her, but, thankfully, the drill-bit headache had let up some. Small favors.

She looked down at herself. Her stomping-boots were coated in oil, her arms were covered in dirt and grease, her tasseled skirt had ridden all the way up to her waist and its tassels had lost their glow, the silly wig was matted with slime, and the casement shirt was cracked and chipped all over.

Watly tried to stand. Everything was stiff and sore. Down Thirty-third Street, Gavy's vehicle was only a tiny dot in the distance, but the other cruiser had stopped and was backing up toward her.

Before she could get all the way to her feet, the vehicle pulled up right in front of her. Its door slid up silently and a tall figure climbed gracefully out. Watly felt almost blinded by Roullic Neets's bright red hair.

He smiled graciously.

"Hello, there, Sentiva," he said, pointing a very nifty ornate chip gun at her face. "Nice hat."

CHAPTER 43

"We've got a fighter *down* on Twenty-eighth Street, Chief."

Fenlocki stiffened. "What's the sitch?"

"Dunno, its sensors are out. I've run a diagnostic and I can't figure. Malfunction, probably."

The chief chewed nervously on yet another sunbean. His eyes itched from all the constant CV mist. "Can you bring it back for repair? I want them all operational."

"I'll give it a shot," the technician said, hands dancing rapidly from one wooden ringlet to another.

"See if we've got the moment it went down on tape. Review the floater lens feeds for that quadrant. I want to know what happened."

Fenlocki resisted the urge to eat another sunbean. He was feeling a little sick. Watching all the blood on the various monitors was not easy on his stomach. It was really awful out there. Why didn't the revolutionaries just give up? Why did they all insist on being killed? Why didn't they just cut their losses and climb back down? That would be better for everyone. This was sickening. It was impossible to look at without feeling one's gorge rise.

Earlier, the chief had toyed with the idea of gassing the whole

Second Level, putting everyone to sleep. Then cleanup could then be easy and bloodless. But that was not by the book. The gas would get into the buildings, and that meant some of the Second Levelers inside would pass out and might bump their precious little noggins on their toilet seats or something. The rules said no, and Fenlocki always went by the raping rules. That's what made him such a raping good cop. He burped and tasted stomach bile.

The door to the control room folded open and Gavy ran in. His long blond lock twitched against his left eye as he rushed. "I'm here. You're terradamn Chancellor is here."

"Good," Fenlocki said, not exhibiting any of the respect he was supposed to give to his superior. "We're ready for you."

"Looks like you're really raping up, Ogiv," Gavy said angrily. He reached up and shifted his yellow bedlock so that it was hanging over the other side of his round face. Now his right eye was obscured by it. "None of this should ever have happened," he spewed out. "And you're responsible. It's a mess out there. There are explosions everywhere, and someone tried to shoot us on the way over. What the rape is going on?"

Fenlocki stepped off the central wooden platform. He found himself talking like a teacher addressing a particularly slow student. "Revolution, O Chancellor mine. Rev-o-lu-tion. You want me to spell it slowly for you?"

"Don't talk down to me, Fenlocki," Gavy said with a sneer. "You are in deep catshit. Have you got things under control yet?"

Now Fenlocki allowed himself one small sunbean. He chewed slowly and leaned back into the rattan railing. What he really wanted to do, what he was using all his willpower *not* to do, was grab that stupid bedlock of Gavy's and toss it back over his bald head. He didn't. He chewed and swallowed. "The fighting machines are doing fine. A lot of the rebels are dead. It looks like most of the ones still alive have fled into buildings. That doesn't mean there aren't still a lot of them, though."

Gavy looked surprised. "Into *our* people's buildings? They can't do that. Are all the Second Levelers okay? Are any of our people dead?"

Now Fenlocki wanted to punch the guy. He restrained himself. "There are lots of raping people dead on *both* sides, Mr. Chancellor. This is a war we have going on here, in case you haven't noticed."

"Well, get the dirty plurites out of the buildings. Get them out and exterminate them. You hear me? This is unacceptable."

Again Fenlocki felt he was talking to a thick pupil. "The machines can't go into the buildings, sir. They are for the streets. That's why you're here. We need *people* to fight this now. Officers and hosts. The hosts are ready. Are you?"

"I don't know why someone else can't—"

"Because, my friend," Fenlocki interrupted, *"you're* the Chancellor. It's your job."

"All right, all right," Gavy said, shifting the lock of hair yet again. He looked absolutely furious. Fenlocki almost felt the man would strangle him with his bare hands any second if he got the chance. It was pretty obvious both men felt like killing each other. Neither moved for a moment.

Gavy took a deep breath and seemed to compose himself just a little, quashing his rage some. "Where's the donor room again?" he asked huskily.

Fenlocki signaled to one of his technicians and the entire far wall of the control room slid quickly upward. Behind it was a plasglass-enclosed chamber equipped with a plush donor chair and hosting device right in the center. "Right here, sir."

Gavy started for the chamber. His face was still red with fury. In fact, his entire bald head was pink.

Fenlocki grabbed his boss's shoulder as he passed. He released his grip almost instantly, realizing he may have overstepped his bounds. "Take it easy with the hosts, Zephy," he said quietly. "Just take it easy, okay? They're people too, not just expendable weapons."

Gavy spun around. His bedlock whipped out and slapped into the side of Fenlocki's face. *"Every* raping plurite is expendable, you bolehole. You said yourself this is war, here."

Fenlocki fished for another sunbean. "Misser Chancellor, I *myself* happen to be a plurite."

Gavy's eyes blazed. "I know, you subspawn. Why do you think we let you have this job? Anything goes wrong, we're all out of here on Floobie-pods in a Jersey minute, you bolehole. You get to stay here and take the heat. Your whole *job* is designed to be expendable, catbreath. Didn't you ever figure it out?"

Then he turned and climbed into the donor chamber.

And Fenlocki shoved a whole bunch of sunbeans into his dry mouth. It wasn't that he was no longer nauseous, it was that— quite suddenly—he *wanted* to throw up. Real bad.

It felt like somebody had just confused things by taking his job and his precious rule book and throwing them out the window. He didn't know what to do. He no longer knew where he stood.

Rape, what a mess.

He needed to get his head together. He just had to get a grip on himself and he'd be fine. Everything would be fine. Gavy was just angry. Gavy was just a bolehole.

"Take over, Leeta. I need some air. I need a break," Fenlocki said, stepping into the hall. "Back in a minute."

CHAPTER 44

It took Alysess a long time to get into the battle togs. Fortunately there were none of those black machines nearby at the moment. If there had been, she'd surely have been blown to pieces as she tried to wriggle into the silver outfit and squeeze on the tight nonslip boots.

She'd had trouble figuring out how to get the clothes off the dead woman in the first place, and then she had trouble figuring out how to get them on herself in the second place. After pawing through the piles of corpses, she'd found one close to her size who wasn't too messed up. The woman had apparently died from a nerve bolt, because there were only two slug holes in the suit—not fatal wounds. One was in the left arm and one in the upper chest, but neither was near anything too important. A nerve bolt must've gotten in to her through the holes before they'd sealed. There wasn't that much blood inside the strange ensemble, and what there was had already dried up nicely.

When the doctor finally got the heavy outfit on, she was totally confused. The helmet had a complicated, ever-changing readout display of some kind projected right on the visor. It took up the entire lower left-hand corner of her vision, and Alysess couldn't make any sense out of it. There were tongue tabs in front of her chin, but she had no idea what they did or exactly how to operate them.

She figured the suit would still help, though. The automedipak feature had apparently sealed the bullet holes tight enough so the thing was still airtight. It was damned cold inside it, so Alysess knew its body-heat-masking layers were still operating. And, what the subs, if she got shot—which was pretty damned likely—at least she was in an outfit that would sterilize the wound, seal it up, and administer local anesthetics. Hey, that way she might not die in pain. Great news. Damn suits were good for something.

Alysess realized she wasn't being very careful. She looked around again, glad to see there still weren't any big black hunks of metal bearing down on her. The ones in this area were apparently well occupied elsewhere.

She looked at all the weapons lying around. There were chip guns and chip rifles, nerve guns and nerve rifles, I-bazookas, gas canisters, mini I-grenades, scrambler rifles . . . quite an assortment. She leaned over to pick up a few, sticking out her tongue from the strain of the heavy tanks on her back. She hit an upper tab.

Suddenly the helmet was filled with static noise. A bright green message lit up on the visor: AUD. MONITOR MODE. Then Alysess heard voices through the helmet's speakers.

"Tavis?"

"Ragman? That you? Tavis thought you were dead! Tavis couldn't get you. Tavis was worried."

"I *was* dead. Twice."

"Ha!"

"Listen, Tavis, make an announcement to any Revy you can get on your speaker. Anyone left alive. I've reached some already myself, and some may be listening now. But I want you to try to contact them personally. I've made a change in the battle plan. Split up. Stay inside the buildings as much as possible. Go through back doors, gardens, alleys, whatever. Stay off the streets as much as you can."

"Do we get to kill the people we find inside?"

"Whatever you want. Guerrilla fighting is all we have now. Point is, have everyone split up and head toward midtown. Somewhere in the mid-thirties between Third and Seventh. The machines have all come from that direction. The command center has to be there. If we can't get to it and shut down the machines, we're raped. Understand?"

"Ragman! Ragman! I shut one down myself! Tavis did! All by myself!"

"How?"

"Shot up at it, I did. Shot up into the place where its head meets its neck. Killed it good!"

"Okay, good, Tavis. Tell the others. But remember what I said about the plan."

"Tavis is a *good* soldier."

"Yeah, bye."

And then there was static for a while. And then Alysess heard Tavis talking individually to some other suited Revies. The conversations were rather garbled and mostly full of Tavis's self-praise and giggles. Alysess stuck her tongue out and played with the upper tabs until her readout said NORM MODE and the sound went off.

She bent over to look at the guns again when Tavis's voice came back, very loud this time.

"Zeppella? You still alive? This is Tavis here, calling you. Zeppella? Yoo-hoo! You dead now?"

Alysess ignored the voice. Zeppella *was* dead. She'd scraped the woman out of this very suit herself. And Alysess wasn't about to answer Tavis. She had quit Revy long ago. She didn't want to have anything to do with it. She just wanted to get to Noonie. And Watly.

Alysess played with the top row of tongue tabs again, trying to remember the first one she'd pressed. She realized monitoring the Revies' conversations could come in handy. Finally she got the visor to read AUD. MONITOR MODE again. There was a whole pile of overlapping conversations going on in her speakers now. It was kind of comforting. Made her feel less alone.

Anyway, it was better than listening to the continuous drone of really bad music that was playing all over the place.

She looked around. Still no machines after her. So far, so good. She had a suit, she had a way to listen to what was going on, and now all she needed were some armaments.

Alysess picked up a chip pistol and a few small I-grenades, snapping the gun and the grenades to her belt. Then she raised up one of the scrambler rifles. An idea was forming slowly.

She'd seen two faces in the upper windows of a building when she'd first come out. And she'd heard an announcement later telling Second Levelers to stay indoors, on their upper floors. *The upper floors.* Why didn't the fighting machines shoot at the buildings? Why didn't they shoot the movement and heat they sensed in the upper floors?

Maybe because they were designed not to. Maybe the gun turrets only shot up to a certain level and no higher. Maybe anything up too high was out of range. It made sense. They wouldn't want those black things to start blasting all the Second Levelers hiding in the buildings above. Maybe the machines were programmed to attack only at street level. Only anything outdoors.

Alysess shouldered the scrambler rifle. She had an idea how she could use it. It wasn't the use it was intended for, but it might work anyway. If the thing's wires were strong enough to hold her weight.

She walked over to the closest tall building on the south side of Seventy-seventh, tried the door, and, finding it locked, blew it open with her newly acquired chip pistol.

CHAPTER 45

Tavis was having a little trouble walking, but IT was still having fun. The suit had kicked in nicely. Aside from the local anesthetics, it was obviously pumping something rather happy into ITs whole system. Something a little goofy and a lot energizing. A euphoric or something. Fun. Ha.

Now both of the slug wounds were completely numb. The whole leg, in fact, was completely numb. But the leg wasn't working all that well. Not—as the Ragman might say—fully functional. The limb didn't hurt a bit, but it didn't move quite right and felt kind of wobbly and loose. Tavis had some trouble balancing on it. It was a little like trying to stand on someone else's leg—someone who had had their joints replaced with thick gelatin.

But Tavis was still making pretty good time. IT had been moving at a steady pace, building to building. IT had a rhythm going. It was developing a lovely ritual. Look out of a first- or second-story window for a machine, size up the street, and—when it looked clear—jump out a door, limp quickly to another building, shoot *that* door open, and dive dramatically inside.

Then—if there were people inside—have some real good fun before moving on. Ha.

In some ways it was a dream come true. There were so very many opportunities for fun here, and carte blanche for having it. Sometimes it was just simple fun: surprise the occupants and kill them gracefully. But sometimes people would be waiting, hiding. They'd have weapons and would want to fight back. Tavis liked that best. Those times, a rush of Tavis Excitement Juice would flow all through IT, mixing with whatever happy stuff the suit was gifting. And Tavis would feel superhuman. And Tavis would kill good. The kills were all a bit quick to be as funly lingering as Tavis would've liked, but they were still good kills. Tavis learned killing could be a real pleasure even if it wasn't slow and artistic. Killing quick and elegantly—in vast numbers—could be an art in itself. Different, but fun.

Tavis was invincible. Tavis was a killing machine ITself. Better than the big black ones. Nothing could hurt IT. Nothing could stop IT. Trembling people in designer clothing would jump out at IT from behind couches or CVs or huge wooden desks. Women, men, children. Perfectly quaffed, squeaky-clean people. Pale people. Dark people. All rich and pampered and soft-looking. All scared bad. They'd have fancy guns in their twitching Second Level fingers. Their timid little eyes would show fear. Great, fun fear. And Tavis would take those eyes out before they even knew what hit them. They were no good at killing, these soft ones. They were soft to the core. And Tavis would bring that softness right out of them. IT'd open them up and bring that softness into the light. Touch it. Play with it. Explore it. Run ITs gloved fingers through it. Throw it around the room. They all had it inside them. None of them had anything different. No matter who Tavis killed, the insides of them always looked the same. It was fun, but it was also a little frustrating. Somewhere, someone was special. Somewhere, someone had something different inside. But until Tavis found that someone, IT was quite happy being a superhuman killing machine. Tavis was the best. Tavis was untouchable.

Tavis would live forever. The machines couldn't kill IT. The soft ones couldn't kill IT. Nothing could kill IT.

Nothing could even phase it. Tavis was on top of the situation. Tavis was a hero. Tavis never got confused, never got discombobulated. Never noncombobulated. Never anticombobulated.

Never excombobulated. Tavis was the most combobulated person in existence.

IT dashed out from another door, angled across Thirty-second Street, and exploded ITs way into another building. After another quick kill full of red, dripping fun, IT crossed through the house to a small back door. Then IT cut across a four-cruiser garage, a lush garden, and a small alley, finally entering another building. This structure, some kind of office, yielded no fun at all. Tavis passed through to the front room, admiring some pretty nifty furniture on the way, knocking some of it over to see how it broke. IT cautiously checked the situation on Thirty-third Street through a large picture window.

Through the lilac-tinted glass Tavis saw two figures in the distance at the corner of Thirty-third and Ninth. They stood by a hovering cruiser. They weren't Revies. They weren't layfighters. They were obviously Second Levelers. They had no protective clothing. No suits, no helmets, no shielding at all.

In fact, one of them was wearing a silly Chancellor Dancer outfit.

Ha, Tavis thought. *Fun to be had.*

CHAPTER 46

Watly needed to live. It was important. It was, in fact, a priority. She had to find her daughter. She had to save her child.

Roullic stepped a little closer. His red hair blazed in the long shaft of orange sunlight that streamed between two buildings. He raised the chip pistol up so it was pointed right where the front echo of Watly's last headache was strongest.

Rape of a way to cure a headache, Watly thought.

"Goodbye, Sentiva," Roullic said, his perfect, surgically augmented lips grinning with obvious relish. Then he chuckled. "I'm about to become a hero. And you're about to meet Cooda, Mam."

"Cruda," Watly corrected habitually.

"Whatever."

Then Roullic stretched out his arm and prepared to fire at Watly's grease-smeared forehead.

"You're a very attractive man, Roullic," Watly said calmly. She was amazed how well modulated her voice was, considering the brutal pounding of her heart.

"Thanks. I know," Roullic said, sounding quite serious. "Isn't it nice I'll be the last thing you ever see? No better way to die, I think."

"You're gonna miss out if you kill me right away, Roullic."

Roullic's grinning lips stretched up a little farther. "I'm rather enjoying killing you, Sentiva. I'm not going to miss anything at all."

"You're going to miss"—Watly tilted her head back proudly—"the best fuck you ever had."

Roullic laughed heartily. His free hand went up to pull on his left eyebrow. He stroked it lovingly between little tugs of the hair. "What a shame," he said when the laughter finally broke off.

"Don't you want to have sex with me before you kill me, Roullic? You're so good-looking. A god, really. Divine. I would worship you. Worship every part of you. And Roullic"—Watly smiled just a little—"I *am* the best. What have you got to lose? I promise you won't regret it."

Roullic's face cringed in disgust. "I *know* you," he said, as if that fully explained his sour expression. He pressed the barrel into Watly's forehead so that it touched the dirty skin lightly.

Watly tried to think. *He knows me? What does that mean? Knows me?* The barrel felt cold and hard.

"No, you don't, Roullic," Watly said quickly. "You don't know me. I'm a stranger. I'm a Chancellor Dancer. A beautiful young dancer. A redhead, just like you. We've never met."

Roullic's pale yellow eyes flashed down for a second in what Watly recognized as the traditional male breast-assessment glance. *I have him!* she thought. *He likes the game.*

"You're Sentiva. I know you," he said, squinting skeptically at her face.

"I'm not Sentiva. I'm a beautiful stranger who wants nothing more than to pleasure you before she dies. Then dying would be okay."

Watly detected a twitch in Roullic's enormous pants bulge. The thing was moving a little, growing.

"A stranger?" he asked, as if trying to convince himself of her part in the little fantasy. "A stranger. A Chancellor Dancer with a blowjobby mouth. . . ."

"Yes. A blowjobby mouth. That's exactly what I have. Everybody always says that. And I give the best blowjobs on earth. Is that what you want, Misser? A blowjob?"

Roullic's eyes looked just a touch glazed. He stared at Watly's lips. "I'm going to kill you right after," he said coldly.

"I'll die happy with your come in my mouth, Misser," Watly said, trying to sound convincingly horny. She smiled just a little and then stopped, letting her expression go blank. Then she tilted her head down a bit—feeling the gun barrel follow it—and looked seductively up through her long eyelashes. She ran the tip of her tongue over the bulge of her lower lip.

The country still rang with that constant piped-in piellna music, sweeping along the streets with obnoxious serenity. Watly tried to sway her hips softly to the beat, wondering if that action came off as sexy or just plain stupid-looking.

Roullic moved the gun so it was pressing firmly into Watly's left temple. "What's your name, stranger?" he asked.

"Aribalitten," Watly said without a moment's thought. She turned up just one side of her mouth, trying to half smile as sensuously as she was able. She very slowly lowered herself to her knees, being careful not to make any abrupt movements that might encourage a squeeze on the gun's trigger. Her right knee popped loudly before hitting the curb. But Roullic didn't fire. He was staring at Watly's mouth, which was now level with his crotch.

"You like the way I look?" Roullic asked, his breathing sounding heavier.

"I think," Watly said, staring up at him, "that you're the most handsome man I've ever seen. I think you're the most beautiful, attractive, charismatic, masculine, sexy creature in the entire world. You *are* a god!" She reached over and started undoing the twist-clips that held Roullic's purple veneer pants closed. The gun barrel was still firm against her head. If anything, it was pressing even harder into the skin of her temple.

"You like my cock, stranger?" Roullic whispered as the thing sprang free and wobbled comically in the evening air.

It was enormous, full of thick veins and crisscrossed with tiny pale surgery scars all around the base and the glans.

"It's enormous," Watly said, not having to lie about that. Then she took a breath and widened her eyes as far as she could. She wanted to look hypnotized, intoxicated by the man's bobbing penis. "It's the most beautiful, big dick that ever existed. It is the quintessential cock. It makes all other cocks that exist or ever did exist obsolete. It is the future of penis-hood. It is tomorrow's cock. It is, without a doubt, the most beautiful tool of manhood in the entire cosmos."

The thing twitched and swelled even further, then rose up and down in a little dance of excited sphincter-muscle squeezing.

"Cosmic cock," Watly murmured with adoration. She touched its stiffness gently. "Cock of the gods." She stroked it softly with both hands, feeling it throb under her fingertips. She saw a little glimmer of pre-come ooze out of the hole on the top. The gun hadn't moved, but Watly could now feel it shaking just a little against her head. Roullic's gun hand was trembling slightly. *Good.*

"Want me to taste you, stranger man?" Watly asked, lowering her voice so it came out husky and breathy. "Want me to put my lips on you?"

"Yes." Roullic's voice came out in a sigh.

Watly had no idea how the hell she was going to get much of it into her mouth. Damn thing was real big. A purple and red stump of flesh that must've been a foot and a half long. Best that money could buy. . . .

"Suck on me." Roullic was moaning.

Sure thing. Watly had no problem with the concept. At this point she'd suck on a small bus if she thought it would save her life. The sucking was nothing to her; it might even be an interesting experience in the end. Trying to blow him didn't disturb her. What *did* disturb her was what she needed to do as soon as the chance came.

As soon as the gun barrel moved enough one way or the other—*if* it ever moved enough—she'd have to do it. Even if the chip pistol only tilted sideways a little—so that she'd get a badly grazed skull if it fired—she'd still do it. She had to.

And it was hard to think about. Maybe even harder, having been a man once. Remembering what it was like to have a penis. Remembering that sensitive, vulnerable piece of self that used to dangle below and fill with blood and aching pressure.

That personal memory made the idea all the more disturbing. Squeezing his balls wasn't such an uncomfortable concept. If the gun moved enough, she would mash the balls with both hands, crushing them with all her might as if she were trying to break solid metal ball-bearings. But that didn't seem so bad. The bad part was the other thing.

When the gun moved, she'd do both things at once. No choice. It was a one-shot deal. She would just close her eyes and do it. Close her eyes and do the ball-mashing thing, yes. But also bite. She'd bite down as hard as she possibly could. She'd clamp and squeeze her powerful jaw muscles as if she were ripping off a particularly tough piece of stale hardloaf.

And that was a disturbing thought. Yet not nearly as disturbing as the realization that she was desperate . . . and that she was actually quite capable of biting off the end of this man's penis if she got the chance.

CHAPTER 47

Alysess caught a great lump of air in her throat.

> *"When I'm down I write to my poovus.*
> *I write to my poovus every day.*
> *When I'm low I write to my poovus.*
> *I write to my poovus and I feel okay. . . ."*

The floating speakers were playing the poovus song. The Watly and Aly song. *Their* song. Some insipid keyboard-created vocalist was droning the lyrics out in roughly the same key as the vapid, uninspired piellna accompaniment. Still, it got to Alysess. They were playing the Watly and Aly song.

Alysess belched out the lump of air and brushed her hand across her eyes roughly. She went back to finishing putting the battle togs back on. She'd taken them partially off in order to remove her bra. She fished in her small doctor bag for Soft pills.

She'd had some Soft pill withdrawal fidgets on her way up the stairs to this roof. If she let them go, they'd just get worse. This was no time to try to kick the drug habit. She popped three in her mouth before sticking the pill bottle in one of her belt loops, putting her helmet back on, and sealing the suit all the way. Then she scanned her surroundings again, waiting for the pills to start working.

She was on the roof of the Seventy-seventh Street building. No one alive had been inside the building itself, or at least if they *were* alive they were hiding. Either way, she'd had no trouble reaching the roof. It had been a pretty exhausting climb up, though. By the end, her hands had started vibrating rapidly and her stomach had begun cramping up—both typical withdrawal symptoms.

But she'd made it. From this forty-story vantage she could see half the country spread out below her. The sun was setting. Shadows deepened and lengthened. At this distance, everything seemed small and unimportant down there. The formerly perfect whitetop of the avenues was now potted and cratered. Little dark lumps were scattered about the streets everywhere—probably bodies. Some were definitely bodies. Alysess could make out tiny arms and tiny legs on some of them, splayed out and twisted at funny angles. The black machines, now looking small and harmless, roamed up and down—about one for every five or six blocks in this area, it seemed. Coppers and cruisers burned on every street. Smoke drifted back and forth, puffed away by the slight breeze when it rose above the first few stories. A few times, Alysess saw some Second Levelers trying to shoot down from their homes at the Revies on the street. They didn't appear very good at it. If they hit anyone, it seemed to be totally by accident.

Every few seconds, Alysess could see small figures dashing from one building to the next. A fighting machine would turn a corner and, somewhere behind it, creatures would scamper about in the shadows. Most were alone, some in little groups. About half were silver and half not. All were headed downtown—toward the gleaming Empire State Buildings.

The twin buildings were still well lit in the golden glow of the sunset, their windows reflecting like bright jewels. *I'll bet it's somewhere next to or inside one of them,* Alysess thought. *The command center.*

The poovus song stopped and another tune started instantly. Even under the constant speaker music, the sound of the gunshots below was still obvious. Some of the scrambling revolutionary insects were still getting caught by the machines, being cut down as they tried to make it to a safe doorway. Their deaths looked surreal from up on the rooftop—like little stylized ballets. The gunshots sounded very gentle and mild—click . . . click . . .

click . . . click . . . click—almost like a finger softly snapping.

Alysess looked at the other nearby buildings. She was high enough to see most of their roofs. On some of them, she could see Second Levelers frantically scrambling into rooftop Floobie-pods. She didn't blame them. If she could, *she'd* get the rape out of the country too.

She watched whole families climb into some of the tiny pods, squeezing themselves in and exhaling so they could get the lid closed. Then the pod would rise straight up slowly. It would hover high for a moment, juicing up and cutting a vacuum channel in the air, and then it would be gone in a second. Most Floobied west. These standard one-shot deals were probably all programmed for Jersey. Straight Manhattan/Shorthills routes. Probably the only kind of international deal a midlevel Second Leveler would cut, Alysess figured. The filthy rich but not the obscenely rich.

A few blocks to the south, one Floobie was juicing about three hundred feet above its pad when the thing exploded. One instant, enormous fireball . . . and then nothing. Alysess glanced around, finally catching sight of a Revy hanging out of a third-floor window with a cycling-down I-bazooka in his hands. He was smiling at the place where the pod had been. It seemed that some of the Revies had started noticing the migration of pods. They'd caught on to the movement above. And apparently the Revies had decided to cut some of the rich and frightened pod owners' trips short. It probably gave those revolutionaries who were pinned in position by the fighting machines something to do with their time. While they waited for the street to clear of black monsters, they could take potshots at escaping upperfolk.

Another Floobie exploded just as the thing rose a few feet up off its pad.

Alysess felt the Soft pills beginning to work. She was more relaxed and steady now. Softed nicely. Jitters gone. She set up the scrambler gun's tripod near the edge of the roof, saving the wire-supply box but tossing aside the actual scrambler and its ringlet-rimmed casing. She wasn't interested in scrambling anything.

She squinted into the oval eyepiece, sighting a rooftop about five blocks downtown, scanning it until she happened on a likely target. *There*. The top of an exhaust tube, ringed with golden ridges. Soft metal.

Alysess checked the charged projectile grapple-blades, verified her aim, and then fired. The rifle made a *pop* sound and recoiled slightly as the projectile and wire shot out. She looked through the sight again, seeing the teeth biting deep into the metal of that faraway exhaust tube. She smiled to herself. Good shot.

The thin wire was taut already, stretching all the way from the side of the long gun barrel to that rooftop five blocks downtown. Alysess plucked the wire gently and heard a deep, metallic note resonate through it.

Her helmet speaker was suddenly alive with sound again.

"Ragman! *Ragman!*"

"Who is it?" The Ragman's voice sounded strained and preoccupied to Alysess.

"It's Flahv! I'm down the street from Empire Two! It's got to be it! I just saw Tavis's blinded fighter go into its base!"

"Good going, my child."

"But Ragman—the place has got the biggest nerve cannons you ever—" And then there was a horrible scream of agony that echoed excruciatingly through Alysess's helmet.

She stuck her tongue at the tabs, silencing the pained shriek instantly. It didn't bother her so much, that piercing death bellow. The volume of it had bothered her more than the idea of it. She was way too relaxed from the first big wave of calm from the Soft pills. She really didn't care too much that she'd just heard some poor slob fry from a nerve cannon. What she did care about was the information she'd just gotten. She'd been right. Right about the Empire State Buildings. The command center was in State Two.

She carefully unraveled the extra wire from the scrambler gun's ratchet hooks and then hit the weapon's cutter blade. The wire sprung free of the gun. It was hard to hold on to and kept trying to slide from her hands, pulling toward the span that stretched to the projectile teeth. Alysess stood up, wrestling with the wire, and turned to the raised door she had earlier used to gain access to the roof. She stretched the slippery, hair-thin wire upward. There was a ventilator node up near the top of the doorjamb. She tied the ridged wire to the node in a triple knot, trying to keep it as taut as possible all the while. When it seemed secure enough, she went back to the rifle, closed the tripod, packed up the wire kit, and slung the whole thing over her shoulder. She knew where she had to go and she knew how she was going to try to get there.

Her off-white brassiere and her medipak were lying on the blue gravel that covered the roof's surface. Alysess left the bag alone.

She needed to travel light now. Or at least as light as possible. She picked up the bra. It was the best she could do, the best she could think of. And all she could think of was the best she could think of.

She slung the bra over the wire above her head. It was an old bra, but it was of tight-weave plasilk—very tough stuff—and it should hold together pretty well under a lot of stress. She wasn't so sure the *wire* would hold together.

Alysess looped the right shoulder strap of the thing twice around her right wrist, gripping the bra cup in her fist. Then she fumbled a while with her left hand, trying to do the same thing on that side. She managed eventually.

She was ready. There she was, strapped to her bra, which was slung over a slim wire that stretched down to a distant building blocks and blocks away. And actually, with the help of the Soft pills, she was feeling just fine. Just fine.

"I am one raping crazy woman," Alysess said out loud. Then she pushed off the edge of the building.

CHAPTER 48

The door opened, making huge waves in the floating dust flecks, upsetting the gentle ebb and flow. Noonie looked up to see Fenlocki trudging into the interrogation room. He closed the door behind him.

"How goes it, kid? Sorry to leave you here like this. Don't know where else to put you. You drawing?"

"What's going on?" Noonie asked.

Fenlocki sat on the far side of the old wooden table that she was leaning against. She was on the one other chair in the room, sitting up on her knees and rocking from side to side. Her elbows were on the table, her hands on her chin.

The chief looked very tired and kind of sad around the lips and eyes. With one long index finger, he leisurely traced a weathered grain of wood that ran across the tabletop.

"People dying. War. It's a mess."

"Where's my mom?" Noonie asked, squeezing her face with her palms.

"I don't know, kid." He sighed heavily and looked straight into Noonie's eyes. His expression was open and honest-looking. "She's probably dead."

Noonie considered the sad-looking man for a while before responding. There were little dark smudges under his eyes. He looked like he needed a shave; a thin, scratchy-looking forest of tiny gray stumps had cropped up on his chin and cheeks, seemingly just in the last few hours.

"She's not dead," Noonie said eventually. She picked up the click-pen and looked down at it.

Fenlocki rubbed his stubbly face slowly with one hand, side to side. "You hungry, kid?"

"No."

"You want to answer some questions?"

"No."

"I need your help, Noonie. We have to stop this. I need to know everything you know. Maybe you can help end all this killing."

"How's my answering questions going to end killing?" She twirled the pen on the tabletop so it spun a few times. Then she picked it up again, gripping it in her small fist.

Fenlocki leaned back and put one large leg up on the edge of the table. His boot looked very big to Noonie. It was shiny and thick and went clear up to the man's knee. The foot inside seemed like it must've been longer than two of hers put together. The foot of a giant.

"I don't know," the chief said. He looked like he could use a nap. "I don't know. . . . Maybe you can tell me who's in charge. Something about their plans. How many people they have, what exactly they want. Why they're doing it this way. Things like that."

"I don't know stuff like that. I don't know any stuff that will help stop it."

Fenlocki reached over and touched Noonie's right wrist. She jumped, almost dropping the click-pen. Her hand tensed and tightened around the pen's shaft.

"You don't know that," he said softly. "You don't know *what* you know. You're Watly Caiper's daughter, and she's a big part of this. You know a lot. I need to know everything you know." He gripped Noonie's wrist a little firmer, raising his eyebrows in the middle so they made a little inverted V. He seemed pained. "I need to try to stop this killing somehow. It's real bad, kid. Maybe you can help me."

Without looking down at it, Noonie slowly twisted the click-pen around so it was pointed right at Fenlocki's face. "Is this the 'terrigation?" she asked, feeling pretty hinky suddenly. "Is this why I'm in a 'terrigation room?"

Fenlocki let go of her wrist and slumped back in the chair. "No, kid. I just need some help sorting this out." He reached into his pocket and pulled out a whole handful of sunbeans.

As the chief chewed, Noonie contemplated shooting him. Maybe if she killed him she could get out. But where would she go? How would she find her mommy? She kept the pen pointed at Fenlocki's lined features. The pinspots cast strong, sharp shadows, bringing out all the rough terrain of Fenlocki's forehead and cheeks. It was a strong, weathered face. A face that looked badly beaten right now. A face that looked sickened by all the violence.

Neither of them spoke for a while.

Noonie broke the silence. "Aren't you going to offer me one?"

He glanced over, looking a little surprised. "You *want* one now?"

She stuck out her free hand, palm up. "Gimme," she said, smiling.

Fenlocki poured a few from his hand to hers. "Not supposed to take sunbeans from a stranger—didn't your mama ever teach you that?"

"My mama's dead, you told me," Noonie said, balancing the little pile of 'beans on her palm.

"Dunno for sure, kid."

Noonie put down the pen so she could pick out the best-looking of the little speckled beans to try first. They were all pretty ugly, but she found one that was the least ugly of the bunch. She put it in her mouth. It was hard as a rock, super salty, and tasted like cat puke.

"You like?" Fenlocki asked, letting his right foot finally drop back down to the floor with a loud thump.

"Tastes yucky," Noonie whined, making her biggest yucky-food grimace and then spitting out the sunbean pieces. They stuck to the table in little moist clumps.

Fenlocki laughed. His eyes squeezed shut and he leaned back in the chair, laughing real hard. "Some plurite *you* are," he finally managed through his giggles.

Noonie was laughing too, still trying to pick any last pieces of bean off her tongue. It was good to laugh. It felt real spaf. She pushed the click-pen aside so it was away from her spit-up sunbean chunks. The pen rolled a bit and came to a rest against the edge of her sketch pad.

"So what do you want to know, already?" she asked abruptly.

Fenlocki stopped laughing and looked over at Noonie. His eyes seemed not so pained now. They seemed grateful.

"Everything," he whispered. "Everything."

CHAPTER 49

The Ragman hadn't felt well since he'd suit-died the second time. In spite of the coolness of his uniform, he was sweating excessively. It wasn't a hot, sticky sweat; it was a cold, clammy sweat. It was frustrating he couldn't get a hand to his face to wipe the stuff off. With the sealed suit on, there was nothing he could do when little rivers of greasy sweat ran down his forehead, gradually surmounted the obstacles of his eyebrows, and finally trickled into his eyes. The sweat stung, making his vision blurry and his eyes feel red and inflamed.

Right after the second death, he'd made it inside a nearby garb boutique and just sat in a corner under racks of expensive clothing for a while. His left arm hurt and his chest felt heavy and tight—like someone small was squatting in it.

Following a short rest and some brief helmet conversations, the Ragman started up again. He had to keep moving, keep heading for the goal. The news from Tavis about disabling one fighting machine had not encouraged the Ragman. From Tavis's description of how it was done, it did not seem very repeatable. One would have to get close enough to shoot upward at the machine's sensor pod without getting shot oneself. One would have to, basically, get right up on *top* of the thing like Tavis had. That was not an easy thing to do. Pretty raping impossible, actually. No, they would have to find a way to get to the command center and shut all the fighters down. It was the only answer.

Though it was hard for the Ragman to admit it even to himself, he knew if they couldn't do that, they'd lose. It was as simple as that. If they couldn't shut down the fighters, there was no way the revolution could succeed. The machines would get them all in the end. The machines didn't get tired. The machines didn't get sloppy.

The Ragman worked his way slowly west and then turned south, toward State Two. He was on Sixth Avenue, being especially cautious. Reports had come in to his helmet speakers that the area near the Empire State Buildings was totally free of black machines. This was not necessarily good news. The Second Level wasn't stupid. There had to be reasons for the lack of machines.

The Ragman could think of two right off. Reason one: the command center was well protected by *other* means. This was undoubtedly true. The last few communications he'd gotten had told of large nerve cannons. And each of those communications had been abruptly cut off. There were surely other defensive weapons as well. Nobody was getting very close.

Reason two was also likely: the command center was defended—or was prepared to be defended at any moment—by *people*. Thinking beings who could notice more than movement and heat. Fallible in ways the machines weren't, but also perceptive and elusive and conniving in ways the machines could never be. People. That would explain the absence of fighters. The fighters weren't discriminating and would kill Second Level soldiers as readily as Revies. Maybe the streets near the center were clear of machines to give leeway to a whole raping army of humans.

The Ragman was pretty sure both these reasons were right. But they didn't daunt him. He kept moving, breathing heavily and trying to shake the sweat from his forehead by jerking his head side to side in the helmet. He wondered if he was dying. It was certainly a possibility. He didn't feel well at all.

He didn't want to die. He wasn't ready. He wasn't done with life yet. There were things to do. Things were not going so well, and he needed to be around to fix them. The revolution had to succeed. It was his dream. It was what he had worked for almost all his years.

Who would lead the revolution if he didn't?

And even if the revolution somehow succeeded without him, he would miss out. That was a scary thought. He didn't want to be gone when his dream came true. He felt like a child being told to go to bed early. He wanted to stay up, to keep awake, to be a part of life, to see what happened. He resisted death like a child resists bedtime: he simply didn't want to miss what happened after. He wanted to be around to see how things turned out. It was not his bedtime yet, dammit!

His heart pounded heavily as he crossed the avenue just below Forty-first Street and hid in the reception area of a posh office building for a moment. The building had no lights on and seemed empty. There was an array of large, abstract-shaped windows facing the avenue, and little clusters of uncomfortable-looking floatchairs were scattered about the central reception desk. The Ragman leaned into a serrated cemeld post near the door, watching the street.

He listened to his own breathing. In-out, in-out, in-out. His chest really hurt. And his left arm, all the way to the hand. He had the shakes now. Pretty bad.

He was scared. Really scared. He told himself to embrace the fear, to feel it fully, to accept it. But he didn't want to. He didn't give a rape about the fear. He just plain didn't want to die, fear or not.

Someone jumped out of the shadows behind the circular reception desk. It was a short man in a yellow business suit. The guy was wielding a small placene pistol. His legs were spread wide and both hands were gripping the gun. His eyes looked terrified. He fired. The slug bit explosively into the cemeld column just next to the Ragman.

The Ragman spun, dropping to his knees, and shot the man in the chest.

The businessman flew back into a group of floatchairs, his yellow suit opened into a bloody mess at the center. He was dead. No breathing, no twitching, no death rattles, no last gasps. No movement at all except for the gentle rocking of the floatchairs under him as they tried to adjust to his weight.

The Ragman stayed where he was, leaning forward on his hands and knees, his head bent down. He gasped for breath. There wasn't enough air in the suit. There wasn't enough air in the whole country. He needed more. His eyes stung bad and his heart seemed to be beating faster than humanly possible. His chest was fire. His left arm was pure pain.

"I don't want to die, terradammit!" he shouted. The sound of his own loud voice bounced around in his helmet, making it vibrate and hurting his ears.

He let his head drop all the way forward so the visor of the helmet rested on the carpet, supporting him some.

And then, for the first time since he was twelve years old, Ragman the Subkeeper began to cry.

CHAPTER 50

Watly Caiper sucked cock.

She wasn't all that sure how good she was at it, but she certainly tried her best. What she *was* sure of was that the damn gun was still pressed into her skull.

Her first cocksucking impression was that Roullic's penis smelled and tasted like rotting sunbeans. Bitter and salty and acidic and overripe and with a strong undercurrent of stale sweat. Something decaying about it. None too pleasant. It might not have been so bad if her activities didn't necessitate her breathing through her nose.

Her lips were getting sore and her neck was getting awful tired of playing fulcrum to her bobbing head. It was damn hard to keep her lips curled considerately over her teeth. That got uncomfortable fast. She tried to vary things some to give herself a rest and catch her breath. She'd stop the bobbing and sucking and try some licking and hand work. Roullic seemed to get impatient with that quickly, so she'd have to return to the more tiring techniques pretty fast. She tried to use the constant, obnoxious background music that flowed through the streets as a guide, bouncing her head in rhythm with the beat.

And the gun was still in place. Trembling and jerking a little, but still in place.

Watly tried pulling on the big, fleshy shaft while keeping her mouth busy on its top. It wasn't so easy. For one thing, it felt a little like patting her head and rubbing her stomach at the same time. She had trouble coordinating her movements. For another, her arms just weren't trained properly.

She remembered how strong and practiced her old male self's right arm used to be. It was as if that masculine hand and wrist and forearm had formed just the right muscles for pole jerking from the years of solo workouts. But her newer, female limbs were not conditioned for this particular activity. She'd never had to make these kinds of rather strenuous repetitions in her whole time as a woman. She was way out of practice. Her arms felt clumsy and weak doing this. It was hard to get decent leverage.

And the damn gun was still there.

She didn't even try to take the big bulbous tip too deep. She knew she wouldn't be able to handle that. She hoped he would be satisfied with plenty of suction and movement, but no depth. Quality, not quantity.

The gun was still right there.

Roullic started gasping and making silly little "yip" noises from the back of his throat. He took his free hand and held the top of Watly's red-wigged head, pressing her closer. Her face was pushed farther onto the penis.

That she didn't like. She'd much rather die from a chip slug in the brain than by choking and gagging on some vain bolehole's oversized wonder-wiener. She resisted the forward push of Roullic's hand but continued all her motions. Her lips and mouth ached badly and her neck started cramping up from the extra pressure of fighting against his insistent pushing.

Move that raping gun! she thought to herself as she sucked.

Roullic moaned and groaned and started saying "Oh-yeah-oh-yeah-oh-yeah" and "Good stuff, sex-wise!" over and over in a little baby voice.

Watly was not looking forward to the inevitable spurt of Roullic-Neets-juice hitting the back of her throat. She could think of many more pleasant things. She imagined the semen would probably taste like decaying sunbeans too—only more so. Rotting sunbeans pulverized into liquid form. Lovely.

"*Oh*, yeah!"

The guy seemed real close to coming, and, quite frankly, Watly would've much preferred being on the other side of the country right now.

"Yeah-yeah-yeah-yeah . . . !"

Yeah, yourself. Move the gun!

The gun was still there, pressing even harder into her temple. The plan wasn't working. The gun hadn't slipped once. And now Roullic was coming to orgasm. And Watly thought Roullic just might involuntarily squeeze the trigger as he came.

In fact, she was pretty damned sure he would.

CHAPTER 51

Alysess was flying.

She was sliding faster and faster, the wind whipping at her silver uniform. She tried not to look down. She couldn't help it. Her feet dangled below her as the buildings sped past; her toes angled inward in an almost comical pigeon-toed point. The streets were a shadowy blur below her. She was way up, higher than she had expected. There was nothing but air between her and the offices and houses that zipped by down there. A Floobie-pod flashed right past her, almost scaring her into letting go of the bra. Everything was moving so fast all around her.

She felt her stomach rising up into her throat and her lower back begin to tickle and arch uncomfortably. This didn't feel so good.

The wire bowed down drastically under her weight, making her wonder if it would hold. It pulled down into a sharp curve at whatever given point of it she moved along. She thought maybe she should have tried for a shorter trip, at least to start. That might've been a good idea. Five full blocks was an awfully long span for one thin, ridged wire. One thin, ridged wire that was designed to carry a scrambling current, not a person.

The building Alysess was nearing grew larger and larger. She could see the twinkling metal of the tiny-looking exhaust tube she was heading straight for.

It felt as if she were sliding down way too fast, and the speed was increasing all the time.

How come I didn't think about how I was going to stop *before I embarked on this particular journey?* she wondered.

Alysess stared at the exhaust tube as she approached, realizing it was going to be a damned hard landing. It just might kill her. She hadn't counted on the speed. The slope between the two buildings she'd chosen was way too great. The angle of the line was just too extreme. She was a raping torpedo, shooting down from one building to another, accelerating with every inch. And if she didn't think of something fast, this torpedo was going to break some serious parts of herself on impact.

She was over halfway there now, flying across the orange skyline, gripping tight to her bra cups and trying desperately to figure a way to slow down.

Alysess could still hear the soft piellna music coming from all directions through the country-wide speakers as she sped down the wire. It flowed out ironically slow and calm in contrast to her fast and precarious journey.

As she grew nearer, the exhaust tube looked larger and more substantial. And damned hard. Neck-breaking hard.

CHAPTER 52

Noonie told Fenlocki everything.

She started by telling him all she knew about before she was born. She told him the stories her mom had told her. She told of how her mommy had been a man, a he-person. And how this he-person went hosting to make money and how one day Sentiva took over his body. And then Sentiva used the body to make sex with her own body—really weird, that—impregnating herself. And then Sentiva killed some important someone while still in the he-Watly body, so everyone blamed the he-Watly. And Watly tried to clear his name by turning the tables and taking over Sentiva's body, but Fenlocki killed Watly's real body right in the middle of it . . . or something like that. So anyway, then Watly was a she and pregnant with Noonie.

"Do you believe this stuff?" Noonie asked.

The chief smiled warmly. "I might be starting to."

And then Noonie went on. She told Chief Fenlocki about growing up. The stories her mom had told her over the years about the subs and the Subkeeper and the revolution. She told him about her self-defense training. About her constant makeup applications and hair-straightening treatments. About her mom's goal and dreams for a fair, peaceful, and just country. About how her mom had wanted to revolt without violence. She told him about her Aunt Alysess and how the doctor would carry information down to the Subkeeper for Mom. And about how the Night Lady had started pushing out of mommy lately.

And she told him, somewhat reluctantly, about how hard it was. How she had to pretend all the time. How she had no real friends. How she had to hide from everyone. How her whole life is a big secret, just like her secret name.

She didn't tell him the Big Secret. The Isthmus secret. The secret of two years ago. The scar-on-her-shoulder-and-arm secret. She didn't tell him anything of that, but then, she rarely told herself anything of that. It was almost as if that Big Secret—the biggest of all—was also a secret from Noonie herself. So, in her mind, she told him everything. Absolutely everything.

She told it all without emotion, feeling nothing inside. No sadness, no emptiness, no longing, no loneliness. Nothing.

"Sometimes," she said, staring up at the pinspots, "sometimes I don't even know who my mommy is." She swallowed and spoke very quietly. "Sometimes I don't even know who *I* am." Still she felt nothing.

Fenlocki looked at her for a while, waiting for her to continue. When she didn't, he pushed his chair back and stood up. "I'll be right back," he said softly, and went to the door.

While he was gone, Noonie just sat and kept looking at the pinspots. She'd stare at the lights themselves and then follow the beams they cast down with her eyes until she reached the little pools of brightness on the floor.

She thought maybe none of this—none of all the personal stuff she'd just said—meant anything to her anymore. She felt nothing from it. It was all old history. Musty news.

Fenlocki walked back in, carrying something dark in his hand. He crossed over to where Noonie was sitting and knelt before her. His eyes were full of kindness and compassion. His expression seemed to alternate from questioning to sad sympathy.

What do you feel sympathy for, Mr. Chief? It can't be me. I feel nothing.

Noonie looked down to see what Fenlocki had in his hand. It was some kind of dark blue cloth. The size of a hand towel. It was wet with some liquid, soaked in something that smelled a little like perfume, a little like medicine.

"What's that?" Noonie asked.

Fenlocki didn't answer. He just looked straight into her eyes and slowly raised the cloth toward her. Noonie pulled back in her seat. Fenlocki stopped, holding the cloth where it was—about a foot from Noonie's face.

"Trust me," he whispered.

Noonie looked at his eyes. She slowly relaxed. She let him bend toward her with the cloth. He pulled the edge of it up through his fingers, making a soft lump of wet blue fabric.

Then he touched her with it.

Her forehead. Her cheeks. Her chin. He rubbed the cloth on her face. He was gentle and loving, slowly cleaning her whole face with the wet fabric. Her ears, her nose, her closed eyelids, her temples, her neck, and then her hands. Every time he pulled the cloth away to turn it, the dark blue was covered with more light flesh tone. The makeup was coming off.

When he was done, Fenlocki tossed the cloth on the table and picked up both of Noonie's hands in his. He was still kneeling before her. "Now you can know who you are, kid," he whispered. "You're Noonie Caiper. Just plain old you. Nothing wrong with that. Nothing wrong with who you are. You're just a great little kid. Nine and a half. Going on ten. You're Noonie. No secrets. No games. Just Noonie. I think that's fine."

And Noonie saw that he meant it. His eyes said he meant it.

She felt herself smoothly sliding into tears. There was no abrupt sobbing or sudden burst of weeping, just a gradual change. She went from feeling nothing to feeling something. Feeling a lot.

Fenlocki pulled her tenderly toward him. "Ca'mere, you," he said. And then he hugged her. And Noonie cried in his arms.

"Everything will be okay," he murmured to her. "Everything will be just fine."

"I want my mommy," Noonie cried, hugging the chief tight and feeling him stroke her hair.

"I know, kid. I know. I'm sorry."

CHAPTER 53

Roullic shuddered in a pre-orgasmic spasm of pleasure. He was real near. Watly braced herself for the feel of a slug exploding her frontal lobes and for the feel of slimy goo squirting into her mouth. She wasn't sure which she would feel first.

"Yeah!" Roullic cried again, shaking all over.

And then Watly heard a strange, metallic-sounding amplified voice coming from just to her left.

"It's *job* sex, isn't it! Gross! A yicky, sticky, quicky! No good, that!"

Watly kept her mouth on the penis but stopped moving. She turned her head a little, still aware of the pistol's constant pressure. Roullic sighed in frustration. All Watly could see from the corner of her eye was something silver.

"If you shot her up a little bit with that gun first and *then* did some of that," the voice continued, "it'd be okay, maybe."

Roullic turned angrily toward the noise. "Who the rape are you?"

"Who the rape are *you*?" the voice singsonged back. Then it giggled noisily.

"I'd get out of here if I wanted to remain alive, existence-wise!" Roullic said angrily. He kept the pistol pressed into Watly's head. His dick throbbed a little in her mouth, obviously wanting her to start moving again and finish what she'd started. Watly kept her head still but gently placed one hand on each of Roullic's testicles.

"Hey," the strange voice said, still giggling. "No need to get cranky-hinky-quirky! I'm just watching. I'm just trying to give a little advice on how to have an *evening*!"

Roullic's whole body seemed to stiffen. He froze. Watly thought maybe he'd stopped breathing altogether. *"You!"* he gasped. "You're the one who raping cut my eyes out!"

"Sound's like me, indeed," the voice said. "Tavis cuts good. Ha!"

Watly's mind whirled. It was *Tavis*!

"You raping tortured me, you bolehole subspawn!" Roullic shouted. Watly could now feel his whole body seething with anger. The penis started to shrink slightly in her mouth.

"I wasn't inside a fade-out host and you *knew* it!" Roullic screamed. "You raping cut me apart! You raping *killed* me!"

And suddenly Watly didn't feel the pistol anymore. It was hard to be sure—the barrel had been pressing there so long that she still felt the physical echo of its cold hardness against her temple. She looked upward. Roullic was red-faced and wide-eyed, pointing the gun way to her left. Pointing it toward the silver blur that was Tavis.

Roullic Neets fired the weapon twice.

And Watly simultaneously mashed those delicate pendulous things of his with both her hands, and bit down on the head of his penis as hard as she could.

Stale hardloaf, she thought to herself. *I'm just ripping off a piece of really stale hardloaf.*

CHAPTER 54

Alysess swung her legs up. They fell right back. This wasn't easy. She swung them again, lifting harder this time. Again they slumped back down.

The buildings flashed by below her. Gilded cupolas and bright red spires flew past. As she slid lower down the wire, all the buildings around got closer and closer and seemed to grow taller and taller. In seconds they were zipping by to the right and left, rising up and passing directly beside her impossibly fast.

Her stomach muscles were not as strong as they could have been. They hurt. It felt like something would pop and snap in her belly any minute. She swung her damned legs up again, lifting with her abdominals, arching her back, and straining with all her might.

Another Floobie-pod rose swiftly up right next to her and then disappeared into the distance.

She was so close to the exhaust tube now that she could even make out the gleam of the projectile's grapple-blades sticking out of its center.

She strained harder and harder, feeling her face get heavy with blood. Her knees rose higher, one on either side of the wire. The pain in her abdomen was excruciating. She fumbled with her feet, trying to grip the line between them as her breath came out in little agonized spurts.

Finally one boot was on either side of the wire. She pressed her feet together hard, squeezing the tiny ridged wire between the edges of her boot's nonslip soles. She brought her knees together too, gripping the line between them, feeling the wire sliding across the fabric that covered her lower thighs and upper calves.

Her stomach muscles protested vehemently, but she kept on using them, holding her legs up and squeezing the wire as hard as she could, trying to create some friction.

The line was whining loudly now, resonating like some bizarre country-wide musical instrument. It was a deep base note: *Waaaaaaaaaaaaaah!*

Alysess felt herself slowing some. But her stomach wouldn't take any more strain. She gave one last desperate lift—everything she had left. She tensed her abdominals, threw back her head, pulled toward her with her arm muscles, and kicked up forcefully with her legs.

Her legs were above the wire now, crossed over it as it whizzed rapidly through them. Her knees were hanging from the wire. She felt a sharp, biting pain as it pressed into the back of her legs. Alysess quickly twisted her right ankle under the wire so that it was looped there. The line was now curled around her legs as she slid across it.

The end of her journey was about forty feet away now, and closing fast. The metal tube gleamed ominously up ahead, large and bone-breakingly solid.

She stretched her legs out before her, trying to lock the joints straight. The wire pressed hard into the tough silver fabric, creasing it and biting painfully into her flesh. But she kept her legs straight. This way she was bending the wire, curling it, slowing herself down a little more.

Twenty-five feet to go . . . twenty . . . fifteen . . .

She let go with her legs suddenly, feeling them twang free of the wire. *Boing!* Her stomach screamed yet again as she held her legs up in front of her. Her knees were bent just slightly.

Ten . . . Five . . .

Alysess inhaled sharply and her boots hit the curved metal. Her legs took the shock, knees smashing violently into her chest.

"Ow!"

She bounced right off the thing, ricocheted back up the wire a ways. For a split second she just hung up there, as if time had suddenly frozen, and then she slid right down again. She hit the tube once more. This time both feet slipped off their sides of the tube. Her legs split wide and she slammed all the way into it with her crotch, hitting it hard with her pubic bone.

She bounced back slightly once again and then finally came to a rest, firmly straddling the golden shaft, gasping for air.

Alysess felt dazed, unsure if she was seriously hurt or not. Her whole body felt really shaken up. The muscles in her legs and abdomen felt ripped and shredded, her entire body was still vibrating from the impact, and her pubic bone was bruised bad. But she was okay.

After a few seconds, she began to laugh. *Damn good thing I'm not a man!* she thought to herself.

CHAPTER 55

Ogiv Fenlocki went back to the control room. He'd been away a long time. He'd been a bad boy, actually. The rules said he was supposed to be in the room the whole time, except maybe to pee. Even that excuse wasn't so great. A good chief of police should be able to hold it in at times like these. His place was at the command center. And here he was, leaving the room for close to an hour to talk to some little girl. Bad boy. Bad "expendable" boy.

Fenlocki climbed up on the central platform and looked around. Things were hopping. The technicians were playing with all the machinery in a frenzy of productive group anxiety. The pinlights above danced in elaborate patterns. Light-keys flashed. The monitors and CVs were alive with activity. Fenlocki could see fighting machines roaming the streets, revolutionaries dashing from building to building, nerve cannons spewing out fire, black fighters sneaking up on people and blowing them to bloody bits, a few staunch Second Levelers shooting down from the upper windows, Floobie-pods zipping away in a panic. . . . Every monitor showed a different scene of mayhem and confusion.

The chief turned to his left. Gavy was strapped into the donor chair in the center of the chamber. His blond bedlock was rolled up against one of his cheeks. He still looked pissed, but now he had donor cables curving up to the back of his reclining shiny head. And, come to think of it, the guy *always* looked pissed.

Fenlocki wondered if the Chancellor had told the truth. Was Chief Ogiv Fenlocki just another slimy plurite to them? Was his whole purpose as chief to be a scapegoat? Did they give him this job just so, should some revolution actually ever succeed, the Second Levelers would have an unimportant head to offer the masses as all the "real" people fled the scene?

Fenlocki had trouble believing that. He'd gotten the job because he was a good cop. He'd gotten the job because he always played by the book. He'd gotten the job because, no matter how unpleasant a given rule might be, he would always stick to it. He believed in rules. They gave life structure. Order. Without them was chaos.

But he felt confused now. He felt disoriented. The talk with the child had just confused him more. He believed her. She told the truth. And if Noonie told the truth, then Watly had been innocent from the beginning. Fenlocki felt bad about that. Real bad. He'd always kind of liked that Watly guy. And he'd even kind of liked the Watly woman he'd met only recently. Liked her in all sorts of ways.

Fenlocki looked from one monitor to another. Was she still alive? Was Watly Caiper/Sentiva Alvedine still alive and somewhere out there? It wasn't likely. Sure, he'd gotten reports back from the auditorium security cops that she'd escaped them. But the way things were out there, chances are she was dead by now.

The chief kept looking at the monitors, half expecting to see Watly there on the projected streets, making a wild war whoop and running toward the command center to save her child. No, she had to be dead. Yet this Watly person was a damn resourceful creature. Fenlocki had learned *that* ten years ago, if nothing else. Maybe she was still out there, breaking all the rules.

The chief felt funny inside. Funny about Watly. Funny about the revolution. Funny about what the Chancellor had said. And funny about what Noonie had said. He *did* believe the child. But believing her just made him feel more funny. Watly had been innocent. And that meant that one of the times he had played by the rules perfectly—the killing of Watly Caiper—he'd been wrong. And the one and only time he'd seriously *broken* the rules—leaving Watly/Sentiva in peace all those years—he'd been right.

What the rape did that say about rules?

But if he of all people started breaking the rules and throwing out the book, what did that leave to go on? Where did that leave him?

Zephy Gavy was giving a thumbs-up signal to one of the control room technicians. He was ready for the modified hosting procedure.

Fenlocki watched the technician engage the hosting ringlets one by one. He felt nauseous again. He felt repulsed by the whole stupid concept of what they were starting. Something really obscene was about to happen. It made him sick. But he felt hopeless. He was stuck. He had a job to do. What else was there for him to do but the job he was hired to do?

Another technician, Mobben, turned from his console to look up at Fenlocki. "Chief! You're back! We were getting worried. You got any orders? Any changes?"

Fenlocki leaned into the rattan railing and watched Gavy begin the donor process. Zephy's body went totally limp. The blond snake of hair on his face unraveled and hung to the side. It was as if he were dead. But Fenlocki knew the Chancellor wasn't dead. No, indeed. His mind was very alive. So alive, in fact, that in a few moments his nasty little brain would be controlling the bodies of close to a thousand hosts. Quite a technological feat. Quite a marvel, really.

"Chief?" Mobben said again. "*Chief?* Any orders?"

Fenlocki slammed his fist on the rail, sending tremors through the caning below. "Yeah! Yeah, I got an order!" he shouted. "Somebody bring the kid some dinner! She hasn't eaten since raping breakfast and she doesn't like my sunbeans!"

Mobben looked confused. He did a goofy double take back to the console and then to the chief. He swallowed so hard, Fenlocki could see his little Adam's apple bobble. "Uh . . . should I give her a nutri-gruel packet and a straw?"

"No, terradamn you!" the chief yelled, his knuckles white as he gripped the rail. "She's a person, just like you or me. You get her a raping tablecloth and a raping napkin and a raping knife and fork. Then you get her a glass of juice and a plate full of good stuff a kid would like. You hear me? Like a decent human being. Got that?"

Mobben nodded timidly.

"Then do it *now*!"

Mobben took off his headset and slithered out of the room,

giving Fenlocki a look that seemed to say, *You're acting awful loopy. Methinks you've had one sunbean too many!* He closed the door very softly behind him.

Fenlocki almost ran out and called Mobben back into the room. It suddenly struck him that maybe giving the desperate, frightened, bewildered little girl a knife and fork might not be the best idea. But he let it go. She couldn't hurt anybody much with those. First off, she was just a little kid.

Second, the utensils weren't very dangerous. Fenlocki was familiar with the silverware the command center's cafeteria always supplied. It was made out of cheap, bendable metal. The fork tines were always pretty dull, and the knives, though relatively sharp, were thin and lightweight. And they had very short blades.

CHAPTER 56

Alysess had never killed anyone. She'd never even injured anyone, with two exceptions. The first exception was the one time she slugged Watly Caiper in the jaw some ten years ago. Watly had been a man back then, and he'd really pissed Alysess off. Mainly just because he'd gotten her involved in the whole mess to begin with. So she hit him in the chops. But she'd felt bad and guilty about that one little jab in the face for a long time after. She didn't like hurting people. She'd much prefer doing the opposite. That's why she became a doctor.

The one other time she'd tussled with another person was not long after that slug-in-the-kisser incident. Alysess had ended up grappling pretty damn fiercely with Sentiva Alvedine. The male Watly had gone up to Second to find a donor room, and Alysess had stayed down with Sentiva. They were in a First Level hosting room, and Sentiva was unconscious. She'd been knocked out with a blast canister, and Alysess had prepped the woman for a little "revenge hosting."

What happened was, Sentiva started to wake up well before Watly's donor signal came in. And Alysess had to hold the angry, groggy, incredibly strong woman into the hosting chair's metal plates—leaning on her, sitting on her, pushing her, shoving her hard, fending off blows, and offering a few back.

It got pretty nasty. By the time Watly's consciousness finally entered and took over the damn woman, both Sentiva's body and Alysess's body were badly bruised. There were cuts and scrapes and lumps all over the both of them.

Yet, if Alysess *hadn't* fought with the woman, Watly would not have lived. She didn't know it at the time, but as she struggled to keep Sentiva in place, up on Second Watly Caiper was being fatally shot with a nerve gun. If Alysess hadn't physically forced Sentiva to stay against the hosting plates, Watly's projected consciousness would not have had any place to go. And Watly Caiper would've been gone forever.

But that fact still didn't make Alysess comfortable with the violence. She didn't like violence. She didn't like violence of any kind, but she particularly didn't like the idea of being violent herself. That was an almost intolerable thought. She considered herself a good person, a gentle person, a very moral person. More moral, certainly, than the Ragman. More moral, even, than her love, Watly Caiper. Hurting someone else, *killing* someone else, was not something she ever wanted to do.

Alysess wondered, as she made her sixth modified trip sliding across a scrambler wire, what she would do if she had to kill someone or die herself. Could she do it? She hoped, unlikely as the odds might be, that the question would never come up. She hoped she could continue her rescue mission without ever having to face the problem.

So far, so good. Since she'd first climbed up that ladder through the portal to Second, she had hurt no one. She had fired her weapons at no one. She had been physically threatened by no one. She had, she realized, been damn lucky so far. But would her luck hold out?

Alysess landed smoothly on a Forty-sixth Street rooftop near Seventh Avenue. After her first nightmare ride, she'd finally gotten the hang of this wire-traveling. She had the technique down. First she'd sight a building just a little shorter than the one she was on. Then she would shoot the projectile blades at something that stood tall on the far side of that building's roof—a doorway or pole or high exhaust pipe. Then she'd be off, sliding smoothly across the wire. Near the end of the trip, she'd raise herself upward with her overtaxed arm muscles. And when she got just above the near side of her destination's roof, she'd lower herself and start pumping her legs—running right along the roof's surface, slowing herself down. Sometimes she slipped, sometimes she stumbled, and sometimes she ran smack into the pole or doorway. But it worked pretty well, especially since she wasn't going nearly as fast as before.

Each time after landing and disentangling herself and her bra from the wire, she would check to see if there was another likely target to head for next. If not, she'd have to break into the building she was on, climb down the stairs, dash across the street if the coast was clear, and start all over again.

She didn't like doing that. She much preferred conducting her southeasterly journey from roof to roof, never going indoors, never going on the streets, never running into any other people. She liked being way above the fray. It felt safe. It felt as though she were just an observer, a large bird flying over a battlefield. Soaring along on its own separate mission.

Every time Alysess had to go down onto the streets and into the buildings to search out a new starting point, she felt very hinky. So far, the only people she'd run into had been Revies, layfighters, and the occasional timid Second Leveler. The Second Levelers she encountered thus far always seemed more afraid of her than she was of them. They'd scurry away into the darkness like kitchen roaches. Up till now, her luck had held.

As she set up the scrambler gun's tripod for the seventh time, she wondered how long that luck would continue. Eventually someone was bound to try to stop her. Someone was bound to try to kill her. And what would she do? Was she even capable of defending herself? Would she be able to shoot another human being?

The only image in her head she could even tolerate along those lines had to do with Noonie and Watly. She thought maybe, if it came down to defending one of them, she could kill. She could, just possibly, kill for her baby or kill for her poovus. But for herself? Could she take another person's precious life just to protect her own? Did she even have that right?

By now Alysess's body felt like it had been *through* a war, instead of *over* one. Her arms were killing her, her belly was incredibly sore, her legs were throbbing, and her pubic bone still hurt like crazy. But she kept on. Sliding and sliding and sliding. Skimming over the surface of Manhattan, like a flat stone skipping over the water.

The country was getting dark. The sun was now only the top

part of a sinking orange ball that Alysess could see very fleetingly between buildings as she zipped by them. The streets below were shadowy and ghostlike. All the colorful buildings started to look gray and dingy in the half-light. The whitetopped avenues were just dim, pale veins in the shadows.

The closer Alysess got to the State Buildings, the more revolutionaries she saw in the darkness below. Every time the hulking shape of a black fighter left a street, she could make out whole swarms of tiny dark figures dashing from building to building down there, heading south. Sometimes the fighters backtracked and cut down every person on the street. But there seemed to be less and less of the machines as Alysess got closer to Thirty-fourth.

The suit speakers were full of noise and conversation. She heard chatter about huge nerve cannons, she heard death screams, she heard bloodcurdling war yells, she heard gunfire. And she heard worried voices wondering about the Ragman. Apparently no one could reach him and no one had heard from him in a while.

Alysess tried not to think about that. It was not her concern. She was not a part of Revy. She had quit that world. She was on her own private quest. She had no time to worry if old Ragface was dead somewhere below her. That just wasn't her prob.

CHAPTER 57

Watly's eyes were closed.

She heard Tavis scream metallically to her left. Then Roullic screamed. Then the gun clattered to the sidewalk.

And Watly tasted blood.

No come. No joy-juice. No sickening, decayed-sunbean-flavored Roullic jizz . . . just blood. Cloyingly, nauseatingly sweet blood.

She released her jaw muscles and unclasped her hands quickly, as if both her mouth and fingers had been burned. She spat out something. And spat again. And spat again, feeling her stomach clench up as if about to explode in a great gush of vomit. She took a few deep breaths, listening to the moans and gasps that came from both directions, and then finally opened her eyes.

Roullic had fallen back and was rolling around on the whitetop. He was clutching his groin with both hands, and there was a sea of blood streaming through his clenched, pressing fingers. The chip pistol was on the ground right next to Watly. She snatched it up and stood, her knees popping loudly. She felt dizzy and distant from herself. Her mouth and chin was covered in stickiness and her head felt like it weighed about fifty pounds.

"Tavis is shot! Ow, ow, ow! Not a good thing, this. Not allowed, this!"

Watly turned to see a silver-suited creature half sitting up by the curb. Tavis was leaning back on locked arms, legs splayed out in front in a huge V shape. The front of the suit was open in two places. There was one big jagged hole of redness in the left stomach, and one bloody opening right in the middle of the chest between the breasts.

"*Ow*! Tavis shot *twice*! Bad enough Tavis shot, but twice is two times too many!"

Watly walked over toward Tavis on rubbery legs. She couldn't see the face behind the helmet, but she could recognize that weird half man/half woman voice easily. She hadn't seen Tavis in ten years. Tavis the weird one. Tavis the strange, scary beast. Yet they'd been through a lot back then. Watly almost felt a fondness for the genderless creature. Or at least a sense of sympathy over the bad wounds. Really bad-looking wounds.

Tavis started clumsily lifting up a chip rifle as Watly approached. She stopped a few feet away from the splayed creature.

"Yicky, icky, sticky mess, Tavis is. Red not fun when it's from the me inside. Red not a good thing when it's from Tavis. A target I am *not*!"

Watly thought Tavis was trying to aim at her with the weapon. But the silver-covered arm was twisting to the side. Tavis leaned to the left, balancing on the left arm, and aimed the gun toward Roullic's tortured, twisting form.

"You did a bad thing to Tavis! Tavis is not supposed to be hurt! You hurt me! You've been untoward. Nontoward. Antitoward. Extoward. Not toward at all! *Ha*!"

Watly saw Tavis fumbling with the rifle's trigger, trying to balance the weapon with the one hand so it was aimed at Roullic.

"See how *you* like it! See how you like getting shot!" Tavis said, the voice sounding weak through the suit's speakers. "How does *this* feel?"

And Watly turned to look at Roullic Neets. She made no move to stop Tavis. She felt numb. She just watched, holding Misser Neets's gun in her hand, still tasting his viscous blood strongly in her mouth.

The entire lower part of Roullic's business suit was covered in blood now. He was still moaning softly, curled toward them next to his floating cruiser. The cruiser's door was still open, as if waiting for Roullic to climb back in. That didn't look likely.

Roullic was in obvious agony, his red-coated fingers still mashed firmly into his crotch. His body was shivering and trembling all over. Watly scanned his shaking form from top to bottom. Then she looked up again at Roullic's agonized, deathly pale face just in time to see it burst open from one of Tavis's high-powered chip slugs. One second there was a face there, clenched in a grimace of excruciating pain, eyes squeezed shut and jaw locked, forehead veins bulging with pressure . . . and then there was an explosion of flesh. The face disappeared into a irregular soupy mess of stringy meat and bone and blood. Roullic's body spasmed violently four times and then went limp.

"How do you like *that*? Not so fun, is it?" Tavis said.

Watly turned away from the mutilated body to look back at Tavis. The recoil of the rifle had knocked her/him flat on the back. The two gaping holes in the silver suit were now overflowing with sticky redness. The hole in the chest seemed to be pumping the blood out in regular little spurts. It ran down Tavis's sides to the road surface.

"Tavis hurt bad," the suit's speaker said softly.

Watly walked closer and leaned in. "Hey, Tavis," she said in a quiet greeting.

"Who is it?"

"It's me. It's Watly Caiper."

The helmet turned slightly toward her, and Watly thought she could just make out two shiny, catlike eyes through the tinted visor. "Watly Caiper? Ha! Watly Caiper! *Everybody* wants Watly Caiper's head. Good guys and bad. You're in deep catshit, Watly Caiper."

Watly squatted on her aching knees and looked down at Tavis's wounds. She was no doctor, but to her the bullet holes sure seemed like fatal injuries. The one between the breasts looked like it was real near the heart, if not actually *in* it.

"You're dying, Tavis," she said softly.

"Tavis doesn't die," the metallic voice replied. "Not in Tavis's repertoire. Tavis is invincible."

"Doesn't look like it to me," Watly whispered.

"Wanna bet?"

Watly looked down at Tavis's body. The lump of the breasts, the slight bulge at the groin of the suit. The wide female hips and slender waist. Watly's eyes uncontrollably fixed on the crotch area. There *was* some kind of lump there . . . or was that just the wrinkling of the material?

"What are you looking at?" the suit speaker squawked. "Don't you *dare* look at Tavis! Don't you dare look under there just because I can't move right now! It's Tavis's secret!"

Watly squinted into Tavis's helmet visor, trying to get a fix on the vague eyelike shapes within. "I was just wondering. . . ."

The sound of breathing through the suit's speaker was getting very labored and slow. "Don't you dare. Never tell. Tavis's secret. Kill you if you look."

Then there was no sound for a while but Tavis's irregular breathing. Watly thought maybe she/he was unconscious now. The only movement from Tavis's body was the tiny rise and fall of the chest and the continual spurt of blood from the holes.

Tavis moved an arm abruptly, grabbing Watly's wrist. "What do you see? What do you see?" he/she hissed out.

Watly blinked. "What do I see where?"

Tavis moaned as if Watly were being very slow and stupid. "In *me*. Within. The bullet holes."

Watly looked down at Tavis's wounds. "Blood," she said simply.

"*Within*. Within." Tavis groaned, sounding frustrated. "Is it different in there? Is it . . . is it *special*?"

Watly tried to see Tavis's eyes better, but they were obscured by the visor. She was sure the strange genderless creature was dying. "Uh," she said, looking back at the bloody injuries. "Uh . . . let's see. Yeah. Yeah, sure. It's special in there."

"How? How is Tavis special within?"

The strange sexless voice sounded desperate. Its tone was almost religious. Watly sensed that this was a deeply important question to Tavis. She didn't know what to say. "Uh . . ."

"Is there blood?" Tavis asked. "You said there was blood."

"I was wrong. There's no blood."

"No blood?"

"None. Just . . . silver fluid. Like mercury. Bright, beautiful silver liquid."

"*Yes?*" Tavis gasped. "And what's *within*? Guts? Organs? Yicky, sticky mess?"

"No. None of that," Watly answered. She paused for a second, thinking. "I can just see inside, Tavis. There's *light* in there. A bright, golden, spectacular light. Within you. No blood, no guts, just a beautiful bright pure light. It's incredible."

Tavis trembled all over. Watly wasn't sure whether they were death throes or some kind of ecstatic tremors. "Yes yes yes yes!

I knew it. It's *me* that's different. *Tavis*. All this time I've been looking in others, and it's *me* that's special."

"Yeah," Watly said softly. "Sure."

And Tavis went limp again. The creature's chest stopped moving, but the blood continued to flow regularly out of the wounds. Watly figured he/she was dead. It was over. Much as she wanted to, she wouldn't look to see what was under that pants bulge. She'd respect a dying person's wishes. The secret of the creature's sex would die with the creature.

Suddenly Tavis's head sprang upward sharply. "Watly Caiper, huh?" Watly jumped back, startled. "Watly Caiper? Ha!" Tavis's voice was suddenly playful and energetic. Maybe even cruel in its gleefulness. "I know something you don't know! I know something you don't know!"

Watly pulled back even farther, momentarily frightened by almost-dead Tavis's burst of energy. "What? What do you know?"

There was a loud giggle from the suit. It sounded crazy, maniacal. "Your daddy's dead. I watched him fry. Eiter. He burned in the Man-With-Hat-On. He died nice and slow. He screamed a lot. I watched it all. It was fun. His skin bubbled off real slow. Real slow, it burned off him. Ha."

Watly felt strange suddenly. The dizziness that had been there before seemed to envelop her. She felt lost. Adrift. Not angry, not sad, not upset. She just felt a strange kind of hopelessness wash over her. "Oh, damn," she muttered. Tavis's head slumped back to the whitetop. Now the creature really did look dead. Happily, contentedly dead. Happy to have the last laugh, to get one last knife thrust in.

"Lost my chance," Watly said to herself, trying to stand. "Lost my one chance to have a dad." Her head started to hurt real bad again. The hopelessness that grew in her felt like a familiar—and almost comfortable—blanket. "Oh, damn."

Instantly, as if she had just now woken up, it hit Watly what she had done to Roullic. Not what *Tavis* had done to him—that seemed almost merciful—but what Watly had done. The savageness of it. The barbarism. She still tasted blood on her tongue. She no longer knew herself. She'd lost herself. She'd lost everything. She'd lost her chance to have a father. The dying Tavis had shown her that. And why would Tavis lie about that? Just to be cruel? No, it had to be true. She'd lost the Dad-chance. She'd lost Alysess, her lover. She'd lost her daughter to the clutches of the enemy. And she'd lost herself. Lost her very self in violence.

Tavis's blood no longer spurted out, it just spread slowly down the silver suit and pooled up on the whitetop. And Watly's legs seemed as if they didn't want to support her. Where was she? What was she doing? And what was the use? What was the use in anything?

Her head was pounding really bad now, and she felt her lips start to move without her control. It didn't really matter.

"Shhh . . . shhhort . . ." she heard herself say. It didn't matter. Nothing really mattered.

"Shhhort blade . . . Whhhatly . . ."

The street spun around her. Her head felt enormous, like it was stretching to ten times its usual size. "Whhhatly . . ."

Go ahead, Watly thought numbly. *Go ahead and take the body, Sentiva. It's yours.*

Watly thought she was hallucinating. Thirty-third Street stopped spinning, but there was something strange going on down at the end of it. There was a huge crowd nearing her. Over a hundred people, men and women of all ages, marching right up toward her. They had First Level faces and wore First Level clothing, but they were marching in perfect unison. All of their feet were hitting the road surface at exactly the same time. Their eyes looked glassy, as if they were all dead inside. And each of them had guns and rifles. The weapons were held up, sweeping side to side in perfect sync. And each of them was wearing a shiny yellow hosting cuff.

An army of hosts, heading right at her.

Sentiva pushed hard against Watly's mind. Watly felt her aching brain caving quietly in to the push, push, push. And the battalion of host-soldiers drew nearer.

Watly felt she could hardly think at all anymore. In fact, the only thing that came to mind was, *Well . . . I'm toast.*

CHAPTER 58

Alysess was stuck again. She had to go back down to the street. Back down to real life. Back down where the war was. Where the danger was.

It was frustrating. She was so close to the State Buildings now, it almost seemed she could reach out and touch them. About two more short wire trips should do it. Three at the most. But she had to go back to the street and find a tall building with better prospects to aim toward. At least she hadn't seen any of the fighting machines around in quite a while. This whole area seemed clear of them.

She trotted across Sixth Avenue, scanning the street carefully in both directions as she moved. Way up ahead, she saw some Revies walking downtown. About fifteen of them. They seemed pretty fearless, walking calmly in the center of the street. At this point, it seemed they were confident about the lack of black fighters about. And they must have figured they weren't yet near the nerve cannons everyone was talking about.

Alysess stopped in the shadows of a garish, purple- and orange-sequined doorway that led to an autorestaurant. She looked up to see which was the most likely building nearby to

work from. There were a couple of prospects. A lot of buildings
around were tall enough, but it was hard to tell if the angle was
right, if the path would be clear.

Alysess stepped out of the autorestaurant's doorway and
walked two doors down, still looking for the best starting point for
her next journey. The piellna music continued playing loudly from
every direction. Alysess was getting pretty damned tired of
hearing it. It was as if the whole war had a bad, incongruous sound
track grafted onto it. She glanced down the street again, surprised
at what she saw now. Way behind the revolutionaries, there was
a crowd coming up the avenue. From this distance, they looked
like First Level layfighters. But they were all walking the wrong
way; they were coming *from* the State Buildings' area, on an
intercept course with the Revies. The revolutionaries stopped and
seemed to be staring at the people approaching them. One of the
Revies even appeared to be waving at someone in the throng.

The crowd of people continued uptown. They seemed to be in
some kind of formation, marching up the avenue in strangely
synchronized steps, their bodies separated by what looked like an
exact arm's length each. There appeared to be about two hundred
of them. As they advanced, a few of their numbers broke off from
either side to go inside the buildings they passed. They split off
from the procession in groups of two and three with perfect
rhythm, walking zombielike into the nearest doorway. And the
rest kept coming, marching like automatons. They got closer and
closer, and Alysess could now see that they all had something on
their wrists that reflected brightly even in the dim light. It looked
almost as though this was a mob of people wearing hosting cuffs.
A mob of hosts.

Alysess was about to step out into the street to get a better look
when the marchers started shooting. All fifteen of the revolutionaries were cut to pieces instantly in a loud volley of perfectly
synchronized chip fire. They fell and tumbled in a heap. Dead.
And the marchers kept coming. Slow, plodding, perfect steps.
They almost seemed to be marching to the beat of the gentle
piellna music, the war soundtrack.

Alysess reached behind her and threw the door open. She dove
into the building, not caring if it was tall enough or well-
positioned enough or not. It would have to do. She had to get off
the street.

It was almost pitch-black inside. Alysess stepped cautiously
into the darkness. She could see a few shapes. Chairs, maybe. A

round desk. She walked farther into the room, stepping very slowly and carefully. She had to find the stairs. She had to get to the safety of the roof. The safety of her wire. She wished she could see better. She wished she had the time to wait for her eyes to adjust. She wished she had a raping light or something. It was too damn dark. And the dark was dangerous.

She stepped on something. Then something else. Something squishy. Then she almost tripped on something. Why was it taking so damn long for her eyes to adjust? Rape.

Someone grabbed her foot.

Alysess fumbled for her chip pistol. Where had she put it? What side of her belt was it on? The grip of the disembodied hand was hard and firm around her ankle. She tried to shake her leg free. It didn't work. *Where the rape is my gun?* She felt the grenades hanging from her right belt loops, but they were too powerful to be any use at this range. Where was the raping gun? There it was, hanging low on her right side. She tore it free of the belt and stuck her gloved index finger into the trigger ring. Was this it? Was this the test to see if she could kill or be killed? Was this the moment she had worried so about?

Alysess pointed the gun downward, toward where the hand seemed to be coming from. The grip was relaxing just a little on her ankle. Her eyes began to clear some, able to make out more and more in the darkness. Whoever held her was facedown on the floor, wearing silver battle togs. And no helmet.

"Who?" Alysess hissed, still pointing the gun down at the head of whoever grasped her ankle.

"Uuuh . . ." the head said. It was just a moan. A tired, sad moan. Alysess let her finger relax from the gun's trigger.

"Who is that?" she asked.

And then a very soft, almost indiscernible voice came back. "It's me."

"Me who?"

"Rag. It's me. Rag."

Alysess squatted, squinting into the dark shape below her. "Ragface? That you? What the rape happened to you? Where's your helmet?"

She helped the limp form turn over and pulled him to where he could lean against a nearby column. "Couldn't breathe in it. Not enough air," the Ragman whispered.

"Pretty stupid, Ragface." Alysess snorted. "Your whole communication stuff is in the helmet. Nobody could get you. They're worried about you."

"Alysess?"

"Yeah, it's me," Alysess said. She leaned in so she could see him better.

"You back in Revy? I knew you'd come back."

"No way. I'm not back."

"What are you doing here?"

"Tripping on you, it seems." Alysess snorted again. It felt good to snort. It felt particularly good to snort for the Ragface, for some reason. She looked at the man's bearded face. The Ragman's features were becoming clearer to her. He looked real sick. His face was pale and greasy-looking and his eyes were dark and sunken. All the wrinkles around his mouth seemed deeper.

"What's happening out there?" he asked. His voice sounded hoarse and full of extra air. She hardly recognized it.

"I dunno. You sure did start something. The entrails sure have hit the fan, you old fart." She saw that his dark eyes were desperate for information. He was begging her to fill him in.

"I *dunno*, Ragface," she said to his unspoken question. "The Revies think they lost their leader, I guess. But they're going on. They think you're dead."

"I am dead."

"What happened to you?"

"I'm dying."

Alysess finally realized why she still couldn't see very well. The terradamned visor she wore was *tinted*, for Cruda's sake. She unlatched her helmet, broke the seal, and pulled the thing off. *Now* she could finally see; now it was evening instead of night.

"You're dying?" Alysess asked, holding the Ragman's eyelids open so she could look at his pupils.

The dark, dilated pupils turned to meet Alysess's eyes. They looked desperate. "Help me, Doctor," the Ragman whispered.

"What is it? Are you shot?"

The Ragman chuckled just a little. Even that seemed painful, though. "My heart," he said. "My raping old heart."

Alysess looked around her, trying to think of something. "I don't have my bag, Raggy. I don't have any equipment. There are no hospitals that—"

The Ragman smiled softly. "I know. It's okay. The suit's been helping. It's got automedipaks. It took care of the pain. I think it's even started me up again a few times, you know? Pretty neat, huh? I helped design these things."

"Come on," Alysess said, lowering him back to the floor. "Put your head down. That's just making things worse."

"I'm dying, Doctor. I'm dying."

"No, you're not. You're gonna be fine. You're gonna be just fine, Ragface. You got a damn fine doctor here. Best in the country." She opened the flap under the suit's left arm, checking on some of the medipak controls. The thing was pumping him full of painkillers and stimulants and heart algens and pressure stablers all at the same time. The natural heartbeat was erratic and weak, the natural blood pressure real low. The suit was basically doing all the work his body should've been. Without it he'd surely be dead.

"I don't want to die, Alysess."

"Yeah, I know. Pretty raping scary stuff. I know." She smiled down at him. "I got the whole speech, remember? But you're going to be fine." She adjusted some of the settings on the suit's drugs.

"You gotta do me a favor," the Ragman said slowly. "You gotta do me something."

"Whatever you want, you old bolehole."

"You gotta lead them. You gotta take over."

"What the rape are you talking about?"

"Revy needs a leader now. You've got to lead them."

Alysess snorted yet again. And then she laughed. "No way," she said. "I'm through with all that catshit."

"You've got to. You've got no choice. You're the only one." She laughed again, even harder. "Why would that be?"

"Because you can make a difference. You can take charge. You have a conscience." The Ragman coughed hard, winced, and then continued. "You have morals. Ethics. You said it yourself. You can make sure we fight fair. You can make sure no more unnecessary deaths happen."

Alysess sighed heavily. "Raggy, old boy, find yourself another flunky. I'm out."

The old bearded face turned toward her. The eyes twinkled in the shadows. "You'll do it. Trust me on that. You've got no choice but to do it. Because you can make a difference. You'll end up doing it simply *because* you have morals and ethics. I know it."

Alysess was trying to get the Ragman's suit's temperature up.

The thing was way too cold for him. "You don't know me very well, then, fella," she said as she played with the temperature gauges. "My answer is no."

"Where's my helmet?"

"Over there. What do you want it for? You'll be fine. I've got everything under control."

"Give me my helmet."

Alysess reached over and got the helmet for him. He told her to reach in and press the fourth tongue tab from the left on the middle row and then hold the whole thing near him. She thought about it for a minute.

"What's that going to do?" Alysess asked finally. "You're not trying to kill yourself, are you?"

The old guy smiled weakly. "No such luck. I already told you. I don't want to die."

She reluctantly did as he had said, pressing the tab with her finger and holding the helmet's opening near his bearded face.

"This is the Ragman, my Revies," he said, his voice sounding surprisingly strong and recognizable suddenly. "I apologize for the long delay in communications. I have been incapacitated. I may not be able to continue. The new leader of the revolution will be Dr. Alysess Tollnismer. Spread the word. Obey her as you would me. She will—"

Alysess threw the helmet across the dark room. It bounced and rolled before stopping. "I already told you no!" she yelled.

The Ragman smiled again. His voice collapsed back to a thin, reedy whisper. "Well, that's just in case you change your mind."

"Rape you!"

"Maybe later. Right now I'm not feeling up to it." His whole body gave a sudden shudder, and Alysess saw the suit's readings going wild. The automedipaks were working furiously to keep the old guy alive.

"Oh, shit," the Ragman said with difficulty. "I really don't want to die, Alysess. Really. I'm so raping scared."

Alysess took his gloved hand and squeezed it hard. "Hold on, there, Ragface. Hang on. You can do it."

"Shit!" The Ragman clamped his eyes shut, grimacing. "Shit! I'm not ready for nothingness. I'm not ready."

Alysess felt suddenly furious. "Nothingness? Now, you listen to me, you old bolehole I-know-everything subspawn. First of all, you're not going to die. And second of all, if and when you do, you don't know *nothing* about it." She gripped his hand even tighter. "You don't know *shit*. You said you were a raping scientist. Well, you want to know what a good scientist would say about death? He'd say, 'I don't know *shit*!' That's what he'd say. Your belief in nothingness is just as stupidly mindless as any other empty faith or belief. *You don't know raping shit!* And that's the truth of it. Admit your raping ignorance, you bolehole! For all you know, you're headed for an afterlife in *spite* of all your raping certainty and all your raping fears!"

She took hold of his bearded chin with her free hand and turned his face gently toward her. Then she spoke very clearly and very, very slowly, staring right into his eyes. "You . . . don't . . . know . . . *shit*! Nobody does. Hear me?"

The Ragman said nothing now. But he gripped Alysess's hand back, and his sunken eyes looked grateful. There was just a little hint of a thank-you smile on his lips.

And then his body shook violently again, and the suit's readings went wild. He was going. Alysess knew it. He was dying. The suit could only do so much. And it had done everything it could and probably for a very long time. Maybe, if he'd been in a hospital . . .

"Oh, damn." The Ragman moaned. "Please . . ."

"I'm right here, Ragman. I'm right here." She reached over so she was holding both his hands now. She gripped them as hard as she could. "I'm with you."

The suit's life-sign monitors were all bright red now. The Ragman's face was a mask of pain that the drugs should have been able to control.

"Oh, damn," he said, moaning. And then he shivered and winced. "The roach . . ." he whispered now.

"What?"

"The damn roach is still alive. The roach is in here with me. Pretty weird concept."

"What are you talking about?" Alysess asked. But she knew the old guy was probably just hallucinating.

"It's climbing up me. Wow."

"I'm right here, Ragman. I'm right here with you. There's no roach. There's no one here but me."

"No, no. *Inside*," he said, sounding impatient. "Not *outside*."

Alysess still didn't understand him. He wasn't making sense. He was delirious. He was hallucinating. And if he wasn't, if he had actually meant something rational, she would never know what it was.

She watched him take one very long, gentle breath. He held the air in his lungs for a long time, and then finally let it all out. The exhale was even slower, even more drawn out. The air eased fluidly out of him. It seemed to relax him, calm him, soothe all his pains, ease all his fears. And he did not inhale again. Ever.

Alysess held his hands for a while. He was still warm. His face was still covered with sweat. His skin was still slightly pink. He still seemed alive. But he wasn't.

The Ragman, the great Subkeeper, was dead. Dead.

Alysess looked around her, wondering what to do. She felt disoriented and really weird in her head and neck and face. She felt numb. *Shock*, she thought to herself. *I'm a doctor, so I recognize it. I'm in shock. Why the hell am I in shock? I didn't even like the old fart.*

And then the door beside her flew open and three people walked stiffly in. They each had hosting cuffs on and their eyes looked blank and doll-like. They held heavy-duty chip rifles, all three aimed straight at Alysess's face.

Shit, she thought. *I'm toast.*

PART THREE

SAVING FACE

What are you, crazy?

OGIV FENLOCKI

CHAPTER 59

The kitchen of the Alvedine residence was on the first floor, a large room behind the sweeping bird-wing staircase, just to the left of the adjoining, elegantly appointed dining room. It was the finest kitchen money could buy.

Watly always liked kitchens—the functional space, the scarred counters, the worn utensils, the smell of meals past hanging in the air, the sweet aroma of meals present spreading thickly from simmering pots and pans. . . .

When Watly first moved up to Second, up to the luxurious Alvedine home, she'd been disappointed in her new kitchen. It had no smells at all. It was sterile and automated and very unkitchenlike. There was no room in it for real cooking—for art, for experimentation.

Most of the appliances were just for show. The enormous, six-legged stove, with its gold handles and bejeweled burners, served no function other than to look expensive and—in Watly's opinion—seriously tacky. The antique-looking sink that sported seven multicolored faucets was not even hooked up to the building's water supply or drainage system. The shiny silver pots and pans that hung over the central counter were totally useless. Though they appeared real from a distance, they were actually one solid, decorative unit and could not be separated or removed. The same was true of the golden spice rack, the wooden drawers and cabinets, and the all-wicker food cooler. Everything was merely ornate set dressing.

The only two objects in the kitchen that served any real function at all were the most unassuming ones: the food dispenser and the garbage melter. The food dispenser was set in the south wall and consisted of a brass keyboard and a three-foot-square folding door. All the automated workings were hidden behind the wall. Unsightly things like the refrigeration bins, the cooking and mixing capsules, cleaning machines, and market delivery tubes were all buried behind the smooth, unblemished surface of the wallboard. The garbage melter was diagonally opposite the food dispenser. It just looked like a large metal box set in the corner. It had a small codelock and a two-door lid on top that opened like a mouth. Like the dispenser, all its innards were hidden—in this case, in a tube that ran down under the floor to the building's lava pipes.

Watly hated that these were the only two appliances that did anything. The kitchen had no warmth, no life. Watly vowed to make it into a real kitchen. To buy a real stove, install a real sink, get real pots and pans, real appliances and cabinets. She wanted the room to be the living, breathing center of her house.

During Watly's pregnancy and Noonie's infancy, Watly fixed the place up. By the time Noonie was one and a half, the food dispenser was hardly ever used. Watly had made the kitchen real. And real kitchens made houses into homes.

And Watly bought a cat and named him Stoney. Animals also made houses into homes. Animals, real kitchens, and people. Stoney was a coon cat, all fuzzy and striped and rambunctious. Little Noonie loved him. It wasn't as good, Watly thought, as having a grandfather around, but it was something. Eiter couldn't come visit ever again. Watly would've liked that. Things might've worked out okay with them after a while, if they'd had time. But they didn't. And that was that.

So, as little Noonie grew older, there was her mama, Watly; there was Aunt Alysess visiting frequently; there was Stoney, the wonky feline; and there was a real, honest kitchen for real, honest cooking.

It was starting to feel like a home. More and more. Until Noonie was seven years old, and the thing happened. But Watly wasn't about to think about that.

CHAPTER 60

Noonie finished her meal. She wiped her mouth on her shirtsleeve and polished off the rest of the mayjuice in two big gulps. The food had been okay, but nothing special. She was used to special.

It was strange to eat alone. No matter how busy Mommy had been, she had always made sure the two of them had dinner together. No matter what else happened, that was something to count on. Noonie couldn't remember the last time she'd eaten alone, if there *had been* a last time.

It was especially strange to eat alone here, in this bare, unfamiliar room. The interrogation room. There were no windows, there was no music player, no CV, nothing. Nothing but the sound of her own chews and sips, and the sight of the strong shafts of light from those high pinspots. And all those soft-looking dust motes floating by.

Noonie missed her mommy. She missed the dinnertimes they'd always had. The quiet talking, the laughing, the stories, the lessons. She missed the other mommy too. The board meeting mommy, the strong, hard one. She missed them both. And she missed her *other* other mommy. Aunt Alysess. The special playtimes. The hugs. The silliness. All three. She missed all three of her mommies.

She would've given anything just to have one of them with her now. *Any* one of them. To talk to. To eat with. Or just to sit silently with and look at the flecks of dust together.

She hummed a little just to keep herself company. After trying unsuccessfully to make a hat out of her napkin, she pushed all the dishes and silverware to the far side of the table, folded the tablecloth, and placed the click-pen and sketch pad in front of her.

She wasn't sure why she hadn't told Fenlocki about the click-pen. She'd told him everything else. *Everything* else, dammit. But a secret weapon should stay a secret. That's why it was called that in the first place. Secret. And anyway, Noonie needed *some* secrets. She couldn't tell absolutely everything. She might need to use the thing. She might even need to use it on Ogiv Fenlocki, though she had an awful hard time picturing herself doing that. He was kind of spaf. Sort of prone. But still, it was good she hadn't told him. A good thing. Some secrets were good to keep.

Noonie opened her pad and started drawing purple monsters, softly humming the poovus song to herself. It was a song she knew all three of her moms liked.

CHAPTER 61

Sentiva Alvedine made a big mistake. Had she just tortured Watly with one last nasty dig as the crowd of hosts bore down on them, that would've been fine for her. Had she said "You're about to die finally, you wimpy little rapehead!" or "Kiss your bole goodbye, you incompetent, cowardly fool!" things would've been different. No matter how cruel, taunting, and inciteful the phrase, no "testosterone-poisoning" rush would've powered Watly's mind to regain control. No flood of male, offended-ego-energy would have poured into Watly so she could take back the body and fight for life.

Any "antler-baiting" statement Sentiva might've offered would've had little effect. Watly didn't have antlers to lock anymore. Years ago she did, but no more. There was no testosterone in her to be poked and prodded to life. She was slipping deep inside herself, giving up, waiting for death, and no male-style attack was going to snap her out of it.

But Sentiva made a mistake. No doubt an inadvertent, inappropriate choice of words. Sentiva Alvedine didn't end up making some inconsequential "head-butting" statement. She had apparently intended to slap Watly hard right before Watly's death—right before *both* of their deaths. She obviously wanted to torture

Watly with one final, pointed verbal punch. One last bit of psychological revenge. But she picked the wrong weapon.

"Whhhatly . . ." Sentiva said.

Watly let her talk. It was almost pleasant to have someone else move her bloodstained mouth for a change. She stared off at the army of hosts as they marched closer and closer. They looked to be almost in firing range now, almost ready to shoot. *Let them come,* she thought calmly.

"Whhhatly . . . we're going to die now. It's time to die."

Watly found that she had no control of her body anymore. Sentiva had taken over, forcing her to stare at the oncoming host-soldiers.

Oh, well, nothing much else *to look at hereabouts. Dead Roullic and dead Tavis, is all.*

"Whhhatly . . . I'm not letting you move. We're going to stand right here and die."

Watly felt extremely removed from reality now. So distant. She hardly heard Sentiva talking through her own lips. Watly was floating farther and farther into her center. Sinking deep within her own mind. She watched the world grow smaller and smaller around her. She became vaguely aware of the music that was still playing all through the country. Kind of a catchy, soothing tune. . . .

"Watly," Sentiva droned, her voice sounding stronger and more in control. "You'll never get to see your precious little daughter again. Poor, pathetic Watly Caiper. What a pity. Mea culpa. Mea maxima culpa. Noonie will have to die all alone. If the police haven't killed her already. I sure hope they tortured her first—"

That was Sentiva's big mistake. That cut right to Watly's primal thing, to Watly's mother thing, to the core of her, to the guts of her mind. *What the rape have I been thinking? What the rape am I doing? Noonie! I have to save my Noonie!*

And suddenly Watly had power—enormous power. She pushed. She shoved hard against Sentiva's surprised mind with all she had. She pushed and pushed and pushed, overwhelming the startled Sentiva with her intense turnaround. She got the body back, *fast*. Her head ached with incredible intensity, feeling like she'd busted all sorts of blood vessels up there, but she was back. She was in control.

"Rape you, Sentiva!" Watly shouted, and then the hosts started firing. Slugs flew everywhere. They exploded into the two dead bodies. Both Tavis and Roullic shook from the impact of gunfire. The slugs slammed into the sidewalk and curb and whitetop all around Watly. Without even thinking about it, she dove forward, aiming for Roullic's open cruiser door. She landed on soft leatherlike and slid quickly to the driver's seat. Slugs smashed loudly into the front of the cruiser. Watly kept her head down, fumbling for the driving ringlets above her. The half-open front windscreen shattered and sent shards of tinted plastic raining down all over her.

She found the main drive ringlet and pulled it sharply downward. The rear cylinders of the cruiser roared to life, making the whole vehicle shake violently. More slugs crashed into the front of the machine, shattering the front end and sending splinters of metal everywhere. The noise was unbelievable.

Watly pulled hard on the kickdown ringlet and the cruiser suddenly shot forward down Thirty-third. She was thrown back into the seat from the force of the rapid cylinder thrust. The sound of chip guns and rifles grew louder, hurting her ears. Something on the front of the cruiser exploded from the gunfire. It sounded like the whole machine was falling to pieces, being riddled into nothingness by a million slugs.

And then Watly felt a powerful lurch as the vehicle plowed into some of the hosts. She was tossed back and forth within the cab as one after another person was slammed into. The cruiser kept going, mowing down everyone in the way. More slugs hit the sides of the vehicle now. Watly threw her hands over her head and tried to curl into a little ball on the seat. The cruiser shot forward, forging right through the crowd. Bodies were thrown this way and that, thumping all over the place. Person after person was hit hard by the shattered front of the rocketing machine. Watly could hear the weight of them as they were struck. *Bang bang bang bang!*

Now the only slugs hitting the speeding cruiser were hitting it from behind. Watly was through! She'd gotten beyond the battalion of soldiers.

She stuck her head up just over the edge of the steering tube and aimed the vehicle left on Seventh. It creaked and moaned in protest, but responded to her control, swerving sharply and accelerating even more.

She was on her way. She was alive.

Watly glanced back. The soldiers were way out of range now. Around the corner and out of sight. But she had another little problem. The rear cylinders of the cruiser had been badly punctured and were now on fire. Bright blue flames danced from the slug holes. They'd probably be exploding any second.

"Shit," Watly said to herself as she wrestled with the reluctant steering tube. "This whole raping hunk of metal is about to blow."

CHAPTER 62

Chief Ogiv Fenlocki didn't really understand the technical aspects of this whole modified hosting thing. He wasn't a scientist. He was a police officer. What he did understand of it, he didn't like. It wasn't like regular hosting. It had been designed, in total secrecy, specifically as part of Second Level's anti-Revy measures. Instead of a normal hosting situation—which always involved two people, the host and the donor—this involved only one donor but many many hosts.

With a regular hosting, the donor's consciousness completely took over the one host's mind and body. It was a total commandeering of a single other person. With this *modified* version, one person could control hundreds, but, by design, only to a certain degree. Right now, Zephy Gavy's mind was spread out over about fifteen hundred different bodies. These host-soldiers were given direction and purpose by Gavy, but they each still had enough of their own brain left to allow a certain amount of independent movement and primitive thought. That way, their objectives were all exactly identical, but they could still operate as individual anti-Revy fighters. They were worker bees now. Cells in one brain, parts of one collective consciousness. They could be coordinated and organized and orchestrated instantly, strategies could be adjusted on the spot, groups of them could even be directed to sacrifice themselves and they could not resist.

This modified hosting was quite a technical marvel. An amazing, baffling scientific feat. It made Fenlocki sick. And the more he thought about it, the sicker the whole thing seemed.

He leaned against the rattan railing and reflexively chewed sunbeans. Every monitor and CV projection before him was alive with new activity now. All the hosts had been sent out to work the sector around the command center. The fighting machines were kept well away as the hosts scoured the nearby streets and entered all the buildings in the area, flushing out the revolutionaries. The Revies caught on the street looked startled and confused. They were being killed in huge numbers. Killed by their own people.

Fenlocki turned to look at Gavy in his plasglass booth. The Chancellor was lying in the chair, hooked up to the shiny donor device. He was still totally motionless. That long, funny-looking piece of dyed hair still dangled limply to the side of his face. He still looked, for all appearances, like he was dead. But he wasn't. Fenlocki knew the guy's mind was quite active, lightly prancing about in every single one of the soldiers' heads. Pretty raping sick.

All those hosts had been First Levelers. They'd been kidnapped years ago—or rather "recruited;" as it was euphemistically referred to. They'd been kept locked up in total isolation all these years just in case they'd ever be needed. A human backup plan. Homo sapiens cold storage kept as insurance. And as Fenlocki saw it, the really sick, ironic thing was that these hosts would probably be the ones fighting hardest *for* the revolution. These unfortunate POWs would be the angriest Revys of all, if they had control of themselves. But they didn't. So they were being forced to fight, kill, and probably die for the opposite side. Pretty raping sick.

The Second Level anti-Revy defense system. Funny how it had seemed so clean in the abstract. So sanitary and simple. For all his years as chief of police, the anti-Revy stuff had seemed perfectly acceptable as theory. Some high-tech fighting machines. Some nerve cannons. Some First Level hosts. A tidy, simple way of dealing with a problem that would probably never arise. Maybe a bit unsavory, but, in a way, very intelligent. Fenlocki had always figured that any rebellion would end very quickly, with very little bloodshed. As soon as any rebels got a look at the fighting machines, they'd give up and run back home. Or, at the very least, if it ever came to actually using the hosts, the revolutionaries would *certainly* surrender then. They'd see they were fighting their own people and stop right away. No one would get hurt, and everything would settle down fast. Orderly, clean, sanitary, by the book.

But it wasn't working that way. None of it was working the way Fenlocki had envisioned it. The revolutionaries were not giving up. The whole island country was a bloody battleground.

Fenlocki looked back toward one of the larger monitors to see a lone bashed-up cruiser speeding along Sixth and then turning east on Thirty-fifth Street. The vehicle looked out of control. It was a mess of busted-up metal and plastic and its rear cylinders were on fire. Damn thing looked about to explode in any second. And when those things went, they really went.

Ah, well, Fenlocki thought, *what's one more death at this point?*

CHAPTER 63

Alysess knew the hosts were just pawns. She had understood what was going on the first time she'd seen them marching up the street.

Here were her friends and neighbors, being forced to fight against their own. They were trapped inside their own heads. Powerless to resist. They were each just people like her, and they had been cruelly overpowered, overtaken, used. Their physical actions had nothing to do with their real wishes, with who they really were inside.

But Alysess didn't think about any of this. She didn't ponder the philosophical kill-or-be-killed question that had been tormenting her. She didn't wonder about her ability to defend herself. She didn't wonder about her ability to fight, to hurt, to kill. She didn't think about the innocence of those three facing her. When the trio of cuffers first burst into the building's reception area, pointing their weapons at her, all Alysess thought about was staying alive.

She instinctively rolled over the Ragman's lifeless body so she was behind the cemeld column. The barrel of her hanging scrambler rifle dug painfully into her thigh. The hosts—two women and one man—began firing almost immediately. The large room became full of the incredibly loud *crack*s and *boom*s of their weapons. Cemeld dust flew. The hosts' slugs pounded into the pillar and thudded into the carpeted floor below. Slugs ricocheted all around.

Alysess pressed her back against the hard cemeld, feeling it vibrate tremendously from the slug impacts. The whole room seemed to be rocking and shaking from the force of the three hosts' continuous shooting. She fumbled with her belt, her hands feeling clumsy and huge. Beside her, the Ragman's dead body jerked from some of the wild, scattered slug shots and ricochets.

The hosts were marching closer. They must've been only four or five yards from Alysess's barely effective haven. They kept firing over and over, never pausing as they neared her slim shelter. Alysess ripped an I-grenade from the belt and held it in her fist. Her hand shook.

A huge chunk of cemeld exploded off the column above her and landed by her feet. They were literally shooting the pillar to pieces right behind her. She twisted the top of the grenade and saw the dotted red line on its readout strip begin to waver and blink. It was fully charged and activated.

The sound of the slug fire was so loud now that Alysess felt it resonate in the bones of her body. It was as if guns were going off inside her, shooting up her spinal column and pounding into her brain. She was only half aware that she'd been screaming at the top of her lungs this whole time—"*Yaaaaaaaaaaaaaaah! Yaaaaaaaaaaaaaah!*"—but she couldn't hear herself at all.

She raised her arm, twisted her body slightly, and tossed the grenade behind her.

The guns kept firing. The column kept shaking and chipping, with chunks being thrown in all directions. White cemeld powder puffed out and rained down on her. Pieces of carpet flew up in the air from the slug shots. There was no explosion. The I-grenade hadn't gone off. How long did the raping thing take? What delay was it set for? *Is the damn grenade a dud?* Alysess wondered as small rocks of cemeld slammed into her elbows and hips and shoulders.

And then there was a sound that made all the others seem like nothing. Alysess's ears seemed to implode inward, meeting in the center of her brain. The whole room lit up in a blinding flash and something like an atomic bomb exploded inside Alysess's closed eyes. The sun had gone nova in this one large Second Level reception room. A wall of boiling air slammed into Alysess's back. She fell forward, landing on her helmet.

She scrambled to her feet, grabbing the helmet up in one arm. There was smoke everywhere. Alysess stumbled left toward the rear of the building. She could see nothing. She was blind.

She ran right into a wall, dropping the helmet. She recovered it quickly, fumbling it up over her head and mashing it on. She felt along the wall for an opening. There was another sound behind her. A rustling noise. And then a gunshot. Someone was still alive back there. Someone was still shooting at her. Maybe even more than one person.

Alysess's searching hand hit air—she'd found a doorway. She dashed through it, hearing more slug shots close behind. Her scrambler rifle swung back and forth from her shoulder. She was in a corridor now, and the air was just clear enough here for her to see a little. There were two old-style elevators at the end of the hall, one of the silver doors open and inviting.

She glanced back over her shoulder, seeing the smoke-obscured forms of two hosts following. One of them had blood and gore all over her face and seemed to have lost half of her cheek and jaw—as well as one eye—onto her shirt collar and blouse. The other was missing his left arm, swinging a blood-spurting stump as he calmly marched forward. And still they fired. It was as if nothing at all were wrong with them. These hosts wouldn't stop unless they were unconscious . . . or dead. *Rape!*

Alysess ran all-out now, pumping hard—straight for the open elevator.

A slug ricocheted off the right side of her helmet, feeling like a hard punch in the head.

As she ran, Alysess prayed to Cruda, she prayed to Terra, she prayed to the memory of that bolehole Ragface—she prayed to any raping thing she could think of. She prayed that the damned elevator was working, and that it went all the way to the roof.

CHAPTER 64

Watly pulled the cruiser's FULL STOP ringlet and, as soon as the thing began to slow a little, she jumped out of the open passenger door. She seemed to be doing a lot of that kind of thing lately. Becoming a raping habit.

She landed on her left ankle, twisting it painfully, and started a familiar, uncontrolled tumble across the hard whitetop. She hadn't even stopped rolling when she heard the cruiser blow up. Damn good thing she'd jumped out when she had. There was a white flash and a loud crunching boom. A piece of hot metal from the explosion hit her squarely in the back, knocking the air from her lungs and making her roll even harder.

Girl, do I need a raping vacation or what? she thought as she smacked into the side of a dead body. This finally stopped her tumble.

Watly lay still for a minute, resting against the dead flesh and trying to catch her breath and pull herself together. The piellna music had gone back to repeating the poovus song again—that old standard. The recorded music must've been on some kind of endlessly repeating loop. She'd heard the song before, not long ago—maybe back when she'd been chowing down on Roullic's flesh torpedo—but she'd hardly registered it.

Now she just breathed in and out, listening. The poovus song. Some nasal-voiced, tone-deaf singer belched out the grand old poovus song. The song Aly had sung to help Watly out of a bad jam more than a decade ago. The "letter-writing" song Aly had hummed while Watly had dangled precariously from a cable outside the window of the doctor's apartment. The song that had said: *I'm gonna try to pass you a note, love.* The goofy love song. *Their* goofy love song.

> *When I'm down I write to my poovus.*
> *I write to my poovus every day.*
> *When I'm low I write to my poovus.*
> *I write to my poovus and I feel okay.*
> *My poovus is best.*
> *My poov' fills my kegs.*
> *My poov' drains the bottom*
> *of life's bitter dregs.*
> *No-ho-ho-ho . . . no bitter dregs.*
> *When I'm down I . . .*

Watly lifted her head up. She could clearly see the top of State Two. It loomed about half a block away, just around the corner. About ten yards ahead of her the totally decimated cruiser still burned and loose, twisted pieces smoldered in a jagged circle all around it. Its fire lit up the area; but then, the area was already pretty lit up. Somewhere along the line, streetlights had come up automatically. Their stark yellow glows cast strange, deep shadows everywhere. Watly would've almost preferred the dark. She was at the edge of Herald Square, a large, empty space that looked strangely barren and evil with all the scattered pools of light.

Watly was stretched out at the northeast side of the square near a large department store. In the store's huge windows were displays of oversized post-Lathone furniture—brightly striped floater desks and fixed pinlights in silver containment cages. Two-legged leatherlike armchairs and copper and brass triangular keyboard stands. Toys of the rich. Some of the large windows were shattered or blown out entirely, but a few were still intact. They looked strange, these perfect, untouched little display rooms. Surreal, tiny, perfectly lit and decorated chambers of the

Second Level good life. The good life Watly had been living for ten years. Her life. Her world now.

The broad, brown doors of the department store folded open. A host walked out, looking blankly around the street, his chip pistol cycling all the way down from some recent kill within. He had the same trancelike gaze all the host-soldiers seemed to have. His dead eyes scanned the area—left and right—and then finally focused on Watly.

Watly suddenly realized that, somewhere along the way, she'd lost Roullic's pistol. She must've dropped it during the excitement. She was weaponless. She froze, feeling almost as helpless, exposed, and at a loss as she had way back when her late father had touched her.

The host stepped stiffly toward Watly, calmly reloading the pistol with a new slug-filled cartridge as he walked. Watly shook her head sharply.

She got up on all fours, her sprained ankle throbbing painfully beneath her weight. The host snapped the cartridge in place and cycled up the weapon quickly. Watly bolted forward in a crouched run, ignoring the pain in her ankle. She sped straight at the host as he began to raise the gun up.

Watly scream-grunted—*"Uuuuuuuuuuuuuuuuh!"*—and leapt forward, elbows up and out. She plowed into the guy as hard as she could, hitting him dead center in the midriff. They were both airborne now, zooming backward from the force of Watly's flying tackle.

And then there was glass. Shattered glass everywhere. Watly hadn't meant to, but she'd somehow sent the both of them exploding through the shards of glass of one of the store's display windows.

They flew violently into a little piece of the good life.

CHAPTER 65

Alysess didn't have time to set up the tripod. She didn't have time to decide what to aim for. She lifted up the scrambler rifle and poked it through the iron fence that circled the roof's edge. She quickly sighted the lower of the State Buildings' two gleaming connecting bridges far, far away. It was the farthest distance she'd tried to slide yet. The rifle popped loudly, spitting out the projectile. The violent recoil from the weapon sent Alysess flying back into the half-propped-open set of elevator doors.

She had no time to waste. The other lift would be up any minute. The doors would open and two zombielike, blood-covered hosts would come out, guns blazing. When she'd first gotten to the roof, she had found some shrapnel from an exploded Floobie-pod and wedged her elevator open so they couldn't use that one to get up, but there still was that other one. Raping lift number two. She'd tried to jam *that* elevator's door closed with some of the jagged metal Floobie-pod parts, but it surely wouldn't hold the hosts back for long.

Alysess let go of the rifle, letting the wire pull it into the fenceposts. It clanged firmly against them, perpendicular to the wire. She had no time to tie off the line and recover the rifle. She'd leave it, letting the weapon hold the wire on this end.

She sealed her helmet on with one hand and pulled her bra from her back belt loop with the other. She heard the buzz of the elevator arriving. There was a gentle *ding* sound, and then the doors ground loudly, trying to open. Alysess heard a loud grating noise behind her, the creak of metal against metal.

She climbed up the side of the fence and swung her leg over the pointed iron spires at the top. Now she heard chip guns going off. The hosts were trying to shoot the door open. Alysess hung with one hand from the top of the fence—seventy stories from the Second Level street—and tried to sling the bra over the wire with one trembling hand. She tossed it gently. The bra hung on the line for a second, and then—as if in slow motion—slowly slipped off the right side of it. Alysess stared down, watching her off-white brassiere flutter gracefully toward the street below. It drifted down like some dying bird shot from the sky and then disappeared from view in the darkness between two streetlights. *Shit!* she thought.

The elevator doors creaked loudly directly behind her. The hosts were obviously trying to force them open physically now. It sounded like they were succeeding.

Alysess looked at the wire. "What the subs," she said aloud, feeling her whole body tremble with adrenaline. "I'll go raping braless!"

She lowered herself and reached for the wire with one gloved hand. Just as the door burst open behind her, Alysess clasped her hands over the thin wire and pushed off from the fence with her feet.

CHAPTER 66

Sentiva Alvedine was not angry. Sentiva Alvedine was not frustrated or upset. In point of fact, Sentiva Alvedine never got angry, frustrated, or upset. The secret of life, she maintained quite wholeheartedly, was to remain in constant control of one's slatternly emotions. The indisputable key to assured survival was self-control. Emotion inevitably befouled one's reasoning powers.

She did not pride herself in the fact that she never got upset, for pride itself was an emotion. She was convinced emotions were a sign of weakness. She held no weakness. For ten years she had been a veritable prisoner in her own body, and yet she remained strong and steadfast throughout. A weaker person would, most irrefutably, have waxed deranged. However, Sentiva Alvedine had never been more convinced of her own lucidity than she was right now.

She did allow herself the occasional foray into two emotional states: amusement and pleasure. She succumbed to these feelings sparingly, understanding they were not as disfiguring to the intellect as feelings such as rage and resentment. Yet they were still hazardous and had to be kept in careful restraint to maintain consistent mental equilibrium.

Right now she was permitting herself a short incursion into
both of these relatively innocuous emotions simultaneously.
Sentiva allowed herself a concise amount of amusement and a
terse twinkling of pleasure.

Watly Caiper had just plummeted through a display window
with a host. Her body—Watly *and* Sentiva's body—was replete
with an abundance of lacerations and scratches from the broken
glass. Unfortunately, none of the injuries were very serious. None
of the punctures looked lethal.

The host, however, was obviously dead. He had apparently
alighted unfavorably on some of the broken plasglass. A long
shard had pierced his neck, extending cleanly out of the anterior
of his throat in a rather ludicrous crimson lancet.

Sentiva felt pleasure at Watly's evident revulsion. Caiper
possessed no stomach for violent dissolution. Sentiva could feel
her stomach bubble with Watly's nausea as Watly looked down at
the bloody cadaver. At that point Sentiva began to grant herself
both the humor sensation and the pleasure sensation concurrently
in moderate amounts. Watly was elevating the host's right arm and
staring at the hosting cuff, her stomach churning even more. She
seemed to be attempting to decide something.

I know what you're contemplating, Sentiva mused, sneering
inwardly. *And you don't appreciate the notion at all, but you're
nonetheless going to execute it. You have no alternative option.*

Then, just as Sentiva had anticipated, Watly selected one of the
longer pieces of sharp plasglass and raised it up. She commenced
to saw it across the firm flesh of the inert host's arm, just above
the cuff. She was sweating prodigiously and her body was having
a difficult time keeping the bile from rising up from her stomach.

Sentiva found all this winsomely amusing. Watly clearly
desired the cuff, but the only way she could procure it was to cut
the carcass's appendage off and then slice off his two middle
fingers. Apparently Watly found this venture rather unpalatable.

Sentiva allotted herself a full three or four minutes of hedonis-
tic emotion during this cuff extraction. It was most gratifying. It
was always rather pleasant to detect Watly's disquiet—corporeal
or cerebral.

Watly was extraordinary puerile. In fact, it was this immaturity
that would irrefutably lead to Sentiva's emancipation. The few
intervals during which Sentiva had been able to regain some
limited command of the body had invariably been either during
some insecure Watly Caiper nightmare or, during waking hours,

when Watly capitulated to feelings of futility. That sense of hopelessness in Watly was destined to arise afresh presently. It was inevitable. At the point of its resurface, Sentiva would seize control for good.

She knew her time would come. For ten protracted years she had known her time would arrive eventually. She had waited patiently. She had watched, listened, and learned. She had carefully disseminated all the data that came to her. Being physically powerless for such a long duration had been, in multitudinous ways, a remunerative experience. Foremost, it had allowed the only instrument at her disposal—her mind—to germinate and flourish as never before. It had facilitated the expansion of her reasoning skills, her deductive processes, and—she resolutely affirmed—her very intelligence. Her cognitive capacity had met the challenge of incarceration and not only endured it, but actually benefited from it. With no sense of vanity or self-aggrandizement, she accepted the manifest truth that she was now a genius.

Sentiva was cognizant of the obvious. The rest of the world was not. One obvious certainty was that Watly Caiper was dangerous indeed. Watly was not dangerous because she was resourceful, or mighty, or shrewd. Watly Caiper was dangerous because she was frail and obtuse. She was emotional. Consequently, she was unpredictable. She could, through a certain kind of doltish dumb luck that continually befell her, cause grave damage. She could—and already *had* in some proportion—defile and contaminate the perfection of the Second Level.

The Second Level had admittedly been seriously wounded. Rebuilding the system would be time-consuming, expensive, and tedious, but not impossible. It could be done. When the insurgence was quelled—as was inevitable—an improved, even mightier Second Level would be raised. Eliminating Watly could only expedite that process.

Therefore, Sentiva was quite amenable to sacrificing her own sagacious mind in order to destroy the woman with whom she shared the body. There was no sense of revenge or hostility behind that willingness. Sentiva Alvedine was above that. Sentiva never felt a desire for vengeance. She never felt rage toward this feebleminded cockroach who retained the reins all these years. Sentiva's willingness to annihilate herself if it marked the destruction of Watly was a well-thought-out, rational strategy. If the opportunity to salvage herself while still eliminating Watly mate-

rialized, she would, of course, hastily take it. That would simply
be prudent. Nevertheless, if that opportunity did not arise, she
would be satisfied with both of them dying for the greater good.
And there was unequivocally no anger involved in that particular
decision.

However, there was an additional, even more fundamental
conclusion Sentiva Alvedine's robust genius had arrived at long
ago. Possibly no one but a mental giant could see it, but it
certainly appeared self-evident. There existed right now one
individual who was much more threatening than Watly could ever
be. Heretofore, no others had seemed aware of this. It was
conspicuously evident, but presumably lesser minds had difficulty
accepting it. Sentiva supposed that it was just conceivable Chief
Ogiv Fenlocki's unsubstantial plurite brain was approaching the
appropriate conclusion even now. Should Sentiva have to perish to
terminate Watly, the chief might attend to the problem of his own
volition. Yet if the course of events resulted in Sentiva staying
alive, she would eliminate the difficulty herself.

The Second Level indeed had a much more sizable menace
than Watly. The Second Level certainly had a much larger threat
than the Ragman, whom Sentiva had observed carefully ten years
ago when Watly had proceeded into the subs that one last time.
Neither the excitable Watly, nor the ineffectual Ragman, nor that
grotesquely unsightly and stupid doctor, Alysess, could win the
revolution. That was conclusively perceptible. To win a revolution required a leader—someone extraordinarily forceful. It required an individual who could not only win the battles, but
sustain the spirit long after the combat ended. It required someone
who could prevent counterrevolutionaries from arising and taking
back what was deservedly theirs. There was such a person.
Sentiva hoped others had finally fathomed that and eliminated that
person. Perhaps Fenlocki had already done so. Sentiva herself had
endeavored to do so earlier and failed.

The most pressing danger to the Second Level was Noonie
Caiper.

It had not unduly taxed Sentiva Alvedine's superior brain cells
to reach that rudimentary conclusion. She had observed the child
growing up. She knew Noonie better than anyone. The little girl
had Sentiva's genes. The little girl had been born of Sentiva's
body and graced with Sentiva's DNA. The child possessed
Sentiva's power and intelligence. And the nine-year-old's life had
paralleled Sentiva's life in a myriad of ways. Noonie had cloaked

her authentic self from the day she was born. Noonie had put a spurious front up all her life. So had Sentiva. True, Sentiva had effected this by design, whereas the girl had done it by necessity, but the results were the same. The child had discovered how to master her own emotions. The child knew how to keep everything locked deep inside. Sentiva was well aware what kind of inner strength and vitality that ability could yield.

The phenomenon that had transpired two years ago involving the youngster had only reinforced Sentiva's judgment of the child. Those were the actions of Sentiva Alvedine's daughter.

Though likely incognizant of it, the girl was the insurrection's most puissant weapon. She had the fortitude, power, and cool-headedness to incapacitate Sentiva's Second Level. Had the youthful girl been raised differently, she would have been Second Level's greatest resource. She could have carried on where Sentiva left off, and Sentiva respected Noonie for that. However, the child had been brainwashed with Watly's skewed version of reality all her brief life. She had been indoctrinated with revolutionary propaganda from the beginning. Therefore, she was on the inappropriate side.

Noonie was, even without her own knowledge or the knowledge of the plurite rebels, the revolution's largest truncheon. If Watly should, by some implausible chance, actually make it all the way to her daughter—or if Sentiva should somehow manage to slay Watly while saving herself—the course of action was plain. Sentiva would kill Noonie. However, if fate necessitated Sentiva killing Watly and thus herself before that action could be carried out, Sentiva would have to assume that the truth about Noonie would occur to someone eventually. Some other individual was bound to be just bright enough to realize the obvious and carry out the child's execution. Perchance Gavy, or Fenlocki, or some member of the Chancellor's cabinet would do it. There was no question that child had to be killed.

A lesser mind might have thought Noonie was too young and small to be dangerous. A lesser mind might have considered the idea of a child being an enormous threat absurd. *What could a little girl do?* a low-grade mind might wonder. But Sentiva was smarter than that. She knew age and stature had nothing to do with power. She knew the child's youth and size were in fact advantages, since they made her appear weak and harmless. Sentiva Alvedine had realized years ago that appearances were deceiving.

Coming across as small and insignificant was an excellent ploy. The small and insignificant make ideal weapons.

Sentiva knew all about weapons. She knew that a short blade could often do more damage than a large dagger. This was partly due to the fact that a short blade could fit and be concealed in places a large blade could not. It was also due to the fact that it could be more readily wielded and manipulated. Further, there was the tendency of a small weapon to be underestimated, laughed at, or dismissed entirely by its target.

Noonie Caiper was the revolution's short blade. And she had to die.

CHAPTER 67

From the time she was five, Noonie had interactive social class two days a week. This was where she had to go be with other children and a teacher. Aside from their being fellow students, it was a lot like keyboard class. The teachers taught history, science, reading, writing, math—all that stuff.

The building was five blocks from her home. It was a large, post-Lathone-style structure balanced on a thin pillar and surrounded by huge flying buttresses that looked like insect legs. The other kids called it "the Bug." Noonie called it "Mutant Monster."

The classrooms themselves were small. Each wooden hall had fifteen keyboard chairs, one solid brass teacher's desk, and two cable-vidsatt projectors. Noonie didn't like it. She barely talked to the other students. They weren't like her. They were young. They were wild and out of control. She didn't trust them. And they made fun of her. They thought she was weird. Sometimes they called her "Rapehead" when the teacher wasn't looking. One of them—Bettle Dolipper—once tripped her on purpose and then kicked her hard in the side. But Noonie always ignored them. She kept to herself.

Noonie Alvedine was an average student. She hated math and science, barely tolerated English classes, and absolutely loved history. Her grades in history, however, were no better than in the other subjects. History teachers found her annoying. She asked too many questions. Bursting with excitement and curiosity, Noonie wouldn't wait to be called on. She would leap up and cross-examine the teacher. She wanted to *know,* to *understand.* It was the only time she participated in school, the only time she spoke up.

". . . so the United States became the United Countries during Cadetime," Mr. Heggie, the Welter-Grade history teacher, droned on with his lesson. As usual, he appeared barely awake. "People saw the wisdom of keeping to themselves," he continued, "of breaking off ties, of smaller, more manageable governments. They realized that being a small part of something big and unwieldy was a dangerous, bad thing. Severing ties is a good, good thing."

"Why were their names different?" Little seven-year-old Noonie asked, forgetting even to raise her hand.

"*Noonie Alvedine.* How many times—"

"Why din' they have names like us? Their names sound funny."

"It was just another way of severing ties, Noonie. Now, sit down until you're called upon. If you go to some of the other countries, like those in Jesusland, you'll hear many of the old names. But most of the United Countries of America wanted to start afresh and disconnect from the past and from each other. They wanted everything brand-new and different."

"How come?" Noonie asked, unable to contain herself.

Mr. Heggie sighed in exasperation. "Because, Noonie, things were bad. There were many bad, bad things happening. Lots of fighting. Wars all around the world. Euroshima."

"What's hor-uh-sheena?"

"Noonie, we covered that already. The bombs in the Outer world."

"No, we din'. Tell about the bombs."

"If you can't be quiet, you'll have to leave the room and go home, Noonie. I've warned you before."

Noonie felt frustrated. Everything was so vague. Everything they taught in history class was murky and blurry. Even recent local history—stuff about Walker Gavy building the Second Level of Manhattan and all that followed—was fuzzy and imprecise. B all sounded, even to a child, like it was half made up. It was as though, when the countries split up and the families split up and everyone gave themselves new names and gave up the old, strange ones, they also gave up on history. They disowned the past. But Noonie wanted to know. It was the only interesting part of school.

"I wanna know 'bout the bombs," she demanded, slapping her little fist down on her keyboard station. Some of the other kids giggled. Noonie thought she heard someone hiss out "Rapehead!" very softly.

Misser Heggie's dark face got even darker. "That's *it*, Noonie Alvedine. You're dismissed. You're going home. I'm marking you as half-day suspended!"

And Noonie, for the third time that month, walked down the aisle of the classroom to head home early. All the kids were laughing. One of the kids stuck out a foot and tried to trip her. Noonie stumbled a little but didn't fall. She wouldn't fall again. Ever.

She walked down the steps of the Mutant Monster building quickly, her face feeling hot.

"Hey, Rapehead!" someone yelled. It was Bettle Dolipper at the foot of the steps. Noonie kept walking. Bettle was fishing something out of his little leatherlike schoolbag, something wrapped in plastic. "Rapehead! Heads up!"

And then Noonie felt something hit her in the arm. It wasn't anything hard or painful. It smacked wetly into her and bounced off. It didn't hurt. She looked down. Bettle had thrown shit at her. Animal shit or person shit, she didn't know. It had thumped off her arm, leaving a brown, smelly stain, and fallen to the sidewalk. "There's your lunch, Rapehead!" Bettle yelled, laughing. He must've been kicked out for the day too. Noonie stared down at the dung for a second.

"I don't eat shit," she said, and started walking again. The minute she said it, she wished she hadn't. *I shouldn't have said anything. Never say anything.*

She heard Bettle running over to the pile of shit behind her. She kept walking, calmly and deliberately, toward her home. Something smacked into the back of her shirt. Bettle had thrown the shit again.

I will not run, Noonie said to herself. *I will not run.* She continued walking slowly away. Bettle did not follow. He just yelled after her. "Rapehead! Rapehead! Eat your lunch, Rapehead!"

Noonie continued on. She was above this. This did not bother her. She was fine. She went home to her huge, elegant house, still hearing Bettle's voice echoing in her head long after she couldn't hear it with her ears. The big house was empty. Mom was still at work and Aunt Aly wasn't coming up till later. The only one to talk to was Stoney, the cat.

And that was fine by her. Fine. As she pulled her shirt off and prepared to wash it in the sink, she barely noticed the faint ache of frustration and anger that seemed to emanate from her chest, in the little indentation at the middle of her collarbone.

CHAPTER 68

The angle was extreme. The ride, incredibly fast. Alysess was sliding down the scrambler wire from a seventy-story-high building to the lower bridge between the State Buildings, which was about forty stories high and a good seven blocks away. Shadowy buildings flashed by below her. She sped downward, her gloved hands clasped firmly over her head, the wire zipping swiftly through her clenched fingers.

Almost instantly she heard slug fire coming from behind. *Crack, crack, crack!* The two hosts were on the roof, trying to shoot her down. *I'm a raping sliding duck!* she thought to herself. She tried to keep her head together. There was no place to hide from the shooting. She was right out in the open, flying across the sky like some living practice target. She hoped she would be out of their range real soon. And that the two half-dead hosts were lousy shots.

Crack, crack, crack! Slugs burned through the air all around her. The sky was full of the blur of tiny projectiles speeding right by her. They were damn close. And getting closer. Alysess felt an abrupt, hard tug at her right sleeve above the elbow. A slug had skimmed by her, grazing the silver suit. Then there was a heavy slap against the heel of her left boot. Another near miss. And then she felt a sudden sharp pain in her buttock, the right cheek.

I'm shot, terradammit! she thought, her eyes fogging up from the pain. The zombie boleholes had shot her in the bole!

Her butt stung rawly. It hurt almost bad enough to make her lose her grip on the line. She slid lower and lower—farther away from the hosts, her hands aching from the strain. And still the hosts shot. Slugs flew everywhere.

Alysess could now feel the wire eating through the material of her gloves. It was sawing right through them, sure to reach her fingers soon.

Great. I'm shot in the butt and any second I'll either get shot someplace a little more important or the line is going to cut my fingers right off and I'll fall umpteen zillion feet to a glorious death. I just hope I land on someone I don't like.

The slug shooting grew sporadic. It seemed they were running out of ammo or giving up. Or maybe dying. Finally the gunfire stopped altogether. She must've been out of range now. Small favors. She was gaining speed rapidly, traveling much faster than she had on that first breakneck wire slide. There was no way to slow this journey down. Her shot-up butt was killing her. And surely the hosts had not given up totally if they were still alive. *Those raping shits ain't done yet,* Alysess thought angrily.

Then, as if in response to Alysess's mental comment about the hosts, there was a great moaning note resonating through the wire. *Weeeeeeeeeeeh!* It was a deep, rich note, deeper and louder than all the others that she'd heard on past wire trips. It sounded like they were sawing at the line with something. The hosts were trying to cut it. That had to be the explanation.

You could save yourselves the trouble, you idiots, Alysess thought pointlessly. *All you gotta do is engage the cutting blades of the scrambler gun. Don't stupid zombies know anything about scrambler guns?*

The wire moaned and vibrated as Alysess slid along it. It would be severed any second, by the sound of it. Her fingers stung from the bite of the line as it broke through the gloves' fabric and dug into her flesh.

She was still about a hundred yards from the center of the golden bridge. Its span loomed below her, stretching from one State Building to another, sparkling from the reflected streetlights below. On either side, Empire State One and Two were lit up brightly from surrounding spotlights. The two enormous buildings grew larger and larger, seeming to step slowly aside as Alysess neared the gap between them.

Alysess's hands were on fire now. The line cut deeply into her clasped fingers. *If I could just hold out. . . . If I can just get—*

Suddenly the wire went slack. The hosts had cut clear through it.

CHAPTER 69

Watly climbed through all the broken plasglass and back toward the street. Fortunately, her Chancellor Dancer stomping boots were thick and solid—otherwise she could've cut her feet badly as she crunched and stumbled her way out of the store window. She had discarded both the node hat and the matted red wig back in the display case with the host's body. Now all she wore were the white boots, the yellow fringed skirt, and the casement shirt. She figured that the casement shirt—like the boots now—might've prevented serious injury when she'd first crashed through. The shirt was very thick placene, molded to the exaggerated shape of a female body much more buxom than her own. Watly could tell that under the shirt her torso was untouched by the glass. Only the shoulder wound still throbbed under the casement.

Other than those clothes, she also wore a rather large—and rather bloody—hosting cuff that flopped loosely on her right wrist. Fortunately, the host had been thick-limbed, so she'd had no trouble slipping the cuff over her own thin arm. There it hung, looking reasonably well attached, at least—she hoped—from a distance. The blood on the cuff was mostly dry by now, but some of it was still moist and sticky. Watly looked down at herself.

There was blood everywhere. Her legs and arms had scratches and abrasions and thin cuts all over them that oozed little red congealing rivers. Fortunately, the host's body had also protected Watly from serious cuts as they'd crashed through the window. This blood was minor blood.

The sight of the blood didn't bother Watly much. In the old days—when she'd been a man—all that blood would've really freaked her out. Especially since a good deal of it was her own. But now, as a woman, that kind of sight wasn't as disturbing. Watly supposed it was an indication of yet another advantage to being female. Women grow very accustomed to the sight of their own blood, she realized. Men don't. Blood is a strange, frightening, foreign thing to them. But when one sees one's own hemoglobin issuing from one's body every month like clockwork, the stuff is no longer a stranger. It loses its ability to shock and disgust.

What *did* shock and disgust Watly was the realization of what she was capable of doing to survive. What she'd done to Roullic. What she'd just done to get the cuff off the dead host. How she'd plowed the cruiser through the sea of hosts before that. She tried not to think about it. She tried not to ponder the apparently innate ability she had to mutilate and maim and kill. She tried not to find parallels to the old days, ten years ago, when she'd killed to survive over and over. The guilt of it all. The revulsion. She tried to think about Noonie instead.

Watly limped diagonally across the square, favoring her unsprained ankle. She was exhausted. She was so far past the point of tiredness that she hardly felt tired anymore. Her limbs kept moving as if they'd tapped an energy source from some other, less-fatigued body. She stared forward blankly, her right hand gripping the host's reloaded pistol as she hobbled along.

The streetlights cast long, dark shadows everywhere, making the scorched whitetop and surrounding buildings appear sinister. Everything around her—the sidewalks, the stores, the empty restaurants, the overturned cruisers, the bodies, the golden streetlights, the tall, gray structures—looked menacing and dangerous. Watly limped slowly onward, one plodding step at a time.

She had reached the intersection of Sixth Avenue and Thirty-fourth Street. She stopped and peered slowly around the corner. There it was. Empire State Two. The building was recessed about thirty feet from the street on the southeast corner of Thirty-fourth and Sixth, creating a circular cul-de-sac before it. Watly knew the

State Buildings both went all the way to the sidewalk down on the First Level. She'd been there in the old days. When the structures had been constructed originally, about a hundred years apart, the first five floors were built wide and then the buildings became narrower above that level, creating the start of the famous State Building taper. But since those thick five stories of both were now below the Second Level, up here the buildings appeared set far back from the street. It made them appear superior, as if they were stepping back to view the world from a haughty distance.

Watly saw that in and around State Two's marble-covered cul-de-sac were dozens upon dozens of dead bodies. All revolutionaries. No blood, no slug holes. Just lifeless people littering the area. Some in silver suits and some in rags and dirty clothes. Men and women, young and old. Not a mark on any of them.

Only one thing could've killed them. Haver nerve guns. But not just any nerve guns. Those shiny fighting suits, just like the one poor Tavis had worn, were probably pretty damned boltproof. Watly supposed they'd been designed to deflect nerve gun fire. So whatever had gotten these people had been more powerful than your standard nerve rifle.

Watly looked at the base of State Two. Yes. That explained it. Huge nerve guns. Enormous. Nerve *cannons*, to be precise. The bottom of the building was ringed with the things. Large silver muzzles pointed out of the stone facing in all directions. Each one was moving ever so slightly, up and down, left and right, as if scanning for something or maybe just constantly confirming its own mobility.

Watly figured if she stepped out into the street, the nerve cannons would blast her. If she tried to get any nearer to the command center in State Two, she'd certainly be fried fast. Each cannon probably shot a spray of forty or fifty high-powered bolts at once, blanketing the whole area. Talk about overkill. There was no way she was going to be able to evade that kind of onslaught.

Watly looked behind her. Way up Sixth Avenue, she could just make out the dim forms of more of those host-creatures as they passed under one streetlight after another. She heard distant gunfire and saw flashes from barrels. A few times she caught glimpses of running revolutionaries trying to escape the incessant attack of the hosts.

Watly turned back to take another peek at the tall, imposing building with its enormous weapons jutting outward from that solid base. *Shit*, Watly thought.

And then she took a deep breath, pulled herself up as tall as she could, straightened the fringe on her Chancellor Dancer skirt, tossed her head back, and stepped forward. She calmly limped around the corner and headed straight for State Building Two.

All the gigantic nerve cannons turned and pointed right at her.

CHAPTER 70

Chief Ogiv Fenlocki wanted a drink. He wanted a drink bad. There wasn't one raping drop of booze in the entire building. Command center rules.

He had never before had the desire to drink on the job. He wasn't much of a drinker anyway. He never drank at home, and only occasionally did he take a glass or two when out at some official party or pompous Second Level event. But right now he could've slugged back an entire bottle of cheap First Level booze if he had it.

He didn't even really understand *why* he wanted a drink so bad. Nothing was so horrible. There was a war on, that's all. Wars were horrible, but they were supposed to be horrible.

People were dying. So? Fenlocki had killed people himself, in his day. Cops had to kill people sometimes. It was no fun, but it was sometimes necessary.

Innocent people were dying. So what? Innocent people always died in war. What the rape did that word mean anyway? Who out there *wasn't* innocent, on some level? And who *wasn't* guilty?

Hosts were being *used* against their will. Yeah? Well? Just like war, wasn't it?

Yet still Fenlocki wanted a drink. He wanted a drug. A bottle of booze or a handful of Soft pills or some inventive, black market narcotic. Why? Why did he want to numb himself so badly?

Was it because he'd discovered he'd been wrong about Watly all these years? So what? People make mistakes. He was human, and humans make honest mistakes all the time. It was no big deal. An error in police work.

And still he wanted a drink.

Was it that comment Chancellor Gavy had made? Was that such a surprise? Such a terrible shock? So Ogiv Fenlocki was a puppet, a figurehead. So they wanted a plurite because, if anything horrible happened one day, he'd be expendable. Was that so amazing? So astonishing? What was the big deal?

And why was his mouth so dry? Why did every sunbean he threw into it now taste so bad?

There was so much killing on the monitors and CVs. So much death. Fenlocki wanted to feel better about it. He wanted to feel better that most of the killing he saw now was conventional killing. The war had changed. It had mostly moved into a five- or six-block radius around the command center. It was no longer largely a war of people against machine. It was now mainly human being against human being. Host against revolutionary—with the machines at the rear, preventing escape, and the cannons at the front, preventing access to the command center.

All he wanted—and was it too raping much to ask for?—was a little drink or two. Something to dull things down a little. Soft him out a bit.

Why couldn't he feel good about the fact that it looked like he was winning? The war would not last long now. It was only a matter of hours. The command center was the revolution's only hope, and it was impenetrable. There were no openings in the stone shielding for the rebels to gain access, and the nerve cannons would keep any of them from getting near anyway. The fighting machines were ready to cut down any revolutionaries who tried to flee the area. And the hosts were winning every skirmish, flushing them all out and driving them either into the machines or the cannons.

The hosts were unstoppable. Perfect warriors. They had no guilt, no remorse, they felt no pain. Or rather, Gavy felt no pain as he controlled them. That was one of the ingenious adjustments made when they'd invented modified hosting. The donor felt nothing, and could make each body fight until it dropped. The hosts themselves, of course, felt everything.

Yes, the counter-Revy forces were winning. Winning easily. Chief Fenlocki would be victorious. Why didn't that feel good? Why did he now wonder, just a little, what the rape side he was really on?

Maybe it was that damn kid. That Noonie Caiper. Her talk had shook him up somehow. The story of her life. One thing the kid had said in particular kept running through Fenlocki's mind. The girl had mentioned, just in passing, something that her Aunt Alysess had said once.

"Alysess once told me her fear," the child had said back in the interrogation room. "Aly said, she said, 'Noonie,' she said, 'Noonie, everyone in Revy is worried about your mother. They're worried about you too. They think you both may have been corrupted. Living for so long up here does things to your mind. It makes it easy to forget where you came from. It makes you forget what's important, what it's like to be a real plurite.'"

And now Fenlocki wondered if there was some truth to that worry. Truth not only about the child, and about the mother, but about him. He'd been a Second Leveler a long time now. This was his world. This was what he was defending. This was what the whole raping war was about. Had he forgotten where he came from? Had he lost a grip on something important over the years? Had he been so busy thinking about his career and his vastly improved life-style that he forgot what it was like to live below?

Fenlocki leaned all his weight against the rattan railing and let his head slump forward. Something hurt in his mouth. It felt as though he might have chipped a molar on one particularly hard sunbean. He slowly explored the tooth with his tongue. It felt rough.

"Chief? Chief?" Mobben was calling from his wicker console. "We got something weird here, Chief."

"What?" Fenlocki said distractedly without looking up. To his tongue, the molar felt like a rocky mountaintop. Huge and jagged.

"Monitors four, welter, six, and nie, Chief. Take a look. One of the hosts is going the wrong way. One of the hosts is coming back to the base. Damn weird."

Fenlocki glanced up at the largest CV projection. It displayed the northwest corner of the outside of State Two. Sure enough, there was a lone female host, trudging blankly toward the command center. Her mouth, chin, and neck were covered with

long, stretching rivers of dried blood. It looked as if she had hemor-
rhaged from within her throat, or maybe as if she had recently eaten
something alive—like she was some wild carnivore. *All* of her was
bloody, arms and legs and even the oversized-looking hosting cuff on
her wrist. She was dressed funny too. Different. There was something vaguely familiar about the filthy, ripped, stained outfit she had
on. A skirt? Who wore skirts anymore?

Fenlocki stared at the projection. "What the rape is she
doing?" he asked quietly, not expecting an answer from anyone.
"There must be something wrong with the donor signal."

The host kept walking, limping steadily toward the building.

"Shall I haver her, Chief?" Mobben asked, his fingers on three
of the firing ringlets. "There must be a host malfunction, Chief.
Shall I haver her with the cannons?"

Fenlocki watched the figure approach the building. The blank,
doll-like hosting eyes. The healthy feminine body. The blood-
covered face and filthy outfit. It looked almost like one of the
outfits those dancers had worn during the election ceremony.

"Chief?"

The host's face neared the CV lens. Thick, voluptuous lips;
bright green eyes; hard, overly strong jawline. Fenlocki recognized the woman now. It was Sentiva Alve— No. It was Watly
Caiper. Watly Caiper trying to come back and get her daughter.
Crazy Watly Caiper.

"Chief?"

She was five yards from the bank of cannons now. Watly
Caiper. Insane, foolhardy Watly Caiper. She looked half dead.
She looked like she'd been through a meat grinder. Fenlocki just
stared at the projection.

"Chief? Shall I kill her? Hey, *Chief* ? Okay, Chief? I'm gonna
kill her now, okay? Better safe than sorry, right?"

Fenlocki said nothing. He kept staring.

CHAPTER 71

Watly was a protective mother. Over the years, she spent a lot of time worrying about her daughter. The times that she'd come home from work and found Noonie already there, kicked out of school for the day, she'd been upset. Not upset because Noonie had gotten into trouble, but upset that the child had been all alone. Such a thing worried her. It didn't matter that the Second Level had a history of being very safe. It didn't matter that there was virtually no crime to worry about. Watly still worried.

"Noonie! What are you doing here?"

"Got kicked out 'gain, Mama. Sorry."

"You should have called me, Noonie. Are you okay? Why didn't you lock the front door? I told you always to lock the front door."

"I'm okay. I washed the kitchen floor and started dinner."

"That's sweet, Noonie. How did you get home? Did you walk all by yourself? I *told* them to give you an escort if they sent you home again. I'm going to have to talk to them again."

The smallest thing could set Watly off. Once there had been reports of a missing child, and Watly had almost freaked out with worry for Noonie. She was instantly convinced that the missing child had been kidnapped. She was sure it was the start of a rash of Second Level child abductions and that little Noonie would be next. It turned out the little boy had just wandered off trying to find his cat and gotten lost. That didn't matter to Watly. Even after hearing the explanation, she made Noonie accompany her to work every day the girl didn't have interactive class. This lasted for over a month. Watly only felt truly safe when the child was nearby.

Even the missing pet situation worried her. A lot of people on Second had cats as housepets. Most would let them play outside, roaming the backyard gardens and safe Second Level streets to their furry hearts' content. Alysess would often joke about this. "If those animals were down on the First Level," she would say, "they wouldn't be people's pets. They'd be people's dinner."

When some of the pets in the neighborhood began disappearing, Watly panicked. Sure, she was worried about their own little Stoney—she insisted he never again be allowed out—but she was more worried about Noonie. In Watly's anxious mind, this missing animal situation was another sign that her child might be stolen away. It never occurred to Watly that the cats might have just wandered off, or that they might have been accidentally killed by an unmanned copper's lift flames.

Alysess thought she was crazy. "Lighten up, Watly," she often said. "Noonie's a tough little togger. She can take care of herself."

Watly wasn't so sure. If anything ever happened to the girl, she would just die.

CHAPTER 72

Alysess thought fast. Or maybe not. Maybe thought had nothing to do with it. Maybe it was some kind of survival instinct that had nothing to do with conscious thought at all.

The wire went slack. She kept flying onward. Her body hurled through space, the forward momentum of her slide still propelling her for a short time. Her stomach flew up into her throat. She spun her arms before her, rolling them over and over in the few fractions of seconds she had. The wire was loosely wrapped around her hands now. She gripped it with all her might between her pained fingers.

And she fell.

She plummeted in a strange downward arch, her body tilted forward like a diver, her fall still affected by the speed and direction she had been traveling along the wire. But now the wire was only attached at one end. And that end was secured to the bridge. She gripped the slack wire desperately.

Alysess flew down and down toward the hard road below.

And then there was a sudden, incredibly violent jolt. Her whole body vibrated from the brutal shock. Her legs flipped upward and then flopped back down, fluttering from side to side like loose cloth. Her arms felt as if they'd been wrenched from their sockets. Her fingers seemed attached by only a few threadlike tendons.

And she was swinging. Swinging for miles and miles, it seemed. The wire was holding, taking the shock of her weight. Buildings flew by to either side in a bizarre upward curve. Way below her, the stone wall surrounding the courtyard between the two State Buildings neared and zipped by.

Alysess strained to tilt her head and look up. She was swinging from the wire in an enormous plunging arc, approaching the welcoming gap between the Empire State Buildings. The pain in her whole body was torturous. Now she could see she was passing directly below the shiny connecting bridge. The bridge sailed by above her, about forty yards up. And then she was swinging back up on the far side. Her body was a pendulum, sweeping back and forth in a tremendous curve between the two huge buildings.

She swung higher and higher on the far side of the buildings and then began to slow. When she reached the apex of the arc she was suspended there for a curiously calm second, and then slowly began to swing back. The speed picked up again. Her hands and arms were in agony. She looked downward as she swooped into the bottom curve of her flight, watching the grass-covered ground glide gracefully by below her. At the lowest point of her swing, she was at least two or three stories above the tree-filled courtyard between the State Buildings. Much too high up to drop from.

She kept swinging, back and forth in a huge sweeping motion. This human pendulum was dangling on a thin wire, swaying forward and back uncontrollably, losing strength by the second.

"What the rape am I supposed to do now? I'm a *doctor*, not a terradamned pocket watch!"

Then she heard a popping sound from above. She strained to look up again. The bridge was filling with cops getting into formation along the bridge's railing. They were lining up one after the other along both edges of the bridge in a carefully spaced pattern of blue uniforms. They were all leaning over, looking down at her. Some had already started shooting at her.

Shit on sunbeans! Alysess thought.

She twisted her body left and right as she swung, trying to make a difficult target to hit. Everything hurt except her butt wound. Her whole rear had gone numb suddenly. *Great. About time the suit kicked in and anesthetized my bole injury. I'll die with a pain-free buttock. Fabulous.*

Her fingers began to tingle against the wire. *What the* . . .

The suit's medipak was activating for her hands also now. The battle tog's medicines were starting to try to numb her painful fingers.

"*No*, terradammit!" Alysess shouted out loud. "Don't numb out my raping hands! I'll *deal* with the pain, you stupid suit! I need my hands! I need to feel! I need to feel the wire!"

But it was too late. Her hands were becoming totally dead as she swung back and forth. She had no feeling at all in her fingers now. She couldn't feel where the wire was. She couldn't feel where it wasn't. She couldn't feel anything. All she could do was just try to keep her hands locked in the same clenched position they'd been in earlier.

More shots rang out, making that strangely nonthreatening-sounding popping noise. Then there was the *whoosh* of nerve guns. The crowd of command center security police above her began to fire down at her twisting, swinging form in earnest.

CHAPTER 73

Watly walked, waiting to die. Waiting for the moment when the cannons would blanket the whole street. Hoping that when that moment came, she would get hit in the head before getting hit anywhere else. She had no desire to die the same way she'd died ten years ago. That was not pleasant. Nerve weapons were not comfortable, quick, painless weapons. They were awful ways to die, and she knew that better than anyone. From experience.

Near the brain, she pleaded silently as she limped steadily forward. *Please get me near the brain.* She didn't want to go through the agony again. She didn't want to feel that unbelievably torturous sensation as a bolt burned slowly up her nerves, up her spinal cord, and finally to her head. She was thankful that pain memories are always vague, distant memories. The memory of the actual event of her death all those years ago was very dim. It felt almost abstract and theoretical. She was glad of that. It was not something she wanted to remember well. Especially not now.

She continued hobbling forward, trying to look lifeless and hostlike, trying to keep her head up and her back straight. The cannons still hadn't fired. She was only a few yards from one of the center ones now. The enormous silver muzzle looked like the opening to some sinister tunnel. A tunnel for animals. A tunnel for crouching dwarves. A child-sized tunnel. *Child-sized*. This made Watly think again of Noonie, and suddenly it wasn't so hard to keep her head high and her back firm.

The barrel of the cannon tracked her, followed her. It was pointing—just like all the others were now—directly at her, no matter where she moved. She walked right up to it.

Nothing happened. None of the cannons fired. She was still alive.

Watly stood there for a moment, directly in front of the barrel, waiting for something to happen. She heard faraway piellna music punctuated with distant gunfire all around her. The dark hole of the barrel remained blank and empty. No flash of fire. No bursting bolts. It was a deep, gaping mouth. A wordless mouth. And she was still alive.

Watly very cautiously and very slowly turned and passed beyond the end of the barrel. The cannon tried to continue tracking her, turning leftward, but she was at its side now. She limped calmly down its length, letting her left hand slide lightly along the silver surface.

She stopped at the stone wall and turned back, leaning against the solid curved base of the cannon's long barrel. She was behind all the huge weapons' muzzles now—right up against the building they grew from. Behind the line of fire. Behind all the gaping mouths. Out of range. She let the hosting cuff fall from her wrist and clatter to the marble sidewalk.

Why hadn't they killed her? Had the hosting get-up worked? Had it fooled the command center? Somehow that didn't seem likely. Even if it *had* fooled them, it didn't make sense they'd spared her. Watly suspected that any host inexplicably returning to State Two during this crazy war would've been killed, just to be careful.

But, whatever, she was alive. She'd made it. She was right up against State Two. Her objective. Watly looked around her. The base of the building was all solid stone. There were no openings. Heavy stone shielding must've closed over every doorway and window at the start of the crisis. The only breaks in the stone were the jutting nerve cannons. Otherwise there was apparently no opening into the building at all. On the far side of the building was a tall wall. It shielded the courtyard that was between the two State Buildings. The wall also had nerve cannons sticking out of it.

Shit on wilted weeder salad, Watly thought. Yeah, she'd made it. She'd made it to *nowhere*, was where she'd made it. There was no way in the damn building. And if she retreated now, who knew if her luck would hold? If she stepped back out into cannon range, *this* time they just might be smart enough to kill her. Whoever was asleep at the firing controls might have woken up by now.

So there she was, her arm leaning into a twenty-foot-long, high-powered nerve gun, her back right up against her destination. She was stuck. Caught between a rock wall and a hardly survivable place.

Watly Caiper let go of the side of the cannon. She slid down the wall and landed hard on her butt.

And she just sat there, waiting for some brilliant idea to hit her.

CHAPTER 74

Sometimes, when they could arrange it, Alysess would time her visit up to Second so she could meet Watly at the Alvedine Hosting Building at the end of the work day. The two would walk home together. If Noonie had interactive school that day, they would all converge at the Alvedine residence at the same time for one of Watly's home-cooked dinners.

These were special times. Family times. There was something nice about the long, quiet walk Watly and Alysess would take home together. It was romantic. And there was something comforting about all three converging for an evening meal to talk about their respective days. Alysess would complain about the First Level, Watly would complain about corporate life, and Noonie would quietly talk about how they never taught enough about history in interactive class. Then Alysess would make them all laugh at themselves, and somehow that made everything all right.

On one of these special days, Watly and Alysess walked home and were greeted at the door by the sound of muffled screams. Little-seven-year-old-girl piercing screams of agony coming from the direction of the kitchen. To Watly it was the sound of the end of the world.

The two mothers ran to the rescue, almost tripping over each other. They burst into the kitchen and at first saw nothing. No one. Then another scream came and they saw Noonie's little legs. Noonie was half swallowed by the garbage melter, only her feet sticking out of the contraption's open jaws.

"Noonie," Alysess and Watly both cried out, and ran to her.

"Help me! Mommies! Help me! *Hurts!*"

They got her out fast, though she thrashed wildly. Her shoulder and arm were terribly burned by the melter and the hair on the back of her small head was half seared off. Alysess quickly lay the child down on her stomach across the cold kitchen floor and pushed Watly away. She whipped her doctor bag open and went to work.

"Hurts!"

Alysess had a burn pack in her bag, but first she whipped open a pain pad and pressed it into Noonie's trembling left arm—the unburned arm.

Noonie let out an ear-exploding screech that blended into a wail and then a series of heartbreaking sobs. Alysess cut what was left of the girl's shirt off with a scalpel and then threw both aside. She tore the burn pack open with her teeth and dumped its contents out on the floor. "Okay, Face. Everything's okay now, Face," Alysess breathed out as she started working on the child's back and arm.

Watly was standing over them, tears pouring down her cheeks as she watched numbly. "She's all right, right? She's okay, right? She's gonna be fine, right, Aly? *Right?*"

"Shut up and hold this, Watly," Alysess said without looking up. Her hands were a blur of frenzied motion with the medical equipment.

Noonie wailed again—more in fear and shock than in pain now. Watly knelt down next to her daughter and helped Alysess press the soft burn plates into the girl's wounds.

"Noonie, baby," Watly said through her sobs.

"Mooooommmmmmeeeeeee!"

After a few minutes, the worst was over. The wounds were treated and dressed, the child was given another pain pad, and the screams and wails softened to whimpers and shudders. Watly was doing a good deal of whimpering and shuddering herself. Alysess's expression was hard and stern with professional concentration. The two women gingerly carried the child into the living room, where they laid her on the wicker couch's soft cushions facedown, her tear-streaked features turned toward them.

No one said anything for a while. They just breathed. It seemed to take all three of them a very long time to catch their breaths.

"How did you open it, Nooner?" Alysess finally asked. Her eyes flashed toward Watly, as if in accusation. Then she turned back to the shaking child and put a hand on her trembling leg. "How did you open the codelock to the garbage melter?"

"Seen," Noonie gasped. "Seen Mommy open it before."

Again Alysess's eyes turned to Watly in anger. "You watched Watly open the melter and you memorized the code?"

"Both mommies," Noonie said. "Seen you both do it. Seen how."

Alysess's expression softened some. There was a hint of guilt instead of anger in her eyes. She stroked the girl's leg softly.

"What were you doing?" Watly asked. "What on earth were you *doing* in there?"

The girl turned her face away. Now all Watly and Alysess could see was the back of her head with its half-seared-off hair. Almost all the hair had burned down to an inch or less. She'd been lucky her scalp hadn't been burned as well as her back and arm. Watly could smell the sickly odor of singed hair. It almost made her gag.

"Saving Stoney," the child muttered. "Tryin'na save Stoney."

"What?" Watly walked to the back of the couch so she could look down on Noonie's face. The girl's eyes were closed.

"I wan'ned to save Stoney," Noonie said very softly. "He burn-ned up."

Alysess stood. "The cat was in there?"

"He burn-ned up like the others," Noonie said. She sounded groggy. "I try-ta save him."

"What others?" Watly asked, leaning down over the back of the couch toward her daughter's face. "Other *cats*?"

"They got burn-ned up. They got all melted up."

Alysess walked over so she was next to Watly. "Noonie, you've been putting cats in the garbage melter? You've been killing cats?"

"Was trying to save Stoney 'fore he melted. Trying to get him back."

Watly whispered softly to her daughter. "How did Stoney get in there? Who opened the codelock and put your kitty in the melter?"

The child said nothing.

"Who did it, Noonie?" Watly asked again. She felt a strange sense of panic building in her belly. "Answer me."

"He was bad," was all Noonie said.

Watly and Alysess looked at each other. Alysess's eyes showed shock and horror. "She's been killing the neighborhood cats, Watly," Alysess said. Her lips twitched. "She killed her own cat."

Watly shook her head. "Noonie *loves* that cat."

Alysess nodded. "Yeah," she said very slowly. "I know."

"He was bad," the little girl murmured again, sounding near sleep. "But I changed my mind. Want him back."

"Watly," Alysess said, her voice trembling. "Watly, we've got to take her to a doctor."

Watly looked down at her daughter. She was so small, so delicate, so tender. Her little wounded body barely took up half the couch. "You're a doctor," Watly said. Her tone was blank. "You're a doctor."

"She needs another kind of doctor, Watly. This is bad. This isn't normal. She needs help."

Watly reached down and stroked Noonie's cheek. "No," she said, as if she were talking about the weather. "She'll be fine. My daughter will be just fine."

CHAPTER 75

Alysess swung wildly.

Chip gun and nerve gun fire rained down all around her twisting form. A nerve bolt slammed into her right shoulder, bouncing off the reflective material of the suit. Another ricocheted off her left thigh. She looked at the trees of the courtyard below her as they whizzed back and forth. They were so far down. So damned distant.

She tried to loosen her totally numb fingers just a little, hoping she would slide gracefully down the wire to safety. Or at least down to some kind of cover. With no sensations coming from her clenched hands, it was impossible to know how much to relax them on the line.

She tried. And slid down some as she swayed recklessly.

And suddenly she was falling. The line lashed at her wrist and arm, unraveling rapidly around her hands as she scrabbled to get another grip on it. But it was gone now. The wire was gone. She couldn't feel it. She couldn't see it. Nothing was holding her. She was plummeting a good three stories to the courtyard below.

As she fell, a slug hit the edge of her helmet and shattered the visor. Another slug slammed into her left arm just below the elbow, breaking through the suit and shattering both her radius and her ulna bones. Three nerve bolts bounced off her legs in quick succession.

"*Rape, rape, rape!*" she yelled as the earth flew up at her.

CHAPTER 76

Chief Ogiv Fenlocki's hands were trembling. He gripped the rattan railing tightly, trying to stop the strange shakiness he felt. Two of his command center technicians were blatantly staring at him, and the rest kept stealing surreptitious glances at him as if he were crazy.

What was so damn crazy?

All he'd said was "Hold it." That was it. He'd told Mobben not to bother with the host. Not to waste the ammo. "Spare the bolts," he'd said. "She can't get in the building anyway." And when Mobben had questioned him further, maybe Fenlocki had raised his voice a little. But not uncharacteristically. Not unreasonably. "Just *drop* it!" he'd said. "Who the rape is in charge here anyway?"

None of that was any reason for the whole staff to be looking at him now as if he were missing a few pinlights in the head.

Fenlocki wondered if maybe he'd said something else, something he'd forgotten. Maybe he'd blocked it out. Perhaps, just as Mobben was about to pull the cannons' firing ringlets, he had blurted something out. He couldn't remember.

But that would explain the strange looks. Maybe, in the heat of the moment, he had jumped in with something like: "Leave her the rape *alone,* already! Let her *be*!"

It was possible. He might've said something like that. He didn't know.

Now, on two of the floating monitors over his head, Fenlocki could see Watly Caiper sitting against the building, resting comfortably next to the huge, phallic-shaped cannon barrel. What was she doing? What could she possibly accomplish out there? One very messed-up-looking, blood-covered woman outside of an impenetrable fortress. What the rape did she expect? What did she want from him, terradammit?

Fenlocki straightened up and wiped his trembling palms on his pants legs. "I'm going for a pee," he said quietly to no one in particular. And then he folded the command center doorway open and stepped into the hall.

He didn't have to pee. He didn't really know why he'd left the room. He just knew he had to get out of there for a minute. Away from the stares and glances. Away from the monitors and CVs and ringlets and levers and keyboards and cables and blinking pinlights. Away from the image of Watly Caiper, just sitting there expectantly.

He wished he could go for a walk. A long, quiet walk through some grassy park. But he couldn't. He was stuck. Stuck here. Stuck in charge.

Fenlocki headed slowly down the hallway, turning right at a juncture. Maybe he'd check in on the kid again. The kid whose name was Noonie, "a contraction of no one." He remembered her saying that long ago. A lie, yes—but a lie with pain behind it. Maybe he'd check on her. No, that would just confuse things more.

And everything felt very confused now.

Fenlocki wandered aimlessly down the corridors of State Two, seeing nothing. Feeling nothing.

CHAPTER 77

Branches and leaves smashed harshly into Alysess's body. She was tossed about, flipping this way and that, snapping thin twigs and bouncing off thick tree limbs. The green and brown arms slapped and punched at her like some bizarre downward gauntlet. Her body was a rag doll, bending and crashing and somersaulting through a large, leafy monster.

Then the branches were gone and she was in empty air again. Twisting through a void. And then some green grass flew up and slammed hard into her numb butt.

And everything stopped moving. Except pieces of dirt and earth and small divots of grass that popped upward and danced all around her. Slug impacts. A shower of slugs.

She was going to die.

Now there was also the flash of bolts striking the grass. They hit hard and burned bright for a second, looking for nerve.

She *was* going to die.

She knew it. They were shooting down on her through the thin cover of tree branches. She couldn't move. She was shot in the butt, in the arm, and in the raping helmet. Her hands were dead and bloody and her body was banged up and beaten to a limp pulp by the malevolent tree. She was going to die.

Incredible fear washed over her. More fear than she'd ever felt. Here she was, down in the lush, walled-off courtyard between the State Buildings, lying in a heap under a huge neo-elm as cops shot down at her. And the fear was tremendous. Overwhelming.

A few yards to her left was a bright white cemeld park bench. It looked absurdly pastoral and serene sitting there among the flowers and bushes. And Aly *knew* she was going to die.

Her body was a mess. The pain was intolerable. The fear was worse than ever.

In one last spurt of desperate energy, Alysess pushed off with her feet and rolled toward the bench. Clumps of grass exploded inches from her face as she tumbled. She landed on her shattered arm in one enormous scream of pain, bumped her broken helmet on the edge of the bench, and slid clumsily under it.

Cruda, I'm dying! I'm raping dying here!

Slugs showered down on the cemeld bench above her. Nerve bolts smashed into it. It sounded like it was being pulverized. Smokelike puffs of powdery cemeld dust obscured everything around the cowering doctor. More pieces of grass and flower petals shot up dimly through the dust.

She was so damned scared. Why did she suddenly know, after all she'd been through, that she was about to die? And die in horrible agony? She was sure. Why was the terror so complete? So uncontrollable? So raping paralyzing? Why did she feel she was sliding rapidly into a deadly panic attack?

And then the small part of Alysess's brain that was still rational, that was not totally crippled with terror, figured it out. She was in an anxiety field. The whole courtyard was one vast anxiety field. This was yet another Second Level defense, another command center protection device.

She was being scared, literally, to death. The courtyard anxiety field must have been activated at the same time as the nerve cannons, to further guard State Two from any invasion. There was no way around it. She was right in the heart of it.

"Oh oh oh oh," Aly gasped over and over.

Anxiety fields directly stimulated the fear centers of the brain. There was no way to block them. And Alysess had never felt so raping terrified in her whole life. And that terror was building, growing, reaching a deadly crescendo.

I'll die for nothing, she thought, trembling. *For no one. For no good reason. And it will be slow and painful. It already is. My life has been worthless. And Watly will die. And probably has already. Ripped apart like that Second Level family I saw at the portal. And Noonie too. Little Noonie—torn to pieces as she screams for me and for her other mommy. They will never know how much I loved them. They will die thinking I have abandoned them. None of us will ever see each other again.*

"Oh oh oh oh oh oh *oh!*"

And the war will be for nothing. The war will be lost. Second Level will win and be rebuilt worse than ever before. Thousands will die and suffer. Thousands I might have helped. I know that. I could have helped. I could have minimized the pain and blood. I could have taken charge like the Ragman wanted. But my life has failed. And my death has failed.

"Oh oh oh oh oh oh pleeeeese! Somebody help me!" she cried out.

And I'm sure there is an afterlife. The afterlife will be eternal torture, eternal pain and agony. A soul-fire that burns in any failure's heart forever.

"Oh oh oh oh oh!"

Even if it's good and pleasant, it's raping terrifying. Existing after death, forever and ever, is more frightening than any nothingness fantasy. To endure infinitely: the worst nightmare of all.

"Oh, no no no *noooooo!*"

Her eyes blurred with tears. Slugs and bolts continued to crash down on the bench above her. Her whole area was being pelted with brightness and streaks of noisy pain. Alysess poked her tongue out, frantically pressing every tongue tab in the helmet. The helmet was full of shattered plastic from the shot-out visor. She had to shove some of the shards aside with her tongue to get at the row of lower, smaller tabs.

"Please!"

Didn't the raping suit have some defense against an anxiety field? Didn't one of these zillions of tabs stop the fear somehow?

There *was* no defense against an anxiety field.

Alysess felt her heart pounding wildly. It was thumping way too hard. It would surely burst right out of her chest in any moment. Her whole body was shaking violently from the terror. The broken arm and body bruises all numbed out suddenly, deadened by the suit's automedipak. It didn't help. It just made

Alysess feel closer to death. It made her feel like her body was slowly disappearing into nothingness.

In the fuzzy distance, Alysess could see a small door to State Two. It was an old-fashioned wooden door. No guards, no locks, no thick bars. They didn't need them. That one tiny door was well protected. No one would ever get to that little entrance with an anxiety field like this operating. So close, yet so far.

Alysess felt her face break out in a greasy cold sweat. Still she fumbled her tongue into the small tabs.

"Help me please somebody help me oh please I'm dying I'm so damned scared please . . ."

And then Dr. Alysess Tollnismer, poovus to Watly Caiper, co-mother to Noonie Caiper, and reluctant newly appointed leader of the revolution . . . went limp there under the park bench . . . and died.

Just died.

All the pain and fear stopped.

CHAPTER 78

Watly didn't come up with a brilliant plan. Inspiration didn't strike, and Watly was smart enough to realize that waiting for it was fruitless. If one waits around for inspiration to hit, one might end up waiting forever. Better to act. Better to go from point A to point B. Better to do whatever the obvious was. Better to do whatever uninspired, simple solutions events dictated than to sit around hoping a spectacular plan would fall out of the sky.

She looked at the building behind her, at the huge cannons jutting from the solid stone surface. Above them the stone wall rose about two hundred feet before there were any windows. It was impossible to climb.

Well, then, she would do the obvious, crazy as it was. Otherwise she'd end up waiting around till morning, staring at her bloody boots all night long.

Watly stood up stiffly. Her joints ached and that old shoulder wound throbbed badly again. She steadied herself against the stone and breathed deeply. Here at the ground floor of State Two there were no inviting doorways or half-open windows. No welcome mats. No red carpets. No little cozy pet flaps. No person-sized ventilation exhausts. There were no openings of any kind into the building. Except the obvious. The suicidally obvious.

Watly stepped forward, careful not to put too much weight on her bad ankle. She walked back down the length of the cannon, limping even worse than before, listing to the right some. The ankle was starting to swell up in the stomping boot. It felt like the boot's tough white fabric was shrinking tighter and tighter around her sprain.

When she got to the end of the long barrel, she turned. She stuck the host's chip pistol into the front of the waistband of her skirt and raised both hands up to grip the bottom lip of the huge cannon's muzzle. Watly did a painful pull-up, kicked out twice with her legs, and slithered up headfirst into the end of the nerve cannon's gaping mouth.

CHAPTER 79

Noonie sat up stiffly. She had been dozing, maybe. Or maybe just daydreaming there in the empty room. And then suddenly a strong sense of uneasiness had washed over her. Something was very wrong. Something bad was happening.

She didn't know where the feeling came from or what it meant. She just felt it. Badness. Badness approaching. Or badness happening. Bad happenings or bad people. Or both.

Maybe she'd just had a bad dream. But the feeling was so intense it didn't seem dream-created. It seemed real. Something was wrong.

She looked down at her pad, which was now full of pictures she hardly remembered drawing. Hours of pictures. The sketches got looser and sloppier and angrier-looking page by page. They were drawings of cats. She couldn't remember the last time she'd drawn cats. She never drew cats. She must have gotten bored. Tired. Tired of drawing, tired of waiting, tired of being in this stupid interrogation room, and even a little sleepy-tired. A little I-need-a-nap-or-I'm-gonna-get-real-cranky tired. It's-been-a-long-day-and-I-want-my-big-white-bed-and-stuffed-animals tired. I-need-Necky-the-giraffe-to-snuggle-with tired.

Before Necky, there had been someone else to snuggle with. Someone cute and alive. Someone furry and playful.

I didn't mean to. I never meant to, she thought, not even sure what she was thinking about. *It was the Isthmus place. It was the rage thing. I didn't do it on purpose. Really. I didn't ever mean to!*

Noonie pushed the pad aside, watching it slide almost to the far edge of the wood-grained table. She held tightly to the click-pen with her right hand. The feeling of badness was still very strong in her throat and the base of her spine.

She stared at the door.

The door's latch was brass-colored and lumpy-looking. It was shaped like a piece of soft clay would be if a big hand squeezed it in a loose fist. It was ridged into little mountains and valleys like a negative palm and fingers.

Noonie heard footsteps in the hallway. Leatherlike soles on the metal tile. They got louder and louder and then stopped.

The door clicked gently and the latch wobbled, lifting up slowly. Noonie gripped the click-pen tightly, staring at the door. Someone was unlocking it. Someone was coming in.

The latch fell back down. The door clicked again and the footsteps echoed once more, slowly fading into the distance. Someone had changed his or her mind. Someone had started to come in but changed his or her mind.

"Misser Fenlocki?" Noonie said very quietly. "Misser Chief?"

But no one was there now. Noonie wondered if anyone was anywhere now. Anyone but her. The Isthmus place began to ache and swell.

CHAPTER 80

Watly twisted around so she was faceup. Then she wriggled until she felt herself sliding deeper down the cannon's barrel.

She had never been one for claustrophobia, but this was pretty extreme. The inside of the barrel was only about two and a half feet in diameter at its widest. It was dark and cold and stale-smelling. Watly had a hard time breathing comfortably. Part of that might've been psychological, but there *was* a slightly chemical odor under the mustiness. The chemical smell emanated from the surrounding smooth metal, almost like ammonia but weaker and less biting.

Watly wiggled more, using her elbows and palms, snaking her way farther inside the large weapon. She was getting a little dizzy from the close quarters. It was very cramped. Very tight. She couldn't even straighten her arms in front of her. She was a human cannon cork. A living stopper. She kept working her way deeper into the tight barrel.

Now I know how it feels to be a penis, she thought to herself.

She lifted her head up so that it was touching the top curve of the barrel. She craned her neck forward, sliding her head along the metal, and looked down her body. Over the rise of her casement

shirt's molded breasts, her feet looking very small and distant.
They were silhouetted against the circle of light that was the
muzzle opening of the cannon. Watly could see the street and the
buildings opposite around the toes and sides of her boots. That
distant, outside world shifted slowly, back and forth and up and
down, as the cannon adjusted constantly.

Girl, this is giving me major willies, Watly thought.

Then she squirmed farther down the barrel. The round hole of
light grew smaller. Watly's head hit something solid. She wriggled forward a little and tilted her head back, looking up. She was
at the rear end of the cannon, right up against the bolt vials. There
were dozens of them, perfectly arranged in a solid wall. Each vial
was frosted yellow with blue code marks and warning labels, and
the ends facing her were hexagonal. They all neatly locked
together to form the smooth, flat surface of the bolt magazine.
Watly squinted at the vials. She could see a faint glow and some
kind of vague, shadowy movement going on within each nerve
bolt container.

If she could get beyond these inactivated bolt vials, maybe
there was a way to get out. Maybe there was an opening in the
cannon on the far side. The bolts had to come in somehow. The
vial magazines had to be reloaded from somewhere. Plus, didn't
a cannon have to be cleaned every so often? Shouldn't there be a
hatch or something that—

Suddenly the whole cannon lurched violently to the left. Watly
looked down through her feet again at the full moon of light. The
cannon was pointing at the corner of Thirty-fourth and Sixth. It
was aimed at the same building edge that Watly herself had peered
around. The barrel raised up some. That smell like ammonia
seemed stronger suddenly.

Watly stared down at where her cannon was pointing, her neck
getting stiff from the effort. She saw a tiny face—a revolutionary's
face—peeking around the corner just like she had. It was a young
man with a dirty sudofeather hat on. His eyes were wide and his
face unshaven. He looked damned scared. Watly could just see the
end of some kind of gun barrel sticking timidly around the
building from near the guy's hand level.

The whole cannon began to vibrate slightly. It wasn't a "heavy
machinery" vibration. It wasn't an "engine starting" feeling. It
was very subtle, just a slight tremble. That ammonia odor now
smelled burned and smoky.

And then it got brighter in the barrel. A light was quickly

growing behind Watly's head. She looked back. The vials were
burning brightly now. Little mini bonfires glowed with intensity
from within each cloudy container. The movement inside every
one was picking up, as if each vial was full of a million frantic,
fragile bugs.

Oh, this was *a really brilliant plan*, Watly thought. *Really
brilliant.*

She looked back down the barrel to see the revolutionary
tiptoeing forward, wimpy little gun out, slinking slowly out onto
the street.

Great!

"Good move, guy! Get the rape out of here!" Watly yelled. But
the man couldn't hear her.

"Hey!" she yelled even louder. "They're about to fry
you . . . and *me* in the process. Get *away!*"

The guy kept coming. Watly clawed at the surface of the tube,
trying to find a lip, an edge, *anything*. She tried to push her way
back out, but the angle was too steep and the barrel too slippery.
Her brow began to sweat. She felt heat radiating from the nerve
bolt vials behind her.

Well, she thought as she slammed her fists hard against the
solid metal surrounding her, *I* said *I wanted to get it in the head
if I was going to get it. And I'm sure gonna get my wish, times a
couple dozen.*

CHAPTER 81

Noonie Caiper Alvedine hated the Isthmus place. She didn't understand it. It was the anger place. The hate place. It was where rage hid within her, all coiled up like a prehistoric snake. It was where fury dwelt, just under the surface.

It seemed like it had sprung up, fully grown, on the day the cats started falling into the garbage melter. But maybe it had always been there. Maybe it had started the day she was born. Maybe it had just been fed over the years. Maybe it had been nourished by all the make-believe. Maybe the fact that Noonie *did* stand for "No one," at least in her own mind, made the Isthmus place strong and heavy with blood.

It frightened Noonie. In the times when the Isthmus place blossomed, she felt out of control. Way underneath the rage and feeling of superhuman strength, there was always just a little baby. A little girl feeling smothered, like she was dying slowly from lack of clean air. But mostly there was power and hate. It was as though someone else moved her, controlled her. Someone else— someone more like the real Sentiva Alvedine she'd heard so much about—moved her to catch the yowling cats, to toss their little squirming, clawing bodies into the lava and watch them melt. To laugh while they died.

She always felt bad afterward. More than bad. Horrible. She *was* horrible. She was bad. A bad, evil, horrible person. Like the pictures she always drew. That's what she was, and she knew it. She was a monster.

CHAPTER 82

Watly always thought that, when it came down to it, dying a second time would be easier. She thought she had lost a good deal of her fear of death. She thought that, if a moment came along when she knew she was about to die and there was nothing to do about it, she would calmly let death happen. She had been there. She knew what it was about. It was about The End, but that was all right. Ends were okay.

Yet Watly was not calm. She was not relaxed and ready to die again. She was frantic. Her heart was bursting with overpumped blood. Her chest was heaving for air. Her hands were scrabbling desperately all over the inner surface of the cannon. She was flailing about and screaming.

The dozens of roiling bolt vials were really hot now, burning the skin at the top of Watly's head. The cannon seemed suddenly empty of air, a total vacuum. Watly felt the tiny hairs all over her body prick up and tingle from static electricity.

"Help me!" she yelled. "Somebody help me! I don't wanna die in here!" Her voice echoed hollowly in the narrow barrel.

And then there was a brilliant burst of light. The light came

from Watly's left—not behind her head. She was blinded by it.
And there was a voice.

"That's about the stupidest thing anybody has ever done," the
voice said.

Watly blinked and squinted. Someone had opened a small
hatch in the cannon's side. There was an incredibly brightly lit
room beyond.

"Give me your hand. *Quick*," the voice said.

Watly blinked again.

"Quick!"

Watly reached out into the light. A strong hand grabbed hers
and pulled her roughly out of the small opening. She still couldn't
see as she squeezed through.

"Close the hatch! Close the raping hatch!"

Watly stumbled backward and fumbled for the hatch handle.
She slammed the curved door closed. The hatch seals set in just as
the crackling *whoosh* sound of the nerve bolts shooting down the
barrel began. She heard distant, muffled-sounding screams. The
revolutionary had been hit. And she was still alive.

"Holy shit," Watly mumbled, trying to catch her breath. She
turned and saw the silhouette of the man who had pulled her to
safety. Her eyes began adjusting to the brightness.

She was in a narrow cannon-loading chamber. It was an
angular room full of pipes and cables and wires and high stacks of
large bolt magazines. A huge magazine-loading machine took up
most of the small room. One of the walls was tilted sharply
inward, but in Watly's disoriented state, she couldn't tell which
one was. She didn't know which was vertical and which was on
the angle. She couldn't even tell if *she* was standing straight or
not.

There were super-strength, clear industrial pinlights in a long
row at the apex of the chamber's pointed ceiling. That explained
the brightness. Her eyes were only now becoming able to see clear
shapes and colors. The human silhouette was gaining definition
before her, becoming a person.

"That has got to be the stupidest damn thing I have ever seen
anyone do in my entire life," Chief Ogiv Fenlocki said. "What are
you, *crazy*?"

He wasn't smiling, but Watly saw concern and maybe even
affection in his face. Honest concern. And confusion. His eyes
looked different. More human. More vulnerable.

"You saved my . . ." Watly started, and then she collapsed back into the side of the closed cannon.

"Now we're really even," Fenlocki said rather coldly.

Watly felt tears running down her dirty cheeks. They felt cold. Fenlocki stepped closer. "You look like shit. You really do." There was something angry in his tone.

Watly cried. Her chest and shoulders shook. That bullet wound under the casement shirt ached painfully as it rubbed against the material. Without thinking about it, Watly raised her arms up. She was reaching out to Fenlocki through her tears. She didn't know why.

"Where's my daughter?" Watly said between sobs. Her hands stretched out limply before her.

Fenlocki stepped gradually nearer. "She's okay. She's safe. Real near."

And then Fenlocki walked slowly into Watly's open arms. His hands hung loosely at his sides as Watly embraced him. He let her rest her bloody face against his chest and cry fully. After a minute of this, he reached his right hand up and cupped the back of her head in his palm. Then Watly really let loose. She wailed. Wetness ran from her eyes and nose all over the front of Fenlocki's blue shirt.

"You're a crazy lady," Fenlocki whispered. "Crazy." He kept saying "crazy" softly, over and over as Watly cried on him. Then he said, "You're messing me up real bad."

Watly knew he wasn't talking about the tears and snot and blood on his shirt. He meant something else.

"I'm messed up bad," he repeated. And then finally he hugged Watly back. They clung to each other hard, Watly crying and Fenlocki murmuring "Everything's messed up" over and over.

After a few minutes of this, Fenlocki said "Sorry" very quietly in Watly's ear. She thought he was apologizing for everything, apologizing for everything that was happening.

"I'm sorry," he said again.

He wasn't apologizing for everything, Watly realized. He was apologizing for what Watly felt against her belly button. Something was pressing into it through his pants. Something firm.

Fenlocki was hard.

"Sorry." He sounded embarrassed. Ashamed.

Watly smiled into his shirt. She felt like she was dreaming. Like they *both* were dreaming. She looked up at Fenlocki's lined face. At the deep nasolabial folds beside his mouth. At the tiny wrinkles around his eyes. At the small sacklike pouches under his lower lashes. This was the face of the man who had killed her all those years ago. The face of her executioner. She kissed it. She kissed the face of her executioner.

And Fenlocki kissed back. He kissed her messy cheeks. He kissed her tears. Her neck, her left ear, her jaw, her temple, her eyelids. And then her mouth. And their tongues came slowly forward and began to dance timidly together. And Watly felt wet and hot below.

The kiss broke for a second.

"This is crazy," Fenlocki said.

"Shut up," Watly said.

She pulled him back to her. Their tongues sparred again, more lustily this time. And then, there in the cramped cannon-loading chamber while a war raged outside, two exhausted, confused soldiers for opposite sides made passionate love.

And the female Watly Caiper finally lost her heterosexual virginity. And it was kinda nice . . . in a weird, dreamlike way.

CHAPTER 83

Watly didn't know what Fenlocki was thinking. They had had sex, and now he was sneaking her down the hallway to a room he said Noonie was in. He seemed withdrawn, maybe embarrassed. He was pulled well into himself. There was a thousand-foot wall around his emotions and Watly couldn't read him at all.

"This way," he said after checking an intersection of corridors to see if it was clear.

Watly limped hurriedly after him. She could feel Fenlocki's warm juices trickling down her inner thighs as she hobbled along. Warm fluids, both his *and* hers, dripping slowly out of her. She wanted, maybe foolishly, to hold his hand as they walked. But she could hardly keep up, and Fenlocki wasn't slowing down for her.

The sex had been good. Different, weird good. It was as if they had both been desperate for contact, for some kind of intimacy, for a break from all the craziness around them. Watly had come. A good, solid come. She'd gotten on top and run her fingers rapidly over that special little button as they'd bucked together. It didn't matter that the fullness—that having a man moving inside her—hadn't been enough. She'd always fantasized that it *would* matter. That she'd feel somehow inadequate that the fucking alone wasn't enough. But it wasn't like that.

She'd played with herself during the sex, feeling perfectly natural, and she'd come real good from the combination of things. And that was fine. Her hands tingled and numbed out in that good, non-numb way, and she saw a pastel rainbow of colors on her inner eyelids. And then, a short while later, Fenlocki rolled them over as one in that tiny cramped chamber so that he was on top. He pounded strongly, passionately, grabbing Watly's butt and kissing her deep.

That was a neat sensation. Her back was pressed into the firm floor. The weight of this big man was on her. Her eyes were open, watching everything. Watching the sweat on the side of Fenlocki's weathered face. Watching the tight grimace of pleasure. Then Fenlocki's legs stiffened and he tensed up all over. He moaned softly—a deep, throaty, male animal sound—and his back arched. He thrust all the way in her, arms squeezing and hips spasming, and he filled her with his orgasm. She could feel his penis twitching deep within her, and it was kinda neat. Kinda wonderful. She was with him through it. She knew what he was feeling. She'd been there.

But the moment passed. They'd dressed in a hurry, not looking at each other and not speaking. There didn't seem to be any good words to use. Watly had thought to put the pistol back into her skirt's waistband, but she felt strange and guilty about doing it, like the weapon shouldn't be necessary now. For some reason she imagined Fenlocki giving her a harsh, disapproving look if she picked up the gun. She didn't want that from him now. Not now.

She left the pistol where it lay on the chamber floor. She knew she'd feel more secure with it—and right now she was feeling very insecure, so she could use all the help she could get. But it seemed wrong, somehow. The chief of police had a gun and she was with the chief. For some reason that felt like that should be enough for her.

At one point, slinking along the corridors, they'd almost run into a bunch of cops who were hurrying along the hallways. Watly and Fenlocki stepped back and pressed themselves into the wall as the police passed. She really wished she'd taken the gun then. She wished she'd had her hand on a cold pistol butt just to be safe. Two weapons were better than one. She'd been stupid. She should've taken it. And she didn't even know exactly where Fenlocki stood or what side he was on.

Watly kept hobbling after the chief, unarmed and unsure of herself. And of him.

"She's in here," Fenlocki said, stopping up ahead in front of a metal door that had a large brass palm-latch. "Hurry up." He was glancing up and down the hall, looking nervous. He seemed terrified of being seen with Watly.

Watly limped toward him and caught up just as he unlocked the door. It folded open slowly.

There was wide-eyed Noonie Caiper, wearing all black, half hidden behind a wooden chair, clutching her pen as if it were a weapon.

Watly's little girl.

CHAPTER 84

Noonie saw the chief first. He looked weirded out. Antispaf. Creepy prone.

Something was funny. His face was gone. His face was blank. Cold-looking. Smeary.

Then Noonie saw Watly. Mommy.

Mommy's face was not gone, if it was Mommy. Her eyes were not blank. They were red and wide—crazy eyes. Her hair was wild and clumped up. Her clothes were strange, dirty like those worn below. She looked distorted, her breasts too large and her legs too long.

And something was really weird about her lower face. It was covered in dried blood. It looked all caked up around her neck. Most of the blood was near her mouth. It looked like the blood had come out of there. Out of her mouth. It was dried in little blackish rivers down her chin and cheeks. But there was an area just around her mouth where there was no blood. It was as if she had reached her tongue out and licked it all off in a little oval around her lips. Or as if someone else had wiped it off her. Or licked it off her.

It made her mouth look really weirded out. Blood, blood, like

Mommy was some raw-flesh-feeding animal, and then an oval of pale, pale skin around her bright red lips.

"Mommy?" Noonie asked, holding really tight to the click-pen.

"Oh, Noonie, baby!" Watly said, and she pushed past the chief and came toward Noonie, her hands stretched out. Mommy's hands and arms were stained with blood too.

Noonie glanced quickly back at Fenlocki. There was a little blood around his face too. His empty face. Dried, smeared blood. Like they had just kissed. Like the chief had kissed Mommy. Or Mommy had kissed the chief. Like he had kissed her bloody face. Licked the blood off Mommy's face, all around the lips. Mommy's face. Or maybe the Night Lady's face.

Fenlocki's eyes were still dull-looking. There didn't seem to be any person behind them.

"*Noonie!* Oh, Noonie!" Watly said, running toward the girl now.

She ran funny. Like a lurching beast. A monster. Like one of her legs didn't work. Her blood-covered face broke into a huge grin. The grin looked big. Too big for her head. And that area of pale skin around the lips made her mouth seem—

"Noonie, I *found* you!"

It wasn't Mommy. It couldn't be Mommy. Night Lady. It had to be the Night Lady. Noonie squeezed the click-pen's end reflexively.

It jumped in her hand, slapping into her sweaty palm with a loud *pop* sound.

And the belly of Mommy's stiff shirt opened into a big red flower. A pretty, dark red flower shone brightly right in the center.

Mommy said "Uhh" real loud and fell forward into the table next to Noonie.

CHAPTER 85

Horror and hopelessness.

A pain so great it made everything that had come before seem like nothing at all.

Watly had been shot in the belly by her own child. Her own daughter had shot her. After all this. After coming this far.

Everything was for nothing. She had tried to get to her daughter. It had been her only goal. It had been the only reason to go on. It was the only thing that mattered anymore, and now even that was taken from her. Noonie had killed her.

Watly leaned on the wooden table, face pressed against the rough grain, and clutched her bloody stomach. The pain in the belly was nothing to the pain in her soul. The wound felt distant, as if it were some other woman's wound. The wound in her heart was worse.

Why, why, why? she thought. All strength left her. She was lost. Lost and covered in darkness. The world was a dark and dead place.

It felt like Sentiva Alvedine hardly had to push at all to take over this time. Watly didn't fight her.

And Watly Caiper could tell, as she slipped deep within the

darkness of her own mind, that this time Sentiva had taken over for good. There was no fighting her anymore. She had won.

And, at that particular moment, Watly Caiper didn't really care.

CHAPTER 86

Fenlocki cried "Oh, *rape*!" and ran over to Watly. *"Noonie! Why?"*

Noonie was crying. The click-pen felt hot in her hand. She had shot the Mommy-person. She had shot her Watly. Her whole body trembled violently as if she were having some kind of seizure.

I didn't mean to—

"Nice shot, child," Mommy said calmly. But it didn't sound like Mommy. It sounded like the Night Lady for sure. It sounded like Sentiva Alvedine.

Mommy, or rather Sentiva, shoved Fenlocki back. He looked confused. His face was almost pure white. White as the napkin and folded tablecloth next to Sentiva's elbow.

"I . . . I'm sorry, Mommy," Noonie said quietly.

Sentiva pulled herself up from the table. She picked something up from the wooden surface, her eyes shining brightly. One of her hands was pressed tightly over the slug wound and the other now held a small knife. Noonie's dinner knife. The short one.

"No problem, child. You did well. You did right," she said without emotion. Even as the blood seeped out between her fingers, her free hand was casually twirling the small knife over and over. "Not necessarily fatal, in my assessment. And Watly has departed for good now. Excellent."

Sentiva smiled coldly down at Noonie and then glanced back toward the chief. Fenlocki was pressed into the wall. His gun was drawn, but he looked frozen in place. His face was turned half away at a funny upward angle and his eyes shifted rapidly from woman to child.

"I just need to disentangle myself of this ineffectual parasite once and for all, child. Just necessitate a second."

Sentiva raised the blade and put it back against her own head, just behind the ear. She squinted just a little, staring straight at Noonie all the while. Her hand shook slightly. Noonie couldn't see what she was doing behind the ear, but the girl did see a sudden stream of fresh blood running down her mother's neck.

"Short blade. This short blade will do nicely," Sentiva said, digging the knife into her own head. "A short blade like you, child."

After a moment, something clattered to the metal floor, landing right in one of the pools of light. Noonie did not look over at it. Sentiva switched hands—still staring directly into Noonie's eyes—and stuck the knife behind her other ear.

"What should I do?" Fenlocki asked softly from across the room. He sounded like he was speaking underwater. "What am I supposed to do?"

Noonie didn't know whether the chief was asking her or himself. She closed her eyes, holding the click-pen as if it were her only link to reality.

Now there was another clattering sound nearby. Noonie opened her eyes again. Sentiva was smiling down at her, blood flowing freely down each side of her neck and streaming onto her casement shirt. The cockeyed smile looked genuine now.

"*Now* I have finally evicted Watly Caiper permanently. Those"—she glanced at her feet—"are your mother. I'll finish with her, and then I'll finish up with you, my sweet little Short Blade child."

Noonie looked down. There were two thin wafers. Each was about an inch wide by two inches long and only maybe an eighth of an inch thick. They were coated in blood and some white, stringy goop, and each one glowed just a little from within. A dim, bluish glow.

That was her mother. Those two creosan wafers were Watly Caiper, Noonie's mom. Noonie's *real* mom. Realer than the Night

Lady, realer than Sentiva Alvedine, realer than the hard, corporate woman Mommy sometimes pretended to be.

Laying on the floor of that room were two small pieces of creosan that held the mind of the mother Noonie loved. The one she *really* loved.

Sentiva Alvedine leaned back into the wooden table and lifted up one of her stomping-boot-clad feet. The table creaked a little. Although the blood seemed to be draining rapidly from Sentiva's face, her grin widened. "Mea culpa, child," she said. "Mea culpa, Short Blade."

"What am I supposed to do?" Fenlocki was still bellowing desperately.

Sentiva stamped down hard with the boot. Directly on one of the wafers. There was a small spark of light that flashed out under the sole, and then a soft cracking sound. When Sentiva lifted her foot up, Noonie saw the wafer was destroyed. It was smashed into two pieces. The soft warm glow had gone out, and thin tendrils of smoke rose from the shattered wafer's broken edges.

Half of Noonie's mommy was gone. Sentiva had just killed half of Watly Caiper.

Noonie shuddered, her mouth dropping open.

"Now for the last of it," Sentiva said, wobbling a little as she lifted her foot again. She held it over the remaining wafer.

"What should I *do*?" Fenlocki cried out.

"*Stop* her!" Noonie yelled back.

But Fenlocki seemed too confused and shocked to move.

And Sentiva Alvedine was already rearing back, grinning very widely now, about to come down hard on that tiny strip of creosan. About to smash the last little piece of Watly Caiper's mind.

CHAPTER 87

Chief Ogiv Fenlocki was a mess inside. He'd been a mess for hours, but now was even worse. When he'd gone down to the cannon-loading chamber and ended up saving Watly, he'd felt messier than ever. Like his mind was turning into something gelatinous. And then they'd had sex.

That had made his head even more muddy-feeling. Because they hadn't just had sex. They'd made love.

He'd felt something strong. Something he hadn't felt in years. Something he hadn't *let* himself feel for years. Since he was young. Young and soft and foolish. A teenager.

He'd felt love for Watly. For her body, her self, for the woman she was—and even for the man she'd been. For the way she moved. For those emerald eyes. For that wily little brain of hers that had evaded him so long. For the love she had for her daughter. For her endurance in the face of hopelessness. For her guts. Her eggs. For that battered, bruised, and bloody body that moved so gracefully above and below him.

And all that had made him feel more messed up than anything. What was he supposed to do with all these strange feelings? What was he supposed to do about the revolution? About his job?

After the sex was finished, he thought he had decided. He thought he had settled it all within himself. Closed and sealed the chapter. He would lead Watly to her daughter. He would reunite mother and child. Then he would sneak them both up to one of Gavy's emergency Floobie-pods—one that was set for some country far, far away. Then he would kiss them both, put them inside the pod, and send them off.

When they were gone—safely zooming somewhere where they could start over—he would return to his control room. And he would do his job. He would do it well and do it thoroughly. It was all he had. It was his foundation. His identity. He would stop the war, stop the revolution, restore peace. Bring things back to the way they had been.

That was his plan. That was the only thing he could think of to do that might keep him from losing his mind entirely. The hardest part of the plan would be saying goodbye. Why did he have to feel this love thing? Why did he feel almost overwhelmed with a romantic kind of love for Watly, and a parental kind of love for Noonie? It confused everything.

And then the child had shot her mother. Right in front of him. He saw it happen. And Watly had pushed him roughly away when he'd come to her aid. The hosting wafers came out—little fragile pieces of creosan. Fenlocki watched numbly as the woman sliced them brutally from her own head. He knew the woman was now the real Sentiva Alvedine. He knew Watly Caiper was in the creosan on the floor.

But he didn't know what to do. Sentiva stomped on the wafer, killing half of his new love. But he loved her body too. What should he do? How could he shoot the woman he had just made love to? How could he cut down the body of this fantastic, sensual creature? What should he *do*?

He felt as though someone had chained him in place, shackled him securely to that dusty wall.

The woman started to come down with her boot again. And Fenlocki just watched. Everything seemed to be moving in slow motion. He watched Noonie's face split into a tortured grimace. He watched her yell out as Sentiva's foot neared the floor. He watched the child's hand flash upward, pen pointed out, and he watched her small fist squeeze the strange weapon's end.

Sentiva's face—Noonie's mother's face—opened up. The chip slug hit her in the forehead just before her foot could crush the wafer. A jagged, sloppy hole exploded her pretty brow and her eyebrows went up to meet it. She looked surprised. A brief flash of something that looked like respect or grudging appreciation passed quickly over her face, and then her eyes rolled up and she fell backward. She landed loudly on the metal, her hands twitching for a second. Blood dribbled from the hole in her head. And then she was still.

She was dead.

Her beautiful, tortured body was limp.

Noonie dropped the pen as if it were too hot to hold anymore. Fenlocki watched the girl crawl forward on her knees.

The child gingerly picked up the one good wafer, held it to her lips for a moment, and then put it in her pants pocket. It was like watching some kind of exotic religious ceremony.

Then the little girl sat very still and looked at the body. The body of Sentiva Alvedine. The body of her mother.

Fenlocki took a slow step forward. The shackles had disappeared, but his feet felt liquid. His head felt ten pounds heavier. The viscous mass that had been his brain was expanding.

The young girl turned and looked up at him. Her eyes were dry. They blazed with something strong. Something animal. Anger.

"Where *were* you?" she asked. Her voice was low and seething. It sounded very grown-up. There was barely contained rage in her level, adult tones. "Where . . . were . . . *you?*"

"I . . ." Fenlocki started, but he had no more to say.

Noonie stood and walked over. She seemed taller now, almost adult-sized. "Give me your gun," she said. Her voice was wintry cold.

"What?"

"Give me the pistol."

"What do you want it for?"

"Just give it. I'm gonna stop all this. I'm going into the control room and stop all this. *Just give it to me.*"

Noonie reached for the gun, but Fenlocki pulled his arm away. He held his hand up high so she couldn't reach it. The child jumped for the weapon twice and then stopped. She stepped up close to Fenlocki, her angry eyes burning into him.

He looked away. "You don't know what you're doing, kid. Settle down. Steady . . . your sockets. Don't bust . . . your . . . power ringlets. . . ."

When Noonie's voice came back, it sounded almost inhuman, like some cut-rate keyboard voice synthesizer.

"I know what I'm doing," she said, and then Fenlocki looked

down just in time to see her expertly kick him real hard in the balls.

He doubled over in sharp agony, grabbing his crotch. The kid snatched the gun from him and sped out the door. His testicles hurt so much he barely registered the sound of the door closing and locking behind her.

"Noooooooonie!" Fenlocki bellowed, his body curled up in a tense ball of pain, perfectly framed by the circle of pinlight he'd fallen into.

CHAPTER 88

Noonie remembered the way. She ran down the hall—the Isthmus place aching and throbbing—and slowed up when she came to the intersection. The halls crossed each other at acute angles, forming a squished X shape. Noonie stopped at the corner, her lungs convulsing in short little breaths, and got on her hands and knees. Creeping forward, she peered around the edge of the sharp left-hand corner. There at the end of the corridor was that normal-sized, unassuming door. The entrance to the command center. Two male guards stood at either side of the door. They looked bored, but relatively alert. Both had on orange and purple jumpsuits with bright blue gunbelts. They each were well armed with rapid-fire chip guns, nerve guns, and big I-grenades.

Noonie looked down at the heavy gun in her hand. Two trained guards with plenty of weapons about ten yards away, versus one little girl with a simple chip pistol. Not spaf.

She backed away from the corner and stood up. She needed a plan. She needed a way in. She was just a little girl. Going on ten. Just a little girl.

Now she had it. An idea.

She turned around, facing the way she had come, and edged

backward until she was almost even with the corner. She was just out of the guards' sight line now. Her small rear was near the corridor's junction.

Noonie transferred the pistol to her left hand. She bent her knees, squatting down on her haunches. *Okay, Noonie,* she thought to herself. *Make it peaky, peaky prone. You can do it. You've been pretending all your life. What's one more little make-believe?*

She brushed her greasy-feeling hair out of her face and pointed the pistol down the hall. The gun was unaimed, facing the general direction of the interrogation room. It was shaking. Noonie bit her lower lip and inhaled deeply through her nose.

"Mommy!" she screamed at the empty corridor. Her voice echoed. "Mommy, *no! Don't! Don't shoot!"*

She squeezed the chip pistol's trigger. The gun made a loud bang, slamming her hand back with its recoil. Noonie instantly pushed off as hard as she could with her legs. She straightened her knees and arched her back. She flew backward, somersaulting into the guard's sight lines. She flipped over twice, elbows out, her right hand clasped over an imaginary chest wound, her face contorted in pain, and her left hand pressing the large pistol into her left thigh where she hoped it was hidden from view. Her legs were loose as she rolled, flopping over and under her while she somersaulted backward. She tumbled roughly across the hallway junction, all the way to the far side, where she landed on her back. Now she was hidden again. She had flipped her way clear across the X in the hallway, a child propelled by a vicious gun blast from her own mother.

Noonie quickly positioned herself on the floor. She opened the front of her black shirt, switching the gun to her right hand, and pushed the hand and gun into the opening of her blouse. She pressed her left hand over the bulge of the gun, hoping the whole thing only looked like two little-girl hands clutching a little-girl wound.

There were rapid footsteps approaching. One of the guards was running down the hall toward her, checking out the commotion.

Noonie lay back, trying to look fatally shot. She lolled her head slightly to the side so she could see better. The guard ran into the hallway intersection, gun drawn. He was looking away from Noonie, toward where the shot had supposedly come. The corridor was, of course, empty. He swiveled, crouching, and moved swiftly to Noonie's side. There was something coiled in how he moved, almost dancerlike.

"Mommy . . . shot . . . me," Noonie whispered with what she wanted to sound like her last breaths.

The guard looked a touch bewildered, but there was concern in his eyes. *Good.*

"Be . . . careful. . . ." Noonie continued, squeezing some tearlike moisture from her eyes. "She's . . . killed the chief. . . . She's trying to . . . get to the . . . command center. . . ."

The guard leaned in. "Let me see," he said, trying to pull Noonie's left hand from her chest. She kept it clenched tight.

"Hey, Jacko! What's up?" The voice of the other guard echoed from around the corner.

"Looks like Sentiva Alvedine's in the building," the guard near Noonie yelled back. "She shot her own togger. The little togger says Sentiva shot the chief too." He tried again to see the girl's wound. Noonie figured he must be starting to wonder where all the blood was. "Come on, little togger, it's okay. Let me see."

Noonie looked over the guard's shoulder. She focused down the empty corridor, letting her eyes widen dramatically in pretend horror. "Look *out*! She's back!" Noonie yelled. "Mommy— *nooooo*!"

The guard twirled around to see. Noonie yanked her gun out from her shirt and shot him in the back of the head. He fell on top of her as the blast was still echoing loudly.

"Hey?" the other guard said. *"Hey?"*

Noonie heard footsteps again. The weight of the dead guard across her stomach pressed into her diaphragm and made it hard to breathe. She felt something wet from the guard's head soaking into her black clothing. She closed her eyes into little slits. She could just barely see through the narrow openings.

The other guard dashed into view at the hallway junction. Noonie watched his blurry form through her just-touching eyelashes. He looked scared. His body spun back and forth as he looked up and down the hall, but he seemed to be looking blindly, too frightened to take in what he saw. Finally his eyes settled on the two sprawled bodies before him—Noonie and the dead guard.

"Shit!" he said, stepping toward them. Then he spun back around, his gun pointing down the hall away from them. It was as if he had heard Sentiva herself walking up behind him, reloading

her gun. Noonie pulled her pistol up from under the dead guard's bulky shoulder.

"Yoo-hoo!" she cried jovially, and when the guard turned back to her, she blew his chest open with a damn well aimed shot. He dropped instantly, too dead to have much of a reaction.

And the blood didn't bother Noonie Caiper in the least. "Guards: nothing. 'Little Togger': two," she said aloud, smiling broadly.

CHAPTER 89

Ogiv Fenlocki was trying to steady himself. He was precariously balanced, and falling now would not be nice. He had moved the table over to the interrogation room's door and put one of the chairs on top of it. Then he'd picked up the bloody knife from Sentiva's still warm hand, trying not to look at her, trying not to look at the dead body of his new love. He'd carried the blade to the door and climbed up on his makeshift platform.

The chair wobbled uncontrollably under him. He slowly reached above his head with the small knife. He was trying to pry open the sealed metal box that was way above the locked door. If he could get it open, he might be able to override the lock—or at least short the whole thing out. Or maybe just raping electrocute himself.

His tongue found his broken tooth and toyed with its rough surface as he worked.

He had to get out. He had to stop Noonie. The kid was wild, trying to mess up everything. The look in her eyes had reminded him of a crazed beast, a domesticated animal who had been brutally beaten so many times that it finally had to explode. She was scary. She was probably going to try to destroy the command center. Fenlocki couldn't allow that. Unsure and confused as he was about everything, he knew that much. In fact, it was nice to have a clear sense of purpose now. It was nice to know he had an obvious path to take: stop the child. Save Noonie from herself and save the control room from her. A clear-cut plan. Simple, clean, easy to follow.

Fenlocki realized, as he fumbled the blade under the lip of the small box, that the kid just might succeed if he didn't stop her. If anyone could destroy the command center, Noonie could.

What was it that Sentiva had called the child? Short Blade? Yes, that was it. Short Blade. Small and inconspicuous, but just as deadly as a sword. Yes. That made sense. The girl was merely an unassuming child, but there was a fire in her now. An unchecked rage. A determination. He'd seen it in her eyes. A killing fury.

"Shit!" Fenlocki cursed as the small knife bent under his forceful pressure on its handle. He turned it over, slowly straightened it, and kept on working, a little more gently this time.

He had to get out. He had to stop the kid. If she destroyed the control room, Second Level would lose the war. The raping command center controlled everything—the cannons, the fighting machines, the hosts . . . everything. Second Level would only have its laypeople and a couple hundred cops to fight with if the center went down. And Fenlocki knew the upperfolk would not make the greatest of soldiers.

Why hadn't they spread out the command center? Why had they centralized the brain of counter-Revy in one place? At one point, that had made sense to Fenlocki. It had seemed right. The command center was impenetrable. Sealed up tight. Solid stone shielding. Nerve cannons everywhere. Anxiety fields blocking any vulnerable sides. Why *not* have one centralized place where all fighting could be coordinated from—as long as that place was invulnerable? Why not?

But they hadn't counted on a little nine-year-old girl. A short blade. A short blade that Fenlocki himself had brought into the building of his own free will.

The lower left edge of the metal box gave just a little. *"Yeah!"* Fenlocki said aloud, feeling pretty good suddenly. He was back. He was playing by the rules. He was going according to the book.

And all his earlier uneasiness began to lift up—to rise from his body and disappear somewhere up near the pinlights. He felt better. He had a job to do.

The sealed box's cover creaked loudly and then finally snapped right off, falling to the tabletop below. Inside the open box was a tangle of small purple and red wires. Fenlocki glanced at the blade in his hand. Its thin tip had broken clear off. He let the knife drop.

Oh, well, he thought absentmindedly as he reached in to the mess of overlapping wiring, humming just a little to himself. *Sometimes a tool breaks when it does its job.*

CHAPTER 90

Killing was wrong. That's what Noonie's mom had said many times. And Noonie's mom had also always mentioned the family legacy. The history. The tradition of nonviolence. Noonie's grandma, Pepajer Caiper, believed killing was wrong too. Watly was always quoting grandma to Noonie. The child had never met Pepajer, but she'd heard endless stories about her.

"Your grandmother often said, Noonie, 'Fight without hurting. Fight without injuring anyone else. That takes the most courage. Be careful you don't turn into what you're fighting against. Never kill, never hurt.' She said things like that often, my baby. And, little Noonie, she was right. She was right about all that."

But when the Isthmus place swelled, none of that mattered. When the Isthmus place ached and throbbed, Noonie was certain that both her mom and grandmom were wrong. Watly and Pepajer. Well-meaning, but absolutely wrong. Killing was a wonderful thing. She had just killed the two guards easily, and it not only wasn't unpleasant . . . it was raping *great*! Spaf to the max. The peakiest of all peaky prones.

There was an incredible release in it. A joy. A feeling of freedom. Of revenge. An ecstatic, thrilling balloon of *richness*.

No nausea, no regret, no guilt. Just a sense of justice. Of equity. Of righteousness. Of payback for all the pretending. All the years of make-believe.

Payback to a world that had just made her shoot her own mother in the face. Payback to the world that had made her kill the cats.

Noonie strapped on one of the dead guards' gunbelts. It was real heavy, full of oversized grenades and slug clips, and it was way too long for her. She doubled it and tied it in a big loose knot at her hip. Then she pulled her black shirttails out and let them hang over the lumpy belt. She looked unnaturally bulgy around the middle, but at least none of the blue utility belt showed.

She pried one of the rapid-fire chip pistols from the second dead guard's hands and held it behind her back. She would have taken both of the fancy chip guns, but they were very heavy and she could only hold up one at a time. She reluctantly left the other gun behind along with Fenlocki's. They sat there in one of the two rapidly widening pools of blood that were slowly converging, connecting the two guards there on the corridor floor.

Noonie walked calmly around the corner and down the hall toward the command center. When she got to the door, she lifted up the gun and gently rapped it against the wooden door's frame.

There was no response.

Once more she knocked politely, putting the gun behind her back after tapping just three times.

When no one answered again, she repeated the procedure, careful to make sure her knocks were still soft and regular. She would continue knocking just like that for as long as it took.

The door folded open a crack. Noonie recognized the face peering out at her. It was Leeta, the woman who had searched her and led her to the interrogation room. She still had that weird, distorting eyepiece strapped to her face. The woman looked annoyed and distracted.

"What?" Leeta said.

"Hi!" Noonie smiled up at the distorted eye. It looked really tiny. "Chief said I could come and watch."

"What are you doing out?"

Noonie rolled her eyes. "Chief says I can watch. Guards say it's okay too. Right?" Noonie looked to the right and left as if there were faces agreeing with her there.

"The chief's raping crazy," Leeta said.

"Come *on*. I'm just a kid. I wanna watch. Chief said I *could*. He *did*. I'll be quiet."

"You're not supposed to be running around out here."

Noonie stamped her feet a little, feeling the heavy gunbelt jiggle against her waist and thighs. "Please-please-please-*please*? Chief says it's okay and he's the boss, right? I'll tell if you don't."

Leeta scowled down at Noonie. From behind her someone called out sharply, sounding annoyed. "Hey, Leet! We need your help back here. Whole bunch of 'em coming into cannon range now. Come *on*."

Leeta started to fold the door closed.

Noonie stuck her foot in it. "Please. I'm just a kid. A little togger." She smiled very angelically up at the woman. "I won't get in the way. I just wanna watch. I'll *tell* if you don't let me."

Leeta sighed. "You be *very* quiet, you hear, kid? One word and you're *out*."

"Promise," Noonie said sweetly as she squeezed in through the door and into the control room. Short Blade was in the command center.

CHAPTER 91

The command center looked different to Noonie. It looked smaller. Less impressive. It was, after all, just a whole mess of wood. A whole pile of levers and ringlets and monitors and keyboards and cables and blinking lights. It was just a bunch of silly workstations, connected into a rough circle and surrounding a pompous-looking wooden platform. Not very spaf at all. Kind of wimpy. Kind of rickety-looking.

Noonie stood near the door, watching. Leeta had returned to her station. The woman's mini-CV projection had flashed back on, and it floated right before her bizarre eyepiece, looking like some strange, tight little pattern of multicolored veins. Probably a road-map readout of some kind. Counting Leeta, there were twelve technicians in the room. They were all either bent over their respective panels or staring up at monitors, CV projections, or pinlight displays. They fiddled solemnly with their dark brown ringlets, levers, cables, and light-keys.

It looked to Noonie like they were faking it. Like they were playacting. It was hard to believe that their concentrated stares and twitching arm movements were actually connected to the war outside. They seemed to be actors, playing the part of anti-Revy technicians.

To the left of all the panels was a large curved glass case or plasglass chamber of some kind. Noonie couldn't see into it. She could only see the reflection of herself on its rounded surface, distorted so that she looked as thin as a stick. As thin as a skeleton. It was too glary from this angle to see what, if anything, lay within the glass booth.

Noonie scanned the control room for weapons. There were what looked like powerful gas canisters under the front edge of each control panel. They were bright green tubes, nasty-looking and, no doubt, very deadly. No, wait. Those weren't weapons at all. Those were some kind of fire extinguishers. There *weren't* any weapons.

Her eyes again passed slowly over the whole room. Finally she noticed a rack of high-velocity haver nerve rifles just to the right of her, near the doorway. Okay, so there *were* a few weapons. But they were closer to her than to any of the technicians. They were set up near the door, where danger might come from if it was to come. And danger, Noonie could sense, was not expected to ever reach the insular, protected environment of the sacred command center.

Yet danger was already in the room. Noonie was it. She was the danger, and she was inside. And the technicians themselves appeared unarmed. Defenseless. No gunbelts. No chip pistols. These were high-echelon scientists. Not warriors. Not fighters. They were mechanics. They were organizers, schemers, tacticians, and strategists. None of these people were soldiers. The room was not designed for soldiers. It was designed for thinkers. For the people who fought the war—*ran* the war—but never got their hands dirty.

If that was really what they were doing at all. If they weren't just pretending. Trying to look busy. Trying to look raping important. Trying to make Noonie mad with their lies and make-believe.

Little Noonie Caiper pulled the heavy chip gun from behind her back. No one noticed. No one bothered with the little girl, standing quietly in the corner while the grown-ups did important things. She was invisible. Noonie held the weighty gun before her with both hands. Her right hand was on the grip, and her left supported the barrel. It felt good. It felt right.

This was better than sex.

Noonie Caiper knew all about sex. She was an expert. The child had never *had* sex, but she knew all about it. You couldn't help but know all about it if you watched CV porn and such. No, she'd never had sex, or even had an orgasm. She was young. But she'd had sexual pleasure. She'd touched herself down there and gotten a warm, runny, spaf feeling. She'd slid down the great wooden bird-wing banister in the living room of her home, feeling the friction and the movement. But she'd never come. She'd never climaxed. And she felt—she *knew*, beyond a shadow of a doubt—that what she was about to experience would be better than the most wonderful sexual orgasm anyone had ever experienced. It was going to peak the peakiest of the peakiest of things prone.

Noonie smiled. "Hey!" she yelled. "Hey, boleholes!"

A few of the technicians glanced her way. The ones who really saw her stared at the gun in disbelief.

"Hey, subspawn," Noonie screamed joyously, "look here! Gonna raping kill you, you little shits!"

And then she squeezed the trigger on the rapid-fire pistol. It did not shoot as she'd expected. It was not a slow, one-slug-at-a-time chip gun. It was not like her primitive click-pen weapon. It wasn't even like Fenlocki's bulky pistol had been. It was a fast-fire slugger, and just a little squeeze made it vomit out gobs and gobs of slugs.

The gun jerked repeatedly, brutally recoiling into her small hands, jerking her aim this way and that. It spat out multiple rounds wildly into the corner of the room, shattering two of the monitors and causing whole clusters of pinlights to burst into sparks.

Most of the technicians stood up in alarm, dropping their charts and ringlets. Some, like Leeta, just turned in their seats, swiveling toward the girl and opening their mouths wide. All their faces were stunned and helpless-looking.

"Ooops," Noonie said, easing up on the delicate trigger mechanism to adjust her grip. "Sorry. Let me try that again."

She bore down on the trigger now, sweeping the weapon across the room. The three technicians on her right burst open. Their screams were staccato and rhythmic. Their stomachs seemed to explode from within and their arms and legs did a goofy little dance of death to the rhythm of the steady slug shots.

Leeta's eyepiece shattered and a great tidal wave of blood washed over it from her face. Then her whole head caved in, in one pulpy hammer-smash of gore. More screams rang out—thumping screams that kept perfect time with the jerking recoil of the gun.

One of the central techies tried to dive behind his chair, but Noonie got him in the neck before he could duck. Then she got the rest of him through the chair itself, watching it burst into splinters in front of his fragile body, and then watching the body itself fracture apart. The two to his left also did a little dance, a twitchy, comical jig that was made all the funnier by the spouts of redness that kept bursting from new holes in their torsos and arms and legs. Someone was on the floor next to them, her hands clasped desperately over her head. Noonie wiped those clenched hands away, watching the fingers fly off and the bulky skull beneath shatter into gorgeous flying ribbons of white and red and gray.

She kept sweeping the gun back and forth, her finger pressed down hard on the trigger, her teeth clenched strongly. She spread the slugs around, feeling the power of the pistol as it spewed out round after round. Blood sailed out from every direction. Flesh ruptured open and soared outward gracefully. Whenever she saw a body part that wasn't red, Noonie would turn the gun toward it until a crimson fountain spurted from it. Great gobs of blood erupted from whatever direction she decided to point the weapon.

It was incredible. Noonie screamed cheerfully—her young, piercing voice louder than all of them—as she spread the slugs around her, blanketing the whole room. "Yeeeeeeeeeeeees!" she yelled. It *was* spaf. It was a great, bright, brilliant white game. The killing game. The revenge game.

Now all the technicians were on the floor in twisted, liquid heaps. Whenever Noonie saw any movement from them or heard a moan, she'd give them another hearty blast until they were still. After a bit of this, the gun stuttered and coughed a little and then stopped. She tried squeezing the trigger harder, but nothing happened. It was out of slugs.

Ah, well, Noonie thought, tossing the gun toward the heap of bodies. *Fun while it lasted.*

She stepped farther into the room. The room was hers now. She owned it. She had bought it. She had just paid in full. Some of the panels and keyboards had busted open and many of the monitors were shattered and floating wildly overhead, their pictures cock-eyed and blurry. She'd done a good deal of damage to the controls with her wild shooting. But not enough. Lights still blinked. Images still flashed. Quite a few of the ringlets and levers and light-keys shifted up and down automatically, as if invisible hands touched them. Some cables coupled and uncoupled by themselves. The command center was still operating, if mindlessly. Noonie wasn't done with it yet.

She glanced at the bodies again. The bugs she had exterminated. The insects she had gleefully squashed under her foot. She'd been right. It *had* been orgasmic. No way real sex was better than this. It had been a great release, a billowing rush of excitement. A widening. A broadening. A mind-opening experience.

Noonie felt a tad queasy and trembly inside, but she knew that wasn't disgust or guilt. It couldn't be that. It was just the excitement. It was just adrenaline coursing in a huge crashing wave through her whole small body. Extra-spafness. The nausea and dizziness would pass. It would pass.

Blowing all the machinery up would probably feel better still. Icing on the hardcake. Noonie reached under her shirttail and got a grip on one of the big I-grenades. She pulled at it, trying to release it from the belt. It was caught underneath the top loop of the belt she'd made when doubling it. Her gaze drifted upward as she struggled with the belt and the hidden release flap. She stared vacantly at her bone-skinny reflection: tongue out and hand fumbling under her blouse.

That is me, she thought, and for some reason she felt even more faint.

Suddenly she noticed the reflection rippling. It appeared as though tiny vertical waves were passing over her image. But they were just small ridges in the glass. The curved plasglass of the booth was sliding slowly aside, revealing a small chamber.

A man stepped out of the chamber. It was Chancellor Zephy Gavy. He yanked a cable from the side of his head, looking like he'd just woken up. Gavy's puffy eyes turned quickly toward the pile of bloodied corpses and then up at some of the shattered monitors.

"What the rape did you *do*, little girl?" he spat, his head tilted back at a sharp angle. The lock of hair wiggled over his right eye.

Noonie's hand tightened around the snagged grenade.

Gavy squinted. Without looking down, he pulled a very small handgun from his front pocket. It wasn't much larger than Noonie's click-pen had been. It was just a stick with a thin wire grip and silver trigger tube.

"You raping *brat*! You sick, raped-up, abominable, catshit

little piece of aborted *subspawn*!" He stepped closer, pointing the tiny weapon directly at Noonie's face. "I'll raping kill you for this!"

Noonie took a step back, slipping a little on a puddle of blood. She steadied herself and spoke as sweetly and young-sounding as she could. "You can't kill me," she said. "I'm just a little nine-year-old girl." *No,* she thought to herself. *No, I am a monster. I am a monster.*

Gavy's round face went bright purple. Thick veins stood out everywhere, sharp contrast to the yellow curl of hair. His whole head looked ready to explode. "Wanna raping *bet*? Wanna raping bet I can't kill you right now, scrotum-head?"

He straightened his arm out, thrusting the gun closer to Noonie. She saw his finger start to bear down on the trigger tube. The grenade was still stuck under Noonie's belt loop. There was no hope she'd get it out in time. She leaned her head forward, bracing herself.

There was a swishing sound behind Noonie as the door flew open. Someone had burst into the room. Noonie looked up, seeing Gavy's eyes flash toward the door for a split second. His gun stayed on her.

"Oh, *damn*!" Noonie heard Fenlocki say as he lurched farther into the room. Then it sounded like he was tripping and half falling as he bolted around the central platform and came toward them.

Gavy's eyes and gun stayed on Noonie. He turned his head slightly and directed his voice over her shoulder to where the chief was. The bedlock fell away from his face a little. "You see what she did?" Gavy yelled, his face even darker now. "You see what your little innocent prisoner *did*?"

Noonie could now see Fenlocki from the corner of her eye as he stepped up beside her. His hands were away from his sides—palms forward and fingers spread.

"Now watch *this*!" Gavy continued. "I'll show this little bolehole what happens to bad children."

There was what felt like a very long pause. Finally the chief spoke.

"Don't kill her," he said. His voice was relaxed and controlled, almost soothing, like a parent telling a baby a favorite bedtime story.

"What? *What?*" Gavy yelled back.

"Just do not kill the child, Chancellor."

"Who are you to give *me* orders? Rape you, you raping plurite figurehead!" Gavy stiffened his arm again—stepping right up to Noonie—and pressed the tiny gun into the bridge of her nose. He took his free hand and actually flipped that strange length of hair back over his head. Finally his face was free of it. "Bye-bye, little girl," he whispered.

Fenlocki dove forward. His hand flashed out, grabbing for the gun. Noonie jumped back as the two men tumbled into the pile of bodies. They struggled desperately for the weapon.

Noonie dropped to her knees and yanked violently at the grenade with both hands, trying to free it. The chief and the Chancellor wrestled, rolling over all the blood-covered body parts. The blood hardly looked real to Noonie anymore. It looked like some kind of thick syrup that was rubbing off all over the two men as they grappled. She could see that strange snake of hair flailing and thrashing like an excited tail. Fenlocki had both his hands around Gavy's gun arm. He seemed to be trying to keep the small pistol pointed away from both Noonie and himself. The thing fired once, putting a big hole in the wooden ceiling and sending a shower of splinters down on them.

It suddenly hit Noonie like a brutal slap in the face that there were *other* grenades on her belt. *Dumb*. She let go of the stubborn one and grabbed the one next to it. It popped easily into her hand.

The two men were kicking at each other, biting and flailing and head-butting with all their might. They flipped over the pile of cadavers and disappeared behind it. Noonie stood up to see what was going on.

There was another gunshot. *Pow!*

Then silence.

Total and complete silence.

The movement stopped. Now it looked as though the two men had become part of the heap of dead bodies. They weren't fighting, they weren't writhing, they weren't even twitching. They blended in with the shattered arms and legs and torsos in front of them.

Noonie held the grenade before her, listening to her own breathing.

Some of the broken pinlights and monitors still swung loosely over the bodies, making all the shadows move back and forth. Now it appeared to Noonie that *all* of the bodies were moving. Or maybe it still was none. All or none. *Ghosts*, she thought. *Ghosts coming to get me for what I've done. Did I really do that? Could I have done that?*

Then one of the bodies moved for sure. It looked half buried. The body's hand searched for a hold among all the slippery pieces of flesh and clothing. It was Fenlocki. It was the chief. He wearily disentangled himself from the corpse of the Chancellor. Noonie couldn't see the Chancellor's face, but she thought maybe that was where the gun had gone off. His big, swollen face. Maybe that was where Fenlocki had got him.

Fenlocki's clothing was shiny with the blood-syrup. It reminded Noonie of the way her mommy had looked. The way her mommy had looked right before Noonie'd killed her. *I didn't mean to. . . .*

The chief had Gavy's tiny gun dangling loosely from the limp fingers of his right hand. He stepped over the bodies, the left side of his face twitching some just under the eye.

Noonie twisted the activator ringlet on the grenade, watching its red indicators flash up and down in little dotted lines. For some reason, the lines reminded Noonie of the election tally rods that had raised and lowered way back in the auditorium all that time ago. A little time-setting readout blinked TEN over and over on the I-grenade's side. She held the weapon up, making sure her index finger was firmly pressed into its safety button. If she let go of that, the thing would explode in ten seconds.

"What are you doing?" Fenlocki asked. He sounded exhausted. His shoulders were slumped and his body looked a good foot shorter than before as he stepped clear of the bodies and blood. He seemed such a small, weak man suddenly.

"Stopping it," Noonie said, nodding slightly toward the control panels.

"Don't," the chief said.

Noonie pulled her arm back a little, preparing to toss the grenade.

"Don't," the chief said again. His scrawny-looking right hand lifted up a little, raising the gun some.

"You gonna shoot me?" Noonie asked.

Fenlocki's cheek twitched again. He blinked twice. The gun was still up, now pointed in the girl's general direction. "Just don't," he said.

Noonie glanced at the grenade in her hand. Then she looked back at the chief. "I'm going to throw it. Whether you shoot me or not, I'm going to throw it."

The chief's eyes looked moist. His head seemed to be shrinking down into his neck, growing smaller and smaller. It looked like it was becoming a soft, white ball of flesh. "Please," he said, the gun vibrating in his hand. "Please don't."

Noonie turned sideways a little and brought her arm even farther back. She scanned all the control panels, trying to decide the best place to throw the grenade. "I'm doing it. I'm stopping everything. You can shoot me if you want, but I'm stopping everything."

"Please, Noonie." Fenlocki's voice was very soft. Very breathy-sounding.

"I'm doing it," she said again.

She slid her finger off the safety. The grenade was armed and counting. It had ten seconds.

(Nine . . .)

"The middle one," Fenlocki said.

(Eight . . .)

Noonie glanced at him. His gun was on the floor next to his

(Seven . . .)

feet. He had let go of it. Dropped it. "What?" she asked sharply.

(Six . . .)

"The middle one," he repeated. "Throw it behind the middle

(Five . . .)

panel. That should do it."

(Four . . .)

He stepped to Noonie's side. "Stop everything," he whispered.

(Three . . .)

And little Noonie Caiper tossed the grenade behind the center workstation of the semicircle of panels.

CHAPTER 92

"We're too close," Fenlocki said.

Noonie felt the chief grab her around the shoulders and pull her roughly to the ground. Before she knew it he had thrown his body over hers. She felt crushed under his weight, unable to breathe.

And then . . . life exploded. The world burst. There was a noise that was beyond noise. The sound of planets colliding. The sound of a universe being born. There was no "boom," just an impossible *crack* sound. It was not a sound heard in the ears, it was a sound felt in the bone marrow and in the billions of synapses of the brain. Noonie heard the explosion in all the tiny nerve endings of her hands and feet and the end of her nose. Her whole body was an ear.

The earth shook. Noonie's teeth slammed together painfully. The room went white and things flew everywhere. A wall of heat slammed into the girl, right through the protection of Fenlocki's body. Pieces of wood flew into her eyes and then there was nothing but smoke. The smoke was so thick that Noonie couldn't even see the chief's hair, which was right next to her face.

Two more smaller explosions followed. And then another big one. Each was followed by a brutal, sideways shower of metal, glass shards, and wood splinters. Pieces of machinery bounced off the walls and rebounded with a thud onto Fenlocki's back. Noonie could feel his whole body shudder as things hit it. There was the sound of shattering plasglass. Wood bursting and rupturing. A soft popping noise.

Something else exploded now—something small-sounding that broke apart with a wimpy farting sound. Again Fenlocki's body lurched into Noonie from the impact. She could feel the stubble of his beard scrape harshly against her neck as tiny planets pounded into his back.

There was a loud, bass roar and a blast of even hotter air. It felt as though Noonie's eyebrows were being seared off. She smelled meat cooking. A sweet, expensive smell.

The explosions stopped. The room was just solid white smoke. The only sound now was the loud crackle of flames licking upward.

"Chief?" Noonie gasped out of her empty-feeling lungs. "Chief?" The weight of his body was unbearable now, worse than all the fire and explosions and noise. She wanted to cough, but there was no space for her lungs to heave. *"Chief?"*

The chief's singed hair moved just a little against Noonie's skin. She felt his stomach press even harder down on her as his lungs filled with some smoke-filled air.

"Sometimes," he whispered, "a tool breaks when it does its job."

Then his chest collapsed upward and his stomach pulled back off her some. But he got suddenly heavier. It felt as though he had instantly gained a hundred pounds. As though he had turned to stone.

Noonie struggled to get out from under him, trying to slip to the side. She was pinned. She squirmed a little to the left and pushed up hard against his shoulder with all her might. She shoved and shoved, straining her muscles. Finally he rolled off. His body flipped onto its back right next to her.

Noonie could hardly see him at all through the smoke. She sat up, gasping for air. Fenlocki was just a dim, dark shape on the floor beside her.

But she knew he was dead. There was no life coming from him. There was no Fenlocki-ness left in the body. No sense of Ogiv radiated out.

His body was just flesh now. Empty, limp flesh.

CHAPTER 93

Noonie turned away from Chief of Police Ogiv Fenlocki's dead body. She looked back at the cloudy outline of the open door. Through the thick haze of smoke she could see vague shapes in the hall beyond. Movement. Things approaching. Three cops were running toward the control room. It looked like they had rifles. Nerve rifles. And the weapons were up and ready as they hurried toward her, filling the doorway with their shadowy shapes.

"Place is raping *destroyed*!" one of the cops shouted in a high-pitched female voice.

"Terradamn sabotage!" another one screamed out.

"Who the rape did this?"

Noonie got to her knees and stood up. She coughed hard and wobbled a good deal, but then spread her legs and balanced herself, breathing shallowly. The cops were lined up in the doorway, completely blocking it. Their rifles twinkled bright reflections of the flickering firelight. She saw each of the officers look down at Fenlocki.

Noonie stepped protectively in front of his body.

"Me," she said. "I did. Little togger did. Little Noonie

Alvedine. Noonie Caiper. Short Blade." She noticed she was crying. Funny. Actually crying.

Even through the smoke she could see the fury and outrage in the police officers' eyes. It reminded her of something. Had she looked like that right before she'd mowed down all the technicians? Had her face stretched and distorted into that monstrous maw of hatred? *What am I?* she wondered. *How could I? Was that me?*

"Well, *eat this*!" one of the cops said, and then they all three braced their rifles up against their shoulders and aimed at her.

And the little togger dies, Noonie thought to herself, feeling half dead already.

CHAPTER 94

There was the sound of rapid gunfire.

BANG BANG BANG BANG BANG BANG BANG BANG BANG . . . !

On and on.

But it wasn't the great whoosh of nerve rifles. It wasn't the crackly, electrical sound of bolts streaking down a barrel. It sounded more like the powerful percussive burst of a rapid-fire chip gun. It sounded, in fact, exactly like the noise Noonie's heavy pistol had made when she'd killed the techies.

The three officers began coming apart. Their torsos ripped open as if exploded from within. Slugs riddled their bodies, causing that familiar rhythmic dance and the symphony of blood-spurting. Noonie was stunned. She did not appreciate the sight of death this time.

The shooting stopped, and all three of the cops fell forward as one. *Thump*.

Behind them, Noonie saw a ghost. She didn't believe in ghosts, but there it was. A ghost. Through the haze of white smoke, she saw a bright, supernatural-looking figure holding a pistol. A spirit. Its shiny, white-looking legs were spread far, and one white arm was pointed out, holding a syrup-dripping weapon in its grip. The gun looked like it was the same rapid-fire chip pistol Noonie had left back in that pool of blood next to the two guards.

The ghost didn't move. It seemed to fade in and out of existence behind the billowing smoke. Its body reflected almost blinding whiteness when it crystallized, then disappeared into nothingness in the clouds. Its skin looked metallic now. Shiny silver.

"Thanks," Noonie coughed out timidly into the haze.

"No prob, Nooner-face," the ghost said in a lilting female voice.

The silver spirit slipped the pistol into its belt and pulled off its broken helmet.

It was Alysess.

Noonie felt a big ball of smoky air catch in her throat. Her head spun. She was dizzy, falling into a vortex of smoke.

"Aly?"

"Damn right, Nooner."

Noonie stepped forward, slowly at first. She started by walking, but it ended up turning into a run. She smashed into Alysess, grabbed hard around her silver-suited waist, and squeezed.

Alysess gave her a strong, one-armed hug back. "Careful, Face," she said. "I ain't in great shape. Broken arm, butt shot, numb hands, and all sorts of nasty stuff. Not to mention I just spent the last hour *dying* about seven times in a row. These stupid Ragface suits are crazy. Found a tongue tab that kills you. I was getting pretty raping tired of croaking and being revived by the time the anxiety field I was stuck in finally shut down." She looked back into the control room. "I take it you're responsible for that, Nooner. Thanks."

Noonie looked up at her mom. Mom number two. Alysess's eyes were teary and smiling. She looked near exhaustion, but happy. So happy to be with Noonie. To have found her child.

"Where's the Ragman?" Noonie asked, surprised at how weak and young her own voice sounded.

"Dead," Alysess said flatly. Her eyes shifted to the side.

"So . . ." Noonie coughed. She felt her voice become stronger suddenly. "So . . . who's leading the revolution now?"

CHAPTER 95

Alysess felt good. She had just killed three people, but she felt good. Her body was a patched-together, anesthetized mess, but she felt good. She had survived the anxiety field. Survived by dying over and over. The damn suits were good for some things, after all. She'd made it.

She had found her baby. She had found Nooner-face.

Yet there was something different about the child. Alysess *was* delighted to see her, overjoyed to finally be with her, but there *was* something different. Something beyond the fact that the girl was covered with blood and had no pale makeup on anymore.

There was a subtle change in the look of Noonie's eyes. Shadows seemed to keep passing over them. The pupils were a touch dilated and the irises looked wrong somehow. A little lopsided and fuzzy or something. Even as Alysess watched tears run out from the eyes and down the girl's cheeks, something about those small, childlike eyes reminded Alysess of other eyes. They reminded her of Tavis's eyes. Just a little. Tavis-the-IT's eyes. Alysess couldn't quite put her finger on what it was.

"So who's leading Revy?" the child repeated. Her voice

sounded different too. Colder. Like there wasn't just smoke in her lungs, but a little bit of snow.

Alysess didn't answer her. She just said, "We'd better get out of here, Face. The building is swarming with cops. The Revies are breaking in now. Things'll get bad."

Noonie hugged Alysess hard again. It almost hurt, but Alysess didn't mind.

"Come on, Nooner. We have to go."

Noonie broke the hug. She seemed to be thinking, remembering something. "Just a second," she said softly, and turned back to the control room.

"We have no time," Alysess said, following the girl. Noonie went back through the open entrance to the command center. Smoke still billowed out as the fire roared within. Alysess watched the child step into the haze-filled room, climbing over the three cop bodies, and then lean over one man's body that was just beyond the others. Alysess stayed in the doorway, unable to see who the man was. *Who's she crouching over?* The smoke was too thick to see. The dead guy looked tall. Solid.

The girl reached down and fished into the man's front pants pocket.

"Come *on,* Noonie!" Alysess hissed, glancing back down the hallway to make sure no one was coming up on them yet. She was getting very nervous. "Hurry up!"

"One sec," the child said quietly.

Noonie pulled her hand out of the pocket, cupping something in her palm. It looked like a pile of small stones. She picked two of the stonelike objects out of the palm with her other hand. Then she pinched one of the tiny things between her thumb and index finger. She reached back down and carefully, lovingly pressed the thing to the dead man's lips, slowly pushing whatever it was into his lifeless mouth. The other object she popped into her own mouth. And then Noonie looked like she was chewing on it.

"Noonie?" Alysess asked, wondering what was going on.

The girl dumped the rest of the stone things into her ~~~ pocket, brushed her hands, and stood back up. "You di~~~ me, Aly," Noonie said firmly. Her eyes narrow~~~ loudly on whatever was in her mouth "~~~ now?"

Alysess looked over Noo~~~ far side of the roo~~~

everywhere. The bodies closest to the fire were burning. Cooking. They smelled awful.

"*I'm* supposed to be running things," Alysess admitted finally.

The girl smiled slightly. She turned to her left and pulled two high-velocity nerve rifles from a rack by the door. They looked like the only two that hadn't been badly damaged by the explosions.

Noonie then slung one rifle strap over her small shoulder and walked toward the door, holding the other rifle up for Alysess. "Then let's get to it," the child said with authority.

Alysess numbly took the rifle in her one good hand. She looked into Noonie's eyes, trying to read them. Noonie grinned vacantly and pushed past Alysess.

Alysess turned and watched the girl pass beyond the smoke and start walking down the hall. Her strides were sure and determined. They looked very long and powerful on a person so short.

"Hey, Nooner, wait up," Alysess called. "Wait! Wait a minute. Where's Watly? Where's your mother?"

Without slowing, the girl turned her head slightly as she marched toward the intersection of corridors. "She's okay," Noonie said casually, sounding more like she was pushing thirty than going on ten. "Mom's fine. She's with me."

"What?" Alysess asked, confused.

"She's in my pants pocket," the girl said as she continued.

Alysess stood perfectly still, dangling the long rifle and staring at the girl. *Her* little girl. She felt totally dumbfounded.

"Come on," Noonie yelled as she turned the corner. "We have a war to finish."

Alysess snorted. It was a satisfying, loud one—the first in a long time. Then she hung the rifle strap over her good shoulder and stepped gingerly forward.

"I need a doctor," Alysess shouted after the sound of Noonie's fading footsteps as she limped carefully toward them.

"You *are* a doctor, silly," the girl's voice came back from way down the hall.

And Alysess snorted again. She practically had to trot to catch up with the kid.

CHAPTER 96

The war did not last long after that. The command center was easily stormed now that all its defenses were down. The former hosts joined the rebels, and together they took the Second Level of Manhattan. It was a smooth coup now, led by two people, not one. Alysess and Noonie. Leaders of the revolution. It was nice for Alysess to be a leader for a change. It was refreshing to be making decisions, telling people what to do, instead of just saying "Sure, no prob" all the time. Alysess tried to make it as humane a victory as possible. She tried to fight fair and make her soldiers do the same.

Sometimes they did and sometimes they didn't. She lost total control of them only once. And that one time was, she had to admit, spectacular.

Some of the Revies got it into their heads to blow up the command center. It was already on fire, it had already been emptied of counter-Revies and cops, but they wanted to blow it up real good.

Alysess tried to talk them out of it through her still-functioning helmet speaker, but it was the one time they wouldn't listen to her as they always had to the Ragman. She gave up. She was too far away to stop them. By this time, Alysess and Noonie were in the east fifties. They had worked their way uptown as the sun slowly rose. They'd been coordinating Revies and layfighters, finishing the last couple of battles with straggling police, and trying to round up the last few frightened Second Levelers who hadn't already fled by Floobie-pod. They were too far away to do anything about rebellious rebels.

When the pair of them looked back downtown later on, they caught sight of it happening. The spectacular event, occurring in the orange glow of morning.

There were a number of loud booms and then the right-hand Empire State Building—State Two—visibly lurched downward and to the west.

State Two creaked and groaned and its pointed tip swayed. Then the far side of the huge structure seemed to cave in on itself, slowly collapsing like a house of cards. Flames lashed upward from its foundation. It leaned farther out, and for a moment it looked like it was going to take the original Empire State Building with it. The connecting bridges stretched upward, pieces of gold raining down from them. The old State One tilted a little from the enormous pull and stress. Then the top bridge snapped. It broke at the State Two side and swung slowly down to the left. The falling gold connection smashed sloppily into the original building, busting windows and caving in exterior walls. Billions of shards tinkled downward. Then the bottom span broke, its length splitting right in the middle. Sparkling metal tumbled down from each broken end as they flopped limply to each side.

Alysess and Noonie watched, hypnotized, as very gradually, State Two began to fall. Its right side was crumbling, huge chunks and enormous sheets of stone and metal splintering under the crushing weight. At first it looked like the building would not fall to the side, it would just collapse in place, folding in on itself. But then the point of its spire slowly leaned, scraping across the orange sky of morning. There was a combination grating/crunching/metal-rending sound that filled the air even blocks away. Smoke and massive clouds of dust flew up from the base of the structure as it fell. Its shape distorted as it descended, as if it were reflected in a bending, twisting mirror.

Slowly, unbelievably, this massive building came down, crushing smaller buildings under it. Some seemed to be demolished entirely, others actually looked like they were falling out of the building's way. Most just disappeared completely under the violent shadow of this falling behemoth. There were a series of huge, roaring, eardrum-shattering explosions as it came down. The whitetop shook a little under their feet.

It was a bizarre sight, totally unreal-looking. Even though it was happening right then, right before Alysess's and Noonie's eyes, it was hard to accept. Fireballs and great puffs of smoke sprouted all along State Two's length as it smashed downward. Finally it fell totally out of view, hidden by closer buildings. A few seconds later there was yet another gigantic crash and dust filled the whole sky. More buildings collapsed and fell downward all around where State Two had landed. For a moment it seemed that the whole island was going to be demolished. Then there was another, even louder crash. The street shook violently, almost knocking Alysess and Noonie over.

The building had broken clear through the Second Level. It had crashed down to First, down to the island's original street level.

Alysess didn't approve. It was a stupid, destructive thing to do. She didn't approve, but she couldn't help but feel exhilarated as she watched. She'd witnessed the actual breakthrough of the levels of the country of Manhattan. A huge breach had opened in the division of the levels.

Through the dust and smoke, Alysess could just make out the original Empire State Building. It listed badly to the west now, looking almost as though it too would fall shortly. But it just might hold, a leaning monument to the end of the war.

There would be a lot of work to do. The fires would have to be put out. Massive demolition and reconstruction was obviously called for. There was an enormous amount of cleaning up necessary all over the island. The country of Manhattan was a mess. A patient in critical condition. But there was work beyond the physical. Concerns beyond material matters. There was a lot more than simple repairing, rebuilding, and mopping-up needed.

There would have to be a new government. Some kind of structure needed to be set up. Decisions had to be made. They had to be made soon.

And Alysess Tollnismer was in charge. Alysess and her child, Noonie Caiper. Everyone was looking to them for the answers. A high-strung doctor and a little girl with a glassy look in her eyes. Manhattan's new leaders.

Alysess was worried. She knew very little about kinds of government. About how to set up a new system. And how to run things.

All she knew was what she believed. And what she believed was that *any* system of government worked if most of the people running it were good people. Fair, empathetic, caring, thoughtful, giving, and careful people. And that *no* system of government worked if the people in charge were mainly not good. If they were greedy, selfish, power-hungry, intolerant, and corrupt, things always got messy. This was true for democracies, dictatorships, monarchies, oligarchies, *whatever*.

Alysess thought about all the people she had known in her life. She thought about Watly and Noonie and the Ragman and Tavis and every person she had ever run into on the First or Second Levels. She thought about the actions of the rebels and the actions of those fighting them. She thought about herself. And she realized that, if her theory about governing was right, whatever form of government she decided upon would fail. Any system she chose was doomed.

Because people were messed up. Even *good* people were messed up. There *was* no system yet devised that could overcome the basically raped-up nature of most of humanity. Any system would fail under the burden of humanity's generally crippled nature.

So all she could do was the best she could do. All she could do was try. And that would have to be enough. Doing the best she could would have to be enough.

And maybe that wasn't so bad. Maybe that wasn't so terrible. All anybody could ever do was the best they could do. All anybody could ever do was try, reach, push, and struggle. All anybody could ever do was try for perfection and fail miserably. And that was all right.

Alysess Tollnismer snorted quietly to herself.

And smiled. Damn, but she wanted a Soft pill.

EPILOGUE

Watly Caiper was nowhere. She had no senses, no body. She was floating in nothingness, just a singular consciousness. Something had happened to her earlier. Something traumatic. Sentiva had removed her from the body, and then something had happened. A large piece of her mind, her self, had been lost. A portion of who she was had gone away. Watly hadn't yet figured out what part of her was missing, but something was definitely missing.

Yet what remained of her felt okay. Pretty good, actually. There was no pain, no discomfort, no sense of time passing, just a simple, calm sense of self. Just thought and nothing else.

The limbo Watly inhabited wasn't black. She wasn't suspended in some black void, for blackness would've been something. Suspended would've been something. And there was nothing. No dark, no light, no up, no down. No taste or smell or sound or touch. Just nothingness. Not sleep, not death . . . simply a mind without a body. A "me" without the physical vessel. An "I" cut off from everything else.

The me is not the body.
The me is not the body.

The me is neither hand nor face nor sex.
The me is Watly Caiper, I.
(A sense of self.)
The body is an it.
The body is a that.
It could belong to another.
For the me is a movable thing.
The me is a movable thing.

Watly remembered her old chant. Her old mantra.

She was not afraid. She did not feel loneliness. Somehow she sensed, with utmost confidence, that she was not alone. Noonie was nearby, and Alysess. Her child and her poovus. The three of them had been reunited in some fashion. Watly was sure of it. She had no doubt. Something beyond the five simple senses told her that. Something strong and sure. Love, perhaps. Yes, that sounded right. Love.

And suddenly, Watly was somewhere. She could see. Sort of. Her vision was strange and different, but she could definitely see. It took her a moment to get used to her new eyes. At first everything was streaks and blurs. Even as her sight cleared, it was as though she had no peripheral vision—as though she had blinders on. She was outdoors. On a street somewhere. In the distance, some kind of construction was going on. Watly felt high up, as if she were sitting on top of a ladder.

"Mommy?"

There was Noonie, looking up at her. The child appeared much older. And there was Alysess, at Noonie's side. Her dark, shiny skin looked beautiful. And there was a man, a tall man. Eiter? Yes! It was Eiter with them. Alive. He wasn't dead after all. Old Tavis had lied.

"Watly?" Alysess asked. "Can you hear me?"

"It's my *family*!" Watly said. "My family!" Watly's own voice was unfamiliar. It was like her head was in a bucket.

"Hey, Watly," Eiter said. He was smiling.

"Hey, Dad," Watly said back, and Eiter only flinched a little. Watly laughed.

Alysess wiped away tears. "Hi, Watt. How ya doing?"

"Happy," Watly said. "Glad to be back. I love you, Aly." To Watly, it almost felt as if the part of herself she had lost had been worth losing. It was as if the portion missing was the portion of her mind full of fear and confusion. She felt unburdened. Free. Free to love. Free to care.

"I love you too, Watly," Alysess said.

Noonie giggled. "Me, too!"

"I love my whole family," Watly said joyfully. "Every one of you. And I'm sorry." She felt she could finally understand things clearly now—the things that were important. Alysess was important. And Noonie. Noonie needed her. Why couldn't she see that before?

"Me too," Alysess said. "I'm sorry too."

"Yeah," Noonie said.

"Why not?" Eiter said, looking a little uncomfortable.

"So you're alive, huh, Eiter?" Watly said, feeling relief.

"Looks that way."

"I heard you were dead."

"Wishful thinking," he said with a little smile.

Watly laughed. She looked down at Alysess again. "What happened?"

Alysess took a deep breath. "Whew! Well, a *lot*. The war ended about six months ago—I'll tell you all about it later. Things've been crazy. We've been trying to organize stuff, patch stuff up. Plus heal up ourselves."

"You were hurt?"

"We were all hurt. I got pretty messed up. Eiter here got badly burned before anything even started, so he stayed down on First and waited it out."

Eiter glanced down at his feet. "Ever the hero," he mumbled sheepishly.

Watly looked at her child, who appeared to have grown a good two inches in just half a year. "And Noonie?" she asked. "Was Noonie hurt?"

Alysess and Noonie exchanged knowing glances. They smiled at each other. "Noonie was . . . messed up," Alysess said. "She's working on getting better."

"Yeah, Mama," Noonie said. "I'm workin' on it. Seeing doctors."

Yes, Watly thought. *This is good*. Noonie needed to heal. Noonie needed help. Watly could see that now. It seemed so obvious, she wondered why she had not understood that long ago.

"You guys are incredible," Watly said.

All three of them smiled at her.

"So where am I?" Watly asked finally. Her neck felt stiff. "Who am I in?"

"Well . . ." Alysess said sheepishly. She sounded a little hinky. "I had to put you in someone alive, you know. . . ."

"So who am I in?"

Alysess sighed. "Well, nobody exactly volunteered to be a prisoner in their own bodies for your sake, Watly."

"Alysess, whose body am I in?"

"It's only temporary, Watly. . . ." She seemed to be looking to the others for help. Noonie giggled and Eiter just shrugged.

"So tell me whose body," Watly insisted.

Alysess fidgeted and swung her arms nervously. "It's not exactly a body, my poovus."

Watly tried to look down at herself. Her head didn't seem to want to move. "What the rape did you put me in?"

Noonie giggled again.

"You're in a fighter," Alysess confessed. "It's only temporary, Watly, till we can get you a body."

"I'm in a *what*?"

"I connected your remaining creosan wafer up to the brain of one of the black fighting machines. Eiter helped—he's a great mechanic. It wasn't easy, Watly. We had to modify like crazy. You've got visual, vocal, mobility, audio, *everything*. Eiter even replaced some of the gun turrets with mechanical arms. We worked really hard, Watly. It was the best I could do, for the time being."

"I'm a raping fighting machine?"

"Mommy," little Noonie said, jumping up and down. "You should see yourself. You're really *spaf*. Peaky, peaky, peaky prone!"

Watly finally managed to move her head. She looked down at the huge black metal surface of her body. She flexed one of her five complicated metal arms. She was gigantic. She was powerful. And she was a raping *machine*.

Alysess gulped. "It's just for the time being, poovus. Just temporary. We figured you'd rather be awake and aware *now* than wait around forever for us to find the right host for your wafer."

"Alysess . . ." Watly was almost speechless. She floated herself forward just a little, getting the feel of her propulsion systems. "Alysess, allow me to express my gratitude to you and Eiter by giving you both a hug," she teased.

Alysess blinked. Eiter's eyes widened.

Watly moved her huge form closer. "Come and let me give you both a big bear hug." Watly snapped her heavy metal fingers and twisted her five multijointed arms. Noonie laughed.

"That's not funny, Watly!" Alysess said, stepping backward.

"Just wanna say thanks, Aly."

Noonie was giggling hysterically.

"Back off, beanhead!" Alysess shouted.

"Come on—one big hug for you both. What'da ya say?"

Both Alysess and Eiter ran off down the street. They stopped about twenty yards away.

Noonie climbed up on her mom's front fender and looked into her sensors. The girl was grinning from ear to ear. "Pretty funny, Ma."

Watly wished she really *could* hug now. She wanted to hug her child. "Noonie, baby, we're gonna work everything out. All four of us. The family."

Little Noonie shrugged. Watly saw something wrong with her eyes. Noonie *had* been wounded deeply. Maybe wounded long ago. It would take time, but Watly vowed to help the girl. That was the only thing important now.

Alysess and Eiter were waving at them from up the street. "Hey, Noonie," Watly said, lowering her synthetic voice. "Did Alysess ever mention anything to you about liking machines? You know—really *liking* machines?"

The child giggled again. She sounded more like a kid than she had in years. "Nah. But I'll tell you something," Noonie whispered in her mother's metallic head. "She and Gramps—"

"Gramps?"

"Yeah. I call Eiter 'Gramps.' Anyway, she made sure Gramps hooked up a whole bunch of secret things to you that they wouldn't let me see. Some kind of special parts Aly said were just for her. I have a feeling you're a boy machine."

Watly's laugh echoed in her own head. It was hard to imagine she'd ever get used to the artificial sound of her own voice. "Well," she said, giving Noonie a ride toward where Alysess and Eiter were standing. "I guess maybe this won't be *all* bad. . . ."